C000097470

Signs Of Life

Chris Towndrow

Valericain Press

Valericain
Press

Valericain Press
Richmond, London, UK
www.valericainpress.co.uk

Signs Of Life / Chris Towndrow. – 3rd ed.
Paperback ISBN : 978-1-7392306-0-9
eBook ISBN : 978-1-7392306-1-6

Praise for SIGNS OF LIFE:

"This is not only a gritty Western, it's a love story. It has everything you could want in a brilliant read and more. I devoured [it] in two sittings as it took me to another time and place. A book that will surely bring the love of Westerns to a new audience." *****

"This did everything that I was looking for in a Western novel. Chris Towndrow has a great writing style for the genre and I was hooked with these characters." *****

"This was a quaint, charming book, perfect for anyone looking for a Western fix!" ****

"I don't read very many Western romance novels but I really did enjoy… how the author described the characters, the way of life and the story was full of action and drama." ****

"This is a very character driven story that is an entertaining read. The scenes of town life felt realistic, and the dialogue also felt appropriate to the period. Earl's character growth and evolving emotions felt believable and his road to forgiveness is a major theme." ****

"Everything about this book had me immersed in the story. The authenticity of the dialogue, the descriptions, and the characters all held me right there. I really enjoyed the romance in the story. A Western with heart that had me invested in the characters and the outcome, too!" *****

For Sam

Chapter 1

The flowers were dead.

He'd known they would be; all things wither without love and care.

Squatting down, Earl brushed away the fragments of plant, then used a tarnished hand fork to turn over the rectangular yard of reddish soil. A beetle scuttled away to find a new home.

He carefully unfolded a square of tan cloth to reveal three stems of yellow gaillardia, dug each a small hole and homed them, pressing down the dry earth with dirty fingers.

He rose stiffly and went to where his horse was roped to a dying saguaro. He patted the animal's chestnut-brown neck, returned the fork and cloth to the saddlebag, unhooked his canteen from the saddle and took a long drink.

As the water cooled his throat, his gaze meandered across the familiar surroundings. The lone homestead was the only property in sight on the undulating Arizona prairie.

He wandered over to his companion, who had remained quiet, standing dutifully by his own horse.

'Fill you up?' Earl said.

'Thanks.' Walter's lined eyes creased in long-practised empathy. He proffered his flask.

Earl took it and walked away.

He emptied both vessels onto the turned soil, giving the young plants a good drink to start them on a journey that wouldn't last beyond summer. Still, his objective wasn't the journey, only the gesture.

A hundred yards away, the clear water in the creek ran slow and shallow, and he refilled the bottles. He stood for a while and listened to the burbling. The breeze tugged his straggled, straw-coloured hair as he recalled distant, happier days on this stretch of low bank. A picnic, laughter, perhaps amour. Hard ground pressing rocks into younger flesh which was busy in pursuit of affection.

Before the maudlin introspection became overwhelming, he strode back up the gentle slope to where the mounts waited patiently. He handed across Walter's canteen, affixed the other to his saddle, and returned to his sombre travail.

The two wooden crosses which headed the makeshift flowerbed weren't merely simple shapes. The work of an artisan, they were carved angels with arms outstretched, the folds of their robes intricate in the weathered mesquite. Long legs tapered down, driven into the hard prairie earth many years earlier. Even so, the winter's wind had pushed them off square.

Across the angel's chest, the taller memorial read, "MARY JOHNSON. LOST TO THE LORD 1859. EVER LOVED".

The shorter, standing barely two feet to the crown, was carved with, "ALDEN JOHNSON. LOST TO THE LORD 1859. TAKEN TOO SOON".

Earl straightened the crosses, scooped up a rock, and, wincing at possible damage to his craftsmanship, gave each a few hard raps to regain their stability. Then he tossed away the rock, clasped his hands in front and lost himself in silent reflection.

After a minute, his dun horse whinnied, jolting Earl back to the present day, so he paced across to the ruined house seventy yards away.

Little had changed.

Weeds sprouted enthusiastically from crumbled brickwork, and the past year's wind and frost had eaten away more of the scarred and blackened timbers. A jackrabbit sprang from the interior, startling Earl, and pelted away across the landscape.

At the rear of the house, nature had reclaimed more of the garden. Only the low tumbledown border wall marked out that it had ever been anything but another fifty square yards of anonymous scrub. The husbandry of past flora lived only in his memory. Mary's expertise with the hoe. The neatness of order before the chaos.

A thunderclap belched across the distant mountains.

He surveyed the skies and felt for the direction of the breeze: they'd stay dry. Nevertheless, he strode back to the horses.

Walter replaced his grey Slouch hat, tucking the loose string under his chin. He nodded solemnly and held Earl's hat out.

'We could have done with that rabbit.'

Earl set the wide-banded khaki Western on his head. 'Not today. Not the time. 'Sides, we're home by dusk.'

He untied the reins and patted the animal's hide. The gelding pushed his head against the man's chest, puffing out comforting warm breath.

'Let's go, Jack.'

They mounted up, and Earl cast a final glance across the scene. He eased a heel against the horse's flank, and they moved away, with Walter riding behind.

They rode in silence at an easy walk for five minutes. The horses' tails swished at pesky flies. The abandoned property fell long behind, obscured from view by the undulating land.

Walter pulled alongside. 'I swear there's less of a year every year. Could be only six months we were here.'

'You don't gotta ride out. It ain't like it was. Say the word, and I'll do this my own self next year.' Earl remained grateful that his companion indulged him in this pilgrimage, deferential and understanding.

Walter frowned. 'Just because I don't lay flowers doesn't mean I forgot. But life moves on. A man looking over his shoulder doesn't see where he's heading.'

Earl tightened the reins. 'Well, you ain't got the guilt I got.'

He jabbed a heel, and the horse accelerated into a canter. Russet dust whipped up into a plume which washed over Walter, who spurred his mount onwards too.

The sun warmed Earl's face as they clattered on, the rap of hoof on dirt and grass, hard breaths pumping from the ageing appaloosa's mouth.

The brown landscape gave way to green, and more trees pockmarked their familiar route.

After half an hour, he sensed Jack's pace slowing. Not many years left for this longtime friend. Loss would come again, and the need to seek a new companion.

He steered for a clutch of four broad trees and brought them to rest. They dismounted in the welcome shade, and he hung his hat on the saddle and wiped sweat from his brow. They supped from their canteens, leaning against adjacent gnarled tree trunks.

He inspected the mesquite: this would be good to cut and fashion. It pricked his memory.

'That new shutter holding on fine?'

''Course. I wouldn't hire anywhere else,' Walter replied.

He flashed an amused query. 'Hire?'

'You get my meaning. You do it 'cos you feel a duty.'

'And that's so wrong? Trying to pay back?'

Walter chewed on a biscuit and gave a familiar look of mild disappointment.

Earl looked into his friend's lined eyes. 'I get that you had your fill of me, Walt. I had the fill of me a long time past.'

'I reckon you're as stuck with me as I am with you. Circumstance can better the strongest of men, and I don't want to be torn up guilty from you seeking worse counsel—or drink—this time of year.'

'You talk like this is the only day I'd wind up in the pokey again.'

'You don't aim to—I know that much. It wouldn't solve anything. You quit on drinking, and even a stubborn fool needs a friend. I wish you hadn't had to lean so hard, but what's done is done. I said so last year and the times before. And I'll say so next time. Maybe it's only me you're deaf to. Maybe one day a horse'll kick you in the head, or Mary'll come to you in a dream, and you'll see sense and move on.'

'Can't say I don't wanna. Wanting and getting ain't the same, though.'

'You didn't die that day. Nor did you eat your gun on account of what went on. To my mind, means you got steel—even if it's real deep inside. There's always hope.'

'For what? Can't get 'em back.' Earl's head drooped.

'Sure enough. I mean, hope for starting over. Wearing a smile, not a frown.'

'My humour's my own choice.'

'And you know what I think to it.' With a hard stare, Walter stowed his canteen and climbed into the saddle.

Earl knew the man meant well, beyond his ball-busting. A stern teacher you resent at the time but who gets results you appreciate in hindsight. A feller like Mr Morgan—though Earl had quit long before results could come.

Deep down, he did want to move past the loss, but the final mile of any endeavour was always the hardest. Could he help it if it made him a pain in the ass? Feelings can't be turned off like a lamp.

He could never foresee a day when he wouldn't do right by Mary and Alden—keep their memory alive. Yet, such an honourable task was inextricably linked to remembrance and thus to regret and pain.

They picked up the trail, heading for Walter's ranch as usual, and settled into an easy trek, lolling in the saddle over the bumpy ground. The long-dead riverbed meandered along a shallow valley, sporadically bordered on both sides by trees in varying stages of life.

After a slow hour, the trail morphed into grassy brush, and Earl pushed Jack into a lope. To the north, ahead and to the right of them, the land rose into a ridge. Atop it, maybe three miles distant, another pair of riders were making good speed. A third, riderless horse followed on a long tether. It was the first sign of other folk they'd seen all day.

They were heading westward, towards a boulder the size of a house, which perpetually teetered on the edge of careering to the valley floor. Folks around had called it Tipping Rock for as long as Earl could remember—a landmark aeons older than this annual pilgrimage. A burly man could move the boulder by a small amount, such was its curious fulcrum. Still, the topography meant it couldn't truly be toppled. He'd demonstrated it once to Mary, wanting to show his strength despite being weak with love. He smiled, recalling her amusement at his theatrical bravado. It certainly bested the old homestead's creek for a picnic spot. The view. God's wonderful world before it became less so.

As Earl watched the riders, curious, he strayed from the trail. As he corrected, Jack flashed past a towering cactus, uncomfortably close.

He cursed, then checked behind to see whether Walter had noticed the other riders or was preparing to chastise Earl's near miss. Neither—he was riding single-handed and wiping his brow.

As Earl turned forwards, he was alarmed by a shape moving in the grass ahead and to his left. Jack saw it too, shied, and keeled to one side.

Earl's hands took avoiding action, got crossed up, and yanked hard, veering them away from tall, gnarled shrubs. The horse's head tossed, and its front legs sought footing. Earl evened his weight, dug his heels harder into the stirrups and hauled on the reins. Too late. One hoof rapped against an exposed root, gouging the ankle open.

'Dang to hell!'

They stilled, horse and rider breathing hard.

Walter clattered to a halt in a shower of dust. 'What the hell?'

Earl jabbed out a hand. 'Over there.'

Ten yards away lay a young man, propped wearily against a small boulder, half-hidden in tall thin grass.

Chapter 2

Walter snapped his gun out of its holster. Arrowing it at the stranger, he nudged Dusty into a circumspect walk.

Earl clasped his holstered Colt and encouraged Jack round to the far side of the prone figure, so he and Walter were on opposing sides. If the boy were armed, he'd struggle to hit both men quickly. This was a known ruse amongst bandits— to lay a decoy, catch the travellers off guard, and then the remainder of the party would appear and rob the riders, possibly worse.

Yet the young man had one palm outstretched, fearful. His other clutched the opposite shoulder. Alarm swam on his dirty, fair-stubbled face.

Walter looked him up and down, replaced his gun on his left hip, and then dismounted in one swift move.

'Walt!' Earl warned, not wanting to be hoodwinked.

'What?'

'What in hell you doing?'

'Helping the boy.'

Earl clutched the handle of his ageing pistol. 'Don't take no chances,' he hissed, skin crawling with the sensation of absent onlookers.

'Against one boy? Can't you see he's in a bad box here?'

Earl couldn't deny appearances, but despite the kid's empty holster, could a gun be tucked into his boot top or concealed within arm's reach?

'They'll use this to set you up.'

'Indians?' Walter asked, dumbfounded.

'Dammit, no. Anybody.' The old scourge was long absent—yet not from his memory.

'It's the boy been bushwhacked, not us.' Walter nodded at Earl's hand. 'And when did you ever use that thing anyhow?'

Earl ignored the jibe. Yet, however innocent the scene, his heart thudded. He didn't like it, not one bit. Raiders had broken his life once; it wouldn't happen again.

Walter approached the young man, palms raised in friendship. 'You okay, son?'

No response.

'You okay, son?' Walter repeated. 'Cat got your tongue?'

The boy shook his head and leant backwards warily as Walter advanced.

Earl spied a bag in the dust and inspected the vicinity for evidence of a scuffle or co-conspirators.

Walter grabbed his attention. 'Hey! Boy's in shock here.'

'And Jack got all gouged up for it. Kid spooked him—you not see that?' He gestured to the horse's foreleg. Its hoof scraped the ground in pain.

'I saw fine, and it's a damn shame, but you want to do what's decent here?'

Walter was right. Their deep friendship endured because they weathered these minor storms; they coexisted despite differences and disagreements. Both could occasionally be an ass. Today, as so often, it was Earl's turn.

He retrieved the bag and dropped it near Walter.

'They took his gun, Walt.'

He looked at the boy. His skin was sun-kissed, his hair brown, eyes dark. His outfit was olive greens and tan, topped with a scraggly neckerchief, all spattered with dust. Certainly, twenty-five years their junior, more a boy than a man. Not dressed too fancy, nor a land-loper.

'They take your horse?' Earl asked, eyes darting.

The boy just peered at them.

'Looks like they took his mind too,' he sniped.

Walter knelt and reached towards the boy's wounded shoulder. The boy recoiled.

'We're not looking to hurt you, son. You shot?' Walter cocked a thumb and forefinger, and tapped his shoulder.

The boy shook his head.

Earl continued searching for a threat that hadn't materialised. Instead, there was only a snake, which he kicked at. It slithered away.

'You want to get your thumb out of your ass and help me here?' Walter flashed a raised brow. 'Get from my canteen if you're so damn precious about aiding the kid.'

Reluctantly, Earl unhooked his friend's water vessel and brought it over.

Walter grabbed it, opened it, and offered it to the lad. The latter clasped it with a dirty hand and drank wilfully. With a nod, he passed it back, eyes still wary.

Walter tossed the canteen to Earl and jammed hands on hips, studying their guest.

'He's all abroad, for sure.'

'Horse throw you?' Earl asked the boy, awaiting a lie. An inquisitive face looked back. 'Damn kid's slower than molasses in January,' he muttered.

'All the same, he's hurt and got no ride.'

Earl checked around again, then plucked a discarded black Laredo hat from nearby and tossed it to the kid. The maker was local and pricey, yet the hat fitted neatly: it wasn't stolen.

Earl walked over to his mount. 'Banged up on account of some cripple,' he murmured, patting Jack's neck. 'Sorry, buddy. Made a bad day worse. You and me too old for other men's battles.'

He retrieved the cloth square from his saddlebag, doused it in precious water, and attended to the horse's wounded leg. As he mopped the blood and tied a poor bandage, Jack whinnied.

He rubbed the horse's nose. 'We'll go easy.'

Walter moved close to the boy's face. 'Unless you want to die out here, you come? Okay? You come.'

He pointed at the boy, himself and Earl, then the horses, and lastly, the horizon. The boy nodded.

Walter put a hand under the boy's good armpit and helped him up. The strain across the kid's shoulders tweaked the injury, and his face creased.

Earl watched disapprovingly. 'You take him.'

'Sure, I'll be Good Samaritan. Again.' The look was cutting.

'I ain't after story hour,' Earl sniped.

'Me either. Only civility.'

The boy's eyes flicked back and forth as if the men were playing a game of catch with words.

Walter slid a rifle from under his saddle and pushed it across to Earl's.

'Making me the General now?' Earl asked. He could no more shoot rifles than he could fly to the moon.

'Making comfort for the three of us. Now, help the kid on.'

Walter threw a boot into the stirrup, hoisted himself aboard, then reached down an arm, and between him and Earl, they hauled the kid up behind.

Walter smoothed the animal's neck. 'Sorry, Dusty. Gotta take the weight off your pal Jack.'

The horse gave a hard nod as if he understood.

Earl mounted Jack and eased into a walking gait. Ahead, the kid sat up well, one hand cradled across his chest, the other on the saddle's rear.

As they ambled along, Earl checked for other signs of life—dust plumes, campfire smoke, shapes moving in the brush.

There was nothing. They were safe—for now.

After a short way, Walter swung his reins out left, and they veered from west to southwest.

Earl pulled alongside. 'What gives? We got a new route?'

'He needs a Doc, not a pair of old fools.'

'Old fool yourself.'

'Besides, White Rock is closest,' Walter reminded him.

'Ridgeway is bare another two-hour ride beyond. This is near enough a double-back.'

Walter pointed at where Jack favoured his right leg, the makeshift bandage now half-red. 'We want less riding, not more. I'm two-up, and Jack's hurting. Barely make it before dark anyhow.'

'The kid ain't hurt bad, and I don't got time for a cripple who don't belong out here on his own.'

'What happened to your humanity today? Huh? Maybe he's in shock. Saw a killing. Got spooked real good. Maybe he lost a family?'

Walter's gaze arrow into Earl's eyes, cannoned off the back of his skull and plunged into his soul.

Earl tugged his steed to a halt. 'I can't go to White Rock—you know that.'

Walter eased his reins, and Dusty sidestepped. 'It's the best place. Used to be your watering hole, less you forgot.'

'You after getting me killed on account of this kid?'

Walter snorted. 'I told you many a time to quit on that.'

Earl jabbed his finger. 'You ain't the one with a mark on his back.'

'Dennis Hayes is all talk.' Walter waved it away.

'I don't care about "all"—only words of killing.'

'That was a long time ago. You got me, we got this kid, and I got a notion it's the right place for him.'

'Well, you be sure and get a right good headstone for me.'

Walter merely shook his head.

Earl knew they had to take the shortest route and go easy too. There was no use in worsening Jack's injury while on an errand of mercy—which is what their day had become. It would only wind up with him having to pay a vet.

The boy got lucky that one of his saviours was a good man.

Earl sighed in concession. 'Make down Andrews Creek, find a spot, take a night. Fix us up. Maybe get some answers from the boy. And to White Rock after, if it's the way.'

Walter gave an intense look. 'Was it ever so hard, saving a kid's life?'

'Only the lecturing.' Earl spurred up to a trot.

Walter tilted his head back—for the good it would do, as the kid wouldn't hear either way. 'Excuse my buddy, kid. He means well. Underneath.'

Walter took the lead, and they diverged from their planned route to take the White Rock trail. The ground undulated, as did Earl's mind, which flitted between his spoiled schedule, the kid's circumstance, and whether Dennis Hayes would be standing on the outskirts of town, a shotgun primed for Earl's return.

It made the bile rise—he'd barely suppressed the annual echo of Mary's loss, and now the whole episode reared its head. Though, if hot lead met his chest and empty heart, at least he'd see her again because of a good deed.

It made no difference whether he forgave himself—so he hadn't. Self-absolution made light of things. Death wasn't a light matter. There was nobody on earth to forgive him, and forgiveness after his death would be scant recompense. So, there was no way out. It was his lot to live in limbo, but fortunately he had Walter. Best to try to do right by the man.

He spat away the sour taste of failure.

They dismounted after a long hour, took water, biscuits and bacon from the knapsack—small portions shared between three—then pressed on. Throughout, not a word passed the boy's lips, though neither did he bear any air of furtiveness or duplicity.

After a while, Walter's hand came up sharply in a warning, and they brought the horses to a stand. They'd not long reached Andrews Creek. The water bubbled along, plentiful in its late spring flow, and Earl looked forward to a good soak of his dusty head.

Walter beckoned, so Earl coaxed Jack alongside. The horses butted heads in friendship.

'Gimme the rifle.'

Earl unsheathed it from the saddlebag and handed it across. The kid eased his ass backwards to allow Walter room. Earl gave him the credit of some brains, at least.

As Walter brought the Sharps to his shoulder, Earl found the sightline and the quarry. Not men, or even one man, thank Heaven. Two bighorns—a mother and child, drinking at the water's edge in the shade of overhanging trees.

The gun bucked, and the air cracked.

The mother bolted. The youngling didn't because it couldn't.

Walter handed back the rifle, and with a whiff of cordite in his nose, Earl stowed it.

A nascent smile appeared on the young man's face. He brought pinched fingers to his mouth.

Earl nodded. 'Even a fool gotta eat.'

'And which one's the fool?' Walter left that hanging and urged into a trot towards their dinner.

They roped the animal across Jack's back—it was the only choice—and pressed on for another hour until Walter found a good spot.

Earl was glad to dismount for the final time and lead Jack down to the water's edge to drink. He relieved the gelding of its luggage and gave it many sympathetic pats.

'Fix you up later, buddy.'

Jack replied with a gentle snort.

Earl trudged up to where Walter and the nameless kid had gathered sticks and cleared a patch for a fire.

Nearby, dying shrubs ringed the spot and further away stood a clump of Palo Verde and Joshuas. Barrel cacti bedecked the area, and a few early-season cicadas sang.

He unpacked his bedroll and laid it beside Walter's, then collected both canteens and refilled them at the creek. He brought Jack closer to the camp and roped him up on a rogue saguaro amidst a thickish patch of grass. The horse ate hungrily.

'Watch for snakes, y'hear, Jack? Don't need you in a fever and all.'

He pulled off his spurs and massaged his ankles, then grabbed the flint and tinder from his war bag and went to start the fire.

He watched as Walter tossed his hat on the ground beside the saddles, loosened his faded yellow necktie and ran a hand through his thick black hair. Mary's hair had been dark too, thinner, longer. A lost sense beneath Earl's fingers.

He shook that away and continued working the flint. The fire caught with gentle crackles: life from lifelessness. He looked at the kid, expecting a face of wonder, like a caveman or a child.

Instead, the kid ran the edge of one hand across the other palm and flashed an unspoken question.

'Walt?' Earl called.

Walter, drinking from his canteen, looked up.

The kid pointed at himself, then the trees, and repeated the sign.

'You reckon that means… "wood"?' Earl asked.

'Could be.'

Earl picked up a stick, held it towards the kid, and attempted the gesture. The kid nodded.

Walter whistled softly. 'I'll wager the boy is deaf.'

'Shoot,' Earl grouched.

'What's into you?'

'What's into me is I got a slow ride and a hard bed on account of picking up a kid who's a damn fool riding out if he can get robbed clean and leave us to play delivery service.'

'He's offering to help.'

'Damn straight he is. He ain't the saphead not to know a debt.'

'Deaf and slow are not the same.'

'Well, ain't you the medic?' Earl sniped. 'Favours is for gaining confidence. I don't like it.'

'Then make your own damn camp.'

'Cripples is bad,' Earl hissed.

Walter's nostrils flared. 'One. One was.'

'I'm looking after your ass too here.' He blinked away the memory.

'No. You're running from a ghost. Scared, like a kid younger'n this one. He's a right to be worried about us, too, with what he been through. Ever think of that? He's the one with balls here.'

'Let it go.' Earl waved a hand.

'You first. So—you want a fire to cook this butchered lamb, or no?'

Earl sighed. He pointed at the kid—who'd stood idly by as the contretemps passed—made the sign, then pointed at the trees.

The kid nodded and set off on the hundred-yard walk.

Earl laid a hand on Walter's shoulder. 'Keep your gun close.'

'And keep your crabbing distant.'

Chapter 3

Earl gathered dry grass and twigs, and the fire took hold, coiling smoke up to brush the noses of those who'd passed before.

Within minutes, the kid returned with a burgeoning armful of firewood. He worked despite pain in his face, holding the injured shoulder lower. His strength belied his moderate frame—though he'd not been strong enough to fight off whatever had befallen him.

Earl felt a little sorry for the kid. He recalled the three horses on the ridge with only two riders—was it as simple as it looked? Still, he kept his distance, insides churning over the unfamiliar situation. How to interact without a common language? He had nothing to say to the kid and no way to say it, so nothing was what he said.

The kid stayed close to the fire and slowly built it.

Walter brought over the part-butchered lamb, and they rigged up a spit.

The weak sun, obscured by a thickening sheet of dove-grey cloud, slid for the horizon. Mercifully, it wouldn't be a cold night for their impromptu sleepout.

Earl went to Jack, removed the bloodstained cloth, washed it in the creek, cleaned the gouged skin, rinsed the material again and reapplied it.

He stroked Jack's nose. 'Even deep wounds go, buddy. Takes time, is all.'

Next, he made three trips to the copse, working up a sweat as he stripped accessible branches from the trees and bushes. There was an excellent ash tree. He'd fashioned Mary's keepsake box from ash, but the tree back home was long gone. He walked away—no time to cut this one, nor any way to take the trunk back to his workshop.

He dumped the wood, and plopped his aching bones on his bed blanket, which he'd set on the opposite side of the fire from their companion. The kid had pulled off his dusty jacket and shirt and sat cross-legged near the crackling heat. Walter was checking his shoulder.

The coffee pot brewed on a handful of rocks beside the flames—a comforting odour in the circumstance. There'd be no songs tonight, though—too awkward. The fire was welcome and familiar enough, but Earl worried that it signalled their location.

He tried to dispel any dumb notions that this was a trap— but the inner voice wouldn't abate.

Walter sat. 'Shoulder's not broke, I reckon.'

'He cry out?'

'Not sure he can. Most deaf are dumb too, from not knowing the sounds of words.'

'Then he's fool for being out alone and not hearing men who'd do evil.'

'And how are you proposing he gets from place to place? Grows wings and flies? A man can be careful all you want, but an ambush is what it is.'

Earl lowered his voice. 'Real men....' But there were no prying ears, so he spoke normally. 'Real men need to hear.'

'Meaning he'd properly know what a stubborn ass you can be?'

He scowled. 'We brought him, didn't we? Gonna feed him? 'Sides, he uses hands. "Wood", and so forth.' He flitted his hands mockingly.

'Then we're as dumb for not understanding him as he is for not hearing us.'

'We ain't alike, and that's final.' Earl stood.

'Itchy feet today, huh?'

'In need of a wash. You know, for being *civilised*.' He walked away to the creek.

There, he scooped water over his face and hair, drank in cold mouthfuls and let rivulets splatter his faded mid-blue shirt. It lifted five years from him, yet it couldn't wash away disquiet.

He fingered his Colt. Should he leave it here, unseen, so the kid couldn't steal it while they slept? No—Walter would see the empty holster and berate him. Earl had to trust. After all, it was still two against one.

When he returned to the fireside, Walter had poured coffee into two tin mugs, one white, one a faded red, and offered the kid his. The kid put a flat hand to his face, fingers near lips, and moved it away.

Walter pointed. 'At least he's making to talk.'

Earl drank, the hot liquid smarting his throat. 'You so keen—find out the kid's name if we're all gonna be so cosy.'

The kid passed back the empty mug and repeated his hand-from-lips gesture.

Earl caught himself in curiosity about the hand-signing, then berated his weakness.

Walter refilled the mug from the blackened pot.

'I'm Walter. Walter, y'understand?' He drew a "W" in the air. 'Walter. Who are you? Your name?'

The boy danced his hands together as if making multiple signs. The men exchanged a mystified look. Then the boy pointed at Walter and made a "W", essaying the man's lame methods.

The two nodded.

'What's your name, kid?' Earl spoke loudly and glacially as if addressing a dullard. 'Y-o-u-r n-a-m-e?'

Walter tutted at his friend's lame etiquette.

The kid's hands fluttered briefly. It didn't help.

The boy sprang up. Earl grabbed at his pistol.

Walter jolted. 'Jesus! Take it easy!'

Yet, as the boy went for his back pocket, Earl covered his gun. The kid could have a knife in there or even a Derringer. Walter was too relaxed for Earl's liking—as ever. In these circumstances, what was more foolish—being unguarded or circumspect?

The boy withdrew a piece of paper, unfolded it, jabbed a finger at the typeface, and offered it across.

Walter crabbed over, took it, and plopped down in the dust.

The worn parchment was a Wanted poster. The name on it read "'Wild Bill' Hickock".

Earl's eyes flared. 'Wild Bill,' he hissed.

'Wild Bill is long black hair, a moustache, and dead two years.' Walter rolled his eyes as if to a child who asked whether horses could talk.

Earl felt like that child. The river hadn't washed off the day's layer of foolishness.

The kid came over and jabbed at a word on the paper.

'Bill? Yeah.' Walter tapped the spot, then pointed at the kid. 'Bill?' The kid nodded. 'I got you. Good to know you, Bill.'

'Hell of a damn role model,' Earl sniped.

'Who said anything of a role model?' Walter shook the paper as if wagging a finger. 'Maybe that's so he can tell folks his name. Huh? Fact is, we know it's Bill now.'

'I guess.' Earl manipulated the fire spit, then went to his bag, pulled out three biscuits and tossed one to Bill, who caught it one handed.

To the north, the low half-moon behind the clouds bathed the camp in soft light. The fire danced. Seldom had they enjoyed company; certainly, none so unusual.

'You reckon he rode alone?'

Walter found his tin food plate, drew a hunting knife from his belt and carved off a slice of hot meat. He inspected it, then tried it, mouth gaping at the heat.

'Guess so. Not all folks are as kindly to the afflicted. He could be run out of a town or ran himself out from fear or misunderstanding. Some folks don't like his kind, huh?'

Earl sneered but didn't rise to it.

'Wonder where he's from.' Walter stepped over to Bill. 'Where's home? Home?'

The kid couldn't fathom it and shook his head.

Walter looked at Earl, but neither could bridge that divide, so Walter sat.

Earl sipped coffee. 'So, what happens tomorrow? We drop him at the Doc, go back to looking after our own selves?'

'Doc is the right thing, first off.'

'And let's hope you've no need to call the undertaker on me.'

Earl rose, went to the fuel pile, and stoked up the fire. Flames licked the charred carcass. His stomach growled with anticipation.

Bill stood, made a washing motion over his face, pointed at the creek and walked away.

Walter stared pensively. Orange light flickered on his stubbled face and glinted in his kindly eyes.

'Remember Laura Mae Anderson?'

Earl rotated the spit. 'Can't say as I do.'

'Teaches in White Rock. She has a deaf girl. Twenty maybe, now.' He whistled softly. 'Where does the time go? Anyhow, Laura's a good woman.'

'She uses hands and all?'

'Yeah. She said it was a language from the Indian, and white folk are using it now.'

'So, we stole their land—now their hand-talking.' Earl shook his head. 'But he don't look like no Indian kid.'

'Maybe someone learned it to him.'

'And what else did they learn him, Walt? Scalping and all? Stealing?' Earl fixed Walter in a wide-eyed glare.

Walter puffed a familiar irritated sigh.

'Be smart. The kid's nothing like the Mojave who took your family—and you already forgave them. So, he talks with hands—what of it? Laura Mae and Sarah do too, and they're no heathens.'

'We don't know his upbringing, is all. Sure, I got no hate for the Indian, but I got no love neither.'

Walter sneered. 'You had a damn lot of love, as I recall.'

'Mary weren't Indian, dammit. Sure—a drop of blood, but not in her ways. Hell, she were kin to you. I'm talking about raiders and hell-raisers. Sneaky, thieving sons of bitches.'

'Which this kid is suddenly one of? All because he uses the hand-signing?' Walter glanced around. 'If you're that scared, we'll leave him, okay? Then you got your revenge… and maybe your soul will rest, and we can go on with our damn lives.' His eyes flared.

Earl leant away. 'Give over.'

'You sure? You don't want him here, that's plain as day. Look, I'll make like I'm taking first watch tonight, then when the kid's in shut-eye, we'll get gone.'

'What?'

'He'll be no worse off than he was before. We won't have to ride two up and you'll quit on putting fleas in my ear about how Bill's some kinda renegade, waiting to cut your throat. Hell, I'll leave a canteen, so he'll be better than before. Right?'

Earl stared down his friend, dumbfounded and conflicted.

Yet, it *was* a way out. Easy. Some kind of payback. Plus, Walter was the smart one—right? More world-wise. Better educated. Less full of baloney. This way, there would be no need to go to White Rock. No risk.

Tempting.

Walter thumbed over his shoulder. 'Remember—he's a cripple like you said, and it looks like nobody will miss him.'

Earl's throat tightened. 'What's got into you?'

Walter stared for an age, shook his head slowly and laid a hand on Earl's shoulder. The man's eyes were sober but good-natured.

'I was only for showing what an ass you are. I could no more leave this kid than I could've chased you off when you when you wound up in my barn.'

Earl scoffed. 'That makes you an ass right now too.'

'Yeah—but at least I know I am.' Walter retrieved his coffee mug and drank. 'So, I'm not asking you to be nursemaid, only to help me get the kid on his feet. The best start is Laura. We can't ask for a roof for Bill, but if she can talk to him, there'll be answers, and maybe he'll have folk to go back to. *Then* we'll be done. Yeah?'

The grass rustled. Earl watched Bill sit, comfortable in new company.

Walter was right. Perhaps by being calm, Earl could appease him. 'I guess everybody needs a chance.'

'And I got a life to get back to, same as you. A job of work. Ranch doesn't run itself.'

'Wood don't carve itself neither.'

'So, we do our duty to a needing kid, okay?'

'I guess.' Earl nodded towards Bill. 'Want me to give up my plate?'

'No. I see your hunger. You and the kid eat first. 'Sides, I need to make toilet.'

Walter carved off the most-cooked slices and Earl held out the two plates to be served.

He offered one plate and knife to Bill, then sat down with his own. The meat was hot and welcome, bar a gristly slice he flicked into the grass. The canteen's water slid down cool.

Beyond this relief, something inside his skull warned that the kid was now armed. If there was ever a time to cause a ruckus and steal a horse, it was now, with Walter away in the bushes. Maybe this was the weakness the kid had been waiting for? On against one.

Yet Bill smiled contentedly, and, hard as Earl gazed, he couldn't spy malice or plotting. It would be a blessing if the kid were simple in the head—they'd be safer.

Earl had drifted off, thousand-yard stare into the fire's ever-changing dance when Walter's absence weighed heavy, his return becoming worryingly overdue.

He was about to rise and check for problems when movement caught his eye. In his peripheral vision, firelight twinkled off the knife as it arrowed towards him.

Chapter 4

As Bill had probably never heard a cuss word, Earl didn't regret the torrent which spewed from his throat in shock. Nevertheless, his body language made Bill leap up.

He shot daggers at the kid. 'You figuring to gimme a heart attack?' he barked.

Walter arrived at a jog. 'For what?'

Earl pointed at the rattlesnake with a knife skewering its head to the soil. Apart from the fire's crackle and the blood rushing in his ears, all was silence.

'Kid near killed me.'

'Horseshit.' Walter tugged his knife out of the creature and measured his glance. 'Kid near saved your life.' He nodded at Bill, hands together in prayed thanks.

Bill shrugged as if it was all in a day's work, which did nothing for Earl's humour.

'Eat your damn dinner,' Walter sniped.

'You ain't no pa to me,' Earl grumped.

'All the same, you better grow a civil tongue, or you won't have the company of me tomorrow. If Dennis still holds that grudge, you'll want me there. And since when did you do what your pa said anyhow? You're forty-seven years old and a deaf boy not half that is better behaved. Think on that.'

He grabbed the canteen, washed the knife, wiped it dry on his pants, and then used it to carve off his dinner.

Earl kicked the six-foot deadweight reptile away from the camp, grew a pair of balls, went to the kid and muttered,

'Right grateful to you, Bill.'

The kid nodded—Earl guessed he got the sentiment.

So, they were square. He'd live another day—long enough to see Dennis, but maybe only that long.

He sat, reflecting, while Walter chewed through a vast quantity of lamb. The man had only a couple of inches in height, a few pounds in weight, and four years on Earl, but his appetite was disproportionate. Such was the rancher life.

'What if White Rock is enemy to him too?'

'The place he was running from?' Walter shook his head. 'I know most folks there, and Bill's not one.'

'He ain't from Ridgeway.'

'Plenty more towns round about. Doesn't strike me as a grown guttersnipe.'

The boy walked away, patted Jack, and went to a bush, where he took a piss.

Walter drank. 'Walks, eats, pisses, like a regular guy.'

'I got that. Makes me uncomfortable, is all. Like he got a secret.'

'It's not about you. Plenty of people won't have one minute for Bill. We gave him a day. There are enough evil sons of bitches in this world. Liars, thieves, murderers. Cripple he may be in your eyes, but a good kid is how I'm taking him.' Walter shot a look which said the conversation was done, pulled a flask from his waistcoat pocket and poured a measure into his coffee.

Earl shook his head, went to his saddlebag and returned with a brown bag, which he handed across.

'It don't cover the debt for your company again, but I figured it's something.'

Walter slid the bottle from the bag. 'Hard to come by.'

'Jimmy in Ridgeway said you had a bottle a few years back, and I know you're a sucker for something better'n firewater for fixing a coffee....'

'I never had fancy tastes except for a good whiskey.'

'We all got us weaknesses. But not everyone's got someone who sees past such.'

'Nor a friend who'll lie weeks in a barn bed for playing lumberjack for me.'

Earl waved it away. 'I never cared for your old place anyhow.'

'We had good times building it, though, huh? But a bullet weren't much thanks for that steer and what she did, burning the place before.'

'She was good eating though?' Earl winked, chewing on a morsel of lamb.

Walter laughed. 'And she weren't so mad as to make crazy stew.'

Earl laughed, too, though it quickly died. 'A bullet would have cured me of dumb foolery,' he murmured.

Walter clasped Earl's forearm. 'Now that talk is crazy. You living with it every day—and bleating my ear—is a pain in the ass, but nothing so much as seeing you in the ground. You learned the hard way about marking Mary's passing with drinking and railing, but if I have a cross to carry in future years, I'd want you beside me.'

He snatched up his coffee and drained it. 'Besides, you bring me good whiskey, I'd be mad as that old house-burning steer to cut you loose.' He looked Earl straight. 'You really want to clear that debt? Look ahead, not back. Help this kid like I helped you. Everybody makes mistakes. It's only dwelling on them that rots us inside.'

'I ain't begrudging the boy a chance.'

'So—no need for me to sit up the night with a shootin' iron across my knees, to watch against him jumping us?'

Earl sighed. 'I guess, no.'

Walter winked. 'But I'll keep my knife close. For snakes.'

Chapter 5

The camp lay scorched, except close to his makeshift bed, where the grass remained unseasonably lush—a green which tore into his retina.

The primary fire had been extinguished, but wisps of smoke rose from the charred earth over countless square yards. The birds didn't call, and insects were silent.

It was otherworldly.

He rose, trance-like. His stomach swam with bile as he spied the corpses of Walter and Bill, their heads scalped, eyes sightless. The horses lay motionless, caked in litres of their dried blood.

There came a stab of satisfaction that his caution had been proven right—Bill portended trouble—followed by repugnant self-loathing. He wanted to vomit but couldn't; his every fibre knotted like a hangman's noose.

Lazily, he brought a hand to his head and felt for wounds but found none.

He inhaled to confirm he was genuinely breathing. The smell hanging in the impossibly still air wasn't smoke but coffee. A grey pot rested on poor embers at the edge of the mound of ash.

Pain jabbed his ankle, so he looked down but saw nothing untoward.

There were no marauders as far as the horizon.

That pain in his leg again.

He reached out but touched only boot leather.

The eerie tranquillity pressed in as he surveyed the scene.

His leg twitched.

'Earl?'

He looked around for the source of the sound.

The voice came closer. 'Earl!'

There was nobody. His mind cartwheeled, sliding into fear.

'Hey.'

Except he knew the voice. So familiar it was hyper-real.

The next thud in his calf was more substantial, and he called out.

His brain detonated into awareness of truth, and he woke with a spasm, hands smacking the earth to prevent a fall that wasn't happening.

Light bloomed uncomfortably. Gravity pressed down like an anvil. Limbs felt so alien. He spluttered a breath as if surfacing from near-drowning, bursting into air like a cannon shot.

Walter's face appeared. 'Okay, partner?'

Earl pushed himself up onto his elbows, and reality washed over him. The fire crackled, the creek quietly slopped, and the smell of morning coffee was a welcome anchor.

He got his breath, calmed his thumping heart, and swallowed hard, moistening his cracked lips.

'Shit,' he breathed.

'Same old?' Walter's brow was knit.

'Yeah.'

'Thought I recognised you dreaming. Been a while.'

'Probably on account of Bill.' Earl spied the boy chewing on bacon. 'And having… responsibilities.'

Walter gave a sober smile and offered a canteen.

'So start easy with those.'

Earl sat up, then sprang to his feet, keen to shake off neediness. All the same, his back ached.

Camping out on the hard ground was a young man's game. He pulled on his jacket against the cold and walked to the creek. The air was clean and new but couldn't subsume old pain.

He filled the canteen, splashed his face, and took a long drink while he pondered the nightmare. He spat out the rank taste of his friend's apparent death—a passing which would have sated his need to be correct but collapsed his fragile soul.

He checked Jack's leg wound, which had improved.

'Don't go like that. Go quiet and old.'

He paced back to the camp, nodded a howdy to Bill and warmed his palms on the coffee mug. East, thin clouds were breaking into a brighter day.

He sat beside Walter. 'Did I wake you?'

Walter shook his head and munched on a biscuit. 'Your Jack okay?'

'We'll do fine.'

'Figured he should take only Bill, save a few pounds weight. You and I take Dusty and the plunder.'

'Those I know don't gotta give ground to them I don't. Long as we get to town, that's an end to it.'

'You make it into town civil, and I'll spring for pie.'

Earl cast his grounds on the dying fire. 'Whale away. I'm saddling up.'

Earl gathered his bedroll and war bag together, tacked up Jack and fussed him, stroking his big face and the dark patch on his forehead which passed for the letter "J".

The sun said about nine o'clock when they doused the last of the fire and pointed noses southwest.

Earl hated riding two-up. Dusty's spine made his ass sore. Still, it was the right thing to do. The kid rode Jack with care, which was a blessing.

They kept up a good trot for a half-hour before Walter slowed to a restful walk, taking a drink.

Something preyed on Earl's mind. 'About last night—you joking about killing the kid.'

'Why—you wish you'd done it?'

'No. Hell, no. Look, back in the day, you was on my side about not hunting down them what took my family. You regret that? You wanted to revenge but kept it inside?'

Walter shook his head. 'I hurt bad from losing cousin Mary—not as much as you—but bad. Still, an eye for an eye makes the whole world blind. Sometimes a man's gotta draw a line.'

'I'd sooner draw it after finding out what happened, 'stead of living with guesses and empty graves.'

'I'd sooner you forget. Draw that line.'

'It ain't like I can suddenly,' he clicked his fingers, 'Turn it off like a tap, or I would.'

Walter held up a cautioning hand. 'For my money, you don't want to know. Not really. The details, the hurt, it'd be too much. There's reason in everything—even if we don't like it.'

Earl's nose wrinkled in disgust. 'I done nothing to rile nobody. What they done—them Mojave raiders—I'll wager it was payback for some other feller's deeds.'

Walter nodded. 'That's how it used to go.'

'If that's so, whatever sonofabitch riled up the tribe what took my family shoulda drawn a line.'

'The past is past, friend.' Walter nodded at Bill. 'Good deeds are better than bad for making a future.'

'Then I done mine.' Earl searched the distant prairie for signs of White Rock—and an end to this deed.

'Figured I'd stay a night at the hotel,' Walter said.

'You and Bill both?'

'Don't see another way. He's carrying a few coins. I can't expect free board from anyone—for sure, not Laura. I'll talk to Sheriff Bowman. If vagrants set on Bill, and he can give a likeness, we might save another soul. And if they come calling again, have more grudge against Bill, the law should be ready to break up a fight. A man's face on a Want poster gets results. Gets money-seekers out hunting.'

'And if Bill's the cause?' Earl wondered.

'Then he'd be even more of the damn fool you already take him for. Which I don't believe.'

'You always see the good in people, Walt.'

'So I guess Bill's lucky. You'll stay over?'

'I ain't hankering to be at the end of Dennis' gun,' Earl replied.

'I know. But Dennis isn't a young man anymore. And he was never the fastest draw.'

'I'll wager he's had the practice I don't.'

He fingered his holster sadly, not wishing he'd had the practice and regretting he'd owned the gun in the first place.

Walter patted Earl's back.

'True. But maybe he'll see reason and understand the circumstance.'

Earl hoped to hell that was the case.

Chapter 6

Noon was approaching when they trotted past the rough-hewn sign, lolling on poor foundations, which proclaimed, "WHITE ROCK. Pop. 1244."

Earl blew a silent whistle at the town's expansion.

A stagecoach rattled past, showering them with red dust as it accelerated onto the prairie trail. As sparse outskirts began to cluster, Walter slowed Dusty to a walk and crossed the street towards a property. Bill followed dutifully on Jack.

Walter halted at the gate and they dismounted.

Earl wiped his face with a sleeve and forced disquiet down inside. Nonetheless, his eyes darted continuously, watchful for Dennis Hayes. He tied the reins on the low fencepost and rubbed Jack's nose.

The white picket fence needed repair and paint, and the chimney stood askew, but otherwise, it was a pretty place. His own couldn't hold a candle because two women were here—more homely in their inclinations.

'I'll go on.' Walter walked up the front walk.

To either side, spread a small garden. One Mary would be proud of.

It caught in Earl's throat. He took off his hat, reached out and stuffed Bill's into his hand. The kid flashed an apology—he seemed even less familiar than Earl at visiting folks.

As the door opened, the woman's face broke into a smile.

'Walter Doonan, why what a pleasure it is.'

Walter lifted his chinstrap and removed his Slouch with chivalry.

Earl had long seen the irony of a bachelor possessing such charm, set against his own lost cordiality, which the years had blown away. Many times, he'd encouraged Walter to find a wife. Was there a bond that even his dearest—and only—friend had kept in his heart?

'Ma'am,' Walter said.

'No need for your "ma'am". We've been acquainted too long.'

'How are you, Laura?'

'Pretty fine. What's the occasion?'

'Are you in need of occasion?'

'Never.' She looked towards Earl. 'Who are your friends?'

Earl ushered Bill forwards. Laura stepped onto the frontage, and the overhead sun caught her face. Her shirt was marl, crisp and snug to the neck; her skirt chocolate-coloured with a muted check.

Confusion on her face morphed into recognition. 'Earl Johnson, unless I'm mistaken?'

'You have the advantage of me, ma'am.'

He bowed gently by way of compensation for his stiffness and unfamiliarity. He hoped she couldn't see the lump in his throat, which was there for many reasons.

'We met a few years back,' she clarified.

Many years, Earl mused—the days of new marriage when he only had eyes for Mary. Days when White Rock was their nearest town, when he saw folk, and had a spring in his step.

Mercifully, Walter stepped in to save his blushes. 'And this here is Bill.'

'He's deaf,' Earl blurted, then cursed inside.

'Best as we can figure, Laura. Found him out past Tipping Rock, off the trail, abandoned. Maybe robbed.'

'Hello Bill,' she offered. There was no reply. 'I'm Laura.' Her hands flitted.

Silence.

She moved her palm out sideways from her head, almost in salute. 'Hello.'

Her smile was unforced and welcoming. Earl reckoned if it could lift his spirits, it could easily brighten Bill.

They all looked at the kid. He repeated the gesture.

Earl's heart skipped: they had a route out of this mess.

Laura spelt out something on her fingers. 'Bill?'

Earl's brow furrowed, intrigued by the beauty of the actions, then caught himself and fell sober.

The kid nodded.

'Bill it is,' she said to them.

'Not bad for two old fools, eh?' Walter said to Earl.

'That's about all we have, ma'am. No family name, no home, no trade.'

Laura regarded the boy. 'So, Walter, I'd be correct that Bill is the reason for your stopping by?'

'Shoot. The fact is it's like aiming at ladybugs in the dark, fellers like us making sense with the kid or trying to help him, much past dusting down and offering little chow.'

'You're hoping he can sign?'

'He's a good kid, much as we know. Damn near saved Earl's life, too.'

Her face lit. 'Is that so?'

Earl shifted uncomfortably on his feet, called out for being weak, unable to look after himself and needing the services of a deaf mute.

'Walt would have, anyhow,' he said hurriedly.

Walter shrugged. 'Bill took an injury in the shoulder. Thrown, maybe. Not broken, I don't reckon. Or he's the temperament of an ox.'

Laura tapped her shoulder and signed. Bill shook his head and gestured, but without her flair.

'I'll take a guess he's not been around his kind,' Walter said.

'A little rusty, yes. We can get along, though, Bill?' Her hands danced.

Bill smiled weakly, and Earl recognised a gesture from the previous night.

'What does this mean?' he asked Laura, mimicking palm-away-from-lips.

'It means "thank you". And it sounds like he has reason for it.'

'Anybody would've saved a lost kid. Right?' Walter gave Earl a knowing look.

'I reckon so.' Earl scowled, not wanting to be embarrassed in front of a lady.

She looked at the three unexpected arrivals as if weighing them up. Earl prayed they'd made a good impression: this was make or break for an end to the affair.

'I have coffee on the stove.' She stacked her fists and circled one on the other, giving Bill a querying glance.

Bill signed in reply.

'We won't stop,' Walter said. 'You earn a rest Saturdays.'

'Come on in,' she supplicated.

'Right grateful,' Earl mumbled.

They filed in, flanking Bill front and rear. The hallway held two doors to the left and right, an ornate coat stand and a thin side table.

Footsteps sounded, and a young girl appeared. Her face bloomed with surprise, and she stopped dead. Earl wondered why she hadn't come while they were talking at the door, then remembered. All so alien.

'Sarah, this is Walter, Earl and Bill.' Laura signed the same.

The girl, caught in the unfamiliarity, signed with hasty disquiet. Laura replied.

Sarah looked beyond her mother at Bill. She eased closer to him, curious, like a kitten seeing a mouse for the first time. Her face softened. She slowly signed—a small phrase, Earl reckoned.

Bill nodded. Sarah brought her index finger from ear to lips. He nodded again. Her smile was of palpable relief.

Laura gestured into the living room. 'I think coffee is in order for these good souls.'

'Reckon you did good, Walt,' Earl breathed.

Chapter 7

Walter gave Laura the skinny on how they'd found Bill.

Earl's gaze alighted on the various ornaments and effects. There were books and papers, a photograph of Laura with a man—Jim, if he recalled, a nondescript medal and a few wooden toys, presumably relics of Sarah's youth. On the wall hung a pair of tapestries, beautiful and neatly sewn. One depicted a landscape, the other an image of the house.

Earl remained standing, as there were only four chairs. His eye was drawn to the spectacle of Bill and Sarah communicating haltingly. Yet, it was his frequent looks at Laura which caused the most guilt. Barely five minutes had passed, and she seemed to trust Bill more than Earl did after a full day. Maybe you had to be one of their kind to do that.

He felt like an unwilling chaperone, a man out of touch with not only young folk but those who lived in a silent world—one which left a sour taste in his mouth. Were they saying things behind his back—especially unsettling in plain sight? Was Bill already turning Sarah against Earl for things he'd said and done?

Bill couldn't, could he? He'd heard not a word, and Earl had largely remained private in his disquiet. Maybe "hearing folks" were all as one. The "others". The "privileged". Nevertheless, Bill seemed better here, not the burden he had been.

A chair leg scraped on the floor as Bill recoiled from something. Walter stood in a flash.

Sarah signed hastily.

'Not keen to show his shoulder to a lady,' Laura said.

'We figured Doc Cartwright could pay a visit. Give a say-so on his condition,' Walter replied. 'We'll call by. Need to walk up anyhow to tell the Sheriff.'

'You want to catch the men who did this?'

Walter shrugged. 'Long shot. Thugs, thieves. Preying on the innocent, a kid who can't hear danger coming.'

'Well, White Rock is no feather bed,' she replied with a sober expression.

'You and Sarah get by fine.'

'We make our way.'

Earl indicated the tapestries. 'You sew real pretty.'

'That's Sarah. Fine seamstress. Hands are for more than talking, you know,' Laura said.

'You're right on that.'

'We'll leave the kid here a spell. I'll fetch the Doc, get a room fixed.' Walter reached into his pocket and held a coin between his thumb and forefinger. 'This is for trouble.'

She pushed his hand down. 'Put that away. There were days I could offer you a coin.'

He laid it on the table. 'A meal's not free, Laura. That's my word on the matter. You'll be fine? He's a good kid. I don't expect no trouble.'

She acceded with a nod. 'I still have Jim's gun.'

'I reckon you have something better'n that—a reason for Bill to do right by you.'

Earl itched to leave. 'Yeah, a good kid, I guess. Come on, Walt. Affairs to attend to.'

Walter nodded to Laura. 'Anything, you holler.'

She gestured to where Bill and Sarah were engaged in staccato conversation. 'Sarah can make a bad mare do good bidding—a boy should be no problem.' She smiled.

Earl tapped his forehead in farewell and led Walter out.

They left the horses roped up at Laura's and headed up the street. Walter received gestures of recognition, and then he resumed preaching.

'That wasn't so bad, was it?'

'Meeting ladies ain't the issue. It was what if they don't like Bill, meaning we got no way for him. And my history here, which you know of.'

'Come out from under that cloud. 'Sides, the… "meeting ladies" did you just fine.'

Earl stopped dead. Walter flashed a wink.

'And what's that for?'

Walter shrugged. 'I seen that look before, is all.'

'There weren't no look. I didn't give no look.'

'Hmm. Seemed a lot like a look I know from a dancehall a time back.'

Earl shot him daggers. 'Give over. I were civil, is all. Weren't I? You always ragging on me to be such? Laura Mae's a good woman—you said so. I know we gotta take her kindness, so's we can get the hell out.' He looked around nervously. 'Afore another of us needs the Doc. Or worse.'

'Okay, buddy. I'll give it a rest. We do our duty, and then we'll get pie.'

He felt like a kid receiving a treat for good behaviour. 'I guess.'

They trudged along the side of the broad street, where stores were busy with daytime trade. Folks of all ages passed, horses scuffed up dust, and the familiar sounds of civilisation ebbed and flowed.

All the way, Earl watched every man, every window, hand on the butt of his gun. He drank in the place, which had changed so much. Flags hung from a half-dozen frontages, including a new drugstore.

On the far side of the main crossroads, they stepped onto the boards of the jail. In the intervening years, the word "Sheriff" had been stencilled onto new windows.

'Law's pretty fancy now,' Earl mumbled to himself.

With a cursory nod to the young deputy, who lazed against a pillar post watching the world, they passed inside.

In the front room stood two desks, one occupied. Half-partitioned at the rear, the room contained two empty holding cells. Earl didn't remember them so spacious. He didn't want to remember at all.

Sheriff Bowman's moustache was white, five years ahead of his greying mane. The tin star hung lopsided, and the man's round eyeglasses sat likewise.

'Walter, howdy,' he said genially. Then his tone dropped. 'Earl.'

Earl touched the brim of his hat.

'What can I do for you gentlemen?' Bowman continued.

'We found a kid out near Tipping Rock. Busted up in the dirt. Looking like he'd been set on, had his ride and pistol taken.'

Bowman slid out the desk drawer. 'Drink?'

Walter waved it away. Earl held in his contempt. Still, the Sheriff poured a measure. Some things hadn't changed.

There came the noise of boots on boards behind, and Earl covered his gun, wary of an unseen visitor. Yet if it was Dennis Hayes, surely the man would have the sense not to shoot him dead in the sight of the law?

He listened for the click of a hammer. His body flooded with black dread. At least Bill had been left in good hands: Earl's final deed would be honourable, even if imposed.

'Some nerve, Earl,' said the man.

Earl exhaled, though the relief was only partial.

Bowman raised a mollifying hand. 'Here on an errand of mercy, Lyle. Found an ambushed kid.'

Earl inspected Mayor Lyle Potter. The black planter hat and long coat were present and correct, light shirt and formal tie. The man hadn't put on weight—though he didn't need it. More the pity—he was long past due in the ground anyhow.

If there was one man besides Hayes he didn't want to be within ten feet of, it was Potter.

'What kid?' The Mayor's hooded eyes filled with perpetual accusation.

'Name of Bill, we hear. Eighteen maybe.' Walter replied. 'In need of a bath and resting up.'

'He give any descriptions?' Bowman drained his glass, refilled it, and poured an extra for Potter.

'He's a deaf kid, Sam.'

Potter stepped in. 'What's that?'

'He's a deaf-mute. Kinda hoping he'd talk… tell… explain to Laura Mae Anderson what happened. Find out his folks, maybe get him back home.'

'You brought another one of *them* here?'

Earl's lip curled in distaste at the Mayor's tone. He dropped back.

Walter squared up to Potter. 'There suddenly a law against it, Lyle?'

'We've already got *one*,' Potter spat.

'It's only for a spell until he gets fixed up.'

'White Rock is not a town for cripples.'

Earl noted the Mayor's waist; the fancy holster hung under his left hand, its hip slightly higher than the right.

He measured his words. 'Everyone who's hurting deserves a place. He's making no harm.'

Potter span lazily, putting threat into even a simple gesture. 'You might remember whose town this is, Earl. And that you're walking dead.'

'I don't forget nothing.'

'I don't want him here, bushwhacked or not.'

'He's here,' Walter interjected. 'Unarmed and no grudges. Nobody gets thrown out for living and breathing.'

'Know the law too, is that so?'

Bowman raised calming hands. 'If he's no trouble, not walking the streets, not interfering with folk, there's no crime.'

'Twenty-four hours,' Potter said.

'One is fine, but two ain't—that a fact?' Earl asked.

'What's it to you?'

'Not a jot. But Walt did the right thing, and you oughta watch your respect.'

'I said not a word against your friend. He talks and hears as good as any man. Any real person. One who's welcome in this town. Unlike some.'

Earl fixed Potter in his best stare, mind whirling for words of neither retreat nor inflammation.

Walter brushed past the bulky Mayor, tugging Earl's jacket. 'Come on, buddy, we'll be going now.'

Earl abandoned the standoff to follow Walter out into the sunshine.

'Why did I think you wouldn't be a damn fool?' Walter sniped. 'You'd do wise not to argue with Lyle Potter. What's between you is on you. And you already reckon there's a bullet here with your name on. Don't make things worse.'

'My arguing is from him being an asshole. Lord knows how he's still running the show.'

They paused while a horse and trap clipped past, then crossed the street.

'He was born here, has money and enough goodwill toward him to keep on.'

Earl snorted. 'And the balls to call hisself Mayor. Crock of shit.'

'That's your battle, not this town's. Lyle's appreciated for what he does. You see the state of the place. And since when were you the kind to look out for a supposed "half a man" like Bill who didn't belong out riding on his own? Huh?'

Earl grabbed Walter's arm and brought them to a stop.

'It ain't on account of sunshine from the boy—mark me on that. But Potter railing on them women ain't right. What they done today, letting a strange kid into their house, makes them good people.' He looked away. 'Maybe better'n me.'

Earl resumed walking. 'We all need people looking out for us. We all got our bad times, our crosses.'

'No argument on that.'

'Then I'm getting pie, no matter if it's from you.

After visiting Doc Cartwright and asking him to head down to check on Bill, they went for coffee and pie, then walked back to the Anderson house.

Earl stayed unusually tight to his friend, but if he left town without buckshot in his chest, he'd forgive himself a spot of nerves.

He spied the dancehall, and memory tweaked the corners of his mouth. No dancing had touched his feet since Mary passed. No trips to meet womenfolk. Seeking company was different to having it thrust upon him. Yet the interaction with Laura was pleasant despite his admitted awkwardness.

Walter patted the horses. 'I'll take Jack over to the vet. You take Dusty home if you're fixing to rush out.'

Earl shot him a stern look. 'No calling me yellow, now.'

'You came. We did good. I've no desire to see Dennis Hayes take issue with you for a Christian deed.'

Laura emerged from the house.

'Bill any trouble?' Walter asked.

'He's a pretty gentle boy. Doc says he'll mend fine.'

'Makes a man wonder what he did, winding up on the ground like that. You get any kinda story from him? Place to go?'

She shook her head. 'He ran away from home and can't go back. He's been living on his wits a long time, I'd say.'

'In need of a bath and a square meal,' Walter said.

'And folks who know his kind,' Earl added.

'You make them sound like animals,' she replied.

He hated her expression—because he knew that he deserved it. So why did he want to be better in her eyes?

'Earl's not… a born communicator,' Walter said. 'But the Samaritan in him stopped for Bill and saw him right.'

Earl half looked away. 'It's not best convenient, is all.'

'When is?' she asked. 'Good values know no days or seasons.'

Earl's stomach knotted. She knew nothing of his life, his loss—especially on this anniversary of heartache. He glanced around; pretty house, community, and family. Well, Bill had succour and support now, and that was an end to it. The kid was out of danger. The debt was repaid. No point in messing with Hayes.

He unhitched Dusty. 'I'll call back tomorrow. Collect Jack from the veterinarian. Maybe… look in on the kid.'

He mounted hurriedly. He tipped his hat. 'Ma'am.'

Her smile was faint.

He eased the reins back and over, and Dusty got the message, so he pressed them into a trot. As soon as a polite distance passed, they accelerated into a gallop.

Chapter 8

Earl's two-hour ride home to his remote property took welcome attention away from his introspection.

He tied up Dusty at the water trough, removed the tack and stowed it in the house. He left the door open wide and heaved up the wooden shutters on the two windows.

After draining the canteen, he brought his war bag and bedroll inside and unpacked them. He lit the stove, enjoyed a change of clothes and wolfed down a couple of biscuits.

He stood overlooking the sharply curving river, which formed a partial border to the low promontory. The bank was steep but scalable; it only deterred a horseback approach—his decision to guard against an enemy long gone.

The sun tickled his back as he absorbed the near-silence, lifted only by the distant rush of water and a murmur from the chicken coop. It made his stomach jealous, so he went to say howdy to his bevvy.

'Hey, ladies.' He leant on the rail. 'Lucky you don't judge me like some, huh? All the same, I'd take it if it meant company.' He scoffed. 'Listen to me—talking to birds. Least I keep *you* safe, huh?'

He collected five eggs and gave the fence a once-over check. No varmints had tried to break in.

In the house, he put those eggs with some beans on the stove and whipped up a meal. He ate outside on the old felled trunk he and Walter had dragged out a decade earlier. There was a smooth patch where he'd longtime sat his ass down, sometimes musing that this could be a love seat if things were different. Yet, he'd actively avoided love.

At best, his friend took a pew, and another worn area bore witness to the hours they'd passed trying—and failing—to set the world to rights. No—not the world. The world was fine—that's what Walt would say. Only Earl needed fixing.

He sighed.

Walt and Bill would probably be at table in Matthews Saloon.

He wondered if the kid took a drink. How he'd order it. How he'd order anything. How he'd realise if he sat in the wrong seat or looked the wrong way.

Not tonight; Walt would be there to help. Anyway, Bill had accrued eighteen or more years on the planet and slept, drunk and eaten just fine. The boy didn't need babysitting. Even if he needed a caring arm, Laura could offer it now.

He pictured her, and it brightened his spirits.

Two eagles fought noisily overhead.

He hoped there'd be no scrapping in Matthews tonight.

He took his metal plate into the house, washed it off, and then went to his workshop hut next door.

The wood smells never tired him. He peered around absentmindedly and picked up a couple of tools he'd failed to put back in their drawer. The chisel looked dull, so he took out the sharpening stone and worked bite back into the device.

He tested it on the piece of work on the bench, putting more depth into the folds of the half-formed angel's gown.

To avoid straining his back, he pulled up the stool and worked. He switched to the finer chisel to finesse the detail, followed by gentle sanding, then retook the broad chisel to fashion another fold.

He continued, lost in his craft as the sun sank below the horizon.

The clear night gave birth to a veil of unbroken blue.

Earl breakfasted outside, serenaded by birds, chickens and the fire's crackle and hiss.

As he ate bacon, beans, eggs and biscuits, washed down with piping hot coffee, his curiosity moved to Walter's welfare. He wasn't the fastest gun, not even when they were younger, and Potter had a reputation. But then, Walter saw eye to eye with the Mayor a whole lot better than Earl did. Perhaps he'd escape retribution for associating with a deaf kid.

Yet the town was more than two or three men. It was a swirling pot of unpredictability, mixed with the comings and goings of the stagecoach and whatever examples of society it brought. However, one man had made an unambiguous prediction: "I see you in town again, Earl, I'll kill you."

He sighed. It only took a wrong word from a wrong man to a right man to make a right man a wrong man. A wrong dead man or a wrong living man.

Sometimes it was better to be dead than broken.

Earl was broken but would rather not wind up dead—not yet. At least, not thanks to Bill. Bill came already broken. Already cursed. That kind of thing attracted trouble like flies around manure.

He and Walt might have saved Bill's life once, from something as benign as nature, but nobody—not Walter, not Laura, and especially not he—could guarantee it wouldn't need saving again.

Everybody needs saving sometimes.

Good people like Laura Mae don't live on every corner. Nor Mary.

He looked skyward.

Only angels watch over you without interruption. But sooner or later, you have to meet them and offer thanks for getting the spell on earth you did.

Had Bill lived on wits, luck, or the blessings of angels before now?

It was moot—if the kid had done wrong, he'd reap what he sowed. The same is true for all men, hearing or not. Yet Earl hoped not to reap. He was stirring a hornet's nest by even visiting White Rock. Nonetheless, he had to regain his rightful horse and, being honest, excuse his behaviour to a good woman.

He went inside. This wasn't a sweet house, not like hers, with its homely smells and air of kindness.

He gazed across the frankly ramshackle shelf stack he'd made years ago and found something suitable.

Then he saddled Dusty, packed a full bag for good order, and secured the house.

Careful to enter town from the direction closest to Laura Mae's house, he slowed to a walk as he approached. Jack wasn't tied up outside, so he was about to pass by in search of Walter when he noticed Laura tending to her garden.

As he watched her, his spirits fell, knocked by the echo of another woman, another keen gardener. Still, his eyesight wasn't dimmed by his heart's weight, and he took pleasure in what it gazed on—a resonance with a future that hadn't transpired.

He girded his humours, dismounted and tied Dusty to the gate. He self-consciously brushed dust off his jacket.

'Morning.' He rushed his hat down from his head.

'Earl, morning.' She walked over. 'I was afraid you wouldn't be back.' A barb prickled her tone.

'Yeah. It weren't polite how I cut stick yesterday. Right sorry.'

'You did a good thing with Bill. But we all have our lives, I suppose.'

'Walt said you was the best person with folks like that. He's a good judge.'

She frowned. 'I suppose I am good with... people like Bill.'

He hung his head. 'Shoot. I didn't mean nothing by it. I ain't... much for words. With anybody.'

She rested her crossed hands on the top of a white fencepost. Her nails were short; her hands neither strong nor delicate.

'Then you're fine because Sarah and Bill don't use words.'

'All the same....' He stopped, not wanting to dig a hole and lose his sorry ass down there. He scratched his head and offered a lame smile.

She cocked her head. 'So, assuming you were asking after their welfare, your friend and your... wounded lion are fine. You can go home. But it was nice you asked.'

Her smile was thin. She'd seen through him as clear as spring water.

He fumbled in his shirt pocket, pulled out the trinket and gingerly offered it across.

'Ain't much by way of gratitude, but... better'n words I don't got.'

She turned it over in her hand. 'Earl, this is beautiful.' Her face lit. She held the wooden brooch—about an inch across—up to her breast. 'You made this?'

'Not on account of... I mean... Yeah. Just... a thing I do.'

She fingered the carved petals and inspected the fine grain. 'Is this because...?' She eased her head towards the picture-postcard garden.

'I guess.'

'Well, the way I see it, you don't need words when you can use your hands like this.'

He felt as if he'd blushed, barely remembering the sensation. 'Mighty kind.'

A pregnant silence fell, broken only by a pair of mares clattering past. As she watched the horses, he took the chance to note how her brown eyes were mirrored by her chocolate-coloured blouse.

She focussed on him, and he glanced away towards the departing mares, as if caught.

He thought he saw the tiniest flare in her eyebrows.

She coughed. 'I was making coffee. If you were thirsty before going back.'

'I couldn't be beholding.'

She laughed, lilting and warm. 'A blood oath is "beholding". This is only coffee. Besides, Walter will be back from the store for me, and unless I misunderstood, he'll want Dusty from you.'

It had totally slipped his mind. 'That's the case.'

She swung the gate open. 'Come on through.'

He perched on a seat at the table, whose finely wrought tablecloth was trimmed in undulating lace. It was odd to be in a house that wasn't his or Walter's. He visited other properties to deliver his wares, but as a tradesman, not a guest. Cordiality was expected here because of the debt he owed.

'So, you're a woodworker?'

'That's so,' he replied.

She held out her hand. 'I splintered myself something bad trying to repair that fence. So I appreciate your line of work.'

He glanced at the injury, fighting an impulse to take her hand and investigate. Still, the idea had occurred.

She played with the brooch. 'I used to tell Jim he should try jewellery and the like, but there was always a horse to shoe.'

He didn't know the details, but he got the headline. 'I'm real sorry.'

She shrugged, set the brooch on the table, and picked up her cup. 'Time heals all wounds.'

'I guess,' he lied.

'Are you a Christian man?'

'Sure.'

'We're going to church later. To say a word for Bill and so forth. You're welcome along.'

The thought of actively seeking the company of more townsfolk spiked his heart rate.

'By you, but not by some.'

Her brow furrowed. 'How so?'

'I got a… disagreement with a man.'

'Which man?'

'Dennis Hayes. We got history.'

'And you're avoiding him?'

He presumed it was concern, not intrigue—she was a bright woman, and disagreements and brawls were inevitable in menfolk.

'Yeah. For reason why I high-tailed out yesterday.'

She nodded. 'Well, you're in luck. I know Mrs Hayes, and she and Dennis are upcountry for a while at their daughter's wedding.'

He fixed her in an inquisitive gaze. 'That so?'

'So, you won't bump into him at church.'

His every muscle relaxed. There was a stay of execution. But for how long?

He drained his cup. 'I don't like to impose. I… we… already leaned on your good nature.'

'And drunk my coffee.'

It was said in jest, so he showed good humour. 'Fair exchange if I was to mend that fence.'

Where had that come from? His heart and eyes—not his mind—were controlling his mouth, which would countenance that unnecessary time in White Rock was still dangerous.

She waved it away. 'You're no fix-up carpenter for needy spinsters, Mr Johnson.'

'It'd be the least I owe—Walt and I owe. Fetching a kid you're not kin to, ask for your help and so forth.'

'I help young people every day. Nobody teaches in the schoolhouse if they don't want to better folks. So, church is at two-thirty, if you're minded.' She shrugged. 'Unless you have a home to go to.'

He rubbed his stubbled chin. 'Reckon I could offer up some good words for his guidance on the road.'

'With four sets of prayers, Bill will be set well.'

'That's so.'

He rode Dusty up the street, scanning curiously, not warily. Sounds of hammering drifted out from the rear of the undertakers.

He tied up outside the General Store. The paint was new, and the prices a few cents higher than in Ridgeway, but the proprietor remained unchanged. The feminine scent of soap mingled with wood, tobacco, spices, onions and kerosene.

'Howdy, Frank.'

'I'll be a son of a gun.' Frank Wilson was pushing sixty, with a full white beard and elaborate moustache.

'I ain't the second coming.'

'Walt said you was in town.' Frank's eyes narrowed. 'Said you brought a kid.'

Earl's hackles tingled. 'Reckon there ain't no law against it.'

'I guess not. One more in White Rock is one more customer, to take the good of the bad circumstance.' Frank sneered. 'Talking with hands—it ain't natural.'

'You sell to Laura Mae,' he pointed out.

'Well, ain't that great—another cripple-lover.'

Clearly, Lyle Potter had gotten his claws into this man too. Earl measured his response.

'Them kids are nothing to me. I only done what I thought best—giving a man a chance not to wind up buzzard food or in the hoosegow. Now, you gonna serve me, or will I get my wants up in Ridgeway?'

The shop owner sighed. 'What'll I get you?'

'Oatmeal. Molasses. Coffee beans.'

Frank gave a cursory nod and went searching.

The front door opened, its bell tinkling.

Out of habit, Earl's hand came to his gun. Both familiarity and unfamiliarity bred contempt. He turned. Earl recognised the slightly hooked nose, but a once-toddler had grown into a stocky sonofabitch.

'Frank out back?' the young man asked, eyes narrowed.

'Yeah,' Earl replied.

'Okay.'

A pregnant pause.

'You Potter's boy?' Earl asked.

'You Walter Doonan's buddy?'

'Maybe.'

'You bring another deaf fool into our town?'

'You got some mouth on you, kid.' It seemed to run in the family.

'Just looking after the folks in town, like my pa.' The kid kept his distance. 'So I hope the cripple knows to stay in his own lane.'

'What lane would that be?'

'Keeping his hands off my property.'

Earl stepped in. 'What property? Exactly?'

'You want to tell him—the outsider—in whatever twisted way he talks and hears—Sarah is not for plucking.'

A taste of bile washed Earl's throat. 'That so?'

'Yeah. Now, you done being served?'

How did Laura and Sarah tolerate this? Earl was no saint, but the implication of a relationship between the girl and this dirt crawler was a whole other matter. She seemed to have more sense.

Frank reappeared with the items. 'Anything else, Earl?'

Earl shook his head, tossed a few coins on the counter, swept up his produce and went to the door.

'Fifteen cents change,' Frank called.

'Buy the kid a quarter ounce of soap for washing out his damn mouth.'

He clanged the door shut.

Out on the street, he took a deep breath and cleared his lungs of frustration.

Was this the right town for Bill after all?

Chapter 9

Earl found Walter and the kid at the stables. Bill was tacking up Jack. Earl landed firm pats on the horse's neck.

'Jack's fine,' Walter said. 'Vet fixed him up.'

'Thanks. What do I owe for Jack's board here?'

'Abe says on the house, as recompense for what went on.'

'Abe still here?'

'They've not run me out of town yet,' came a voice.

He vaguely recollected the man; black, slightly wiry, scalp-fitting greying hair and stubble. The look of a man with a century of knowledge and deeds in a frame half that age.

'Been... a while.'

'That it has.' Abe pulled off his Derby hat and offered his hand. 'Like I said to Walt, if your mount got hurt helping this kid, the least I can do is show appreciation. Not all folks are so kindly to people like Bill.'

Abe turned to Bill and signed.

Earl assumed Abe had learned hand talking from Laura.

The kid signed back.

'Says he has no home,' Abe said.

'Same he told Laura. Or none he wants to go back to,' Walter added.

Earl took Jack's reins. 'Well, he better fix to find one or Potter'll run him out of town as a vagrant. Then he'll be on his ass in the dust again and looking for more charity.'

'Kid needs a wage. No board without a wage,' Abe said.

Earl mounted up. 'Well, you put a man back on his feet, he's gotta walk—hearing or not—or he's nothing but a burden. And Lord knows I ain't got room for none more.' He tipped his hat. 'But I'll leave a prayer in town for him.'

Earl scanned around. The whitewashed church was busting at the seams, and the seams needed restitching: part of the roof was covered in tarpaulin. It certainly held in the heat generated by a warm sun and many bodies.

Laura sat on the aisle end of the row, intermittently fanning herself with a burgundy-coloured affair, her starched white blouse buttoned tightly to her slim neck. Her hair was tressed up. Beside her was Sarah, then Walt, Bill, and himself on the far end, away from as many eyes as possible.

Earl noted frequent glances in their direction during the service; even the preacher's fulsome oratory couldn't distract every member of the congregation from whatever other thoughts Earl and his companions were triggering.

He wanted to leave. He didn't belong there, not in a house of peace, tolerance and forgiveness—not feeling how he did. Envious. Uncomfortable. Judgemental.

Earl needed a prayer for himself. So, he silently offered one up. Still, he also gave thanks for people like Walter and Laura, better folks than he'd ever be.

Everyone stood for Psalm 23. The words burrowed deep.

How could he excuse his manner in the long shadow of death when Walter, Laura and Sarah had also walked through that valley? They had lost kin yet remained civil, even bright. Why did the rod and staff offer scant comfort to him alone? Were they merely words? Had this only been lip service these two decades? Had something else died that long-past day— his faith?

A real or imagined cold wind gusted past the pew.

He was alone in a room of two hundred people.

They finished the incantation and sat. He alternated his gaze between the pastor, Bill's attentiveness which alternated between the celebrant and Laura's moving hands, and various folks scattered through the room.

He consoled himself that whatever the state of his faith—whether shattered by loss—God still needed instruments of His work, and perhaps on this occasion, he and Walt had been chosen. The least Earl could do to repay that faith was to do a good deed to a fellow and needy citizen.

The deed had been done.

Maybe after so long, he was square with God.

After the service, he wanted to make tracks, but Laura and Walt held back to speak to Pastor Desmond. Besides, he guessed they'd had their fill of him making quick tracks. Besides, there was no rush, with Dennis temporarily absent. It might even give him the chance to behave civilly around folk for a few days.

However, not everyone would make that easy.

Potter ambled out of the open double doors, and the sight of the makeshift quintet sucked the good humour from him as if it had been communion wafers crumbling in a fist.

'Fine sermon, Pastor.'

'Why, thank you, Lyle.'

Potter faced Sarah and Bill. 'Fine sermon, wouldn't you say?' He looked daggers at them, awaiting a response that wouldn't come.

Laura pushed between the youngsters. 'I agree.'

Bill signed to her, a query on his face.

Potter scowled. 'Hands of the red man.'

'Speaking with hands is as much for white folks as speaking with mouths, Mayor,' Laura said.

'And hearing? All that finger flapping doesn't speak to the Lord. The holy word is here,' he pointed to his mouth, 'And they better learn to see it, or the devil takes them.'

Laura flinched, though she tried to hide it.

Earl stepped forwards. 'And any law we should know 'bout attending church?'

Potter fixed Earl in a haughty stare. 'These two ladies may be law-abiding, God-fearing folk, but what vouching can you do for the stranger you put on our town?'

Walter eased Bill away, then eyed Potter. 'The kid's no harm to you, nor anyone.'

'I guess not. No gun, no ears, no tongue.'

'Mr Mayor,' Laura began.

Potter tipped his hat, verging on unexpected cordiality. 'I should be letting you folks run. Stage leaves in an hour.'

'Have a good trip,' Walter said.

Potter turned. 'Oh, it isn't me that's leaving.'

'Bill's not staying longer than he needs.'

'I won't have no-name strangers sleeping on the street. White Rock is a civilised town.'

'He has a bed at the Hotel.'

Potter came closer. 'Well, I can't see how that's possible. See, the Hotel's full.'

'I'm not sure it is, Lyle.'

'Oh, I reckon so. Not a single room left in town.' He withdrew his gold pocket watch and looked at it theatrically. 'Like I said, I should let you folks run on.'

Earl was half in his path and didn't move. His teeth ground.

Potter lowered his voice. 'Pity cousin Dennis isn't here to greet you too.'

'Any man standing in the way of a mission of mercy should shame hisself for it.'

'And you'd know all about shame. Or was it bad luck? Looks like it rubbed off on that cripple, too, while you rode up. Pity again.'

Potter breathed a sarcastic chuckle and strode away.

Chapter 10

Earl walked with Walter. Ahead, Laura and Sarah linked arms. Bill brought up the rear, looking around with interest. Those in Sunday best mixed with people going about their day.

A handful of kids scampered past, their shrieks of fun decorating the street.

Potter's objections—and objectionable nature—were thrown into context with each step. Passers-by had a nod, a smile, even a word for either Laura or Walter. Nobody had much time for Earl—there can't have been more than a hundred in White Rock from the time he was last here. Yet being a stranger didn't make him unwelcome.

A grey-haired woman zeroed in on him. A faint recollection tickled his mind.

'Why, Earl Johnson, as I live and breathe.'

'Ma'am.'

'I thought we'd never see you again and be able to offer our thanks.'

He willed a recall of her meaning—a past deed which held him in good character.

He pulled off his hat. 'It were nothing.'

'My old Pete was buried with that cane you fashioned, he loved it so much. It helped keep him moving about town.' Her head fell. 'Until the end.'

Earl laid a hand on her stooped shoulder. 'Like I say, it were nothing. I'm sorry for your loss.'

'I'm glad to see you in White Rock again, Mr Johnson. You're a good man.'

'Well, I ain't figuring to stay. Just here on a… on an errand of mercy.'

'Then lucky to whoever you help.' She smiled, nodded at Walter, and then shuffled away.

Earl stood rooted for a few moments, then caught up with his companion, all the while wondering who Pete and the old woman were. Lost in the haze of time—pushed out of his mind by bigger and worse things since. If only White Rock was as welcoming to Bill.

However, he and Walt were in it now—they couldn't abandon Bill until the kid was fixed up. It would make Earl look bad, and all the effort so far would be meaningless.

Laura and Sarah had stopped walking meanwhile, and he came alongside.

'Mrs Anderson, ma'am, what causes you to stay here? What did you do that the kid ain't done, so he gets left alone?' he asked.

'We're hardened against those folks now. It's no different to how I could protest about drunks and bar fights that offend many women's sensibilities, but it's wasted breath. No town is perfect, Earl. We get by.'

Laura put an arm around Sarah's waist. 'We've long time wished for another man running the town, but there's no more value wishing for that than there is hoping these youngsters had their hearing back.'

She sighed. 'But we won't do any good standing in the street unpicking folks' character. Besides, Lyle does right by many in town. Made this place attractive to live and work in. Usually keeps vagrants and criminals away. Nobody's perfect.'

'That's a fair state. I get that things between folk can be… personal.'

She exchanged a few signs with Sarah. The girl looked at them all, pondered longer at Bill, and then nodded.

'Come for dinner,' Laura said. 'We can't promise a feast or a bed, but perhaps we can work on an idea or two.'

'We've imposed enough,' Walter replied.

'And yet, of all the places to take Bill, you chose here. My concern is not servitude. You were kind enough to me when I needed some strength, Walter. Outside of Abe, there isn't anyone I'd want looking after Sarah if I was called to the Lord. I certainly wouldn't want her roaming the state, living on her wits. For many years I dreaded her even riding out alone. So, will you answer a lady's offer?'

Earl shared a glance with his companion. 'You reckon I can play nice for a spell?'

'I have an idea she'd whoop you better'n I.'

Laura's eyes twinkled in amusement. He got lost in them for a second.

'Six o'clock?' she said.

'I'll pack manners for both of us,' Walter replied.

She nodded and led Sarah and Bill away.

'The kid must have a trade,' Walter suggested.

'I got work to return to. You and all. Either way, the kid's back on his feet and running his own life.'

'Bill doesn't have a *life*, not here. He got a few dollars and no work. If he's a gambler and a thief, he was either robbed clean or had a safety box somewhere. If he wanted to go, he would. He's either smarter'n a fox, or nothing to his name— no place, no folks, no way to go—like he said. With work, he might get respect. At worst, he gets a horse and a choice of stay or leave. So, to my mind, there's one place to try.'

The stables were diagonally across town, so Earl and Walter cut behind the rows of properties and premises.

Back gardens fluttered with bloomers on the line. Outside one ramshackle house, two grubby children chased each other, squealing.

The men's boots kicked up the dust between the clumps of grass. Nobody found anything to say, knowing Bill wouldn't be able to join in. Earl didn't want to speak—it felt like showing off, and he didn't like the unsettling, self-conscious jangle in his bones. He felt more company when he walked Jack somewhere and didn't feel odd talking to such a companion.

The stables were on a large lot with a corral out back. Earl reckoned the adjacent barn held twenty horses and tried to figure out whether the loft was a place a man could lie his head.

Abe was brushing down a fine leopard appaloosa, its coat immaculate. Familiar odours of equine secretions hung in the air, mixed with the dry cut of straw.

Earl ensured Bill stood front and centre.

Abe paused his chore. 'Walt, Earl,' he said, then added, signing, 'Bill.'

Walter nodded. 'Getting to the point, Abe, we're wondering if you had any work for Bill?'

Abe looked at them in turn and ran a sleeve over his moist brow. 'That so? This paying work, or for keeping outta trouble?'

'First is for the future. Second is for now,' Walter replied.

'I saw the kid tack up before. He got any previous?' He slowly signed some phrases to Bill. The exchange continued.

Earl was a spare part again; they might have been speaking Cherokee. There lay irony. The tribes had brought signs to the white world. People like Potter or Frank Matthews would no more accept Bill than if he'd been Cherokee, Cree, or Mojave from the womb.

Maybe their argument wasn't with the lack of hearing but with what replaced it—the language of their longtime enemies. As if, from their new Reservations, the vast wilds being clear of their kind, they invisibly reached out across the miles and tainted the culture of the white folk.

Earl got a sour taste in his mouth for thinking so cruelly.

'Now, Walt,' Abe said, 'I ain't the owner here, only the help, and I can't vouch for how this'll play.'

'So, you'll give him the job?'

'A week's probation. The kid says he has two years working the stables up at Four Pines, and I got no reason to doubt him. But mark this, if Potter runs him off his property, I ain't arguing. Lyle and I get by, from history, but I need this work.'

'Let's hope Bill keeps his head on and knows what a bounty he's got in you,' Earl said.

Abe nodded. 'Town's growing. Word says they'll be running another stagecoach out of Tucson before long. Mayor might shoot his mouth off about the Hotel being full, but it will be, come summer.' He looked at Bill. 'Hardworking stablehand will make a good wage.'

Earl dug in his pocket and laid a half-dollar in the man's hand.

'I don't take bribes,' Abe said.

'It's on account of livery for Jack and… hoping Bill could lay a blanket in a corner somewhere.'

Abe held up a cautioning finger. 'On the understanding, I don't know a jot about it. I ain't granting anything, but if a kid worked hard of an evening and laid out on straw up in the loft for shelter, and not an eye saw, I'd not be in the place to know, would I?' He winked.

Earl nodded. 'And a second man? For security against thieves and the like?'

Walter looked bemused. 'Did I get something backwards?'

'Take your room, Walt. I ain't riding home after supper, and I've had my fill of Potter's face. I'll settle the kid in here.'

'Thought you weren't no nursemaid?'

'It ain't for company, only purpose. I won't have the evening at Laura's table with your tongue wagging on what a stubborn asshole I am who never did a single deed for nobody. 'Sides, if we prickled Potter, he could send men to teach Bill a lesson to leave. So, I guess I come this far, what's another day.'

'You're a fine man, Earl,' Abe ventured.

'Not God, but not the Devil neither.'

'I'll walk Bill round, explain the workings and such.'

'Mighty grateful to you.' Walter and Earl shook the man's hand. Bill hesitated, then followed.

A spark of hope lit in Earl's belly. He looked forward to accompanying it with a full spread later. A pretty tablecloth. Company. Maybe good deeds were rewarded with more than trouble.

He noted Walter's stubble and scratched his own face.

'Crockett Drake still barbering in town?'

Chapter 11

Crockett Drake, six-foot-tall and one foot of beard, had his chair filled thrice and gave no word about the kid's presence. Earl expected it would be so: the gentle giant with four fingers on his left hand, one being lost in the dumbest saloon brawl Walter had ever recounted.

Drake couldn't afford to lose too many more digits and still razor and cut like a craftsman. He seldom said a word against anybody. In fact, he was only half as quiet as Bill.

When Earl took the chair, a younger man stared back at him from the mirror; youthful for a fleeting moment, the dead eyes of a lost soul who'd longtime wished that the razor slipped and cut his head clean from his shoulders. The echoes remained—forehead creases and eye bags that not even a high-price big-city barber could magic away. Not that he wanted them gone; they were earned, even deserved. The outward embodiment of scars that ran deeper than skin and stayed better hidden from all except Walter.

Anyway, he'd made an effort for the Andersons, and hopefully it would counter his earlier misspeaking. The kid's smartened locks made him look younger and less of a ruffian. If they had the means to spring for a new shirt, he might even pass for dashing. They didn't give Crockett a sob story about the kid's misadventures but were only charged a dollar between three anyway.

As they strolled down Main Street, Walter repeatedly glanced across.

'What now?' Earl snipped.

Walter held up both hands. 'Nothing. Very civil suddenly, that's all.'

'Gotta make a good impression.'

'For Bill, or for you?'

'Leave over. You changed shirt too.'

They arrived at Laura's a quarter before six, the May sun skimming the neighbouring rooftops. Smoke rose from chimneys, and glassy clinks leaked from the saloon.

She'd borrowed a chair from a neighbour, so five squeezed around the small table, which usually sat only two.

The size of the spread made him feel guilty; meat pie and pickles, potatoes and vegetables, biscuits and gravy. Laura was the one owed the thanks for digging he and Walter out of a hole—not of their own making—and yet she was the person offering sustenance. Getting a shave and haircut seemed a poor contribution.

It was noticed, though. 'Can't recall the last time I had three fine gentlemen in the house, all shiny as a new pin.' She signed to Bill, and he thanked her.

The smells in the air were reminders of homeliness and better times. As the youngsters silently engaged, smiles playing on their lips, Earl visited a strange world, one with family around his table and a striking woman toying with the petals of a flower in the tabletop vase.

It dampened his spirits until Laura caught his eye and gave a look of querying concern. He brightened out of courtesy and gratitude for the attention. When she looked away, he admired her attire and deportment.

The conversation was spartan as they ate hungrily. He went to wipe his mouth on a sleeve but noted the napkins and acted like a civilised person who was used to sitting at table and being with folks.

'How come Abe can talk to Bill?' he asked.

'Abe and Jim go way back,' Laura replied. 'Abe was a rock. He helped me convince Potter to let Sarah study in class with the hearing children. Abe wanted to learn, like an uncle she never had. Someone who'd take her for what she is.' She drank, introspective. 'Not everyone treats people like people.'

'No argument on that,' Walter said.

Earl set down his cutlery. 'Maybe Bill'll feel more comfortable talking with him 'bout his folks. Who took his horse. If he has a place to go.'

Her brow furrowed. 'Because life in White Rock would be so bad?'

'Only trying to ease the burden. You put an arm around the kid, but a man needs to make his own way.'

'With respect, Bill is old enough to decide for himself. You can't impose—you're not his father. Why you'd barely give him a second consideration yesterday.'

He hung his head. 'I feel guilty, is all.'

'You'd feel worse if you'd passed by and seen his likeness in the obituary papers next week. A person can only do what they believe is right. I think you both did, and that makes you good folks in my book.'

'Much obliged,' Walter said. 'Bill told Abe he'd worked in Four Pines. Did he mention that to you?'

She shook her head. 'He ran away age ten, before Four Pines. He was shy about it, thinking we'd consider him a cowardly boy and not fit to have at the table. An old lady in Four Pines had taken him in, gave him a roof and some education.'

'Stablehand at ten?' Earl asked.

Laura asked Bill another question. The kid signed—but reluctantly, sheepish.

'He did chores for board,' she relayed. Quickly her hand came to her mouth.

Walter was on his feet, ready to help. 'What is it?'

'She… she caught him trying to steal. A chicken—from her yard.'

Earl thumped the table. 'I dang knew it,' he spat through gritted teeth.

Walter held out a calming hand. 'Hold on.'

But Earl rose sharply, chair leg screeching on the floor, offered a 'Pardon me,' and strode out to the garden.

Night had fallen cold under a clear sky, and his sniping ire turned to wisps of breath in the air. Smoke and sparse embers puffed from Laura's chimney. In the distance, hooves popped on the road.

After a minute, there came a thud, and the door closed behind Walter. 'Now, listen—'

'I knew he'd be a thief. All cripples are, twisted up and revenging.'

'You have no clue about the kid.'

'Yeah? I know plenty.'

'What? About how he was hounded from Copperhead for talking with hands and pulling a knife when things got tough? About walking the land, living off river water and scraps?'

Earl scanned Walter's disapproving face. 'Abe'll not take him now.'

'Relax. Abe won't care two bits about a lad skipping a cog. Mistakes of youth, needing a meal. And he did his penance. He ran chores for three years. Bettered himself. The old lady had no kin. She forgive him? You bet she did. No talk, but she gave him company. Then she up and died.' Walter looked at Earl as if he was the thief. 'And you shame Laura's table with your lunk-headed ways.'

Earl eyed Walter, then gazed out across the tidy garden, ringed by the white posts which stood like ghostly guardians picked out by the firelight from the window.

'She still talking to Bill?'

'She's not a quarter offended as you. She doesn't take other people's burdens like they're her own.' Walter sighed heavily. 'Now, will you come in for pie?'

'Pie and making sorry, I guess.'

'I reckon so.'

He expected tension inside the house, but there was none. Instead, Bill was play-acting how he'd chased that chicken and fallen flat on his face many times. It caused much amusement.

Earl lowered his voice for the apology, redundantly hiding it from the youngsters, then cursed his selfishness. It was simply not into his skull that speaking normally in front of Bill and Sarah didn't amount to bragging—they weren't offended. This tiptoeing of manners made him look more the fool than he would by treating them as equals. Yet, fitting in came hard.

Laura accepted his apology, patting his arm.

They ate. The pie was fine.

'What made him run away?' Walter asked. 'Before—from his real folks?'

Laura put the question to Bill. The lad eyed them in turn, as if seeking acceptance, then signed.

Laura's hand dropped, snagged the plate, and sent the cutlery clattering to the floor. Walter clutched the table edge.

Earl tensed. 'What now?' he urged. 'What?'

Her expression was hard. 'He ran when the Government came to move them into a Reservation.' She looked at him with sadness and distaste. 'He was raised Mojave.'

Walter stood. 'Earl, get the kid. We're leaving.'

'Now listen here—'

'I'm asking nice, for Laura's sake.' Walter turned to her. 'We're grateful as all heck. That was some spread. We'll take our leave now.'

'I think that would be wise,' she replied.

'Bill,' Earl rapped. No acknowledgement. He grabbed the boy's shirt and hauled him up. 'We're going,' he said into the young man's startled face.

Walter fumbled his chair back under the table. 'I'm truly sorry, Laura.'

'It's not your fault. Either of you.'

Bill retrieved his hat.

Earl herded him through the door. 'What in the hell is going on?'

Walter was jumpy like Earl hadn't seen in many moons.

'Bill sitting there in Jim's chair, bold as day—a fine man killed by Mojave. He as good as pushed that fork into Laura's heart. You think she wants an Indian kid at her table?'

Walter spun on the spot and gazed heavenwards as if beseeching the stars for deliverance. 'Maybe coming here was a dumb idea. I need to rest on it. Laura too. We better hope for understanding, or it's back to you and me to watch him.' He pointed. 'Take the boy to the barn.'

He gave a cursory nod and walked away.

Earl grizzled. The silence pressed in on him. The moon was up, but the night wasn't beautiful—not now.

'You dumb fool,' he breathed.

He turned and strode across the back lots towards their makeshift accommodation. The ground was hard and lumpy, like his temper.

Bill walked alongside, his hands jammed in trouser pockets. His face bore the hallmark of a man who knows he's done wrong.

Earl shook his head, dumbfounded. 'You stupid sonofabitch. You gave her one reason guaranteed to close the door on you.'

He shot the kid a glower. 'Some gratitude that is. I wish we'd left you for dead.'

Chapter 12

Sleep passed fitfully.

An occasional night in the open continued to hold a sense of wonderment for Earl, God's sphere beneath his back and the spartan calls of wildlife tickling the quiet canvas above.

A regular night at home offered respite from a day's labour, a soft mattress under his frame. A stable of far-from-silent horses—their scrapings, clumping and farting—was a poor third choice.

Plus, there was his restless mind. The circumstance pinged around his head like a fly in a jar as he tried to square the circle, derive an answer beyond washing his hands of the whole matter and getting back to life. Except, that was the easy way—and what would Laura think of him then?

His hand came to his cheek, startled by the implication: he cared what she thought.

First light came as a blessing. The aura of the waking world seeped through myriad chinks in the building's structure, tiny bright slivers from dawn that portended a clear day. He bathed for a while in the inherent goodness of nature—always a way to subsume ill will and reaffirm that life was a privilege.

There were biscuits and water in his war bag—a poor breakfast, although his stomach was still processing the joys of the previous evening.

Bill lay rolled up in a blanket a few feet away. Swaddled, a babe in a barn because there was no room at the inn.

And Earl, a carpenter.

He smiled. Three gifts would do fine: coffee, eggs, and bacon. Come lunchtime, though, the nourishments would be gone, and his predicament would be unchanged. With the trio of Laura's forgiveness, money, and a horse, Bill would do better.

He watched Bill, absent of other options for filling the early hour, as if hard study of the problem would provide an answer. How could a kid throw a knife so good, survive on his wits so long, make a good impression on the fair sex, and still have a hole where common sense should be?

He shook his head. 'Why you gotta mention that, kid? Look at you—no more Indian'n me. Some folks carry a grudge—you gotta expect that. Hell, why didn't you say some cockamamie story that you fell from the Moon?'

He sighed. 'Breathe this to Potter, and you might as well start walking. Open your eyes. Two good ladies in that house. Angels. And I know from which I speak. I had an angel once. Saved me. Stood me up. Made me better.'

He sat up and wiped the sleep from his eyes. 'Maybe I could use that again.'

He looked at Bill. 'Be smart. Take help.'

He let that hang in the air, unheard and hence unsaid, pushed himself to his feet and dusted down.

After stretching his bones, he took the creaky slatted stairs from the loft to the main space and cut outside. Across the way stood a trough.

The cold water he doused over his head and neck stung to the core; a dose of reality as immediate as the misjudged ballet of a young man's hands. He tousled his hair and drips sneaked down any gap in his shirt.

Abe approached, bearing a mug of coffee. 'Sleep okay?'

'Some.'

Abe nodded, knowing straw was for the animals and the youth. 'The boy?'

'I guess.'

'Something fixing to bother you, Earl?'

'Good deeds make me feel beholding, is all. Sticking your neck out for Bill—a boy with no providence—is swell.'

Abe shrugged. 'Laura did me a good turn, and folks like me don't always attract the best kinda words, so I guess Bill being special makes me feel a little kin. Same as Sarah.'

'Well, I hope he does right by you.'

'Me too. I ain't getting any younger.'

A stiffness twinged Earl's lower back. 'Me either.'

'I'm fixing up breakfast yonder if you want to get the boy.'

'Sure, appreciate that.'

In the stable, Bill had woken, and Earl crudely mimed eating. Bill nodded, so they walked over to the crude shack from which delicious smells poured.

As Abe and Bill's greeting descended into 'conversation', Earl was again the oddity, unable to communicate. So, he ate silently and grew more concerned about what was at stake. Abe had had run-ins with the Mojave in the past, and the fact he and Bill shared a bond would make any breaking of the arrangement hard to take—for Bill, anyhow.

He prayed the kid had mentally joined the fenceposts and would keep quiet about his apparent heritage in order to cling to his remaining friend in White Rock. That, and his job—the door to whatever future he wanted. All Earl could do was hope. Even a Good Samaritan draws a line under his obligation.

They finished up.

'Abe, that was mighty fine. Guess I got another debt to chalk on the board.'

The man waved it away. 'I'll get the kid to repay for you— in muscle. I have some spots in the roof to fix, and my old bones ain't fit to that.'

Bill made the "thank you" gesture. Earl did too—not to be left out, then felt a fool.

'Old dog, new trick, huh?' Abe noted.

'I prefer talking, thanks all the same.'

'Uh-huh. Well, Bill wanted to go over to Laura Mae's a moment. He has a piece to say.'

'I gotta skedaddle, so I'll take him across and make sure he comes back to work.'

The noise of footsteps pattered outside. Alarmed, Earl rose, hoping it wasn't Potter on a random call-by.

Walter nodded in greeting Abe and Bill.

'Morning Walt. What gives?' Earl asked.

'I got news. First, I reckon Laura's fine. Said she wanted to talk.'

'Bill here wants to talk too.'

'That's good. Anyhow, the second is that I got business to get to. Upstate.'

'Well, don't that beat all. Hell of a moment to pick. Running out when this whole thing is on the edge of a pin.'

'Not exactly a time of my choosing.' Walter scowled, then shook it away. 'Now, we gonna broker this peace? I'm saddling Dusty. You bring the kid down.'

Earl crudely beckoned Bill to follow over to the stable. There, he packed up his things and prepped Jack, fussing the horse as if they'd been parted for days. He climbed into the saddle and thumbed the kid to do likewise. Bill reached out a hand for help up behind, and Earl offered it.

'Come on, Jack.' He tapped a foot into the horse's belly. 'Let's get this shitshow on the road.'

They ambled through town, and he tried not to catch anyone's eye, hat pulled heavily down over his brow. It would be dumb luck if Dennis arrived in the final minutes before he cut out for good. He didn't want to have to leave Laura so abruptly again.

She was at her gate, talking with Walter, when they arrived. The kid jumped down athletically.

Earl pulled off his hat. 'Morning, ma'am.'

'Morning, Earl,' she replied.

'Walt said you had a piece to say.'

But whether it was worry, impetuousness, or plainly that he hadn't heard, Bill didn't let her speak but struck up with a few signs. She watched, perplexed, then motioned for Bill to stop.

'What'd he say?' Walter asked.

'He says sorry for causing a ruckus at our table, and his heart is full of gratitude for what we've done for him. He said he'd leave us alone if that's what we wanted.'

'He's manners, I guess,' Earl said. 'And a roof at the stables, which is better'n none.'

She raised a hand. 'It's okay.' She heaved a breath, on the verge of her own confession. 'Sarah and I talked. Sometimes it's not us old folk who are the wise ones.'

'True enough.'

She brushed a stray lock behind her ear. 'For years, we've fought prejudice and wondered how people could be so small-minded. Then we do the same to this young man. Mojave killed my Jim—there's no argument about that and no forgiveness coming. But they are gone now, and besides, Bill is no more Mojave than any of us. I might as well be against him for being a man because a man was the type who took Jim. And you, Earl—I took offence at your reactions— so I was no better. I told Bill we've no argument with him in this town or this house until he has a place to go.'

Earl's heart soared to the clouds; his shoulders seventy pounds lighter. It was all he could do not to punch the air.

It was over. The misfit fitted somewhere.

Duty done, problem solved. Time for normal life.

She signed a few more phrases to Bill. He nodded in thanks, then offered his hand. She shook it.

'You were smart,' Earl said, close to his friend's ear. 'She's a good woman, and this is the right place.'

'I won't claim much but luck and gratitude.'

'No, Bill, I can't,' she said whilst signing.

'Can't what?' Walter asked.

'He wants to give a token of his appreciation.'

Bill opened the top button of his shirt, reached into the gap and fumbled something out—a neck chain bearing a small silver amulet. He unhooked it, gathered it, and laid it in her open palm.

Earl's heart pattered like the rains of a storm.

Bill signed.

'Ma left me this.' As Laura spoke his words, her face creased into warm appreciation.

Earl bent closer, his nerves jangling as if he stood on a precipice, staring into an abyss.

His brain went into overdrive so fast it could have torn his skull clean in two. His chest tightened. He put out his hand as if seeking balance with both feet already firmly planted. His back grazed Jack's flank.

'Earl?' she said, worried.

He looked at the three of them as if in a dream, the tail-end of the unreal nightmare from that morning at the campsite. The past and present were fused like a mythical beast which was alarming and impossible in equal measure.

A bell that would grace the finest church clanged in his head. He gripped and tugged at the reins. His knuckles thwacked the horse's hide. His foot pawed at the stirrup. With almost catatonic motion, he mounted.

Their faces gawked at him. His mouth was too numb to speak, his chest rigid.

Instead, he jabbed Jack unusually hard, fought his balance as the horse crabbed sideways, then grunted loud encouragement, and they accelerated away, spraying dust plumes in their wake.

Walter inspected the coil of metal in Laura's palm, then took the amulet between his thumb and forefinger.

'Walter?' she asked, dumbfounded and nervy.

The words fought past a blockage in his throat. 'I gave this to cousin Mary on her wedding day. Token of my happiness for her and Earl.'

Walter watched the disappearing ochre cloud on the roadway and sighed. He looked at the startled kid, then at her.

'I think we know who Bill's father is.'

Chapter 13

The ride passed quickly, unnecessarily hard on Jack, and yet felt interminable. In past years, twisters plied the state with less energy and destructive turmoil than Earl's mind.

At the homestead, he dismounted gingerly, aching from the unfamiliar pounding, and apologised profusely to his equine companion. He let Jack loose in the small corral, and it drank with gusto from the trough.

He kicked the fencepost, jabbing pain through his boot.

'What in the hell're you doing?'

Jack merely lifted his head and locked a large eye on him.

''Cos it can't be—that's why.'

There was no kick hard enough to cast out his seething disbelief or calm his boiling innards, so he dashed into the house.

He pulled off everything bar his underclothes, darted out and plugged down the steep rough-hewn steps to the river. There, tensing against the torture, he plunged in. The chilly water knocked the breath from him, a vain attempt to extinguish the fire which burned inside.

He thumped his backside onto the rocky riverbed and submerged his head, numbing his face and stabbing shock into his skull. He gulped down mouthfuls of the clean liquid, flushing his chest and guts with the cold. Then he surfaced and held there, shivering, using his palms as support, lounging back yet remaining tense against the flow.

He didn't know whether to cry or yell—nobody would see—but he was too cold for either. The sky crushed him with myriad possibilities and impossibilities.

He sat, scanning the green-brown landscape and the blue firmament. Grass and twigs coursed past. Nearby, a single leaf eddied by the bank. Its crimped edges rotated to and fro, caught between the inexorable pull forwards and a strange undercurrent holding it still.

He closed his eyes, focussed on the sound of the water, and willed nature's soothing tones to cast out the internal raging as if a puff of wind could fell the tallest burning tree.

The cold abated in his body.

When a measure of calm descended, he pawed to the narrow, inclined bank and lay there, feeling rock and grass press into his back, as if a drowning man ashore.

The breeze took moisture from him, but he didn't languish, gripped by a desire for distracting enterprise. He couldn't resolve the situation by thought and worry.

He paced up to the house, pulled off the soaking long johns, dried himself and put on fresh clothes. It went some way to erasing an invisible stain.

Afterwards, he mixed up a plate of bacon with beans and washed down the ensemble with steaming coffee strong enough to float a colt.

The noonday sun had pushed the mercury up, but he went to the toolshed, found an axe, tested it on his thumb, and carried it to the corral. There, he tacked up Jack with a harness, and they walked towards the copse a quarter mile from the house.

'Lord's testing me is what it is.' He patted Jack's neck. 'Put temptation in my way and spoil it by lies and things what can't be. Make me look an ass in front of a good woman.' He laid his head against the warm brown hide. 'It ain't fair.'

He had no more words. He could talk all day yet not believe the apparent truth. His mind was useless; it was better to exercise his body productively.

He went to a preselected tree, set aside his jacket, and worked the trunk with the axe. The few chirping birds mixed with the slap of Jack's grazing.

Halfway through, he took a rest and drank deeply from the canteen. Yet the interruption from travail allowed his mind to wander, which he didn't want, so he resumed his task, hefting the axe again and again at the mesquite, the hard clacks carrying across the peaceful soundscape.

After a few minutes, as he paused to wipe sweat from his brow, something caught in his peripheral vision. He rested the axe head on the ground.

'Never any damn privacy when a man needs it,' he muttered.

Walter stopped a safe distance away—from falling temper rather than falling timber—and dismounted. He let the rein slack, and Dusty munched on the woodland floor.

'I got nothing to say to you,' Earl called.

'If you were a stubborn pig-headed fool for nigh-on twenty years, that's nothing to what you are now.'

'He ain't my boy. And that's an end to it.'

Walter moved to civil distance. He didn't rise to Earl's anger. 'You know that's not true.'

Earl cast the axe aside and approached to arguing distance. 'I never drew on you, Walt. It oughta stay like that.'

His friend eyed the holstered gun and sneered—an echo of Potter's in a face Earl loved immeasurably more.

'And you had a son who was dead to you. That doesn't have to stay either.'

'He ain't my boy, and you can't prove it.'

'The necklace—'

'He stole that,' Earl snapped. 'He already admitted on being a thief. He's a no-good lying cripple.'

Walter squared his shoulders. 'I oughta punch you in the mouth.'

Earl yanked up his sleeves. 'So, lay me out.' He put his dukes up.

'That's Mary's necklace, my hand to God.'

'He's dead. My boy is dead! What part can't you get into your damn skull?'

Walter pointed at the partially severed trunk. 'Seems like there's more brains in that tree than in *your* skull.'

Earl rushed forwards and grabbed Walter's lapels. Surprise filled the man's face.

'You wasted your damn time riding out here to lecture me,' Earl snarled.

Walter lowered his voice. 'Yeah. But I still came.'

'More fool you.'

Walter took Earl's wrists and pushed them away. 'I don't reckon there's any more fool than the one I'm looking at.'

'Go to hell,' Earl spat.

'And I would, too, to climb down, rope you and haul you up out. To the real world.' Walter jabbed a finger at the ground. 'This world, which is no kinda hell, 'cos you have a lost boy returned to you.'

'It. Ain't. True.'

'It's a damn sight truer than the lies you tell yourself. Told yourself every day for near twenty years.'

Earl swung out. Walter feinted, easily avoided the lazy fist, and stepped back.

'I say again, Walt. Lay me out.'

'No, 'cos it's what you want. It's what you deserve, and you know it.'

'What I deserve is the world to leave me the hell alone. Not send a thieving deaf-mute claiming to be my boy, for Lord only knows why.'

'He said he's twenty this year. Alden would be the same. You blind or dumb?'

Earl's eyes flared. He leant in, swung again, and missed.

'I don't want Bill as my kid,' he rapped, steadying his balance.

'You ever think maybe he doesn't want an asshole like you for a father?'

Earl stepped in to reduce his range. Still missed. He dusted himself off, despite there being no dust, and calmed his heaving chest.

'Then we're all good, ain't we?'

Walter turned to go. 'Maybe I am a fool— trying to give you back some of your life.'

'I didn't ask for it back,' he spat.

'You're one stubborn, ungrateful asshole.'

Earl jammed hands on hips. 'Your business here done?'

'Yeah. I got better places to be.'

'And you call me coward, running out on a situation.' He curled his lip in disgust.

'I got a letter this morning. My dad passed. I'm heading to Garrett Falls. Taking the stage to Phoenix.'

Earl's arms fell by his side. The wind left his sails as if the eye of a storm had snapped across the men.

'Shoot,' he breathed. 'Reckon I'm sorry.' He hung his head.

'Well, we were close. Closer'n some fathers are to sons.'

Earl's eyes narrowed. 'Don't think I don't get the meaning.'

'So maybe I was wrong to think I taught you better. Walking out like that—not just on Bill, but Laura Mae? High tailing with no word?' Walter sneered. 'And she called you a *good man*.'

Earl darted forwards, making to raise fists again, but gave up and heaved a weary sigh. 'If you came here for helping, it ain't doing no good.'

'You loved Mary, and you disowning Bill is tramping heavy boots on her memory. Still, I come, beating words into your skull like a mesquite log, hoping there's a bug of sense in there, burrowing to get out.'

'I say again—we don't got no proof.'

'Then I don't believe there's any proof in the world will make you open your heart.' Walter shook his head in despair. 'Being away from Bill—Alden—before is what got you like this. Are you looking to do it again? Huh?'

'Me being away is what got Bill like this.' Earl kicked the ground. 'Assuming it's the boy, like you reckon.'

'No. You being away didn't take his ears.'

'Then what did?' Earl rapped. 'Huh?'

'Maybe you want to talk to him. Find out.'

'I can't talk to him.'

'Why? You not got the means, or you not got the balls?'

Earl clenched and unclenched his fist. Walter shook his head sadly. Earl had lost count of how many times he'd seen that.

'I gotta look after my own skin,' he protested.

'And Laura doesn't run a house for runaways and orphans. Only one of you is kin to Bill.'

'He's safe there. I ain't.'

'Like he was safe in the crib that day?' Walter's gaze burrowed into Earl's retina.

They mentally circled each other.

Earl's teeth set on edge. 'Reckon you oughta be going now.'

'I reckon so.' Walter went back to Dusty and took the saddle. He adjusted his hat and gave a last patronising look.

'Safe trails,' Earl said flatly.

'Maybe I'll see ya.'

Earl picked up the axe, listened to the dying swish of the horse's legs on the grass, and then swung away.

Chapter 14

Laura ate slowly. The food was fine, although she'd overdone the carrots, distracted by the heavy atmosphere and her ranging thoughts. If there were a million questions, she'd barely cogitated on the first dozen.

Sarah pushed aside her clean plate. "You okay, Ma?"

Laura nodded lazily.

Sarah signed again. "You fibbing? You got the blue devils."

Laura laid her cutlery on the half-empty plate and gathered her hands. "Why does a man run like that?"

"He had a shock."

"People get shocks. Like when your father died. Did we run?"

"Mr Johnson is a… complicated man."

"You see everything, honey."

"How would you feel if Pa walked in, plain as day?"

Laura's heart cracked a little. 'I wouldn't believe it,' she said and signed.

"So we shouldn't go railing on Mr Johnson for his shock."

Laura pushed away her plate, appetite gone. "Walter is a good man. If he's stood by Earl all these years, it means he's a good man too."

"And Earl… Mr Johnson is grieving."

Laura ruffled her daughter's blonde curls. "Everyone does—for something."

"Why is he not joyful now?"

"I don't know. There's… hurt inside him. Or more. Poor man."

She sighed and went to the kitchen, where she washed up the plates and cutlery. Sarah came alongside and laid a comforting palm on her mother's shoulder.

Laura's hands slowed to a stop in the basin. 'If Jim walked in, I wouldn't believe it,' she reiterated aloud. 'But that's not to say I wouldn't jump for joy.'

They tidied up and sat in the living room. The fire leapt and crackled. Laura spied the amulet on the side table and caressed it in her hands.

Sarah looked over. "Do you think Bill stole it? Found it?"

"I don't know. But it would be some coincidence. It's beautiful. Jim would have been proud to make something like this."

"Ma, do you want me to stay away from Bill?"

Laura fingered the worked metal—a gaillardia, if she wasn't mistaken. Had Bill gleaned it was her favourite flower? Was this a ruse to lull her and Sarah into a false sense of security—currying favour, so they let down their guard? But a boy raised by Indians? Possibly indoctrinated in hatred towards white men, schooled in theft, deception and revenge?

She closed her eyes and forced away the cruel thoughts. How would Sarah and her generation become more tolerant and compassionate if this was the example she saw?

A knocking noise.

Laura opened her eyes. Sarah was tapping the table—her way of getting attention. "Ma?"

"It's fine. I'd rather you spend time with Bill than Tom Potter."

"Me too."

"Keep a watch on Bill. I wouldn't want him to do wrong by Abe. He needs a job if he's to have a future. You have your sewing."

"Perhaps he needs schooling?"

"He hasn't had the opportunities you have. Or real parenting."

"Do you think he will get that?"

"Will Mr... Earl see sense?" she queried. 'Who knows,' she breathed. She set down the amulet, feeling it wasn't her place to wear it, as if treading on Mary Johnson's grave. On the table lay the carved brooch he'd brought. Again, it represented a gaillardia.

Too much coincidence, she mused.

"Will he come back?" Sarah asked.

Laura thought about Earl's reaction, his eternal paucity of conversation and the prospective return of Dennis Hayes. Earl didn't seem like a coward, yet his absence from White Rock for many years spoke volumes.

She'd shrunk in on herself too when Jim died, and become bitter for a time. The difference was she'd passed through that dark spell, and Earl had not. Perhaps because she'd had a young Sarah to care for.

"I hope so," she signed. Why? she wondered. For Bill's sake or her curiosity as to what lay beneath Earl's gruff demeanour.

Sarah sat on the arm of Laura's chair. "He makes beautiful things."

"Any man who works so well with his hands can't be bad." She clasped her daughter's delicate fingers. 'Hands do God's work.' She stroked Sarah's face. "Nobody should lose their child."

"Perhaps Bill won't be lost."

"I know. But it's not our place to say."

"Don't be sad, Ma. Let me play for you."

Sarah sprang up and went to the corner of the room. She pulled out the stool, hinged up the lid of the upright piano, and settled herself.

The notes rose and kissed the air as Sarah's fingers danced. The beautiful melody filled the room, then the house.

Laura rested her head against the chair back.

'Who needs words when we have hands?' she murmured.

Chapter 15

Bill's mind blazed. After Laura had explained the significance of the amulet and the logical conclusion, he'd excused himself from the house. He didn't want to be shut in a room of worried looks and well-meaning suggestions. He needed to work it through, to get used to the fact—or at least the possibility that he had met his father.

What did Earl's hasty departure say about the man's character, intentions and conscience? Bill had done well enough without Earl for almost his entire life, so if the man never returned, maybe he'd lost nothing.

Yet, at minimum, Bill had to make his own way and repay the faith and kindness Earl and Abe had shown.

Silently, as there was no other way, he groomed the leopard appaloosa. He'd noticed Abe giving this animal special attention and wanted to make a good impression by lightening the man's workload. In a town with few allies, he had to keep every last one. With every brush stroke, he counted his luck and looked forward to real dollars in his hand, to opportunity.

For every day he'd cursed heaven for his difference and wondered how a loving God could do such a thing, there were days like today when man's humanity to man made life more than bearable, actually enjoyable.

He found a knot in the mane and worked it out. After a minute's calm, the horse jolted as if distracted.

A familiar overweight man strode towards him.

People usually wore one of two expressions around Bill: warmth or disgust. The man showed the latter, apparently pretending to be a windmill:

Lyle Potter waved his arms as if shooing away horseflies.

'What are you doing to my horse?!' He stopped a safe distance from the deaf stranger. 'Who gave you rights to tending to him?'

The stablehand set down the brush and moved his hands.

Potter spat on the ground. 'None of that heathen work!' He swatted at the hands, and the man stepped back. 'I won't have you around my property.'

The interloper looked around—possibly for help, a place to run, or a no-doubt lame excuse.

'You understand, cripple?' Potter raised his voice. 'Leave my property alone!' He tugged his gun from its holster and waved it in dismissal.

The horse whinnied at the noise and sidestepped as if spooked. Potter backed away, not wanting to receive a kick to make his day even worse.

Without warning, the boy lunged forwards.

Potter tugged the trigger. The bullet tore into the earth near the kid's feet, and its loud report lit up the area. The horse reared. Potter backed off, stumbling.

The boy flinched. His body slapped backwards into the horse. He spun in alarm, flailed his hands, snatched the reins and tugged harshly downwards.

'Leave off!' Potter rapped.

As the boy wrestled the horse to calm down, Abe ran up.

Potter jammed his gun back in its holster and thrust an accusing hand at the boy. 'What's all this, Abe?'

'I might ask you the same!' Abe panted, eyes wide. 'What the hell do you think you're doing?'

'I won't have this freak around my horse.'

'You won't have a damn horse if you keep shooting for nothing.'

'He rushed me.'

'An unarmed man rushed a gun? Even for you, that's a hell of a story.'

He stepped into Abe's personal space, gripping the gun.

'You watch your mouth.'

Abe held the stare. 'I won't have guns fired on this property.'

'My property.'

'By deed, yeah, but not by care. A gold mine you bleed dry for liquor and whores.'

Potter snarled. 'I never touched a whore. I better this town.'

'And spit hate.'

Potter pushed his face close to the creased dark skin of his accuser. 'You're lucky for two—the boy can't hear, but he can see, or you might be kissing the dirt.'

'I make it three.' Abe stood his ground. 'That you and I go back aways and have things in our heads which need to stay.'

That was unarguable, and Potter hated that Abe had that knowledge.

He eyed the boy and pursed his lips. 'He here on your say-so?'

'He works hard and saves my bones.'

Potter nodded slowly. 'He's a no-good cripple. One step out of line, and I'll have him on the next stage out of town. You hear? He touches my animal again, he robs a single brush, I hear one word against him from folks who stable here—I'll put him on your horse, Abe, and whip the animal into running, so he won't stop 'til Tucson, and you'll be down a horse and work your wage to buy another.'

'He's a good kid,' Abe protested.

'Him here is asking for starting fights. I hope his wits are sharper than his tongue.'

'His wits don't cut half so bad as some men's tongues.'

Potter's hackles rose. He wanted to grab Abe and show him the error of his ways. He couldn't, not with the cripple boy watching.

'Like I say, you watch your step. And the kid's.'

'We'll do as we are done to. White Rock is a town of good people—like you say. A man has a right to work and a bed for an honest living.'

'And half a man too?' He looked Bill up and down: the kid stood there like a lox.

Abe noted the scar on the back of Lyle's hand. 'No man is perfect.'

Potter gritted his teeth, reached out and stepped forwards. The kid thrust the reins into the Mayor's hand. Potter dutifully passed them to Abe and glowered at the kid.

Then he wagged his finger like a kindergarten teacher, turned and left.

Chapter 16

The smell of wood varnish tickled Earl's nose as he applied a second coat to the hand-turned chair leg. He'd considered, those days ago, suggesting to Clay Gabbitt he ought to replace all four with sturdier legs if his wife was going to keep eating like that. She'd only snapped one, but he feared for the life of the remaining three—and the new one he'd fashioned. Still, if it came to pass, it would mean more welcome dollars in his pocket.

A shadow from the open doorway fell across his bench.

He'd expected it, though not this soon. He raised his arms and submissively turned in case it was Dennis or Potter. Unlikely—they'd never visited his house. However, things were different now. Nothing was certain anymore.

'That'd be some heck awful day I held a gun on you,' came a familiar voice.

Well, there's perspective, Earl mused. Their friendship hadn't sunk that low. Not yet.

He lowered his hands. 'Don't be saying you rushed back on my account.'

Walter stepped into the small workshop. 'Not yours, but somebody's.'

Earl's arms prickled in the tense air. 'How's your ma?'

'Sad. Alone now. But she has her boy.'

'She's lucky.' He resumed varnishing.

'I knew you'd still be here,' Walter said eventually. He tossed his hat on the bench, knocking Earl's hand—deliberately, taunting him?

Earl bit back ire. 'A man has work and a life.'

'Kid could be dead by now.'

Earl span. 'Lies and baiting words,' he said through thin lips.

'In the calaboose even. Who's to say not kicked out of town? Or cut and run? Like his pa.'

Earl darted close, holding up the brush like the weakest weapon. 'I ain't his pa.'

Walter took Earl's wrist and lowered it. 'I'm done with this.' The voice was low, even, and cut through with unwavering intent to win. 'Mary was my cousin, and that makes Bill some kin to me. If you want to be blind as the boy is deaf, then it's my notion to do right in your stead. You rail on your father—and look at you.' His glance reeked of disgust. 'He was so bad, huh? Yet you're the model, the perfect man?'

Earl whipped his other hand up, but Walter caught the wrist mid-flight and cast down both arms as if trying to smash crockery.

'Why did you want kids? Huh? To show you could do better? Care more? Right? I'll bet that part of you didn't die that day. Our Mary is looking down, rejoicing that her boy's not beside her. And wondering what happened to the man she married, I reckon. A quarter Mojave she was, fighting insinuation and prejudice all her life but turning the cheek, trying to be a better person than them who'd hate. You? Hating every day, blind to the gift she sent back.'

'You sonofabitch!'

Earl charged, ready to topple Walter, pin him down and land a clean punch in that dirty mouth. Split his lip and let the blood of lies soak the dirt.

Walter dodged. Earl clean missed, barrelled through the doorway, cracked his shoulder on the jamb and tumbled to that same dirt. Grazes stung his palms and the brutal sun burned his retina.

He lay there, chest thudding, sucking dirt.

Walter stepped outside as if he was lazily taking the morning air.

Simmering, Earl pushed up onto his elbows. Walter reached down. With a sigh of defeat, Earl let himself be hauled up. He inspected his scratched hands and dusted down his shirt and pants.

'I don't hate him. I just… I can't talk to him, Walt.'

'Sure you can. I went to see *my* pa. No talking to him now, but I went all the same. And you *can* talk to Bill. You got help for doing so.'

'Not talk. *Talk.*'

'About… things what happened?'

Earl clutched at his ruffled hair. 'What if I tell him, and he hates me? If he sees what a testy, railing ass I am? And it ruins him? Makes him angry and closed up?'

Walter smirked. 'Then we'll know for sure you're his father.'

Earl pulled away, the words biting at his marrow, and turned his back on the truth.

'I don't got the right to have him in my life.' He looked around at his property. 'Such as it is.'

'But it won't be like this. It'll change you. You do want another chance at life. You said.'

Earl looked at the ground.

Walter sighed in defeat. 'I pass on your regards?'

The question hung there for a few seconds.

'White Rock ain't a good place to me,' Earl protested.

'A man can catch a bullet in any town. As can any kid. Which of you has more balls right now?'

Walter untied Dusty from the hitching post, gathered the reins and set the first boot in the stirrup.

Earl's lip curled, but he couldn't deny his friend's assessment. 'Walt?'

'Yeah?'

'You won't look at me the same, will you?'

'I only ever give you honesty, so... no. I won't come along next year. I can't face Mary, knowing you'd abandoned your own son. But this isn't about me.' Walter shrugged. 'Do what you want.'

'That'd be us? Really?'

Walter's eyes darted. 'I dunno.' He straightened his hat. 'I gotta go.'

Earl died a little inside.

'Hold on. Gimme a minute.'

Before they left, Earl asked if Walter wouldn't mind them swinging past Clay Gabbitt's house. If Earl's conscience took him to White Rock, he might as well pick up a few bucks from a customer on the way.

That errand complete, they made good time. Coming in from the south, they passed the water tower, its vane spinning lazily. The squeaking iron had a menace to it—one that was all in his head. Dennis wasn't due imminently, and neither Laura nor Bill was likely to offer comparable confrontation. All the same, butterflies were having a high old time in his belly.

'Walt, you said your piece, and this ain't your battle to fight no more. I gotta foul or fix this myself. Only wish I had the slightest clue on what to do.'

Walter tugged Dusty to a stand. 'You got figuring to do, that's for sure. And no, I won't speak for you, but I have my hand here if trouble comes calling.' He patted his gun.

'Right back to you.' Earl glanced reflectively at his own holster. 'I guess.'

'Kind words win more hearts than bullets.'

'Ain't for winning hearts,' Earl protested, feeling seen.

'Really?'

'Give over. It's for Bill.'

'Hmm.'

They dismounted outside Laura's, and tied the horses to the stabling post.

Earl tapped gently on the door, afraid someone would be home, and he'd have to deliver an apology he hadn't prepared, despite it being due within ten seconds.

Laura greeted them with a smile. 'Gentlemen.'

'Ma'am,' Earl replied—stalling. Plus, two days absent of her radiance and goodness had him flustered.

'If you're here with an apology, Earl, you can save it. The day Abe stood on that spot and told me Jim was dead, I slammed this door in his face and ran to the back room.'

'Except I didn't lose. I found.'

She nodded. 'I'm sure you have an eloquent explanation ready, and if that's so, keep it for Bill. He's more in need than I.'

'From him being mad as a nest of bees?' he asked, fearful.

'No.' She gestured inside. 'I have coffee, and pie leftover from dinner.'

The men exchanged a look.

'Can't say I don't got a spot in my belly,' Earl said. At the threshold, he paused and faced Laura. 'I'm sorry for my running out.'

'The fixing is in the coming back, not the words.'

They took seats in the dining room, set themselves up with pumpkin pie and coffee, and heard that Sarah had gone to the stables after school to check on Bill.

'The boy doing okay?' he asked.

'Mostly. He had a run-in with Potter, but that was only a matter of time.'

'He hurt?'

'No. Abe stood by him. It's on my mind to give Bill the full book on... being in the same town as certain people.'

'Every town got certain people,' he suggested. 'If it ain't for being deaf, it's for being bow-legged or quarter Indian or such.'

Her face creased into amused curiosity. 'Not a whole, not a half, just a quarter?'

'My Mary was quarter Mojave on her pa's side.'

Her shoulders fell. 'And I got wound up tight on the suggestion Bill's one whole—which he never was. This apology is mine to give.'

He waved it away. 'They took from you—you got a reason to hate too.'

'And you have a chance to take back what was lost.'

Earl toyed with his cup. 'If it's true. The necklace and all.'

'So,' Walter said, 'If we could rest on your good nature a spot, Laura, and get more words from Bill through your lips, we'll all rest easy knowing the truth. If it isn't true—if he wears a mask to set about making trouble—that isn't right. If he's preying on good nature, stealing that amulet like it was a chicken, I'll march him up to the Sheriff in a trice.'

'If that were so, we wouldn't hold you guilty for bringing him here, I hope you know,' she replied.

'Not a man alive who don't make a mistake,' Earl said.

Laura straightened her back. 'Well, don't we all get so down in the mouth? Pie is supposed to cheer up folks, not cause worries and regrets.'

Earl laid his fork on the table. 'And it was fine. You're some cook, Laura.'

Her smile returned, like a golden dawn on a winter's day.

'Well, don't be shy on calling round. The stove is on after school, and besides pest control, that fence needs fixing.'

'Then I'd fear for the size of Earl's gut,' Walter said.

'Hey, less on my gut,' he retorted, smoothing his waistcoat.

'Pie for chores is no sin,' Walter said.

'Give over on "chores for the good lady". I ain't no fixer-upper.'

Laura took up the carved wooden brooch. 'No, but a little carpentry for a man who does work like this? I'll have the prettiest fence in the whole county.'

Walter laughed. Earl glowered, a tinge of redness in his cheeks. His brain stumbled for something to dig himself out of this cul-de-sac of a stitch-up.

Footsteps rapped in the hall. He looked around.

Bill entered the room, with Sarah behind him, and stopped dead. A smile left his lips. He stared at Earl, then Walter, and back to Earl.

'Afternoon, Bill,' Laura said, signing.

The boy replied with similar.

Sarah eased past the blockage in the doorway and sunk into a chair. She watched with keen blue eyes.

Earl was like a green cowboy at a steer roping, the audience growing eager by the minute. What could he say— and how? His mouth moved silently.

Bill took a tentative step forwards, looking at Laura as if for guidance.

Earl glanced at Walter, Laura, then Bill, and still came up empty. He moved towards the boy.

Bill pointed at Earl and signed something to Laura.

'What?' Earl tensed, heart fluttering.

She licked her lips. 'Bill says… he says… "Are you my pa?"'

Four pairs of eyes burrowed into Earl. All the moisture evaporated from his throat.

He nodded reluctantly. 'I guess… maybe.'

Chapter 17

Laura rose sharply and fussed about, clearing away the plates and mugs.

A collective sigh washed over the room, but Earl remained tense. He wasn't ready to submit to affection—the boy was still a stranger. He'd no more embrace Bill than he would Laura.

In any case, his name wasn't Bill. It should be Alden, and if he'd held up a murdering no-good like James Butler Hickock as any kind of model, it would be something for Earl to exorcise from the boy if he was to be any kind of son.

Laura ushered "Bill" into the seat she'd vacated. She ground two fists together. He nodded.

Earl had seen that before—one of maybe four words he could "say" to the kid. Hardly the basis of more than a passing acquaintance, certainly not a familial relationship.

To live silently under the same roof, point and mime like a fool, just to get by? He couldn't imagine day-to-day activities, let alone any discussion about the past, present or future. This was an unfamiliar sense of guilt and discomfort, replacing what he'd longtime carried.

He sat.

It was reminiscent of the barn dance of '54—he and Walt on one side of the room, looking at Mary and her friends on the other side; the gulf of the sexes, his nervousness at approaching, lost for words. Except it was worse here, as words would achieve nothing.

The sides of the canyon were steep and forbidding. Only one thing—one person—could bridge them.

'Is the kid—is Bill—getting by at the stables?' he asked Laura, pointing lamely between them, asking her to 'interpret'.

She cottoned on, smiled at Bill to warm him up, and signed. He replied.

'Except for Potter, he's doing well. He says Abe is a good friend,' Laura said.

Sarah signed.

'She thinks he could use another blanket at night.'

'Sure, sure,' Earl said hurriedly. 'I'll go by the store.'

Bill signed.

'He asks if it's the necklace that makes you his father.' Laura's brow creased in compassion.

'Only if he didn't thieve it.'

She put that question to the kid, and the response was extended.

She narrated. 'Bill can't promise, to his dying day, but one of the tribe elders took it from his mother's neck after she passed.'

A tsunami of sorrow crashed across Earl's being.

He looked away, not to see or hear those words in the air. He'd assumed that Mary had died—Alden too—but not admitted it. Not really. Now a witness had voiced the facts.

He fought back the tide and listened.

Laura continued. 'He says another couple in the camp raised him. When they were being removed to go to a new Reservation up in Colorado, a ruckus broke out. Some of the Mojave protested. Bill saw the Government people were like him, but looked suspicious of him. He'd always felt he didn't belong. Some of the tribe would tease him. This repatriation—it felt like he was on the wrong side of that prejudice—'

'Even at ten year of age?' Walter interjected.

'He may not have been schooled, but he's got some senses in there.'

She focussed on Bill's hands. 'So he saw a chance, took a horse and left. Nobody chased him. The Mojave knew he wasn't right there. The Government men didn't care where he belonged. They had bigger issues.'

Bill finished. He studied Earl's face for a reaction.

What *was* on Earl's face? The same as in his heart—regret—which lived there every day. Something else crackled through his body. Reticence. He tried to mask it with a smile and a nod. Bill responded in kind.

'So, what's the word, buddy?' Walter murmured.

Earl turned away from Laura. 'What, you want me to throw a party? Whoop and holler?'

'Some folks would.'

'I ain't some folks.'

Walter sighed. 'And like I said, I'm not fighting this battle no more.' He stood, touching his brow. 'Laura, ma'am, you're God's angel to Bill and us. I'll be leaving now. Can't speak for Earl.'

Earl bolted up before he was left floundering again.

'You know where the door is,' she said. There was disappointment on her face—the first time he'd noticed it, but not the first time it had been there.

A tinge of bile hit his throat like his conscience had turned to stagnant water and invaded his mouth.

'Don't forget that blanket,' she added, words sharp as knives.

There was an expectation in the kid's eyes.

The kid.

Earl had to stop thinking like that. Bill was much more than a kid. He knew exactly how old he was. To the day. To the hour. Because he wasn't just any kid. He'd cried, suckled and smiled under Earl's roof. A roof that Earl had brought crashing down.

That had to be undone.

'Come. Come stay with me,' he blurted. He looked at Laura and jerked his head towards the k— Bill.

She eyed Earl with suspicion, so he nodded encouragement and pointed. Inside, the weight of responsibility squeezed his fragile heart.

She signed to Bill, who held up a hand, put the first two fingers together and snapped them onto his thumb.

'He says no.'

'No?' Earl sank into the chair, pilloried by a single word.

Laura translated. '"I see it you trying to do the right thing, but it's not what you want. I don't need pity. I want a job, and schooling, even if I have to lay on straw. You saved my life, and I have to make it even. I have past sins, and I don't need to be beholding".'

Earl's heart fell through the boards. *His* were the past sins, and he was trying to make amends. Bill couldn't know how herculean that task was.

Walter moved closer. 'Boy's got reason. He can't ride to and fro town every day from your place.'

'It ain't 'bout that,' Earl insisted.

'Being rejected, huh? It's a real kick in the craw.'

Earl opened his mouth to slam a rebuttal back in Walter's face but saw Laura, her palms loosely together as if in prayer.

He jammed his hands in his pockets and stepped to the window. A pony and trap kicked up dust on their way towards the town intersection.

He pondered.

If Bill wouldn't leave White Rock soon, Earl needed to figure out a way to escape the shadow of death so he could stick around too. Bill had made the whole endeavour harder—but it had been dumb to think this was ever quick and easy. If Earl truly cared, life had to stop being about him.

Chapter 18

Walter drank deeply of his beer. Earl sipped a ginger ale. The hubbub played; the chink of glasses, laughter, the coarse background of a piano Earl swore needed tuning. He looked around, hurrying the steak with his eyes alone.

'It's good you saw right,' Walter said.

'Deception is what it is.'

'Keep your voice down. You done enough causing a fuss in this room.'

'Don't think I don't know it.'

'Difference is, you and I are used to fighting, and we do it real calm like.' Walter smiled.

'You make us sound like squabbling kids.'

'Fine by me. Kids use words. Men use bullets. Words, I can handle. Don't be cut too deep. A boy pushing his pa away is… well, you know some about that. Besides, he's only turning down a roof—not you.'

Earl shot a piercing stare deep into Walter's grey-blue eyes, their lids heavy with the years—and the extra burden of conversations like this. How much they'd aged each other, despite their steadfast mutual improvement and support.

In lieu of pointless rebuttal, he took a long draw on his drink. The short silence was broken by the arrival of fat steaks, and each gratefully sunk their knives into it.

He was halfway through filling his belly with the most tender meat—better than got served in Ridgeway, he had to admit—when a familiar voice cut the dedicated hush at the table.

'Fast work, getting that cripple kid work in my town.' Potter and Bowman stood nearby.

Earl put down his knife. 'Abe were needing, the kid is able, and that's an end to it.'

'Needing? Or bribed, Earl? From your pocket. Or maybe your schoolteacher friend flashed Abe her titties to get another retard a place in town.'

He stood in a flash. Walter's cutlery clattered down. Potter's hand slapped onto his gun. Two men at an adjacent table stopped talking and looked on.

'You take that back,' Earl said, calm as he could.

'Or what?'

'You speak ill on that woman or that boy, you'll answer to me.'

Potter scoffed. 'Answer?'

'That's so.'

'A lot of care for folks you don't half know, Earl. Maybe if you had as much care for your own family, they wouldn't be dead. And cousin Dennis wouldn't be ready to see you right for what you did.'

Fire lit inside Earl. He fought with every fibre to retain his temperament, grasping the small mercy that Potter didn't know Bill was his son. That needed to stay under wraps.

'No law against caring for folks. Protecting them from men with no good grace.'

'Men of no good grace?' Potter sneered. 'Like you? Coming here that day, causing trouble. Then now, bringing the weak and afflicted? Polluting the town?'

'This town got polluted long afore I came. Stench in the rafters is worse than in the gutter.'

Potter jabbed out a hand, aiming to sock him in the shoulder, but Bowman intervened, pulled the Mayor back a step, and received a devil's glower for his trouble.

'You watch your big bazoo,' Potter told Earl.

'Likewise.'

'Pardon me?' Potter moved in, squared up.

Walter rose—one peacemaker on each side was only fair.

Earl's gaze didn't waver. 'Bill is a good kid. You lay a hand on him, you'll answer to me.'

'That so?'

'I'll shoot you, not a second thought. Hell, I'll shoot you in the back or sleeping.' Earl scratched his holster.

'That old gun of yours? That'd be some sight. All rusted up. Like you. You're all talk.'

'I talk, I walk, I fight my fights,' he said—in counterpoint to his track record.

Potter tucked two fingers into his waistcoat pocket and drew something out. His tone was measured, startling in its innocence. 'This pocket watch has more chance of killing me than your gun.'

'I guess we'll see 'bout that.'

'You draw against me, and I'll shoot that gun right out of your hand.'

Earl nodded. 'Then sleeping it is.'

Potter gazed for an eternity, then turned to Bowman.

'Witness that as intent, Sam. You'll know where to look if my bed runs red. See that he gets the gallows.'

'Come on, Lyle.' Bowman grabbed a fat arm and encouraged Potter away.

Earl watched him go until a hand pushed him back into the seat.

'Eat your supper,' Walter said.

Wordlessly, he obeyed. Second by second, bite by bite, his temper evened.

'I won't have us run out by that sonofabitch.'

Walter frowned. '"Us?". That's a word.'

'Not you and me. Me and the… me and Bill.'

Walter's eyes creased in pleasant surprise. 'Maybe there's hope for you after all.'

Earl lay in his long johns, head propped up on his folded arms, looking down his chest at his companion.

The single lamp flickered, throwing undulating shadows onto the wall. Distantly, the saloon piano and hubbub seeped through the smartly decorated walls. This was one of the new rooms: the place had doubled in size since Earl last stayed. He had to give Potter this—the man ran good enough premises.

'Figure I owe you 'til my dying day.'

Walter frowned. 'It's not like I keep score—the back and forth.'

'Weighs like the whole earth, owing and all. Now we owe Laura Mae too.'

'Everybody has gratitudes and owings. Children to parents for the gift of life. Parents to kids for laughter and love. Those that are saved to those what saves them. You wear yours like a noose, not a blessing. Life's goal isn't a level balance or staying torn up inside for not getting that level. Not yours to judge. It's the Lord's. Only to live life right and do good by others.' Walter pushed up onto his elbows. 'Picking up Bill is that deed. Stone's rolled back. Boy's come again to be at his father's side.'

'Trying to make it right, ain't I?' Earl protested.

'If you want my two cents, you oughta find out what made Bill come to be deaf. Then you might realise you did no wrong.'

'Excepting I did.'

Walter shook his head. 'No man can see the future, and all men leave their womenfolk at home. You're no better, no worse—I said it a thousand times. I was away two hours when that steer wound up burning my old house. Did I get riled up on it? No. I built again—we did, you and I. You build now—with your boy. So you gotta stay in town a while? What of it?'

'Gonna cost dollars.'

'I wasn't aware there was a price on love.'

Earl's eyes narrowed. He sighed. 'Bullets come cheap.'

'And grudges get forgotten.'

'That's some gamble.'

'So cash in your chips and quit the game,' Walter scoffed. 'We'll do your work. Raise the boy, do right by Mary.'

Earl sat up. 'I ain't for bobbery.'

'Because of not having another room?' Walter smiled.

Earl nodded sagely. 'Yeah. I can't lose you, Walt. Owe you my damn life.'

'I don't want you cold in the ground, neither. Just to… be smart.'

'Yeah.'

The clock ticked.

'Long time since we shared a bed,' Walter mused.

'Circumstance and bright ideas make it so now.'

'Until Potter catches on.'

'Screw him. Johnson is the name on the register for that next room.' Earl jerked his head backwards. 'And Johnson sleeps there. No lying going on here.'

'Nor here.' Walter reclined. 'It's late, and I recall you snore on a full belly, so I'm shutting eyes.'

'Sure.' Earl slumped onto the pillow. ''Sides, you always need a piss in the night.'

'Stable's just next door,' came the drowsy reply.

'You're an ass, Walt.'

'Yeah. Now turn out the light.'

Chapter 19

The following morning, Laura left the house with Sarah, and they met Bill at a quarter before ten. He'd scrubbed up pretty well, and the fact he'd made an effort raised a smile. Still, he was in dire need of a change of clothes.

By way of offsetting a maternal desire to look after Bill—because he was homeless, motherless, and needed a signing companion—she allowed the youngsters to converse privately. It raised another smile: her daughter had someone her age—and situation—to be with. Yes, a couple of friends from town might stop by the house, but the interaction was sparse. One of the girls, Lola, knew some sign language, but not enough for conversation. Mostly they sewed keepsakes, played the piano together, or silently read their books. It made more for presence than companionship.

Sign language by osmosis happened in a few places in town—a reflection of the community's general good nature. To her mind, it was no different than helping an older soul with their groceries or chopping wood for Vernon Prince, who'd lost the use of his right arm in a riding accident.

She left the youngsters behind as they dawdled—the trio wouldn't arrive at the schoolhouse like a family. That was fine—she didn't want to set tongues wagging.

She tried not to dwell on the fact that Bill was an unknown quantity. It would have scared her too much.

There were enough reprobates in the world, like those who killed husbands, wives or marooned hearing-impaired boys on the unyielding prairie.

Did this mark the beginning of an end? Would Sarah now have a better go-to companion than her mother? Was the writing on the wall for the "best friend" part of their relationship?

Her mind fast-forwarded to Sarah's last day at home. The empty nest. The future as a greying widow. Perhaps her students would keep her young? The joy of teaching and learning, improving lives, and seeing youthful faces light with understanding. It would be nicer to have a companion, though. Life is always better that way.

She shook it away: maudlin, presumptuous, one-dimensional. In the meantime, Bill's presence precipitated Earl's, and four were stronger than two against the pockets of ill will. If Earl was willing to risk a confrontation with Dennis Hayes to help Bill, she should equally take small steps of bravery.

At the schoolhouse, she set up the desks with study materials, watching as Sarah and Bill took seats in the second of four rows of four desks. The young man drank it all in; this was likely his first real school experience.

Yet, academic matters and the personal factor were wholly different. As evidence, Tom Potter's flashed double-take was a down-to-earth bump. He forced a smile towards Sarah but a scowl at Bill.

Laura feared the green-eyed monster. Tom's brain didn't run especially fast, and she held little hope for his performance this lesson, given he'd squander energy shooting evil glances at the twosome and mentally filing every second to replay it later to his father.

She girded her loins: there was no point worrying about things you couldn't change.

Besides, she could expel any pupil who disrupted the class—although that would be a last resort. Teaching Tom was virtually a prerequisite for her presence in White Rock. Life was a tightrope act, but Bill's presence acted as a gusty wind, making balance difficult.

As the lesson started, three of the fifteen were absent, which wasn't unusual. This skewed the class older—the youngest was Ella at ten, and Sarah the eldest at twenty-one.

She introduced Bill to the class, bypassing details and favouritism. The response was predictably mixed. As always, Lola stood out, offering a basic signing of, "Hello, I'm Lola".

After a few minutes, Bill signed a question. Laura replied in words and signs for the benefit of everyone. It was a simple question, so a few tuts rang out. Soon came another query. Sarah chimed in, and three-way signing broke out.

Tom Potter looked up from his desk. 'Mrs Anderson, can we move on, please?'

'Patience, Tom.'

'Let them figure it out later,' Ira said.

'Yeah, in bed,' Devin piped up.

They all sniggered.

Laura was ready to ball them out but held in her frustration. She recapped the point, chalked a question on the board, and then toured each student to offer assistance.

Still, her mind drifted. Yes, she should—and did—take each pupil on their merit and learning pace, but how would Bill cope with the other lessons?

Earl swung the sledgehammer and clubbed the head of the fencepost. It gave an inch. He glared at the ground, curious at their laborious progress.

Walter rearranged his grip on the post, Earl swung, and the rap clattered their eardrums. Twice more, but something was amiss.

He set the hammer's head on the ground, pulled off his hat and wiped his brow.

Walter drew a forearm across his head. He stepped to where a jug of lemonade stood on an old rickety table, poured them a glass and drank. The warm liquid was a poor substitute for coffee, but they'd consumed all of what Laura had left for them. Despite her invitation to make as many pots as needed, they didn't want to push hospitality too far.

Earl looked away, past the house, up the street. 'Wonder how the boy's doing?' he said, primarily to himself.

'The boy? Meaning your boy.'

'Sun's not past noon and already balling time?'

Walter shook his head in familiar despair. 'I reckon your head would stand up a good long fence.'

Earl thwacked his glass down on the table. 'You ain't got the job of talking to him.'

Walter gave up. He wrapped his arms around the partially-driven post and heaved it out of the dirt. Then he knelt, peered into the rough hole, dove his hand down, rooted around, and with huffing and puffing, wrenched something from the soil. He tossed the stone aside.

He stood, quickly scuffed the knees of his pants and glowered at his friend. 'I know some about stubborn rocks standing in a man's way.'

Gone two of the clock, lunch in the saloon having passed without incident, Earl parted company with Walter on the excuse of an errand to run.

When his friend was out of sight down Main Street, he jammed his hat low over his brow and set off.

While Laura had offered to keep her ear to the ground and warn of Dennis Hayes' return, Earl remained on edge because the man could arrive aboard any stagecoach, any day.

His time to fix things up with Bill and find a permanent solution was short, but how short?

The clock on the white wooden fascia of the schoolhouse showed past eleven-thirty, as it had done for years. Maybe it was left that way to suggest it was always time for learning.

He pulled off his hat, roughly neatened his hair and eased open the door to the single classroom. Thirty-five years since he'd been in such a room, and not for long enough even then. Some things endured; the smell of books, the sense of smarter folk than he.

Laura was alone; the pupils had left—as he'd planned. She was on the verge of departure, arms full of books.

'Earl?'

'Laura, ma'am.'

'The deference is charming but unnecessary. Just because you're mending my fence doesn't make you a hired hand.'

He dipped his head. 'Right sorry.'

'Here to help me with these things?'

'No. That is—I guess. I mean, no, I will, but—'

'You're here for something else,' she said, sparing his blushes. Almost.

'Yeah. I—' He swallowed and dug deep of courage and humility. 'I'd be real grateful if you'd learn me on how to talk to the—my—boy.'

She smiled broadly and set down the books. 'Is that right?'

'I figure I oughta.'

'Oughta?'

He corrected himself. 'I figure it's right.'

'Well, it would be my pleasure.'

'Oldest fool you ever had for learning, I guess.'

'Oldest? Yes. Fool? I'm not so sure.'

'Well, I feel like it.' He kicked his feet like a truanting teen.

'We'll begin with the alphabet.' She gestured loosely to a pupil's desk. 'Take a seat.'

He looked at her, a rabbit in the gaze of a wolf. 'You mean—?'

She slipped instantly into schoolmarm. 'What's the matter? Too soon for you? Better things to do?'

It was as if Walter had conjured up a lost twin, another person placed into Earl's life to keep him on the straight and narrow through less-than-gentle persuasion and an understanding of—but not being swayed by—his bullshit. Yet when she looked disapproving, it triggered a part of his brain he'd long forgotten existed. He'd be a heel to consider putting up a fight. She deserved better. In fact, she deserved more than he'd probably ever be able to muster.

'I reckon not.'

She gestured again. 'We'll go slow.'

He sat.

It felt otherworldly. Embarrassing. Yet positive.

She perched on the edge of the teacher's table and eased her maroon skirt up a few inches to make it comfortable.

Reflexively, he sat up straight. He'd never sat up straight during class. He'd barely paid attention to anything more than Laila Browning and trying to glimpse her unmentionables.

Laura held up her right hand and closed it into a fist with the thumb protruding. With her left, she pointed at him.

He copied the symbol.

'A,' she said.

They repeated it.

He hoped he'd be alive long enough to get to Z.

Chapter 20

Bill ran his fingers over the knot in the wood. Everything had its imperfections.

It was dark and shaped like a teardrop, where a diagonally-sprouting branch had been trimmed away. Darker than the surrounding grain. A Mojave amongst a sea of whites.

In the past, he'd trimmed many twigs and branches from logs. There were foraging or firewood trips with one of the tribe or, very occasionally, his father.

Except not his father. Just a man, an apparent knot on the trunk of the country. A man unlike him. Bill had lived as an outsider in a group of outsiders. Now he was a different kind of outsider. Yet he'd been cared for previously, and there were signs he'd again found an accepting bosom.

He knew that he and his birth mother had been taken from their home, but not discovered exactly where that was. As such, he didn't dedicate his life to finding the place as there would likely be nobody and nothing there. Still, as he travelled, he kept an eye out in faint hope. He knew it was within a few hundred square miles of the Mojave camp, not elsewhere across the vast country he'd heard of.

When the ambush happened, he'd been on a new route, allowing that spark of hopeful discovery to remain. At worst, he'd find a new place to call home. He'd tell all this to Earl when the time came. He might also find the courage to ask why Earl hadn't come looking for him and Ma years ago.

He didn't remember Mary, but he'd summoned the courage to ask the Chief's wife about her. They'd only said two things; kind and blonde. Kindness wasn't unknown to them, but fair hair marked her as White.

He couldn't grieve because he had scant memory to taint with loss. If he possessed anything, it was curiosity—about an absent future. Those moments of wondering waned over the years as the travails of a self-sufficient life became all-consuming. Curiosity about the future was time better spent elsewhere.

The tribe hadn't said what happened to his father, so he assumed it was to spare him the pain of hearing about a killing. Now he'd met Earl—against all the odds—he didn't want to cause an argument by dredging up the past. All the same, he was keen to know about his young life, and that fateful day of the raid. It must have hit Earl so hard, so he sympathised, but dearly wished that his father would brighten up now. Life was uniformly better, wasn't it?

He didn't want to cause a fuss about the ambush. That was done, and the outcome more than made up for the event. He wanted to let it lie. After all, he'd been less than law-abiding in the past. He certainly didn't want to risk having to go up against those robbers—or make Earl do so.

The past had to be left behind, as best as current circumstances—and other folk—allowed.

He fingered the knot. Silently.

A shadow fell across the stable wall. He turned.

Sarah stood there, partially silhouetted against the sun-drenched compound beyond the door. The light glowed on her wavy blonde hair, giving her a halo.

She held up a pail and pointed behind her.

He nodded, understanding.

She'd explained that she helped Abe not for money but for the enjoyment of being around the animals. Still, she was here, and he had no axe to grind about that.

Bill watched her go. Then he pinched the nail between thumb and forefinger, hefted the hammer, and drove the nail half into the wall, good and strong, and away from the knot which would bend it, harm its progress. The reverberations echoed silently through his arms.

He tested the nail's strength, then hung a set of loose reins on it.

Being around the stables made him keener to have a horse of his own again, and this would be the first he'd owned through merit.

He scrutinised the dozen or so occupants of the stables. To take one would be the easy option, but the wrong one. Thieving is only workable until you get caught or become a victim and realise how the other man feels. He'd hit both those marks before now.

Someone appeared, a face he recognised—Tom Potter, clearly with something on his mind. The issue would be that the fool had no idea how to convey it.

Three things perennially made Bill nervous; communications barriers, a problem he was unaware of, and anyone carrying a gun who seemed unafraid to use it.

Tom Potter possessed a clean sweep of the three. He was also taller and heavier than Bill.

Tom approached, gabbling and gesturing animatedly.

With intermittent past practice, Bill had gleaned a few words of lip-reading when he tuned into the person, and they made an effort—like with Mrs Walker.

Tom didn't care. He treated Bill like an imbecile. The voice was unmistakably raised and urgent, but it was as valuable as barking at a knot.

Tom pointed out the door, cupped his palms on his chest and waved his hands across each other. He made a kissing gesture against the back of his hand and wagged a finger vehemently.

This was followed by clear disparaging signs against Bill's ailment, and again with the chest cupping and hand waving.

Bill would have been deaf *and* an imbecile not to get the point. The point was redundant, but the inference raised his hackles—a sweet girl like Sarah would never have leapt into any kind of relationship with Bill based on a few hours together.

But Tom continued with the notion that Sarah wasn't available because she was already *his* girl. This came as news to Bill, but he was in no position or mood to refute it. She'd barely looked at Tom at the schoolhouse, and if he were such a jealous lunkhead, she wouldn't have stoked the fire by sitting beside Bill.

It was all very fishy.

Nevertheless, not wanting to get his block knocked off, Bill held up his palms peacefully and nodded.

This placated the hornet.

Bill wrapped up the exchange by nodding, signing Yes, pointing at Tom, then out the door, and finishing with a flourished phrase on his hands. As he did so, a smile crept across his lips: his private victory over aggressive offenders.

Tom darted in and grabbed Bill's shoulders. He shoved, made a loose approximation of Bill's sign-off, and jabbed him in the chest.

Holy smokes. Bill didn't know how, why, or when, but by extraordinary bad fortune Tom Potter knew the sign for "Eat shit, asshole".

He brought his dukes up, but Tom's fist moved quicker. The blow to Bill's stomach landed as hard as any man's, and he went down, rapping his forehead on the wall of the nearest stall and crumpling into the pungent straw.

Now Tom's defences went up, preparing for reprisal.

Wincing in pain, Bill pushed himself to his feet, unwilling to be defeated in the first round.

A silhouette appeared and crystallised out of the backlight. Sadly, Bill's head movement gave the game away. Tom wheeled, dodged Abe's outstretched arms, and flailed away another punch. The man went down.

Bill's eyes widened. He was definitely into something now—an altercation not of his own making. He didn't want to fight Tom: his new companions deserved better. However, Tom did want to fight—because it would prove that deaf kids are scum and need to be taught a lesson.

Bill put his dukes up and stepped to the side. Tom mirrored.

Abe writhed in pain.

Bill feigned a punch, which was easily dodged. Tom jabbed for his head but missed.

In Bill's peripheral vision, another silhouette flashed. He studiously ignored it. He darted left, ducked for no reason, and stepped left again. Tom followed, swirled on the spot, and flashed out a right which missed Bill's ear by barely an inch.

The silhouette was a person now, with an object in their hand.

Bill weaved to keep his opponent's attention.

The empty pail caught Tom across the back of the head, and he went down like a sack of grain.

Sarah dropped the pail as if it was hot. She looked at Tom, and her hand came to her mouth.

Bill wanted to rush in and give an embrace of thanks, but he withheld—it would appear weak. Instead, he darted to Abe and helped him up. There was no blood on the man's dark face, although a bruise might show.

"I'm fine," Abe signed, pushing Bill's hands away, but his face betrayed hurt pride. He eased his backside onto a hay bale.

Sarah was beside them, worried as she eyed Bill's forehead.

"What?" he asked.

"You're bleeding."

"It's nothing," he gestured, though his head thumped.

She shook her head sternly, tugged a white laced handkerchief from her pocket and reached towards his injury. He recoiled. She responded with a matronly look, edged with tenderness, put a steadying hand on his upper arm and dabbed the handkerchief to his forehead. He winced in pain. She rolled her eyes. He must have flushed pink at the show of pain and at the attention.

Abe pulled an expression of interest. Bill dismissed it. Sarah saw and frowned. He smiled to mollify her.

She removed the cloth. "You're hurt. Don't be a boy about it."

"Okay," he signed meekly, feeling about half his age and in the presence of a mother he'd never had.

She picked up the pail, skirted the unconscious Tom Potter, and skipped out the door.

"Who started it?" Abe asked.

Bill pointed at the defeated pugilist. "He. I swear."

Abe rubbed his jaw. "Help me get him up."

They sat Tom on the hay bale against the stable wall. Abe held Bill's head and examined it. "No blood. He'll remember it tomorrow, though."

"Good," Bill signed.

"What was his beef?"

"I think I spoke to his girl."

"Sarah?' Abe shook his head and looked with disdain at Tom. "Stupid boy."

Sarah reappeared. She'd brought water, and beckoned Bill to sit on a stool, where she tended to his grazed brow. He fought the embarrassment as he watched her dainty hands and tried not to meet her blue eyes. If Tom had a beef before, it would be nothing compared to now.

Tom woke, stood groggily, withstood a brief interrogation from Abe, and then left at pace. If he'd had a tail, it would have been between his legs.

"Imagine being laid out by a girl," Bill signed.

Sarah pursed her lips.

"Young lady," Bill corrected.

She smiled. He willed her to finish nursing. Whilst he felt the most cared for in years, he didn't want her caught in a storm between two men, neither of whom had any claim on her.

She stepped away. He touched the damp spot on his head; his finger came back clean, although the cuts throbbed from a sharp rap on rough wood.

"Thank you."

"I hope I didn't hurt Tom bad."

"I hope I never make you angry," he signed, eyes wide in good humour.

"I hope so too."

The threesome headed for the Hotel. Abe insisted on seeing Bill back to his room without further kerfuffle.

A way short of their destination, Potter approached, his face echoing his son's disquiet.

'This kid fixing to fight my boy now, Abe?'

'He didn't start it.'

'In a pig's eye. You're lucky I don't fire him.'

'You're lucky I was there to intervene,' Abe retorted.

Potter gave Sarah a look of distaste. 'Cripples having to gang up on my Tom.' He tutted. 'And a girl, too. Never be a lady, fighting like that.'

'Your view's your own, Lyle.'

Potter turned to Bill and raised his voice. 'And don't think I don't know you took a room last night. Making Earl Johnson do your dirty work, looking to slip me on by.'

'Man's got a right to room his boy, Mayor,' Abe insisted.

'His boy? How d'you work that?'

Abe cursed inwardly, sensing he'd overstepped a boundary of confidence. 'Nothing.'

Potter inspected Bill. 'Now, if that don't figure,' he muttered. 'Well, if you weren't out before, you are now.'

'Out of what?'

'Terms of trade of that Hotel is to refuse entry to any man, any person, any… cripple we say causes issue. And starting fights is issue.'

He moved into Bill's personal space and inspected the newcomer's facial features. 'If I don't know much, it's a fact that Earl Johnson married a half-breed Mojave piece, and on these black eyes of his, this kid has Mojave blood.' He stepped back dramatically. 'So I serve notice he's barred from the Hotel. We don't house thieving red sons of bitches in a respectable place of business.' He stared at Abe. 'I make myself clear?'

'Crystal,' Abe replied through gritted teeth.

'And all three of yous, leave my Tom alone.'

Abe didn't rise to this lie. He simply nodded curtly and ushered Sarah and Bill on down the street. Inside, his gut churned with regret.

When they arrived at Laura's, she immediately caught sight of Bill's injury and darted forward.

Earl exchanged a worried glance with Walter. His fist clenched: the kid had been scrapping. What the hell kind of son had he inherited from the wild prairie?

'What happened, Abe?'

Abe recounted the events, signing as he spoke. Bill and Sarah interjected with additions, which he voiced for the benefit of Earl and Walter.

Earl breathed relief that Bill was the innocent party. 'Potter's got no right,' he growled.

'He's every right,' Laura replied. 'As much as I have to exclude a pupil, or the saloon has to eject a drunkard. Only difference is Bill here has not done a thing wrong.'

Earl sighed heavily. 'I guess. What the heck's to do?'

Sarah signed to her mother, who was somewhat alarmed. Sarah countered with supplication on her face. Laura signed to Bill, who looked at Earl as if seeking advice or approval.

'What gives?' Earl asked Laura.

'She's worried Tom will find Bill sleeping in the stables, and who knows what might happen. You already found him bushwhacked.' She ran fingers through her hair. 'Sarah wants to sleep in my room with me and give her bed over to Bill. Just for a day or two until this mess is straightened out.'

'I ain't sure on that.'

'Neither is Bill. He doesn't want to… impose. I think that's his father talking.'

Father. The word hit Earl square in the chest.

'Well, I ain't the judge. It's you what's being imposed on. I'd take the boy, but there's a wage to earn and schooling to do. If there's a place in town, that works all ways.'

'There's an open barn, a dirty street, or a woman's bedroom,' Walter said. 'Better than trail-side, I guess.'

'Not a woman's bedroom like that,' Laura said. 'A bed in a room. Given over by a girl who wants what's best for a person who needs protection from wrongdoers.'

'I don't rightly know my answer,' Earl said.

'With respect, it's Bill's place to answer.'

'He'll get more'n a scratched head for any shenanigans.'

'I'll tell him.' She signed to Bill.

The boy looked at everyone, rested on Earl, and finished on Sarah. He put a hand on his heart and bowed to Laura.

'You're not outta the woods yet,' Walter murmured, patting Earl's shoulder. 'Fact is, I reckon that fence is only the start of your paying back to this good family.'

Chapter 21

A storm had raged on the night after Bill left the tribe. He never used the word "escaped" because he hadn't considered himself a prisoner at the time or in retrospect.

As he'd lain under the lamentable shade of an overhanging rock, getting marginally less quickly soaked than if he'd been out on the plain, he'd wondered who the Lord was angry at to have sent this cataclysm upon the neighbourhood. Who was at fault—those who kidnapped then nurtured him, the Whites for driving out these apparent marauders, or he alone for absconding with no regard for gratitude or farewell?

This night passed infinitely more physically comfortable but no less strange or mentally bothersome. His mind whirled like those clouds which had hurled down silent thunder and shocking lighting.

He was glad for an absence of friends—friends who would surely mock him for lying in a girl's bed, or corpse with insinuations about an illicit liaison. He shivered with undeserved embarrassment.

By the light of the candle's flicker, he noted the girlish items bedecking the room; hand-crafted drapes, a soft toy, a painting of a cactus in Sarah's younger brushstrokes, home-made cushions and linen, a child's wooden rocking horse, a pair of dolls dressed in Sarah's handiwork....

He'd only seen a room like this once, and that memory made the circumstance prey on his mind even more.

As he lay there, under sheets that had touched her, on a pillow where she rested her head, factions warred over conflicting emotions. He felt dirty, ashamed, guilty, utterly indebted, out of place, nervous and, worst of all, aroused.

His mind needed to be stilled, made light. Mrs Walker had told of folks who counted sheep in their mind to aid sleep, so he blew out the candle and, with many blessings to count, began to number them.

On waking, it took Bill a few moments to recall where he was. The new silence he bathed in had neither the aura of a tepee, a night under stars or storm, a lodging, barn, hotel, woodshed, nor an abandoned ramshackle homestead. Maybe this was what a home was like.

Quickly he dismissed it because this wasn't his home—only another lodging, one step on an unknown journey. The next task was more pressing—navigating a house of two ladies without embarrassing them in the hours when washing, and unmentionables had to be both undertaken and avoided.

Mercifully, all passed without incident.

After a cordial but odd-feeling breakfast, the three walked up to the schoolhouse.

By luck or judgement, Tom Potter wasn't in class. Bill joked with Sarah that he was probably sleeping off the wound she'd inflicted. Initially, her face swam with guilt and worry, but she buoyed. He asked if she'd inadvertently 'taught' Tom the signed phrase which started the affray—and she sheepishly admitted it was.

He calmed her: Tom had been spoiling for a fight, and if a scratch on the forehead was the price Bill paid for defending her honour, so be it. She blushed.

Laura brought their attention back to the day's topic, so he sat straight and faced front. He had to be as good a pupil as a stablehand and lodger. There could be storms without mercy on the prairie, and cold rocks were no match for a real bed, even one so girlish.

When school finished, he and Sarah let the other pupils leave, then helped Laura tidy up. Her gratitude was evident. Such tolerance, understanding and budding affection were in direct counterpoint to Earl—and Bill could make a direct comparison as the man walked into the classroom at that moment.

There was the customary 'Afternoon, Bill,' from his lips— Bill had learned to read that, followed by something of a surprise, a signed Hello. Yet there was aloofness and an expression permanently carved from plains rock.

Part of Bill felt sad, sorry, and overwhelmingly aware of his own imperfection. It was hard enough to come to to terms with Earl's existence, let alone their inability to communicate.

Despite this disappointment, a grain of hope remained. As he left the room, allowing Sarah out first—like the gentleman he aspired to be—he was certain Laura was helping Earl to learn the alphabet.

Still, it would be many weeks before Bill could directly ask the litany of questions that had bubbled up during the past years and, more keenly, over recent days.

Chapter 22

Earl met Walter in the saloon for breakfast that Saturday.

For the first time since returning to White Rock, he relaxed into the surroundings.

Walter drained his coffee mug. 'I'm heading home for a few days. Old Man Harper is looking to take a couple of my bulls for studding, and damn if I don't need the money.' He looked around. 'A bed and three cooked squares a day are all well and good, but I'm hardly sitting on a mountain of gold.'

'Town living burns a hole,' Earl agreed.

'I'll come back inside a week, check in on... circumstance.'

'Which should be my lookout.'

'By rights, yeah. But even St Paul had to be on the road first.'

'Hey—I'm on the road,' Earl protested.

'Reckon I dragged you out there, too. Took your horse and left you—like young Bill.'

''Bout which I was an ass.'

Walter stood. 'It's not me you gotta make peace with.' He laid two coins on the scrubbed wooden table. 'Pass my regards and departure.'

'That I will.'

Earl watched his friend go, desperately hoping he'd return before Dennis arrived—though he was too ashamed to say as much out loud. It didn't stop him from feeling exposed.

Winding up in a box comes to every man, but now would be an unfortunate time. Years ago, he'd have willingly stepped into the six-foot hole, terminally sleepless and desperate for release from his torment. He'd have been with his family again.

Except he wouldn't—not then, not now. For all his reservations about Bill, one fact remained: his son was alive. Someday, Earl might finally realise he hadn't indirectly killed the boy that fateful afternoon.

Someday.

Amidst the buzz of mid-morning street life under an unseasonably warm sun, he spied a familiar figure gliding up from the edge of town, a pail in one hand and a parasol cast over her shoulder. He let a carriage pass and crossed the wide dusty roadway.

'Morning, Laura. Bill okay?'

'If you mean any disturbance, no. He's quite the gentleman. If you could be proud, you should.'

The pail was half-full of water, with a dozen flower stems lying against the side. A trowel was fastened to the handle by rough string. It rapped against the pail as the water undulated with her body movement.

'I reckon so.' He pointed. 'You want I carry that for you?'

'A chip off the block, is it—chivalrous for a lady?'

'I'm not wishing the boy to be alike me. Kid has enough problem—' He stopped, but too late.

Her face creased in a worryingly familiar way. 'Because he's deaf, you mean?'

'Shoot. I—'

'His lack of hearing doesn't define him. It's not who he is. Spend some time with him, and you'll discover that.'

He nodded meekly. 'Yes, ma'am.'

'Don't "yes, ma'am" me, Earl. I'm not your—well, I suppose I am your teacher. What I mean is I'm not your mother or your wife. All I may be is a woman carrying a pail that a good man offered to hold not long ago.' She raised her eyebrows expectantly.

He relieved her of the cargo. 'Where we headed?'

Her face fell serious. 'The cemetery, if you'd be kind.'

That was a slight kick in the gut for his attitude and the echo of his circumstance.

'Be a pleasure.'

She led him up Main Street and turned left onto Gulliver, absentmindedly twirling the pale blue parasol as if she were a lady being escorted to church.

He wondered how it would appear to passers-by, but as she talked more about how Bill had settled in, he didn't give it another thought. Tongues always wagged, so a spot of gentlemanly conduct was no more noteworthy than a new boy in school or youngsters letting off firecrackers for kicks. Anyway, it felt good to be seen with her, however undeserved her company was, and despite it continuing to unsettle his conscience.

The cemetery lay set back from the road, separated by a low wall. At the midpoint stood an open gateway beneath an iron arch bearing rusted lettering, which proclaimed to those with a scant sense that this was White Rock Cemetery.

As she forged ahead, he followed dutifully, preparing words of sympathy. Yet, he became distracted by the haphazard rows of headstones and was mentally transported many miles away to two simpler memorials.

Soon she halted. The parasol slid down her arm and bumped to the earth. He darted in, concerned. She covered her face with her left hand.

The headstone lay flopped on its back, cracked in two. The legend remained visible, but the destruction was no less repugnant. All nearby memorials were untouched.

He dumped the pail and, on instinct and kinship, clasped her shoulder. Inside, he raged.

She smoothed her head, then scrunched her hair in annoyance.

He wanted to pull her close, knowing how a maelstrom would erupt if he found Mary's grave desecrated—especially by a known assailant. Yet the gesture would be presumptuous—too forward and out of place.

'This was as good as my doing.'

She shook her head. 'You carry enough weight in your heart. Don't carry more for me.'

'We brought the boy. Doubled your burden—on account of those with minds for hating.' The words soured his tongue, describing himself barely a few days earlier.

'And I had enough time to refuse that burden—which is nothing of the kind. Doing so would be admitting defeat, giving in to naysayers.'

He pointed at the broken stone. 'I'll fix this.'

'It's not your place.'

'It is so. To give back for what you do for my boy and putting up with my baloney.'

She picked up the parasol, its edge scuffed with ochre from the dirt. 'Grief isn't baloney. It just takes people in different ways. Some bleed quick and short, some long and slow. What's important is you don't run out on Bill. My work is living, not crying. Looking forward with what Jim left behind—our Sarah. I see him in her face, her goodness, every day.' She gestured downwards. 'This is a darn shame, a cruelness, but Jim wouldn't want me—or you—raging against whomever it was. An eye for an eye makes the whole world blind.'

'You got a strength that can make some men feel weak.'

It wasn't a mollifying sentiment—he did feel weak, yet she strengthened him somehow.

She gave a slight shrug, then looked past the standing stones and crosses, out to the land beyond, where rock outcrops stood like statues.

'Jim rode out that day as a favour to Lyle Potter. No, not a favour—an understanding. The Mayor had let us stay, with our wicked hand-signing ways, for Jim's skill with a rifle. He could ride and hit a Mojave galloping at a hundred yards.'

'All the same, it went bad.'

Her shoulders slumped. 'Jim wanted the best for us—a nice house we'd made, a school to teach in, a workshop where he could smith. He had a baby girl to provide for. So now that's my work: to do what's best, be strong, not give in to darkness and greed and those who don't know better.'

'That being so, taking in a boy with Mojave blood—Mojave what took your devoted—is forgiveness enough the Lord would look most kindly on.'

She met his eye. 'Mojave took your wife too, and by the looks of it, a too-big piece of your good soul. You've as much cause to fear and hate them as me.'

Sympathy plucked at his heart. 'Hating is their right. We took their land, and then we pen 'em up like sheep. Stealing, burning—we made that. So, I know why they done what they done, and I got no choice but to reap that and make a life anyhow. Hating back? Empty as a creek in high summer.'

He took off his hat and fiddled with the brim.

She tapped his arm. 'A man's character defines him, not his blood or afflictions. The person who broke this stone, they could be black or white or red, old or young, blind or sighted. What matters is their heart, which is colder than the earth.'

'That's so.'

'And they are certainly not as good of a person as you or Bill. Nor is anyone who judges or excludes people based on their difference. We are all God's children. We all have shortcomings—whether they are visible or invisible. Some people need to learn to live and let live.'

'I reckon not much changes in this world.'

'Yes. All we can do is hope.'

'Well, you give Bill and me hope, Laura. And we're mighty grateful.'

'It's my pleasure, Earl.' She puffed out a heavy breath, drawing a line under things. 'Now, I came here to fix up these flowers. Will you hold my shade for me?'

He held the parasol over her, all gentlemanly-like. 'It'd be the smallest thing.'

She bent, pulled a single stem from the pail and twirled it.

'This is the same as that brooch you kindly gave. And Bill's locket.'

'It were Mary's favourite.' He fingered the corner of his eye.

'And mine.'

'I think you would have got along,' he reflected.

She knelt and roughly pushed the pieces of the headstone together. 'You and Jim likewise.'

A shadow passed across his mind. 'I don't reckon anybody 'cept Walt would come to my grave.'

She stood, sadness in her eyes. 'I will. But I don't want to have to.'

'I'm not hankering to be down there, but Bill wants to be in town, so I gotta stay.'

'I'll talk to Elizabeth Hayes when they return. All will be fine.'

'You're some teacher, some woman, Laura, but if your words are faster than a man's gun, that'd be some kind of miracle.'

She rubbed his shoulder. 'You got your son back. Perhaps miracles come in twos.'

Chapter 23

God hadn't taken Bill's hearing; Earl knew that much. The boy was born bright, beautiful and perfect. Had the Mojave beaten the boy for being White and caused his hearing loss? He doubted it: they had chosen to take Mary and Alden rather than burn them inside the house. He'd often debated which would be worse—not to know their fate or to have found their charred remains?

His throat tightened in remembrance.

Would Bill understand why they had been taken? Earl knew of Whites being removed to be surrogate squaws, even babies to be raised as Indians. Mary's heritage, which was visible in her beautiful dark eyes and dark hair, probably counted in her favour. It didn't matter: the taking was done. What remained was Bill's deafness—caused through accident, illness or wickedness.

Earl had to know, to lay his conscience to rest. Answers, not reparations, were needed.

Yesterday, after seeing Laura in the cemetery, he'd been struck by the notion that a new shirt might show he was trying to be a better man. So, that morning, he got used to the feel of his dark brown apparel while taking his old shirt to the laundry, checking in on Jack at the stables, and enjoying a pot of coffee in the saloon.

Now, he waited outside the church. The arriving congregation trickled past, most offering him a cursory nod.

Bowman and Potter, inseparable, lumbered up the street, clocked this figure in unusual attire, and were their usual genial selves—Bowman touched the brim of his hat, and Potter looked through Earl as if he wasn't there.

Soon, he spied Bill, Laura and Sarah coming up the road. The young folk were engaged in staccato signing, and Laura walked by their side. She wore a mid-blue blouse, a wide-brimmed hat with a red gaillardia stem in the band, and a long navy skirt over black boots.

Potter was quickly forgotten.

Her face broadened into a smile, as this wasn't an arranged meeting. The youngsters signed "good morning", and he replied in kind.

Laura touched his arm. 'I didn't teach you that yet.'

'Guess I been spying, by chance.'

'A smarter person would say it's because you care about the boy.'

'I figured I'd walk in with Bill—if he's minded to let me.'

She signed to Bill, who looked at Earl and nodded.

'Perhaps you're starting to pass muster,' Laura said.

Sarah tugged her mother's hand, a girl in a young woman's body.

'Nice shirt,' Laura said as she was led away. The rim of her hat passed in front of her face like the moon eclipsing the warmest of suns.

He gestured Bill ahead. Then, awkwardly like an executioner leading a prisoner to the gallows, he laid his hand on the boy's shoulder and left it there as they went inside the wide-thrown double doors.

They took the back row, behind judgemental eyes. A faint whiff of paint hung in the air.

Mayor Potter sat in the front row, looking like the cat who got the cream, and soon Earl discovered why. The service acted as a dedication for the church's new roof, which Potter had funded.

The man gave a short oratory, during which he sang the Lord's praises and his own in equal measure. Earl's stomach boiled to the verge of devouring itself.

The donor himself revealed a plaque. The congregation applauded—bar four people.

Bill stood during the hymns, but unable to sing, he followed the words in the book he held, running a finger along the lines. Earl was struck by how the boy matched the correct pace, finishing a verse when the singing paused, as though Bill sensed the movement of Earl's body or felt the resonances of the distant piano. Of course, he might have attended church since leaving the tribe—whether a resident or stranger in any town—and had committed to memory the rhythm of every song in the book.

Earl had much to learn.

Occasionally, forwards and to the left, Tom Potter and another youth subversively glanced round, sniggering and making mock hand gestures. It stuck in Earl's craw. He hoped Bill hadn't noticed but reckoned the boy had learned to let such taunts slide off him like water from a moleskin coat. Earl would have to do the same, as knocking their heads together would have more far-reaching ramifications.

As they all sat in silent prayer, he wondered what thoughts Bill was sending up. Possibly wishing his father was something less of an ass.

So, Earl asked the Lord to make him less of one. He had reason to be. The past belonged in two places alone—in the past and his heart.

Except when it reappeared, lying hurt in the dust, deaf and needing.

They filed out.

He led Bill down the three broad steps and waited for the ladies. Presently they came.

'Now, shall I set a fourth place at dinner?' she asked.

His search for a reasonable and polite refusal was interrupted by the approach of Lyle Potter.

'Miss Anderson.' Potter touched the brim of his hat.

'Mrs Anderson. Miss Anderson is my daughter. What can I do for you, Mayor?'

'Regarding school. I'm getting word the new boy is disrupting the class.'

'Really?' she replied sweetly, though Earl saw steel in her eyes. 'I find that hard to believe.'

'You find it hard to believe that two members of the class, who can't possibly learn at the same speed as the *normal* children, are causing distraction and delay to others' rightful education?'

'Two of the class hardly constitutes—' Laura began.

'I simply won't have this town becoming a home for cripples, Mrs Anderson. I won't stand for you creating a deaf school by stealth. And a filthy Mojave boy too. Thieving heathen murderers.'

Her eyes flared. 'Well, that's where you're wrong. Bill—'

'Is an outsider and a half-blood Indian. This speaking with hands is spreading like a plague—a plague sown by evil heathens.' He jabbed a finger towards the youngsters. 'These… two… will be privately tutored, or you'll be looking elsewhere for another job.'

'That's blackmail,' she hissed. 'People have a right to communicate.'

'A schoolteacher must impart good practices.'

Laura's lips pressed tight, white in apparent anger as she sought a reply.

Earl could stand it no longer—beyond insulting the youngsters, it was hurting Laura.

He stepped in. 'Now listen here.'

Potter swivelled. 'This doesn't concern you.'

'You're talking 'bout my boy. Making it my business.'

'Not if you'd stayed out of White Rock and kept that stranger from corrupting an upstanding establishment. You've enough nerve anyway coming here—Dennis has about as much time for disruptive influences as I do.'

Earl clenched his fist but held back. People were still on the street. He wanted them to be aware that their Mayor was the aggressor and not give them any reason to consider Earl the more unsavoury character.

Potter cocked his nose at Earl and eyed Laura. 'That's the position. You'll inform me of your decision after school tomorrow.' He touched his hat. 'Good day.' He strode off.

Earl's heart wept a little for her.

His jaw worked. 'Of all the men to say this is a good town. Acting like that under the gaze of God.'

Laura encouraged him away. 'The other cheek, Earl. It's what we live by.'

Chapter 24

Laura pulled off her hat and set it on the side table. She'd remained silent all the way home, and Earl had let her as he, too, churned over the words and obstacles cast in their path.

He followed her to the kitchen, where she raised undue clatter, bringing together coffee grounds, water, pot and stove. He was minded to go out to the wood shelter, unleash the axe on some unsuspecting timber, and dissipate his rage through innocent destruction.

'Tom Potter's doing, I'll be bound,' she said by way of an opening remark.

'All the same, your load is doubled.'

'And with you here, my benefit is likewise. Potter and his boy are swinging away now, afraid. They have more than me to contend with.'

Earl considered that the first phrase could be interpreted as a compliment, and it warmed him.

'I don't get the Potter boy. One day, railing at Bill, pretending on protecting Sarah for hisself. Next day, as good as pushing her in the dirt for wanting an education.'

'There was never a coward who wasn't a bully.'

'He makes out they was courting. Or did I get that backwards?'

She set the pot on the stove. 'His imagination is as active as his temper.'

'That so?'

She leant on the side drawers and mussed up her hair to release it from the tightness of being under the hat. It was tied up at the back, but bangs softened her gently lined forehead.

'About two years ago, a young mare kicked up at the stable. It had Sarah trapped in the corner, could have trampled her, knocked her clean out. Tom heard the fuss, caught the rope, and got that horse out of there. Thinks he saved Sarah's life.' Her chest fluttered.

'Don't sound like courting to me.'

'It isn't. Wasn't. But he asked to take her to the Fourth of July dance, and I said yes—I owed the boy. So, they went, and he tried to kiss her, and she had none of it because he's not the right kind.'

'Damn straight.' Scarlet coloured his cheeks. 'Pardoning my language.'

She dismissed it with a wave. 'He walked her to school for a few days. They took a ride out. Being tall, he figures he's like an older brother. Anyway, all kind gestures are for one thing—the same as any man wants with a woman.'

'Having his way.'

'And more—for bragging rights. Because he'd be the boy who took a deaf maiden as his payback for saving her.' She looked at the floor. 'In his eyes, Sarah's not a girl anyone wants, and she'd be grateful for any boy to lay with her.'

'Son of a—'

He caught himself and flashed an apology. He really had to work on his language around her.

'So Tom walks around with seeming ownership of Sarah, marked as the boy she'll give her thanks to. Now he'll cause stink like a skunk to keep your son away. And tell tales, and perhaps you'll up and leave. And would he ever marry her?' She rolled her eyes. 'Not while the world turns.' She chuckled. 'Not that I'd allow it anyhow.'

'I ain't minded to leave while the boy's happy and working a job, even if I ain't the one giving him a roof—though I plan to, soon as I can figure it. Anyhow, beats me why Potter'd let his boy near Sarah, what with his railing against the afflicted every hour of the sun.'

'Because the first boy who did everything his father told him would be the second only after Jesus himself.'

He sighed. 'Which is what I got now, I guess. A kid who won't do the right bidding.'

'You'd rather have no son than an imperfect one?'

'That'd be a lie.'

'Good. Then don't be fooled by my Sarah. You've missed eighteen years of mischief and back-chat in Bill, and don't think she's always been God's angel because of a pretty face and a good heart today.'

'There's more'n pretty faces and good hearts in this house. There's steel as good as any blade.'

He realised the inference, and she turned away to the stove—perhaps to spare a blush. His heart leapt, so he chastised it. It wasn't right to compliment either her steel or rich beauty—because it could be misinterpreted as courting behaviour.

She took the coffee pot into the lounge, where the youngsters stopped conversing. Bill directed what appeared to be a question. Earl was getting used to recognising a query in Bill's face. Maybe he could actually do this… communicating.

The dialogue continued. Bill dove into his pocket and thrust a coin in her direction. Reluctantly she took it, poured the coffee, handed Earl a mug and pulled up a chair.

'What'd the boy say?' He sipped the brew.

'He offered to leave town rather than cause problems at school.'

A tiny ember in his heart caught alight. 'Kid knows 'bout doing right.'

'I said not to go, not for our blushes. Home school is fine for Sarah. She's old enough. She has been for years, but staying home would make us more insular. Many children don't attend some days. A person has to want to learn.'

'Except Bill wants to leave.'

She shook her head. 'He wants to learn, to earn his way. But he knows he doesn't fit, and it seems he puts my and Sarah's welfare above his own.' She sipped her drink. 'Wherever he learned that, you should be indebted to them.'

'Reckon I am.'

'So, I'll school Bill at home for as long as he wants.'

'It ain't your place. This ain't his... home anyhow.'

'Home should be where a person is happy. Unless he hides it well, he's happy here.'

'But you sharing a bed and all?'

She fell reflective. 'I held Sarah in my bed plenty of nights after Jim died. She held me too, in her own way, though she never understood. She's a caring soul at heart.' She forced a smile. 'Besides, I can't cast Bill adrift, whether he's kin to you or anyone.'

'I swear I'll make things right. I'll find a space, and you can go back to your lives.'

Laura indicated where Bill and Sarah were in silent conversation. 'You mean, you want to take away this?'

'If there were another place in town, that'd be fine, but money's the hitch. Hotel won't take Bill, stable is no proper comfort, and it'll sit better with many folks if two kids not courting weren't sharing a house. A few days, I'd grant your kindness, but if he wants this to be his town—having a friend, a teacher, work and all—I gotta find a better way.'

Laura nodded, pursed her lips, and went to the window.

Earl watched the youngsters. Within a week, Bill had developed more kinship than he'd probably had in his life. Earl's dormant parental instincts nagged him to do what was right for the boy.

Trying to prise Bill away from town because of his own history and prejudices was doomed to failure. He couldn't regain the lost years by exerting his will now. Sarah was like a lifeline for Bill. If only it didn't feel like Laura was salvation for Earl himself as well.

Laura turned. 'Jim had a forge at the back of the stables.'

'But whatever smith took his place works there now?'

She shook her head. 'Emmet has his place across town. The forge is empty. Potter let me keep it,' her head fell, 'Even after Jim passed.'

He reached out a comforting hand but stopped short.

'You reckoning to take a brush to the place and make the kid a room?'

'I think with your carpentry and my… homemaking, it would be better than the barn.' She offered a hopeful smile.

He nodded. 'And neither of us would be beholding to you no more.' He pointed at Bill and Sarah. 'But I think he'd come by every day if he were welcome.'

'And you?' She arched her brow suggestively.

He swallowed, unfamiliar with the attention. Safer to be reticent, though—even if it was due to practicality, not habit.

'Call by? That be nice. But stay? No. One day I'll shoot more'n my dumb mouth off in this town, and Bill gets to be another person tending to a grave, and I got too many years knowing that's a poor way to spend a life.'

'As you will. My weakness is only wanting the best for good folk.'

'Ain't no weakness from where I stand. Weakness is in hate, not love.'

'So will I school you here too? In our little… project?' She cycled through A, B, and C on her hands.

'Sure. Lotta catching up to do. Things I gotta say. First question is if he'll take the old forge.'

'Then I'll ask him.'

Chapter 25

Bill slept more soundly on the second night at the Andersons'—though it was relative. He'd passed nights under the stars where the only trouble on his mind was the next day's eating or whether he'd be jumped by roving Mojave who'd get lucky they found a prey who wouldn't hear them coming.

Sarah's room had a faint perfume. A soap, perhaps, or scented talc. His closest sense memory was Mrs Walker's aura of lavender—a stronger tinge that permeated her house.

He'd no recollect of his birth mother's scent. In the camp, the air flitted with wood smoke, cooking odours, pipe smoke, horse dung, or, sweetest of all, the welcome petrichor following a drenching. He couldn't hear the rain drumming on the canvas or rattling on the ground, but he'd peer through gaps in the tent as the drops bounced up from the hard earth.

As he lay there, inspecting Sarah's room, he felt conflicted about moving to the old forge. The comfort of a real home was soothing, but the sense of being a visitor, tiptoeing around kindly people, niggled him.

His presence also risked bringing more turmoil to the household, through rumour and sniping, from people like the Potters. He didn't want to make the Andersons' lives worse after they'd made his better.

Soon, the aroma of coffee and bacon snaked under the gap in the door. It puffed into the room's clear, feminine air and tickled his nostrils, teasing him to rise from the bed and seek out the source.

After breakfast, Abe called in to give Bill his first week's wages, and Bill delighted in the rub of the cool coins in his palm. The first tangible tendrils of hope.

When Abe left, Bill pressed half his wages into Laura's hand and didn't take no for an answer. Her gratitude manifested in a tentative gesture towards an embrace, but she opted to clasp his hands.

Afterwards, she suggested they walk into town. Sarah could drop a piece of embroidery work at Mrs Jackson, and they'd stop at the Bank to deposit wages, then pick up supplies at Wilson's Store.

Bill pondered whether he'd soon be citizen enough—here or anywhere—to have an account at the Bank. First, he'd need to get and keep the necessary dollars.

A half-hour later, they promenaded up Main Street, tens of folk buzzing along boarded sidewalks. The sky was a canopy of motionless oyster grey, so Laura forewent parasol or bonnet, and Sarah wore a jacket which gave her a mature, womanly appearance. It made him walk taller and feel even more drawn to her.

He waited outside a house situated down a small side alley while the ladies visited Mrs Jackson. He assumed she was a hearing woman, and Sarah needed Laura to help communicate.

They passed the barber's shop, and Abe waved through the window as Mr Drake lifted the man's face and expertly drew the cutthroat over his chin, carving out the first line of skin from a sea of white foam.

Bill focussed on the chatter in Sarah's hands as she poked fun at passers-by.

He didn't catch all the names nor understand some of the words, but the gist of her good humour came across. Now and again, she'd touch his arm or give a gentle shoulder nudge.

At the Bank, Laura suggested he remain outside. Strangers, especially men, often raised concerns, as they'd sometimes be up to no good. Withdrawals were to be accompanied by paper slips, not a Colt's unblinking eye.

Bill waited on the edge of the sidewalk, leaning on the rail where four horses were tied up. He recognised one from the stables—a plain grey mare with a rough white crescent on its forehead. It was a docile animal, so he happily petted it— caressing the soft hair on the back of its ears, sensing its warm breath tickling his hands.

This might be a good horse, he thought. Come the day, any individual he chose would need to be attuned to touch and gesture more than voice.

The Bank building, new and four-square, stood near the edge of town, with only a gunsmith, undertakers and two unidentified properties beyond it. After that, the road ran out into the open country, with mountains in the distance—dark clouds heavier out there, squatting low over the peaks like a hen on her eggs.

Two men approached on horseback. Their dust trail waned from a cloud to wisps, and they manoeuvred their mounts towards the Bank's railing. Their faces were furtive, and Bill knew their voices were low from the movement of their mouths.

Bill slid behind the grey mare, watching over its back as the newcomers dismounted and tied up. They were older than he but not Earl's age, clean-shaven, tan hats. One horse caught his attention; piebald, with two full black legs at the front, two full white at the rear, and one ear of each.

He recognised it.

Its rider set his boots on the sidewalk. Maroon boots with tan laces.

Bill furtively studied the man, and recognised him too. His eyes darted in worry. He slid further behind the grey mare, patting its neck to keep it calm.

The men's heads were together in conversation. They could shout for all it mattered to him. They looked up and down the street. He ducked as their gaze passed him.

He knew why they were here—and needed to act. A hearing man would call alarm. An armed man would draw his gun. A lawman would use his badge.

Bill was none of these.

His heart thundered in his chest. He glanced around, seeking a solution.

The men drew their guns, kept them low, and walked towards the Bank.

Never in his life had Bill wished more to be able to yell. His mind raced. Every second was torture.

Sarah and Laura were in the Bank. The Bank was about to be robbed.

He was helpless. But there were others.

He darted around the other tied-up horses, urgently unhooked the reins of the two new arrivals, yanked hard and set off at a run, drawing the startled mounts away from the premises.

His feet pounded the street as he ignored looks from pedestrians—many of whom must have considered him the criminal—until he skidded to a halt outside the barbers' red and white striped boards.

Abe caught his eye immediately.

Bill windmilled his arms, reins flying around his head, and crudely signed, "Bank. Robbery. Help."

Abe bolted.

With shaking hands, Bill wrapped the reins around the nearest post. He was running again when Abe reached his side, tugging paper from the neck of his shirt.

Four units down, the Sheriff's door stood ajar. Abe broke away, clattered up the steps, had his head inside the office for barely five seconds—yelling for assistance, Bill assumed—then worked to catch his youthful companion as they covered the last hundred yards.

Short of the Bank's frontage, Abe stumbled to a halt, startled. He grabbed Bill's shirt, stopping him in his tracks.

Abe signed, "Gunshot. Dangerous."

The deadliest quiet, the silence of injury and death.

People on the street hurried away. A woman scooped a young child into her arms and sought cover. Sheriff Bowman trotted past, panting, gun drawn, unfazed.

The building was thirty yards away.

Sarah was in there. Gunmen were in there.

So Bill ran.

Chapter 26

Earl was at the laundry, collecting his old shirt, looking the best it had in weeks. The timing was ideal because his current attire had picked up grease stains at the forge. One of the churchgoers—he didn't catch her name—recognised him and asked if he'd heard about the robbery his boy was involved in.

He didn't stop to hear the details but caught, "Go to Laura Mae's", as the door closed behind him. He broke into an even jog. Curious looks tracked his progress. A man cussed as he was forced to step aside.

His skin prickled, and his mind juggled two thoughts: Bill tried to rob the Bank and is dead, or the boy tried to rob the Bank, and I'll damn well kill him myself. Either way, Earl foresaw an examination of the bottom of a whiskey bottle for the first time in many years. Or maybe the woman was stirring up trouble—insinuating the deaf-mute stranger must be behind all the evil deeds in town.

Earl prepared to deliver a reckoning to someone.

As he barged brazenly through Laura's front door, his chest heaving so hard with worry and effort that he could hardly speak, he arrived in the room to find three upright, intact, and relatively calm people. His relief that Bill was unharmed spoke volumes.

They looked at him as one. First, he sought Bill's face and found neither regret nor explanation.

'What happened?' he asked Laura, too brusquely.

She gestured for him to calm down, which was futile until he discovered what triggered him to bolt down the street, a clean shirt flapping like a sail in his arms, the world's first apparent laundry thief.

'There was a robbery at the Bank. Sarah and I were inside. Bill was outside.'

'Was there shootin'?' he snapped.

'Yes.'

His jaw dropped, and his heart swelled with care.

'And you was inside? Without the boy? What in God's name for?'

She laid a hand on his arm for stillness. 'For doing our chores in town, like regular people. It's nobody's fault.'

'Mrs… tongue-a-waggin' from church reckoned Bill were involved. Reason I come down here like a new-branded steer.' He heaved a gust of relief.

'Bill *was* involved. He recognised one of the men, ran to Abe for help, and Abe called Sheriff Bowman.'

Flummoxed, Earl looked back and forth between Laura and Bill.

'Recognised?'

'Bill knew the man's horse from a year back. He saw it after a hold-up in Washburn. And he was right. William Petrie is wanted on three counts. Well, he was.'

'Hope he gets the gallows, shooting at innocent folks and women and deaf girls—'

'He's dead, Earl. Cal Prince shot him right there. Three counts are all well and good, but Cal Prince is fast, and he has a lot of money in that Bank, and he didn't want it taken.'

Earl let that sink in. 'And the other feller?'

'In the jail cell. Listen, alive or dead criminals are not what makes the day. Your Bill ran in after the Sheriff. While there was still an armed man inside.'

She stepped closer as if to protect her words from unhearing ears. 'He took their horses. He thought lightning-quick, and he cut them off from escaping and raised the alarm. And he came in, unarmed, worried for us.' Her face was beseeching.

'Reckoning to… save you,' he said robotically.

'Because he thought one of us might have been shot. And because he's a good boy—*your* boy—and he cares.'

'Well, tell him not to be a fool running at a loaded gun, on account of….' He looked at Bill, hung his head, and quietened his tone. 'On account of I can't lose him again.'

'Are you sure?' A glimmer of knowing schoolmarm appeared in her face, followed by a crease that belied teasing.

'I already got Walter for ball-busting, if it's all the same,' he hissed.

She signed to Bill.

Bill observed Earl's face, then raised an open hand, fingers up, and touched his thumb to his forehead.

"Pa?" Laura whispered.

Earl knew only a few signs, but he had the right one. He held up a fist and nodded it forward.

Bill lowered his hand, stepped forwards and offered it to shake.

Earl held it firmly, then, as his heart swelled, pulled Bill inwards, and wrapped him in an unashamed embrace.

Laura piled the table high for lunch.

As they ate, drank, talked and signed, he had a moment of stepping outside himself, a man at the room door, looking at a family that wasn't and never had been—an echo from a future that had long passed into impossibility. It was sobering but warmed him.

With full bellies, all four walked over to the forge and made plans.

The room was dark and dusty but not tiny. Bill would be decently accommodated when the detritus was cleared away, a broom pushed around, and a bed added.

Earl said he'd go home and fashion a simple bed frame, return with tools to fix the leaky roof, and the women would try to make it homely. Those were easy steps. Simple chores and furniture were in the purview of any person.

Winning hearts and minds was different, not counting dodging Dennis Hayes' gun.

Chapter 27

Soon after three o'clock, there came a rap on Laura's front door, and out of curiosity, Earl followed Laura to see who'd come calling. He reckoned the newspaper, maybe with a photographer too?

"DEAF BOY FOILS ROBBERY".

He'd clip that cutting out, fold it real careful, stow it in a thin box he might fashion from finely-chosen ironwood, take a ride out to the old house, dig a spot beside Mary's memorial, and bury the box, so she would know about her son's deed and be proud.

Except it was a part falsehood; she didn't lay there. That spot was undoubtedly many miles away, somewhere on the wide anonymous scrub, left behind by those who'd taken her. Invisible, unknowable, unmarked. Instead, he should point his face to Heaven in search of her. Perhaps take that box, set it to burn and let the smoke and ash rise to her.

Unless she already knew what had passed, looking down on events, her bountiful heart filling with love for the boy she'd left behind, and rejoicing to see his heart was good too.

Earl hoped she also held forgiveness for his foolhardiness and would be joyous at the reunion. What about his consorting with Laura, though it was merely friendship? That was a tougher ask.

The door opened with a creak.

There was no photographer there, nor reporter.

Instead, there was Sam Bowman, and beside him, a taller man with wire spectacles and the lined, high forehead of sixty or more years. Further behind, inside the gate, Lyle Potter held a commendable distance though his disparaging haughtiness carried across.

'Afternoon Laura, Earl.'

'What can I do for you, Sam?' she asked.

'Hoping we could have a word with the boy—that is, your boy, I believe, Earl.'

'Regarding what?' he asked curtly. 'And who's this?'

'Harrison Fulwell, manager of the Bank,' came the reedy voice of the other. 'I'm here to offer young Bill my congratulations.'

Earl looked behind them, seeking any trap, any contrary evidence. 'For what he done?'

'A deaf-mute foiling a hold-up is some deed,' Bowman replied.

Earl's skin goose-pimpled at two of those words. Yet not a fortnight before, he'd spewed them like grass seed. However much he banished them from his vocabulary, they'd still crest his ears until his dying day. That was a battle he couldn't win.

'I'll call him.' Laura went inside the house.

'The other feller admit on riding with the dead man?' Earl asked.

'This was his first, by all accounts,' Bowman replied. 'Not even a loaded gun—all for show. Living in the shadow of William Petrie. A one-time job for paying debts and moving on. I'll give him three nights for penance.'

'Three nights? For that?' Earl's face set hard.

'Kit Harman made his peace and set us straight on the deeds Petrie bragged about. He took no hostage, fired no bullet.'

'The Bank has concurred,' Fulwell chimed. 'We lost no men, no funds. We'll lose no custom.' He peered inside the house. 'Thanks to Bill.'

Earl seethed but held his tongue. It wasn't his position to determine justice for Kit Harman. He didn't want to soil this positive moment or start a confrontation on the steps of a happy house.

Bill appeared, with Laura's hand maternally on his shoulder.

Earl pondered her bottomless well of care, and whether he could ever offer such true parenthood as she seemed willing to give?

Fulwell held out his hand and raised his voice. 'The Bank wants to thank you, Bill, for what you did today, raising the alarm, stopping the hold-up, and saving us many thousands of dollars.'

Bill scanned the faces, then took the man's hand.

Laura quickly signed for him.

Fulwell pulled some paper dollars from his tight black waistcoat.

'And this is by way of a reward.'

Bill tentatively reached out, looked at Earl for approval, and, receiving a curt nod, took the five ten-dollar bills and held them like eggs.

Then he snapped from a trance and signed, "Thank you".

Laura voiced the words for the visitors' benefit.

Earl experienced a feeling he didn't ever remember: pride. He patted Bill's shoulder.

Sam Bowman eased forward, glancing behind as if revealing a secret. He dug into his jacket and emerged with five more papers.

'Petrie had a price of a hundred on his head. Cal Prince shot him but reckoned the boy deserved half for the bravery of running in to protect these women and other folks with nothing but bare hands and not even hearing. So,' he flustered the money across, 'Giving the kid benefit for being on the right side of the law.'

Earl whipped the cash into his pocket, knowing whose eyes were searching. 'I thought worse of you, Sam.'

'Cal's who you should be thanking. This isn't my doing.'

Laura sighed. 'Gratitude was ever so hard.'

Earl drew himself up. 'Good of you to stop by, Sheriff.'

Bowman got the message and headed away. Fulwell tipped his hat and followed. Potter let them out the gate, then walked up to the house.

Earl eased Bill backwards, away from the line of likely fire.

'Congratulations from the Mayor himself? We are honoured,' Laura said with lilting mockery.

Potter ignored her and directed his attention on Earl. 'Way I see it, a hundred dollars buys a fine horse for a kid to ride out of town and start a life.'

'Maybe, maybe not,' Earl replied.

'I got word the kid wants to camp down in the old forge.'

'It's my place to give,' Laura stated.

'Debatable. What gets me is you'd give so much kindness to a boy you don't know. You might ask yourself how the kid knew those men before? What's to say he's not like them?'

'He ain't like that,' Earl snarled.

'Hell, Earl, you didn't raise him! The plains did. He could have consorted with criminals for years.'

'Maybe I take as I find—and you should too.' It was a lie, and shame ripped through Earl at his past self. Yet, he could clearly have been a worse man.

Potter nodded sarcastically. 'I do. You've a lot of time for cripples—for a man who made my cousin one.'

'Such kind words about your kin,' Laura interjected.

The Mayor worked his jaw but left her jibe alone without a glance. 'Dennis is sure looking forward to seeing you again.'

'Is that so?' Earl asked.

'I got word he's returning.'

'Got word?'

'I sent my congratulations on his daughter's wedding.'

'And told him to take the first stage back?'

Potter merely smiled. 'Hard lines, Earl. Got your boy back, and soon enough, he'll be an orphan. A week, I'd say.'

'We'll see 'bout that.' But Earl didn't believe his own bluster.

'It comes to something to wish a man dead,' Laura sniped.

Potter shrugged. 'Neither man nor boy is compelled to stay in White Rock.'

'But we are free to,' Earl replied.

Potter stepped closer, whiskey breath on Earl's nostrils, and spoke low. 'Thirty days. Today's good deed gets him thirty days to put his life in order and saddle up. Any trouble, laying a hand on my boy again or such, fifteen days.'

Laura brushed in. 'Duly noted, mister Mayor. Now get off my property.'

Earl smiled inside, as if to say, "That's my gal"—which she wasn't.

Over coffee, Earl shook off Potter's ultimatum. The conversation turned to Bill's new shot at independence. He was happy to move in immediately—even before the bed was brought. A few straw bales would be fine.

Earl recalled his younger self, huddled in a corner of Walter's barn. Running from home and living on his wits had been no fun, and stumbling upon this kindly soul—who gave him lodgings and work—was the genesis of his new life.

The mystery resurfaced: Alden had been taken at only six months old, and the Doc hadn't said anything was wrong with the baby's hearing—so how did Bill come to be deaf?

Earl debated whether the issue was sensitive. Then, as communication and understanding held more import than the risk of disagreement, he put the question to Laura.

'How will knowing make a difference?' she replied.

'It ain't from thinking it can be fixed or getting a reason to curse the Lord. I gotta know, is all. If I don't ask, maybe the boy thinks I don't care, and that ain't so.'

'Okay.'

After an exchange of signs with Bill, she heaved a sad sigh. Sarah fell sorrowful. She tentatively reached for him and patted his shoulder. He replied with an awkward smile.

Laura faced Earl. 'There was a raid on the camp where Bill was kept. White folks, out for revenge, he was told. There was an explosion nearby. His ears were young and tender, I suppose....' She trailed off and shook her head.

Earl gritted his teeth. 'Poor kid,' he mumbled. 'Without that raid, I reckon he'd be fine.'

Her brow furrowed: he'd unwittingly belittled the boy's deafness. Again.

'I meant—' he began.

She waved it away. 'I understand. I'd be lying if I hadn't had moments when I wished Sarah could hear—especially when she was younger. Now, I simply accept. You will too.'

'Should'a left those people alone. What'd they do to us?'

'Us? Took loved ones—that's true. But other people had reasons to war against the Mojave too. We forgave. Not everyone is so charitable. "Us" and "them" is what caused this.'

'Us both losing. 'Bout the same time, if I heard right.'

She did the sums in her head. 'I suppose it would be.' Her cheeks drained. She signed to Bill, he replied, and Laura's air of worry leaked onto Sarah's face.

'The Mojave camp was way north, by the river. Now, don't get ahead of yourself, Earl, but I have a recollection that Jim said their raid was to a camp north of here.'

Earl sprang up, startling all three. 'Tell me 'bout that raid.'

Laura calmly stepped over and gestured for him to ease up. 'Nothing is for certain.' Her voice was low and soothing.

'All the same, I got a duty to find out. Maybe it's nothing, then all well and good, or maybe it ain't and folks gotta answer.'

'For a man running scared from a threat of revenge, you certainly fire up your cause quickly.'

He opened his mouth for a retort, then snapped it shut. A rejoinder had once left his mouth in the direction of Dennis Hayes, and how had that turned out? It would be more criminal here because Laura was only trying to do the right thing.

Instead, he went to the window and watched the world, nerves jangling.

She came to his side. 'The raid was on Potter's say so, and, yes, it was in sixty-one. Early spring. The year before, Mojave robbed the stage carrying five thousand dollars of the Mayor's gold into White Rock. The man's not one to let go of a grudge. Or money.'

'It ain't right.' He thumped the window frame.

'Potter pretended the posse was to revenge the death of the brother whip that day. He said it was his duty to find justice for the man's kin in town. But really, it was to get back his money. Potter's father worked as a forty-niner and made a handsome strike. So, from father to son came the money, and if Potter wanted to stay money-bags head of the town, he had to have it back. Some are blind to it, but I see.' Her lip curled in disquiet. 'Ten in the posse. Only Abe, Potter and Dennis came back. Abe told me some of it. He knows what happened.'

His teeth ground. 'Greed's a scourge and makes men evil sons of bitches—pardon my tone.' He shot a familiar grimace of apology.

'Don't mind it. Greed sent the posse. Greed killed Jim.'

'Potter get the gold?' Immediately he regretted such a tasteless question.

'Most. He gives to the church because he's such a sweet, God-fearing community man.' She rolled her eyes, which raised his spirits.

Her proximity was tickling his nose with her scent, and with every day—if not every hour—it was getting harder to deny his attraction. All the same, he shoved it deep down inside, because such matters were unimportant right then.

'Then I figure to talk to Abe. Hell knows I can't ask Potter 'bout it, and I gotta be sure.'

'Go careful with the outcome. Don't be rash. You're cared about.'

By how many? he wondered.

Chapter 28

Bill sat cross-legged on Sarah's bed, fidgeting at the hole in the thigh of his long johns. Outside, the sun had long passed the horizon, and the house was losing its warmth to a starry night of cool air.

Spread out on the floral bedsheet were two rows of five ten-dollar bills. He'd never seen so much money, let alone possessed it. It was a little scary.

Earl—the word 'father' wasn't yet in his everyday mind— had allowed Bill to do as he pleased with the money. Bill wanted a horse—not for an escape route, merely for freedom, a sense of accomplishment and proof he was no 'boy'.

Bill tried to imagine his father's voice. Was it gravelly, as if dragged over stones like the man's life had been? It certainly didn't possess the evenness and calm of Laura or Sarah.

He'd watched the man's tanned face, tried to look behind the lined eyes, and studied the movement of his lips to sense tone. The grit and anger of the initial acquaintance had gone—but Bill always feared ire in any face, as it usually meant the person wasn't thinking straight. Misunderstandings led to confrontations even amongst the hearing. When tempers were short, scant time or willingness was given over to including him or compensating for his deafness.

He rubbed a bill between his fingers.

Should he pay Earl for making a bed frame, or would that gesture imply distance between them? Should he accept the bed as a gift from father to son? Either way, he'd need to save a few dollars for a mattress.

Certainly, he'd get new underwear and something for Sarah by way of thanks for letting him take her room. In the bathroom, he'd found two bars of soap. One was larger, the other—Sarah's—nearing its end. He'd matched its scent to her, especially earlier in the living room when Earl and Laura were in the kitchen. As he'd counted the money for about the tenth time, she'd looked on, sharing in his contentedness. She'd signed, "My hero"—finger-spelling it, correctly assuming he didn't know the word. Then she'd nervously given him a loose embrace, her blonde curls brushed his cheek, and her clean scent washed over him.

For a minute, the hundred dollars was forgotten.

In the morning, Laura went off to the schoolhouse, leaving him with Sarah. She sewed for a while, her slim fingers expertly dancing over the fabric. Earl had gone home.

He caught her attention. "Would Abe sell me a horse?"

She paused her work. "There are four in the corral."

"I've seen them. Would I be allowed?"

"Yes! Shall I come, or do you not want a girl there?"

"You can always be with me."

She blushed.

They stood at the corral fence, assessing the four horses. One nannied another, trying to fend off his advances. The third repeatedly brayed, occasionally darting up and down parallel to the far fence. Too penned in, Bill thought. It longs for the open. Too flighty.

The fourth grazed calmly at the bales. He'd idly marked out this one before, hopeful but disbelieving he could earn enough in such short order.

He asked Abe whether the fourth was for sale.

"Would you like to try him?" Abe signed. "A man can't choose his horse on looks. He must be ridden. The bond must be there."

Bill looked at the man's kindly face and noted a few biscuit crumbs caught in his navy necktie.

"Can I?"

Abe nodded. Sarah bounced on her feet and clapped her palms silently together, equally invested in the process.

"I'll fetch him. I call him Tanner." Abe walked off.

"I'll get a saddle," Sarah insisted. Before Bill could protest, she darted away, skirt kicking up behind her, towards the tack store.

Abe roped up the horse and led it over.

Sarah, slight as she was, had no trouble scurrying across the compound with the saddle. He was perplexed how a girl who worked so delicately possessed such hidden strength. Perhaps it matched her personality—and Laura's: feminine on the outside but steely against the forces which lurked.

The three of them fixed up Tanner, and Bill greeted the gelding profusely. He tried to push his thoughts into its huge brown head, willing it to be a good mount.

The warm air battered Bill's face as he rode, out past the eastern edge of town, first at a canter, then a gallop. Tanner ran strong and eager, undoubtedly enjoying the exercise.

The old reins, mottled and cracking beneath his fingers, undulated with the horse's bobbing nose. He switched to single-hand and tugged the brim of his hat down against the afternoon sun, veering north to keep it from his eyes.

Just in time, he saw the narrow creek, gripped the reins and jabbed Tanner's flanks. They sailed over undaunted.

The scent of smoke tickled his nostrils. A homestead stood some way off, chimney pouring grey into the blue above. Not wanting to encroach on any unmarked private property, he eased the reins over and headed back west.

"I hope you're less than a hundred bucks," he thought as sweat glistened on the animal's neck. He imbibed its odour and the joy of earned freedom.

Neither Sarah nor Abe were at the corral.

He stripped off the bit and reins, patted the horse's neck, gathered up the tack and strode to the storeroom. The store had two parts—the outer block for the main items and a small room behind for tools and spares. He saw a flash of clothing through the doorway, so he set the saddle down and went forwards.

He stopped dead.

Tom Potter had Sarah against the wall, one hand on her chest, his face weaving as he tried to meet hers. Her mouth hung open in a silent howl of distress. Her hands flailed uselessly; Tom was easily thirty pounds heavier.

Disgust had seldom entered Bill's young life. The shapeless darkness which perpetually existed in opposition to those like himself and Sarah was made form, alarming and frightening in equal measure.

He had to act. But his opponent could punch, was cornered—discovered—and wouldn't hesitate to come out strong. If Bill missed a bob or a jink, he'd be laid out, which would do Sarah no good—because Tom would return to his task and show even less mercy.

The idea repulsed Bill. This was worse than the Bank—it would leave her with a deeper mental scar than his death at the hand of a gunman would have been. She was too perfect to spoil.

He took a deep breath, then rapped on the door jamb.

Tom's head whipped around. He pushed away from Sarah. Her eyes were on stalks, her hair messed, blouse askew.

Bill's heart bled.

He backed away, into the open area of the main storeroom, with saddles and tack on three walls. The answer was simple: he had to take Tom's attention. As cockily as he could, he beckoned for Tom to fight him. After all, the bully would want revenge for the previous encounter.

Tom charged, readying a fist.

At the last second, Bill pulled his body out of the express coach's path, leaving a leg dangling.

Tom caught on and lifted one leg. But the second snagged Bill's outstretched foot, and Tom toppled forwards and spread-eagled on the dusty wooden floor.

Bill scanned urgently around but found nothing of use, so in improvisation, he sat hard on Tom's shoulders, pinning him.

At the Coopertown rodeo, he'd watched, wide-eyed in youth, as fit, practised men with fancy shirts and cleanest hats rode the bull for up to fifteen seconds. After about three seconds on bucking Tom Potter, Bill readied a mollifying sucker punch to the man's neck—which he would rather not have done—when something bumped his back. Tom heaved in pain and battered the floor with his fists.

Bill craned his neck round. Sarah was astride Tom's backside, surely—hopefully—inflicting discomfort. Her eyes were pink with the dawn of tears. She forced a weak smile as her body jittered in shock.

He wanted to ask if she was okay, but she wasn't and would only say Yes to put a brave face on things.

"Get Abe?" he signed high in the air.

"Can you hold him?"

"No."

She glanced around, and her face creased in thought. Tom bucked violently. He was probably cussing hard, and Bill thanked the Lord it would pass Sarah by.

"Let him go," she signed.

"Let him go?" His face was aghast.

"He won't tell. He can't. He was bad, but beaten. He will never tell. It would be too much shame."

"But we will tell."

She met his gaze but avoided the question. Tom wriggled like a stuck pig.

"If we stay, Abe will come, and know the truth," he signed.

"If we tell, or Abe tells, Tom will behave worse. We must be better than him."

His heart sank. Surely they couldn't let this evil ape go free?

"Are you sure?"

She nodded sadly. "Now, before he does something bad."

This was her town, her tormentor, and her nightmare. So he helped her to stand. Tom bucked his freed legs.

She reaffirmed her decision, so Bill sprang up, shielded her from Tom and cautiously put his fists up. Inside, he quaked.

The defeated assailant lay there, awaiting further retribution. Then he scrambled to his feet, flashed the hardest of stares at them, then jogged out of the cabin, checking both ways as he left.

Bill unclenched his fists and calmed his breathing.

Sarah was lost in a distant world of shock and revulsion, panting as the nerves ebbed. She caught his eye, her face creased, then she piled into his chest and held on like a drowning person does a rope.

Tentatively yet willingly, he clasped her soft shoulders and simply let her be.

Chapter 29

The house had never felt empty before, but it did now.

For eighteen years, it had been home to only one person; the ideal size, no space for guests—nor had Earl a desire to accommodate any. It had only ever been meant as a new start, a roof over his head, after the old place was torched.

Now he judged it small and empty, a house but not a home. Experience of a loving, inviting household had done that.

He toured the outside, poking around the workshop and its adjoining covered wood store. Sawdust and shavings flitted like summer snowflakes in the light breeze.

Would Bill ever live here?

He was reticent about accepting any offer of accommodation. The boy had his life and needed his privacy. He'd been beholden to nobody for many years. The time when he most needed a father had long passed. They communicated only brokenly. Bill's job wasn't suited to a solitary home on the prairie.

Was it even feasible?

Earl could break his back rearranging the house, only to have his son hear the rancorous, shameful truth of his kidnap and storm off. Bill might prefer the unpredictable familiarity of his recent existence to the emotional discomfort of sharing a roof with the father who had abandoned him.

The boy who was Bill… and Alden.

It remained fragmented in Earl's mind, a broken pot whose jagged edges matched, although he couldn't—or hadn't been minded to—put them back together.

A baby had disappeared, years had evaporated, and a young man had appeared. There was no through-line in his heart.

Part of him wanted Bill to declare his manhood and already-found independence by making his trail and stopping by to see his father on occasion. After all, some bond was better than none—which is what he'd endured until now.

He pottered into the workshop.

The bed frame was taking shape, occupying much of the space. Everything else had been pushed aside, physically and metaphorically. He'd be later than expected with his three commissions. Poorer in the pocket but richer in spirit—which mattered more.

He spied the incomplete angel cross, rudely shoved onto a shelf.

Mary.

His heart weighed heavy.

In his mind's eye, the two finished crosses stood on the prairie, the wind tugging at the newly planted flowers.

Bill.

His heart felt lighter.

He thought of White Rock, of the house. He wondered what Bill would be doing. And Sarah. And especially Laura.

Why was Laura not so burdened as he? She grieved. Perhaps the bright light of her daughter kept her spirits up. Maybe Bill would lift him likewise.

He spied the unfinished cross again. He reached it down, then ran his hands over his work.

It gave him an idea. Then another.

The following day, Earl packed the war bag full to bursting, taking a change of clothes, tools and a good sum of food and water. He roped the angel cross to the lower half of the saddle to keep it from rapping the horse's flank as they rode.

He shut the house, mounted up and walked away.

He took the ride easy, following a well-worn mental path. Apart from one stagecoach passing by in the distant east, betrayed by a dust plume, he didn't encounter another soul. He could fall unconscious, still mounted, and when he woke, Jack would have arrived at the right spot.

As always, when the old house hove into view, his demeanour darkened like the building's blackened stone walls. Instinct said to tour the ruin, but he told instinct to go fish: he'd done his annual wallowing already.

He went to the pair of graves. The flowers were still strong, like his memories. He took a moment to acknowledge Mary, hat held across his belly.

'Found our boy, love,' he muttered. 'Reckon you made a good kid. He's… different. Imperfect.' He cleared the lump in his throat. 'Like me.'

After a small silence, he replaced his hat and stepped across to the grave marked by an angel bearing Alden's name. He hesitated, concerned this was a desecration, then steeled himself and worked at the wooden shaft. He eased it from side to side, took hold of it in the crooks of his elbows and heaved up. It loosened somewhat. He repeated the manoeuvre and the pointed end lifted from the dirt, taking the cross into his arms.

He didn't want to leave it there, burn it, break it, or toss it amongst the ruins like a vandal. That would have been disingenuous. So, seeing value in the wood itself, he unroped the other piece of cargo and tied them up together.

Then he apologised to Jack for treating him like a packhorse, promised a long drink at Andrews Creek for his trouble, and pressed a worn boot into the stirrup.

From the saddle, he surveyed the scene again. Appearance said his soul's burden had halved, but it didn't feel so. Was he on the right path? Talking to Abe was paramount. The truth must be heard, however unpalatable.

He tapped the horse's belly, and they moved away.

Chapter 30

Bill watched Sarah at dinner, nervy and curious.

For days, he'd studied how she held herself, interacted with hearing people, and switched between attentiveness and seclusion. She had spent all her years with family, while many of his days were alone and certainly absent of those who could truly communicate with him. If he remained deaf for the rest of his life—which he'd long accepted—he wanted it to be as little of a barrier as possible.

Deep down, he didn't understand why Sarah wanted Tom Potter's assault to remain a private matter. The man needed to experience justice. Yet, Bill was an outsider. When he left White Rock, Sarah and Laura would carry on their lives, and she must have considered that Tom being scorned and defeated was better than judged and indicted. Or maybe he'd never see justice, so why bother telling?

Either way, Bill mustn't let slip what he knew.

As darkness fell, he walked to the forge to spend his first night. It didn't have the homeliness of the Anderson house, but it was a place he had control of, rather than being at the whim of others. He'd taken the stability of Mojave life for granted, and it had been abruptly removed. He'd taken Mrs Walker's roof over his head for granted, and she'd up and died.

If Mayor Potter left him alone, even this small room was a sanctuary.

Sanctuary?

Did he want to live in a town where he needed a bolthole? He had Tanner now, a chance for freedom again. He'd see Earl, somehow, whatever transpired.

There was nothing else for him here.

Except there was.

One person occupied his thoughts as he drifted off to sleep.

In the morning, he went to Mr Wilson's store. The town was becoming more familiar, and he walked with growing confidence. Occasionally he'd receive a tip of the hat or a bob of the head. For the last few years, that had been the most he could expect wherever he went. People wouldn't stop and chat if there were no way to talk. Familiarity—not friendship—was his apex.

He took a few things back to the forge, then went to Sarah's house.

She was at the piano. She looked so pretty it almost took his breath away.

He entered deliberately, waving as he'd become accustomed. He'd learned it from watching Laura—she never wanted to startle Sarah, nor would she approach from behind. In this respect, they needed to be treated like horses. Once he'd walked behind a mare and received a kick in the thigh for his trouble, he never did it again.

Sarah stopped playing. "Hi."

He was curious about the attraction or the point of the endeavour, especially as music was for the hearing.

"Why do you play?"

"Why?" Her brow knitted as if the question was ridiculous. "To feel. To feel beauty."

"Not to please your ma?" He pulled a chair over.

She shook her head. "That would be silly. If she wants music, she can play. It is... like a game. Learning, feeling." She tapped her fingers together. "It keeps me flexible for my work."

He pointed at the sheet of lines and dots. "You read?"

She nodded, danced her finger across the top line, spelt, "C-C-D-A-F-A-G", and then touched the keys in turn.

The stool was set high, and her left leg pressed against the piano's frame.

He pointed. "Is that how you feel?"

"And in my fingers. And with loud notes, through the floor." She wore no boots.

"You are very clever."

"It's only practice. Like sewing, riding, learning to sign."

"I guess."

She beckoned. "Come, try."

"My hands are too slow and big."

"You've seen Mr Rawles play in the saloon. The piano is not only for ladies." She patted the wide stool beside her.

For a second, nerves held him back. Then he remembered yesterday's embrace, her need for a friend. She hadn't been uncomfortable, and, after a few seconds, neither had he. So, he sat.

She extended an index finger and pressed down sharply on a particular key, gesturing for him to do likewise.

He felt a tiny vibration.

She pointed further up the keyboard. He picked a key and struck it. The difference was barely discernible. He tried another.

No, he simply didn't get the appeal.

She took his left hand and laid it, upturned, on the underside of the keyboard. She'd not held his hand before. Luckily it only trembled after she let go.

Then she played a note on the extreme left, the centre, and finally—reaching across his body— the extreme right. Her hair tickled his neck, and goosebumps leapt to attention.

"I feel," he signed shakily.

She smiled. "Take your boots off."

He did, then retook his place, perching away from her on the edge of the stool, so one buttock half-floated in mid-air. He replaced his hand under the keyboard and rested the other on the endboard.

She played. Her fingers weaved and skipped. He studied her face and its concentration as she summoned the movements from memory. Last, he closed his eyes and took in the minute changes in the vibrations and rhythm, letting them soak into his being.

It was a dance of energy, ebbing and flowing. Occasionally her arm brushed his, her scent wafting in and out as she swayed. Mrs Walker's flowers tickled his memory.

He experimented with the pressure and position of his feet on the floor—widely or closely spaced, arched or flat.

Soon came a stillness, and he opened his eyes. Hers sought opinion.

"I know now why you play."

"Don't give up, Bill. Find what brings you joy, however strange it may be to a hearing person. They don't know what it's like for us."

He shook his head pensively. "Thank you."

"No, thank you. You saved me. Twice."

"You let me stay."

She stood. "I made you something."

He smiled. "I bought you something."

Her eyes widened. "You go first."

"No. Ladies first."

She smiled and skipped out of the room. His heart jumped. He fumbled his hair to neaten it.

She bounced in, carrying a large, folded square of cloth. It was tan, like his shirt. She unravelled it. It was a bedsheet, simply sewn around the hem, plain and masculine—not flowery and girlish like the one he'd slept under in her room.

"For your new room."

He beamed. "Thank you."

"My hero. Again." She looked down, sheepish, then darted in and pecked him on the cheek.

Vibrations coursed through him like a symphony no pianist could master. He reddened, set the bedsheet across a chair back, then, to distract from his self-consciousness, pulled the small paper parcel from his pocket and proffered it.

She took it gingerly and unwrapped it as if it was a jewel.

He tensed. Would she be disappointed it wasn't? It was only soap.

But she held it to her nose, found its scent familiar, and bit her lip, almost coquettishly.

"That's so sweet."

"I saw you needed it." He shrugged.

"You saw in the bathroom. You saw in the Bank. You saw in the stables."

"Seeing, I can do. Hearing is not so good."

She nodded vehemently, her mouth pursed in sober but happy reflection. "And you care."

He swallowed, dredging up a truth he'd begun to acknowledge. "What happened—those things—are because I'm here. Tom hurting you. You leaving school. I can buy a store of soap, but it won't stop the things. But if I leave, it will stop. I make people mad, and it hurts you. I don't want you hurt."

"It will stop, Bill, it will. Don't go."

He shook his head gently. "You are precious, you and your ma. One more deaf person is too much for White Rock."

She quickly placed the soap on the piano top, grasped one of his hands, squeezed it, and shook her head. Then she let loose and signed, "Don't go because of me."

"I can't stay forever." Yet he wanted to. This was impossible.

"Don't go."

"You have your ma, and Abe, and the town, and your work, and the piano and—"

"Not one true friend." Her eyes explored his.

"We'll still be friends," he signed.

She stood back, heaved down her shoulders as if gathering herself against attack, and painted a solemn expression on her face. Then she brushed her hair behind one ear and found a smile.

He much preferred it when she smiled. Light from the window caught behind her, offering an angelic glow as it had that time before.

She licked her lips. "Would you like [—]?"

He frowned. He racked his brain. "Don't understand. Don't understand that word."

She tried again, but still it rang no bell. He shook his head.

She finger-spelt it: "C-o-u-r-t." Then she spelt out the last three words. "Would you like to court me?"

Was this a family word? A hearing word? A town word? Certainly, not a Mojave term, nor any of the few Mrs Walker had imparted.

"C-o-u-r-t?"

Her expression moved to sympathy, understanding that their lives differed despite sharing the same base affliction. He might as well have asked her to fashion a new axe head or hit a poised snake with a plate knife in the half-dark.

"Is it bad?" he asked.

That brightened her. "No. It means… be together some. Sit. Talk. Walk. Care. Be like what Tom Potter thought he was with me. But is not." She stamped her foot. "Is NOT."

He swallowed. His body fizzed. "Together. Like...."

She nodded, reticent.

Instantly he looked away, around the room, anywhere, fearing a rush of embarrassment or nerves. The dots in his mind joined so quickly that they encircled the earth in the blink of an eye.

She took his hands and sought his attention, finding it uneasy and curious. He moved his hands to take hers and enjoyed their soft smallness. He breathed in her air and sensed a particular silence, a pocket of their soundless kingdom inside the world at large.

It was too real, and what he had known he wanted but would never admit to.

"I never did c-o-u-r-t before."

"Nor I, that I cared for."

He considered. "Then we could... kiss?"

"If Ma says so."

"Ma?" This was a whole new development.

"You must ask permission from Ma. It's just how it's done."

He frowned. "You are not teasing?"

"I wouldn't."

"What will she say?" He bit his knuckle. This was a barrier to kissing this beautiful girl—something beyond his own inexperience and worry.

"You have to ask."

"And Earl—Pa—do I have to ask him? And the Mayor?"

She gave a silent laugh. "No, silly. Not even Earl. But I think... he would like it."

"We don't talk much." His face fell.

"He is hearing. He can't help it."

That raised a smile. "I should ask both together. So Laura can speak the words to him."

"That is a good idea. So, you will ask?" She put on impish expectancy.

"Yes. I will ask. And if they say 'Yes', I can court you. I would like that."

"I would like that too, Bill." Her eyes explored his.

"Then I can look after you. And stay."

Their hands momentarily fell silent.

"You were worried I wouldn't be safe with you here," she signed.

He nodded.

"You could help me," she added.

"How?"

She led him into the kitchen. After a nervous glance around, she opened a drawer.

At the back lay a gun.

He flashed her a surprised expression.

She lifted the gun out and closed the drawer.

"That belongs to your ma," he signed, caution in his face and anxiety in his bones.

"For our protection. For my protection."

"I understand. It's wise."

"But I can't shoot. I want you to teach me."

He stepped back. "No. What would she say?"

"She won't know. It will be our secret." Her expression supplicated him.

"We already have one secret."

"And Tom is someone I need to protect myself from."

He shook his head vehemently. "You can't shoot him."

"I don't mean to. But if he comes here, and I'm alone…." She squeezed his hands. "I want to be safe. Even as a warning. You want me safe—if you care."

"I do care, Sarah."

"Then, show me. Let's go now before Ma comes."

He sighed, unable to argue the point. If he was partly the cause of her concerns and endangerment, he needed to be part of the solution. Besides, she'd never truly use it. It was a sop to her worry.

Perhaps this marked the first lesson of courting: the gal is in charge, and a man has to keep her happy. Still, he'd rather keep her happy with kisses and presents than guns and ammunition.

Too late: she'd lifted down a biscuit barrel from the top shelf and unloaded a box of bullets. He hoped Laura didn't keep a tally of how many were inside.

Chapter 31

Earl rode into White Rock early that afternoon and stabled Jack while Abe kindly took the crosses into the storeroom.

Back in Abe's shack, the man brewed coffee.

Earl pointed to a shape in the outer reaches of the lot. 'That a wagon?'

'What's left of it.' Abe chewed on his jerky.

'For sale?'

'Ain't worth a hill of beans. You make it run, it's yours.'

'Sure?'

'Eyesore, to my mind. Firewood, come Fourth of July.'

'You got yourself a deal.'

'If you're looking to haul folks, they'd better be brave. I hear you're some carpenter, but even so.'

'No, just some gear. I'll bring the kid's bed from the house. Fair if I raid your toolshed for loaning, fix the thing up?'

'That's fine.'

Earl sipped. 'I got a question for you, Abe.'

'Shoot.'

'You rode with Potter's posse in sixty-one?'

Even the mention of it aged the man in moments. 'Against my judgement, yeah.'

'We talked to Bill about where the Mojave had him camped, and it's my reckoning it's the same what you raided.'

'Past Four Pines, fork in the river.'

'Ain't familiar. But the kid said river, way north. Did you dynamite the place?'

Abe's eyes flared. 'No. It wasn't no massacre.'

'Okay—but was there some kinda explosion?'

The man's head hung. 'Yeah. Yeah, I guess there was.'

Earl's soul creased. 'How come?'

'I don't know. I heard a blast, but we were gone by then—Jim and me took the gold clear away.'

Earl blew out a disappointment. 'Dang.'

'Why you ask?'

'If that explosion went on, it might explain Bill's situation.'

'About how he comes to be deaf?'

Earl nodded.

Abe's mouth hung open. 'Look, I'm sorry if—'

Earl held up his hand. 'Don't bother yourself. You're a good man, and I know any bad deed weren't on your say so.'

'It was sure as hell on Potter's.'

'Well, I'd be a fool to even speak of it. It's hard enough getting civility out of the man, let alone a story.'

Abe sipped his coffee pensively. 'I sure wish I could help. Only other person who rode away that day ain't in town.'

'Then it's a dead story.' Earl cast the coffee dregs on the earth, forlorn.

'Oh, he'll be back for sure.'

'That so? Would he know what went on?'

'I figure he would. He was helping Potter use up all his bullets on the Mojave who stole his gold.'

Disgust coated Earl's windpipe. 'Who was it?'

'Dennis Hayes.'

There could have been jugglers and acrobats performing in Main Street, chorus lines of talking horses, or a raging gunfight, and Earl wouldn't have noticed. His brain was full to bursting, wrapped up in the conundrum.

Not only did he not want a bullet from Dennis Hayes, he also needed answers. If the man held a grudge against him for a saloon accident, it was nothing to the reciprocal ire Earl would feel if the man had taken Bill's hearing. One thing was certain: their meeting must not end in Dennis being put in the ground. At least, not until the story of that posse raid had been entirely told.

How? He couldn't out-draw the man. He wasn't smart enough to verbally outmanoeuvre him. Walt wasn't in town to offer his counsel. Yet, Earl couldn't leave without the matter being concluded. He owed so much to Bill; this was the least he could do in repayment.

He wondered what would be easier to take: finding an answer and living with the temptation to give payback where it was due or hitting a dead end and remaining curious and unsatisfied for his remaining days.

The immediate and tricky task was the same: getting on Dennis's good side before the man cocked his hammer.

Approaching Laura's house, the lilt of music crested his ears. He eased open the front door and stepped into the living room doorway.

Sarah and Bill were on the stool, her hands on the keys, his attention studiously on her fingers and face, one palm resting on the piano's frame.

Bill happened to turn his head, saw Earl, and jumped up like the stool was on fire. Sarah stopped playing.

Earl gestured for calm. "No matter," he finger-spelt. He was keen to learn more word signs; fingerspelling was already tedious, and he was nowhere near a good pace.

"Hello, Pa."

That word again. But it was only that; certainly, no true bond.

"Hello, Bill. Sarah. You play?"

Bill shook his head.

"You learn?"

Bill made the see-saw sign for "maybe".

Earl gestured for them to continue. They sat, but further apart than before. Was there something between these two? The boy was no fool; Sarah was charming and pretty, with an echo of her mother's steel.

Sarah resumed playing—a simple tune, one he recognised.

He was taken back more than two decades, watching Sarah's hands as Mary's, which had danced over their piano in the old house. She'd always seemed transported to another world. At the same time, he'd gazed on, unselfconscious about taking in her form, grace, and beauty.

One winter, she'd ground him down. As the snows and storms restricted his travels, and he was minded to do less in the cold workshop, they'd spent more time in each other's warmth, and she suggested he use the hours profitably. He'd protested that it was merely her way of fending off his frequent desires and advances, but the result was the same.

He recognised this tune because he could play it. Or the Earl of past days played it.

He moved closer, watching Sarah's fingers, dredging up his memory of the necessary movements, and found his right hand by his side, tapping imaginary keys.

Bill caught sight and flashed a querying raise of the eyebrows—the signed adjunct for a question—and indicated where Earl's hand had fallen still in embarrassment.

"You piano?"

Earl gestured over his shoulder, "Past".

Bill stood and gestured for him to sit. Earl didn't want to but was wary of disappointing his boy. Or maybe, deep down, he wanted to impress or at least feel relevant. Maybe this marked the start of a connection, one based on a wholly polarised experience of music.

His larger frame, a half-head above Sarah, made coexisting on the stool somewhat socially awkward, but he swallowed his pride. He cracked his knuckles painfully, tapped a few keys to get the feel of the instrument, then forced up old muscle memory and strung a few notes together. While he noodled around, Sarah's left hand tapped out a simplified bass line.

Soon he gravitated towards the previous tune, and she used that visual cue to dovetail the whole bass line into his right-hand melody. In a half-minute, they were playing in sync. A smile crept across his lips. He'd always imagined Mary teaching the daughter that they'd never had.

Bill stood beside of the piano, hands on the lid and the end rail, watched their playing, and then closed his eyes.

They went around the tune twice—Earl was about three-quarters perfect on the second run, then finished with a dramatic lift to signal the end.

Sarah smiled, and he nodded, paternally tapping her back. Then she looked past him, and her expression hardened. He swivelled.

Laura stood in the doorway.

He rose sharply as if guilty. 'Afternoon. We... uh... that is—'

Her face softened as if she'd seen a shooting star or witnessed a lamb being born. 'Why, I never would have thought.'

'I ain't a patch on Sarah, not even back aways.'

'You're quite the surprise. With every day.'

He was sure he blushed. 'I don't know 'bout that. I did some learning. When I were a younger man.'

'And now you're learning to sign. As not so much a younger man.' She touched his upper arm. 'It's never too late for fresh things and new starts.' She gathered herself. 'Anyway, my manners—coffee?'

'That'd be kind.'

He needed to relay what Abe had revealed but wanted to wait until the youngsters weren't there.

She left for the kitchen, and he tried to figure something to say—sign. The twosome darted looks in his direction, then at each other, exchanging quick phrases. He imagined it's what kids half their age would do—messing around, private jokes.

Laura dashed into the room and rapped a biscuit barrel down on the piano lid.

Sarah jumped as if shocked by the noise and grabbed Bill's hand: these ten-year-olds had been caught at something.

'What's the matter?' Earl asked.

Laura's face was thunder like he'd never seen. She signed furiously, a jaggedness about her movements that leaked her thoughts as if they were words ringing in the air.

He wished he could tune into the conversation:

"Was this you?" she asked Sarah.

"Yes, Ma." The girl hung her head.

Bill saw her body fizzing with nerves. His pulse raced: he'd really gone and done it now. He'd broken something precious or stomped on a newly planted flower.

"I saw it moved. Did you steal? Did you give it to someone?"

"No, Ma."

Laura's eyes were on stalks. "Did you use the gun?!"

"I can explain—"

"You better had."

"We went shooting. Bill was teaching me."

She flashed her attention at him. "You? Corrupting my daughter?"

"Teaching, ma'am. Only a little."

"What gives you the nerve? The right?" Her mouth hung open.

"I wanted her to be safe from people like Tom Potter. After what happened."

"By putting a gun in her hand?" Laura clutched her head in shock. "Guns are dangerous. They're not for girls like Sarah. She can take care of herself fine."

"It was one time. I didn't mean harm."

"I darn well hope so."

Bill flinched at her ire. His heart was sinking fast. It had ridden the crest of a wave. Now it was drowning.

"I only want her to be safe," he beseeched.

Sarah took a step forward. "It was me. It was my idea, Ma. Don't blame him."

"I blame you both. Imagine what could have happened!"

"It's not like that!" Sarah stamped her foot. "I wanted to be safe. I asked Bill to teach me. I told him to keep it a secret. He didn't want to. You keep the gun—you want to be safe too. Don't tell me I can't be. It's not fair."

Laura's chest rose and fell.

Sarah reached back. Bill squeezed her hand supportively. She replied, then released her grip to sign.

"Bill offered to leave town if it would keep me safe. He doesn't like what's happened. So, because I want him to stay, I thought if I learned to shoot, I would feel safe." Her shoulders fell. "And I thought you'd want me safe too, Ma."

Laura sighed. "I do. But it's not Bill's job."

"Yes, it is," Bill interjected.

Laura's eyes flared. "Pardon me?" she signed more gently.

Sarah flicked a look at Bill.

"Yes, it is. I want to court her." He swallowed hard, regretful. It shouldn't have come out like that.

Laura's expression morphed to mild disbelief. "Pardon me?"

His legs felt weak. He puffed out a breath, drew himself up, laid a hand on Sarah's arm, and then signed shakily, "Please, Mrs Anderson, I'd… like permission to… court your beautiful daughter."

Earl saw the verbal conflagration subside like a candle flame snuffed out. Laura's hand came to her chest, her body shocked, struck—but with an appreciative smile on her lips.

Earl moved closer. 'What happened?' He tried to meet her eyes, which was no chore.

She didn't respond, as if in a daydream.

Then she turned. 'Bill and Sarah want to go courting.'

He felt kicked in the stomach but by a bale of the softest, most striking petals. His mouth moved soundlessly. His mind whirled. His heart tried to get a signal through, reminding him that courting often leads to happiness.

Something moved in his peripheral vision.

"Can I, Pa?" Bill signed.

The boy clearly cared for Sarah. Earl experienced an odd sensation: fatherly pride.

'What was the ruckus?' he asked Laura.

'They… he… made a mistake. Because he cares about her.'

'Can't say I ain't noticed a kinda meeting of circumstance between them.'

The youngsters held hands and offered hopeful faces.

Laura licked her lips and sighed. 'It can't be said they're not good for each other. What do you think?'

'I ain't the one for making the decision. Choice of the girl's parent. Always was.'

'Do you object?'

'With due respect, heck no. But Bill and me ain't figuring to ride in here and mess up your lives.'

'Not a jot of a mess as I see it.' A twinkle flitted in her eye. 'You both brought care and kindness.'

'He steps out of line, I'll give him leather—no mistake on that.'

'I think he's more likely to be upstanding and look to be bettering himself.'

He smiled, reflective. 'Courting can do that to a man.'

'So, we're agreed?'

'I'd have a stone heart to fight young love.'

She nodded.

As if through an unspoken connection, they raised their right hands in unison, made fists, and bobbed them forwards.

Chapter 32

Bill shook Earl's hand, and Laura pulled him into a loose embrace. Sarah sprang into her mother's arms, then shook Earl's hand, bobbing her head in thanks.

Then the pair darted from the room, leaving only air in place of contentment.

'What did they do?'

'He taught her to shoot my gun.'

He sucked in a breath. 'Shooting is for life and death, not for quarrels and such. Even the winner loses, I reckon.'

'I believe it came from a good place. He cares. It's not wrong to want to protect the ones you love. And me? I assumed it was his fault—that *he'd* corrupted *her*. I mustn't judge him by his past. He's a new man now.'

She sighed, then brightened. 'It was sweet he asked you too. He has a good heart. Like his father.'

He turned away. 'I don't figure that.'

Was forgiveness that easy? Letting go of a mistake borne from trying to do the right thing?

She clasped his arm. 'You judge from inside. I see from outside. For a boy who wasn't parented, he's not done too bad.'

'I guess.'

'You're a stubborn old mule, Earl Johnson.'

He chuckled. 'Then I reckon you do judge pretty good.'

'This won't happen overnight—you know that? And Bill's past isn't lost just because you weren't there. He can tell you, and you can share in that. Even better, you can create new memories. Good ones—to push out the bad ones.'

'That'd be a way to go.'

'Always.' She smiled. 'Did you have a reason for calling by?'

He shifted on his feet. 'I did come by to bring something for you.'

'So we're all winners today, by the looks of things. What did you bring?'

'Don't be expecting fancy dresses and the like. That's courting behaviour. I got something for… by way of giving back for what you lost.'

She looked around the room. 'I don't believe I've lost a thing.'

'It's… best you see it. I'd not do its describing justice.'

'Well, now I am intrigued.'

As he carried the item from the stables to the cemetery where they'd arranged to meet, it began to feel like a present rather than a duty or a favour. Abe had provided a burlap sack, making the imminent handover even more like gifting.

As he approached the graveside, she stood in silent reflection. He wondered how often she came here, and counterpointed it with his own, much longer, annual pilgrimage.

He waited in her peripheral vision until she came back to the world.

He pointed at the broken gravestone. 'I figure me and Bill being here is part, if not all, the reason for this cowardliness.'

'All the same, it's not your duty to buy a new stone.'

'Take this with gratitude, and let's speak no more 'bout it.'

'Thank you.'

So he untied the sack and wheedled the wooden memorial out.

She took in its form, the inscription he'd newly carved—copied across by memory from the defunct item, and the beauty it held compared to the neighbouring stones and crosses.

Her face flushed pink, and she clutched both hands to her heart, fit to swoon. He quickly set down the angel and took her shoulders in support. She looked at him, then at the cruciform carving, and wetness appeared in her eyes as she sought reply.

'Earl Johnson, that may be the kindest thing a soul has ever done for me.'

'I figured I were the right one for fixing up such.'

'Words can't express how special it is. You're some craftsman.'

He wanted to brush a nascent tear from her eye, but inspected his feet, embarrassed by the compliment and keen to hide his fondness for her.

'We all got something.'

'Well—wait—did you do this in two days?'

'Heck no. All but the inscription was waiting on the name. I done it a while back, after… others. I were saving it for me or Walt, whoever went first.'

Concern replaced the tears. 'No? Why Earl, don't wish your life away.'

He picked up the cross. 'My life ain't worth much anyhow. Broken as that old stone.'

Now she grasped one of his shoulders. 'None of that talk. I'm allowed to come here and cry for Jim—but not for you.'

He flashed an apologetic expression. 'I guess.'

'I choose deference. Gratitude. I choose to move on. To be an example for Sarah. To hold onto sadness, but not as a burden. I only wish you would too.'

'I try. Reckon I'll do better.'

'Good.' She took a deep breath. 'Now let's set this straight.'

With permission, using half the old stone as a mallet, he carefully drove the stake of the angel's legs into the ground in the appropriate place.

She rubbed his arm in thanks. 'As I say, this is something special. I won't forget.'

'Not forgetting is the purpose.'

Her smile was tinged with sadness. 'Yes.'

'I figured I'd get buried by Bill and Mary, but now I ain't sure. Guess I oughta decide quick.'

'Don't talk like that.'

He pulled off his hat and scratched his head. 'Would you promise me one thing, Laura?'

'What's that?'

'I spoke to Abe 'bout the posse raid. He reckons it could be the same as what came to Bill's camp, took his hearing and such. But he don't know. Only one man—excepting Potter— knows 'bout any dynamite being used. That'd be Dennis.'

She went to speak, then fell sullen.

'So,' he continued, 'I need to talk to the man. If I don't, and he shoots me dead, I'd be real grateful if you'd get the truth from him and keep it as you see best. Maybe not tell the kid, less he comes out shooting and winds up like his father.'

Her brow creased. 'You have a fine way of making a woman sad.'

He laid a hand on her arm. 'Would you do that for me?'

She sighed. 'I'll say yes, but it won't come to pass.'

'How can you know such?'

'Because we'll find a way.'

'It ain't your place to fight my battles.'

'It concerns Bill's welfare, and now he's courting with Sarah, it makes it my battle too.'

'I guess.' He glanced towards town. 'It'd be good to know the character of the man, what his temper's been like these years. If Dennis is the killing kind and all.'

'Then you should talk to Frank Wilson. They take a drink sometimes.'

'Shoot. Another man I gotta make mends with.'

'If you're serious about making a future in this town and helping your boy, you have to make nice with people.'

'I make nice,' he protested.

She noted the new angel cross and smiled. 'Only with people you like.'

'I won't deny that.'

'Make nice with Frank and Dennis, and you'll save those people you like from having to bring two posies of flowers up here.'

Chapter 33

Bill slept under Sarah's gifted sheet that night. Although the forge was still spartan and the bed a makeshift affair, it gave disproportionate comfort.

As his hands rested on the material, then caressed it, he imagined Sarah's fingers on the same cloth, some days earlier, as she fashioned the simple article for him. He touched it lightly as if stroking her instead. It kindled and worried him in equal measure.

He worked in the stables until Sarah arrived at lunchtime. Laura had agreed that the couple could ride out together, on condition they returned for dinner, took sufficient provisions, and carried no gun. He promised to take the best care of her daughter. In response, Laura hugged him—the fondest gesture yet.

Sarah had packed a simple picnic, and the afternoon was set fair and warm. Her cream outfit made her appear more beautiful than ever—or was that because they were courting and he was allowed unsullied appreciation of her form?

Bill brought Tanner out, saddled up. She needed no support to mount, being an excellent rider, but he couldn't help offering assistance. She took his hand to be manoeuvred behind him on the saddle and gave it a peck before letting go.

Bill had never spent seventy dollars on anything, but Tanner was worth twice that.

The corral had been the horse's straitjacket, and Tanner rode strongly. Bill revelled in a warm wind on his face, mottled reins jinking in his grip, and the comforting clench of Sarah's arms around his waist. Occasionally she loosed her hand and indicated a direction change, and he eased Tanner's guidance across, learning how much rein the horse needed to do his bidding.

They rode for close to an hour, pausing midway for a shared drink from the canteen.

About a half-mile out, he saw their destination. She'd stayed coy, only revealing it was a place she liked to visit for peace and seclusion. The black gape in the low cliff grew more prominent as he slowed to a canter, then a trot, and finally, a walk as the ground became less navigable. Tanner picked through the uneven boulder-strewn scrub until the going was too hard, and then Bill pulled the horse to a stand. He slid down, offered a hand, and Sarah dismounted into his arms.

They led Tanner up to the cave's mouth, which stood about three metres high at the apex and four metres wide at the bottom. It was teardrop-shaped but jagged, like a prehistoric flint or arrowhead. The sun caught the cave entrance at an angle, throwing half-light and half-dark deep into the interior.

"Are there b-a-t-s?" He finger-spelt the last—knowing the creature but not the sign.

She smiled. "No. But there are… monsters!" She wriggled her fingers menacingly, grabbed his waist and tried to tickle.

Or, he assumed it was tickling. He'd seen one of the tribeswomen do it to her youngster, and the black-haired boy had enjoyed it, pushing out a long, unheard laugh.

Bill had never been tickled. He didn't know what to expect, but it didn't hurt, and he didn't laugh. It felt... different, so he smiled because he thought he should.

There were no saguaros nearby, so he looped the reins around a boulder with a notch in it, not wanting to risk Tanner being schooled enough to be ground-hitched and stay put. Being stranded on the plain once was plenty, and whilst it would be with Sarah this time, he'd promised Laura everything would be fine.

He unslung the small picnic and blankets and followed Sarah into the cave.

It didn't run very deep—maybe ten metres. After widening, it narrowed sharply, the roof falling, until the black gash that angled back into the rock was barely a few hands wide and a metre tall. No direct sunlight reached this far, but it was bright enough.

"Do you like it?" Her light dress stood out against the charcoal hues of the cave wall.

"Yes. How did you find it?"

"Ma and I were out riding one day when I was little, and Pa had... gone. We talked. I was sad. Sometimes I come here when I'm sad."

"You're not sad now?"

"No. I'm happy." She stroked the wall. "It reminds me of the world in here. Darkness and light."

"Sometimes, it's hard to find a place of light."

"Do you feel bad about what happened to you? Do you want to find who attacked you on the trail?"

He shook his head. "No. It's the world balancing. I did my share of taking."

"It can't have been easy, living like that." She stroked his cheek, making his nerve endings crackle.

"I wouldn't go back. Not now."

They worked together to spread out the blankets on the dusty ground. He suspected the wind never whipped it up, and Sarah had smoothed it out over the years.

He imagined her here, taking a break from being an outcast in a hearing world. He'd had such days of low mood when forces railed against him—except his coping had sometimes been through push-back, not introspection. A cruel generalisation, he knew: boys fight, and girls cry.

Inside the cave mouth was a recess in the wall, blackened by campfires. He pointed.

She nodded. "Will you get some wood?"

"Yes."

"There is some at the back, I keep for always dry wood, but we need more."

"I will hurry back."

The small fire crackled as they sat on the blankets, ate and drank.

"You owe me nine kisses," she signed. "One per stone."

"What?"

"Remember—you said one kiss for every stone I hit when I was shooting."

She was right. He glanced at the cave mouth. "What if someone comes?"

"Ma would not let us ride out if she disapproved. They know what courting means."

He hung his head. "I never kissed a girl before."

She lifted his chin. "Bill, do you want to be courting? Or was it a trick?"

He shook his head vehemently. "I do. A lot."

"So I want my nine kisses for shooting good. I want a man who keeps promises and doesn't tell lies. We don't have to tell the whole town you kissed me."

"They have enough hate for me anyway. Kissing would just be another sin."

"The whole town doesn't hate. Only some folks."

Bill grimaced. "Tom Potter would be mad if he knew."

"He can go to hell. I won't not court a boy I… like a lot."

"I like you a lot too."

She cocked her head. "So, it was nine."

Something unknown shuddered through him, but she'd leaned in, very close now, so he quickly kissed her once. Warmth radiated from his lips into every inch of his body.

The second kiss passed slower. The third, fourth and fifth were similar but on the heels of each other. There was no displeasure on her face, so he wriggled closer and kissed her twice more.

For the eighth, he laid a hand on her waist and let the squeeze of their lips last many seconds. The smell was like living inside the headiest posy. The taste was like nectar from the finest bees.

Lastly, he put both arms around her and didn't even try to count the time.

When they broke off, he took her hands—partly from affection but mostly to stop her speaking. He wanted the fervour to dissipate and the reality of it to sink in.

"That was nice," she signed. "I liked the last one best."

He smiled. "Me too."

This was affection, he realised. A new emotion to add to his experiences.

He let it wash through him as he pushed his mind out, beyond lips, mind, and body, then out from the cave, across the prairie. They had a unique, private quietness, even within their everyday existence of silence, inside the stillness of the cave, amongst the calm of the wilderness, held in the landscape of the territory.

Chapter 34

After the youngsters returned that evening, Laura cooked for the foursome. Earl found it oddly normal—despite having no frame of reference.

Through dinner, the silence was unusually pervasive. Nobody mentioned where Bill and Sarah had been or what they'd done. Instead, Earl and Laura exchanged the occasional knowing smirk. It was easy to bond about something everyone held in common.

When the table was clear, Sarah took Bill's hand, and they excused themselves.

Earl and Laura sat in the living room and sipped lemonade. A fire crackled in the hearth.

'Why the long face?' she asked.

'Figuring Bill ain't gonna come stay with me, no time ever.'

'I can't say I'd blame him—if this is courting sticks. If it truly does, they'll want a place of their own. It might work for a while here—the forge is certainly no home.'

'All the same, I need to be talking to the boy. You ain't my servant and messenger.'

'So commit to your lessons, Earl Johnson. And spend time with Bill. You might be surprised what can be done without signing words.'

'Yeah.' His head lolled. He ran a hand through his hair.

'And now what is it?'

'Someday, kid's gonna ask. 'Bout what happened. Rips me up inside to say.'

She moved to the nearest chair, like a priest stepping into the confessional booth.

'You just tell him,' she said softly.

'And if he hates me?'

'That's the chance honesty takes. Or you keep it locked inside, and it rots your gut until you die. No—the moment before you die, when you regret your silence and wish you'd trusted in love and forgiveness.'

'You're some wise woman, Laura.' And real handsome, he wanted to say. And understanding, patient, and a million other qualities he didn't dare flatter or embarrass her with.

'Well, I travelled that road. When Sarah grew up, I had to tell her Jim was dead because we gave in to Lyle Potter. We could have left town, but we'd finished this lovely house, and Jim's smithing was earning good wages. I could have said we didn't have a choice—but we did.'

'She coulda hated you but not run. Little girl needs her ma and a roof. Bill don't need those.'

'Let me ask you this. By keeping quiet, who are you protecting—him or you?' A schoolmarm query rested on her face.

'I guess.' He knew the answer.

'Tell me. Call it… practice.' She touched her chest. 'I'll promise you it's a million times worse inside you than it truly is. Pour it out. Move on—it's best.'

He sighed. 'Walt's the only one what knows.'

'The difference is he carries it like a secret, not a boulder.' She laid a hand on his. Even that touch was an unguent on his wound. 'If you don't tell *me*, you'll never tell Bill because there's no chance I'll hate you. I've known Walter for many years, and he's a good judge of a person. He'd never be a longtime friend to a cold killer or a stone-hearted rabble-rouser.'

He downed the rest of his drink, part of him wishing it was whiskey for courage. Shame was on the horizon—did he want day or night?

'If not now, then—' she began.

He quickly took her hand, fearing she'd leave the room just as he stepped over the precipice.

'That week, I got a job. Rich feller. Forget the name. Good job. Good pay. We had Bill—Alden—but a few months. I saw dollars. I took a ride into town. Needed a gun. Mojave was seen around. My old gun were beat up on account of using it for hammering. Some days I were a lazy asshole.'

He winced—again. 'Pardon my language. I wanted a good gun. I earned it. Got it, and all. And I took a drink. And a meal. Bath and a shave at Drake's. Supplies. A fresh sage hen for good cooking. New bloomers for Mary. And I rode back like a doting man. A man who reckoned he were owed a good time with his beautiful wife while his boy slept in the crib.'

He tipped the cup to his lips, but it was empty. He rapped it down on the table, cursing neither it nor her—only his fallibility.

She loosed her hand and squeezed his. 'But they were gone,' she murmured.

'Taken and gone. Mary's horse dead. Flames licking the roof.'

The image burned in his mind's eye, never having left. The echo slammed back: the moment his heart had turned to ash and blackened his soul.

'All for a damn gun!' He thumped the arm of the chair. 'Away on a high old time, buying a weapon for killing, and leaving two to die.'

He rapped the chair repeatedly, so hard he'd break either it or his bone.

'Thinking of me. Leaving them no defence against the enemy, what came and took them for their revenge or needs. No man by their side. 'Cos, I am no man.'

He sprang up, went to the hall, tugged his holster belt from the wall hook, threw open the door, darted to the garden and hurled the weapon into the log pile on the far side. Blood pumped, his chest heaved, and his teeth were clenched so tight they might break. Even the chirrup of cicadas didn't calm him.

On the horizon, the colours of peach and orange signalled dusk.

When he turned, she stood there, arms limp by her side, warm concern etched on her face. He could only bear a glance—then tried to pass by her into the house.

She caught his shirt and stopped him.

'I'm leaving,' he muttered.

'No, you're not.'

Now he searched her face. 'Why?'

He was wound tight as a drum. A lesser man would have shoved her aside or done worse.

'Because that won't fix it.'

'Maybe I don't wanna fix it.'

'Well, I'm not giving you a choice.' She took his hand and marched him inside.

His mind whirled with surprise, confusion and worry.

In the living room, she stood him foursquare opposite.

She raised a hand, made the fist-with-thumb-out for "A", held it to her chest and moved it in a couple of circles.

'Now you,' she instructed.

Stupefied, he copied. It wasn't difficult to master.

'Good.' She stepped closer.

'What does it mean?'

'"Sorry".'

His shoulders fell. He repeated the sign. 'I'm real sorry.'

She shook her head. 'Don't tell *me*. I'm not the one who's hurt. Tell it to yourself. Apologise—then forgive yourself.'

He nodded. 'I guess.'

'I meant now, Earl.'

There was no mistaking the seriousness of her tone nor the underlying reason: she cared. She wanted to fix him. He'd been broken for twenty years, and she'd had enough of it after only two weeks.

Why had he done this to himself? Cowardice. Refusal to admit failure. Imperfection—the confession he'd breathed to a mound of stones. Laura was flesh and might judge.

Judgement was due. Overdue.

He made the sign. 'Sorry.'

She nodded. He repeated it. A smile broke on her lips.

He rotated his fist, round and round. 'Sorry, sorry, sorry.'

He turned the words inwards and pushed them down his throat, into his heart, stomach and gut. He willed them to flood every inch of him. As it did so, the rancorous guilt poured the other way, subsuming his torso, causing him to judder as if on the verge of tears.

She caught him before he'd even begun to fall, drew him in and let his chin rest on her shoulder.

'I'm sorry, I'm sorry, I'm sorry,' he babbled.

She stroked the back of his head. 'It's okay. It's okay.'

Laura made coffee, good and strong. The hot liquid in his throat was ambrosia after the torment of the last minutes.

She collected his gun. He'd not damaged it—though it made no difference: the appendage never got used anyhow.

They stood in the kitchen. She'd regathered herself so quickly, which he credited to many things, not least the legion of grouchy schoolkids she'd dealt with over the years.

Inside him, myriad emotions battled for control, but relief won. The rock in his heart had cracked—not broken or powdered, but it was a start.

Maybe that's all he was—another grumpy boy who wouldn't speak up or who was throwing two decades worth of hissy fits for refusing to see facts. She'd roped the steer and got it to walk on tiptoes in one fell swoop.

She was an angel on earth, like another he'd known before. But something else lay unsaid.

'He'll be wanting to know why I didn't come searching.'

'I'm sure he will.'

'But one man against a whole Indian camp? Suicide. Though lotta days I wished I had, and died trying, to let it all go.'

'Then you wouldn't be here. And Bill would. So you made the right choice. Perhaps it balances out.'

'With Mary gone?' He shook his head. 'No.'

'Look around you. I lost one and gained one too, and we do fine. Past is past. Future is future. So, I'll see you every day for lessons, okay?'

'Sure.'

'But first thing tomorrow, you visit Frank Wilson.'

'That I will. And after, I'll fix to get the wagon running so's I can bring the bed in from home.' He'd told her about the wreck Abe had gifted him.

'You should get Bill to help you.'

'And talk to him how?'

She shook her head, amused. 'And there was me thinking carpentry was tools and sweat. You make it sound like a sewing circle. It'll be good for you two. Anyway, he'd be a fool not to do anything which gets him a better night's sleep.'

'That's a fact.' He drained his mug. 'On which, I should get to the Hotel. It's late and been a long day.'

'A good day,' she suggested. 'Love started today.'

He imagined she meant Bill and Sarah.

Chapter 35

Earl was dutifully at Wilson's General Store the moment it opened.

First, he soft-soaped the man by purchasing generously. Then, with no other customers on the premises, he enquired—as politely as he could—how Dennis Hayes was doing these days.

Things passed well, given the circumstances.

From there, he went to the schoolhouse for the appointed lesson before the pupils arrived.

'Well?' she asked.

'Dennis is a man of his word, by all reckoning.'

'A word which lasts eighteen years?'

'Can't know for sure, but I don't expect the man to be buying me boot polish and whiskey on account of blinding him.'

She sat at a desk and gestured for him to do the same. His knees scraped the underside of the woodwork.

'So, tell me about it. If I have to defend you to Elizabeth and Dennis, I want a clear conscience.'

'It ain't your place to defend me.'

'Then why do you ask for my counsel?'

'Because Walt ain't here, and without another friendly gun to face down the man, I gotta use brains and words to fix this, and besides kindness and steel, brains and words are what you got. 'Cos I don't.'

She smiled. 'That's very sweet. But say things straight, okay?'

He took a deep breath. 'After Mary passed, a year to the day, I come to town. I took a drink. Lotta of drinks. I were cut bad. Real bad.' He closed his eyes and forced the memory out. 'Dennis were there. After the posse, this musta been, 'cos I reckon he got hurt that day.'

'He got that nasty scar on his face.' She stroked the desk. 'Some got worse,' she mumbled.

'Laura, I—'

'No, go on.' She smoothed her navy tunic and painted on an encouraging expression.

The saloon came alive, the clamour inside and outside his skull. Deep gashes of loss in his soul. A fuse so short it would take his arm off before he threw the dynamite.

'I forget my words that night. Maybe I spoke on the man's cut-up looks, maybe not. All the same, he called me coward and Mojave-lover and said words alike Mary being a part-Indian made her better off dead.' He rapped on the table, hearing those insults again.

She bowed her head.

'And I got the first punch—what I never did afore to no man.'

'In the eye?'

He shook his head vehemently and shoved his chair back, startling her. He turned away at making the offence and inspected his boots.

'Dennis went over, only not to the floor. Corner of a table went smack in his face.'

'So—an accident,' she said.

He couldn't look at her, so he focussed on the chalk marks on the board.

'A gone eye is a gone eye, and it were gone, 'cos the Doc couldn't do nothing for it.'

He wanted to spit on the floor, but this was like her second home, let alone being in her company. 'And this is the man you look on now. Who got riled up and brawling, hit a man and was took to the cell for a night. A sorry asshole thrown out of this good town for being hateful and taking a man's sight for ragging on the best woman who ever lived.' Present company excluded, he wanted to say.

She approached, her tone as if becalming a spooked mare.

'An accident. A mistake. An error of judgement. You're not the first man to put a fist on another. Think how it could have been worse.' She noted his gun.

He pushed at it as if trying to hide it. 'I never drew since the day it were bought. And I never took a drink since that man lost his eye.'

She squeezed his arm. 'Because you're trying to make amends. Like at the cemetery, when again you weren't responsible for what happened. Good deeds fix things better than loud words. And you're a good man.'

He mustered a glance. 'I still never figure how you think that.'

'You think your heart is gone, that it was taken the day the Mojave came. When you were simply out getting nurture and protection for those you loved. And later, you try to do right by an apparent boy stranger, then by a widow, and now you apologise for an out-of-character moment.'

'On account of apologies maybe got a tiny chance of stopping a bullet. Only chance I got, I reckon.'

'Then perhaps you should try a good deed for Dennis Hayes and tip the balance in your favour.'

He sought meaning in her face but came up short. 'I don't get how to do deeds for a man who ain't here.'

Her brows arched. 'You fixed my fence.'

He was about to point out that she was in town when he'd repaired her property—but a man didn't need to be home for his fence to be accessible.

'Dennis got a broke fence?' he enquired hopefully.

'No. But his porch is a long-time rotten.'

He wanted to clutch her in his arms by way of thanks. Instead, he straightened his back, smoothed his jacket and cracked his knuckles.

'I'm right grateful for your good sense and quick thinking.'

'It's nothing. Only be sharp about it. You have perhaps three days.'

He tipped his hat. 'I'll get the wagon fixed up for bringing wood.' He turned for the door.

'Earl?'

He looked back.

"Signing?" she gestured.

'Shoot.'

She made the "watch" sign for him to pay attention, held out a fist and pulled it towards her. Perplexed, he repeated the gesture, assuming it was what she wanted.

"Good," she signed. "'Wagon",' she said. 'Add it to your vocabulary.'

"Thank you."

'Now, sit. We're running short of time since we used up some of the lesson trying to help you stay alive long enough to use these signs with your boy.' She added a typically beautiful smile to take the edge off the jibe.

After 'school', he passed by the Hayes house to scope the task. Being close to potential nemesis sent a shiver down his spine.

Laura was correct about the state of the porch, and he saw where Mrs Hayes has nearly put her foot through a rotten board. He surreptitiously took rough measurements, figured out the effort needed, and chuckled forlornly. If this were a paying job, it would be very welcome.

From there, he went to the stables, where Bill proudly showed him Tanner. The kid had chosen well.

Afterwards, they walked over to where the open wagon stood in scrub grass. One of the wheels lay clean off, planks were missing from the load bay, and rust caked the ironwork.

"We f-i-x?" Earl signed.

"Why?"

"Moving... s-t-u-f-f. Your bed."

Besides the alphabet, question words with facial inflexion, and a few verbs, Earl stumbled through some basic phrases, but the finger-spelling was tiresome. It felt like solo pumping a handcart down a rail track in pursuit of a flat-out dangler.

Bill nodded. Earl patted him on the back, and they went to gather tools for the restoration.

That afternoon they worked together, man and boy, replacing the planks, scrubbing the rust, fixing the wheel and greasing the axle. Later, they heaved the wagon up by its arms and gave it a rolling test. It ran fine, so Earl broke into a run, and Bill followed. They dragged the cart across the compound, he panting hard, Bill taking it in his stride.

When they tugged against the momentum and brought their wagon to a stand outside the stables, they'd done more than complete a project; they'd created a moment.

He embraced Bill, and they slapped each other on the back.

Laura was right—being sad amidst this was a waste of life.

Chapter 36

The next day, Earl made an early start, hitching Jack up to the wagon and taking a sedate pace home. Credit to his handiwork, everything remained intact. However, he winced a few times over rocks and as the wheels yawed through the shallow water of Holland Creek.

At the house, he rustled up a pot of coffee and gave the wagon a once-over with the complete set of tools from the workshop. After a heavy lunch, he separated the bed into its three components—head, foot and slatting—and loaded them onto the wagon. He added the planks of wood for Dennis' porch, fixings and a few tools, and then pointed Jack's nose towards town.

'Good deeds lost lives afore. Hope one can save me now.' He smoothed the horse's neck. 'Or you won't be carrying this dumb old load of flesh again. Abe'll look after you, and you can go quiet and old like I said.'

As he lolled along, he wondered why he hadn't invested in a wagon earlier. Although he specialised in small pieces, not wanting to be a fence-and-furniture handyman, he could upscale his skills. Maybe even, as years advanced, he'd be wise to move away from intricate carving towards larger pieces—broaden his horizons.

Heck, if Bill showed interest, maybe they'd join forces. He'd attacked the wagon project with gusto, and if Earl were honest with himself, he'd want his boy to do something more worthy than being a stablehand all his life.

He chuckled: a father for barely two weeks and already disappointed with his boy's career choice. No wonder the kid wasn't keen to live with him.

Laura had coffee and biscuits ready, which Earl took gratefully after he'd left Bill and Sarah at the forge to dress the bed. Laura made good coffee; none of the belly wash some folks did.

She suggested they practice signing. He was concerned that Dennis' stagecoach came closer every hour, and time for such diversions was wasted: dead men didn't need sign language.

'Every day's a day for learning,' she chided.

'You'll have me at the piano next,' he joked. 'I barely got out the saddle.'

'Bill's been playing—or trying. If you want a bond, there's a chance. Sarah and I passed many days on that stool. You can't beat teamwork like that. Teaching and learning are what keeps a mind young.'

He pointed. 'You oughta tune it up. G sounds a mite flat.'

'Well, I never did. The perfect ear, is it now?'

'I don't know 'bout that. I could fool around in there for you.'

She waved at the piano. 'Be my guest.'

So he opened the lid, had a pry around, then went outside to the wagon and lifted down his toolbox.

He dug past a couple of seldom-used tools to find an old tuning lever. He'd never had the heart to throw it out, having been a wedding gift from Mary's father, "So she and Earl would always make beautiful music together". If he'd cleaned and tuned their old piano once, he'd done it a hundred times. He'd never claim to be pitch-perfect, but close enough was better than most.

Some while later, he gave the keys a glissando, found it improved, and tried a run-through of the tune he'd played with Sarah.

By the end, Laura was standing at his side. 'You know "Clementine"?'

'Blindfold, back in the day.'

'Perhaps you'll end up teaching me, rather than the reverse.'

'I only got 'bout a dozen. I'll never make the concert hall.'

She sat beside him. 'You create plenty of beauty with your hands anyway, Earl. Work, play, and soon talk. So, give the old girl a run—show me your chops.'

He caught her drift, thought for a moment, and then gingerly embarked on the tune.

After a few bars, she joined in with her right hand, an octave higher than his, adding a quirky layer to the melody. He quickened, chasing her hand up and down the keys, faster and faster, the odd bass note going awry. But her smile encouraged him, and he teased her, increasing the pace.

He quickly jumped down an octave, and she followed, taking his original position. After a few bars, he jumped his hand back, narrowly missing hers as she leapt to the right.

He'd always considered Mary's piano ideal, but here and now, it paled in comparison.

At the end of the tune, he looped immediately to the beginning, laughter on their lips as he varied the pace, switched octaves, and even eased his shoulder against hers to unbalance her. For a couple of minutes, they were acting half the age of the other occupants in the house rather than twice their years.

He finished with a flourish, and they burst out laughing.

'You're a wicked man.'

'You made me play,' he retorted.

'I didn't make you cheat and fool.'

'You said, "give the old girl a run".'

Her eyes flared with mock indignation. 'I meant the piano!'

'Sure. Must'a got all mixed up.'

'I say again—you're a wicked man.' She sprung up from the stool and stopped dead. 'Walter.'

Earl spun. Indeed, Walter stood at the doorway, wearing an amused smile.

'We been… playing some,' Earl blustered. He stood, self-consciously smoothing his shirt.

'Uh-huh.'

'You get a fair price for your bulls?' he asked, desperate to change the subject.

Walter entered the room. 'A goodly sum. The kid okay?'

'Bill and Sarah are courting now,' Laura said with an edge of motherly pride.

Walter gave Earl a look of amused approbation. 'Is that so?'

'He asked for a blessing and all.'

'He's looking to care for her. Like a good man does to those he loves.' She winked at Earl.

He rubbed his cheek absentmindedly, hoping to brush away the redness that was surely there.

Walter nodded. 'And you tuned the piano, less I'm mistaken?'

'I figured if Sarah wanted to learn Bill, I should give the instrument a fix-up.'

'You've not played in, what, twenty years?' Walter suggested.

'I'll imagine it's all the extra dexterity Earl's learnt with his signing,' Laura said. 'Coffee, Walter?'

'Very kind.'

She sashayed past Walter to the kitchen. He studied Earl as if judging a truanting schoolboy.

'What?' Earl snipped.

'Pretty good playing, the two of you.'

His eyes narrowed. 'I smell your meaning.'

'She's a handsome woman.' There was a deliberate off-handedness slathered in insinuation.

'So what's been keeping you apart all these years?' Earl gave as good as he was getting.

'Oh, I'm happy as I am. Always have been.'

'And I was too, so lay off your needling.'

'"Was"?'

Earl closed the piano lid. 'She'd never figure to be doing with me.'

'Is that so? You know, buddy, you're as blind as your boy is deaf.'

'I see real good, Walt.'

Walter put his index finger to Earl's forehead. 'Then maybe it's this instrument needs a fix-up.'

They walked from Laura's up Main Street and left down Mountain Avenue with Jack and the wagon in tow. Earl had recounted her suggestion about soft-soaping the would-be killer.

Had Walter deliberately stayed away these past days, forcing Earl to ride the runaway train of emotion alone, like a mother bird that pushes the chick out of the nest and hopes it will fly before it plummets to its death? It didn't matter: Walter was back now. Earl had an ally in town. Maybe just in time.

Walter offered a more-than-courteous nod to a woman they passed, and it was met with an equally enthusiastic smile.

Earl recognised the lady. She was roughly Laura's age, with long hair, and her matching scarf and skirt were a distinctive bright burgundy. Had Walter been sandbagging? Earl wouldn't raise the topic yet—perhaps it was a mirage created by his fondness for Laura rather than a nascent bond between his friend and another.

Earl halted Jack. The wagon gave a final creak and came to rest.

'You speak to Frank Wilson?' Walter asked.

'He said there's been no more fights picked.'

'I don't know Dennis like Frank does, but I'd put odds of fifty-fifty at best. Easy for the man to ride out to your place and kill you sleeping—which he's not done. Everyone draws a line.'

'You know his words, Walt. If I come to town again, I'm a dead man.'

'Maybe so. Hayes was happy to back up Potter and kill as many Mojave as was needed. He musta been mad as a hornet to get cut up like that, doing Lyle's bidding, but he couldn't revenge on his kin—so maybe you're the next best thing.'

'Excepting his fall were an accident. Shooting up a camp for that sonofabitch—kin or not—were a dumb risk, and he got his deserves.'

Walter sighed, pulled off his hat and scratched his head. 'I know you're asking me to back you up—'

'I ain't meaning fight my battle.'

'All the same, my insisting brought us here, so some weight is on my shoulders. You don't want a second gun watching over you—that's fine. But I'll stay in town 'til the man's back.'

'If whatever town we pitched up at with Bill, Hayes was the answer to discovering who and what took Bill's ears, I reckon I'd need to ride in and try to make peace with the man anyhow. This way, I got the mercy of time to figure a plan and the brains of a good woman to suggest it.'

'Did you ever think to leave and get a friend to ask Dennis about the posse?'

Earl frowned. 'What happened to you ragging on me to take ahold of my life? You want I should be beholding to you for more? You already as good as saved my boy from buzzard food.'

'All I'm saying is, finding out is finding out—from whoever. You're so sure Dennis will shoot you on sight—you don't think I'd rather that not happen?'

'Like I say, I gotta do it.'

'Then, fine.'

A pang of melancholy hit Earl. 'Would you look in on Bill if it come to it?'

'It won't come to it.'

'All the same….'

Walter shook his head in resignation. 'You gotta hear it, so, yeah, I'll see right by the boy, best I'm able.'

'You're a wheelhorse, Walt.'

They offloaded the new planks onto the scrub ground beside the Hayes house, and then Earl rode Jack back to the stables and put the wagon alongside the forge. Walter made himself scarce to run errands.

Earl walked back to the site of his pro bono project and began work.

The early stages felt peculiar—pulling up the rotten planks was as good as wreaking destruction on the property of a man who'd sworn to kill him for even entering the town. What if Dennis turned up now when, to all appearances, Earl was causing further injury to the situation?

He couldn't help constantly surveying the street. Yet, all remained calm throughout the afternoon of hard labour.

One or two passers-by threw odd expressions his way and a man by the name of Delmar Grant probed him on the nature of his business.

It started accusingly, moved into understanding, and then came an appreciation of Earl's good deed. Earl didn't say he was doing the work to save his skin, and it ended with Grant saying he might be in touch about some carpentry chores of his own. Earl refrained from remarking that he might be dead by nightfall.

At around four o'clock, he was sitting on the step, taking a drink from his canteen, when he noted a familiar shape ambling up the street.

He peered into the heat haze. Potter was pushing a contraption he'd never seen but heard folk tell of—a wheeled chair. Sitting in it, and yawing on the uneven roadway, was an old woman who was seventy-five if she was a day. Ma Potter? Of course, the man must have a mother, but did she possess the man's objectionable character and turn of words?

Ma was asleep.

'Fine day for a walk,' Earl said, opting for a pleasant opening gambit.

'What in God's name are you doing? Who gave you permission to even walk on Dennis' property, let alone pull it apart?'

'In God's name, I'm turning the other cheek, Mayor.'

Potter strode up. 'Breaking a man's house?'

'Fixing a man's house,' Earl corrected.

'Well, you finally did run mad.'

'Just trying to be neighbourly. He's your cousin—you not want the best for him?'

Potter shook his head in disbelief. 'I've seen some dumb things in my day.'

'Mrs Hayes near broke her leg on this old porch. I hear Dennis is no keen man for chores.'

'What the hell will he do when he finds out what you've been at?'

Earl stood. 'Well, he's sworn to shoot me dead anyhow, so I'll take my chances this don't make it worse.'

That fairly poleaxed the rotund troublemaker. 'Aren't you the brown-nosing sonofabitch?'

Earl stepped closer. 'Like you buying a church roof to make popular with the good people of this town?'

Potter's nostrils flared. He leant in. The brims of their hats touched. 'I hope they bury you close by here, so I don't have to go far for dancing.'

Again, Earl forced down his temper, knowing he was already standing here because of its legacy. 'After I'm done, you got any fixing up I can do for you, Lyle?'

Potter's mouth opened and closed. He stepped back. 'Sure. Come by and lay a hand on my property any time. I flat out dare you.' He gripped the butt of his gun.

Earl held in a smile and indicated the old woman snoring gently. 'Don't wake Ma with a shot now, Mayor.' He tipped his hat. 'I got work to be doing.'

He turned away, picked up his hammer, and, without checking Potter's demeanour, drove in the next nail like it was piercing the man's skull.

Chapter 37

The following day, having accepted an invitation to take a well-earned break from carpentry travails, Earl rode up to Laura's house with her horse in tow. Hester was kept in the corral behind the main stables, not fully liveried like the post and stage horses. Sarah and Laura shared the animal, with Laura's previous mare having died two years before.

Laura met him outside the gate. They filled the saddlebags and then mounted up.

She led them away, out past the town boundary and turned a sharp south towards distant low hills. Recent low-pressure weather had waned, and the sky was a milky blue. Fair for a trip out, but not too hot to make a lady perspire on a midday ride.

He kept Jack a length behind Hester's pace, off to the side for a clear view, away from the dust thrown up by her hooves, moving his attention between the scenery, the way ahead, and Laura's form. The wind tugged her charcoal skirt, and her gloved hands bobbed with the undulating reins.

Mary had loved to ride. When she felt impish, she'd challenge him. Sometimes it ended in victory, sometimes in defeat, and sometimes—best of all—it ended in a secluded spot, burning off some loving energy.

He cast away the mental image—it was wrong to compare then and now. Still, he had.

After twenty minutes at a good clip, the ground rose, and Laura slowed, heading up to a copse.

The thicket sprouted near the edge of a steep drop overlooking a river valley. They dismounted under the cluster of Palo Verde and hitched the horses. Jack and Hester began to get acquainted.

He patted Jack. 'Don't do anything I wouldn't.'

He took in the view, pulled off his hat to air his head, and went to Laura. 'Mighty fine spot.'

She pulled off her riding gloves and untied her bonnet.

'One time, Sarah and I were up here while a storm raged across the valley. Eight years old, she was, perhaps. The lightning forked, and she squealed like a darling.'

'You get a bucketful?'

'No, we got the wind, though. Blew her hat clean off. She chased it around like a naughty hen. I laughed. I shouldn't have.'

He let out a heavy breath, bereft of such fond times with a child. 'Men may dig mines, but memories are better'n gold.'

'Well, seems you're a poet too.' She flashed a smile, took off her navy cape and folded it.

'I speak as I find, that's all.'

'That you do. That you do. Come on.'

They laid out rugs under the shade, unpacked the lunch things, whipped up a fire and sat. His self-consciousness reached a new peak. Company always meant Walter Doonan, not a lady. He felt like a show pony: best manners needed.

He watched while she made coffee, taking any secret opportunity to drink in her beauty. He wondered whether she had ever done similar. On their wedding night, Mary had called him "the handsomest man in the whole state"—but that was a lifetime ago. All the same, even with his courting skills rusted up so grimly, he swore that more than once he'd detected romantic interest in her words and gestures.

He coughed involuntarily to expel such idiotic notions. This was merely a friendly picnic.

Not for the first time, she sprang a tutorial on him, first making the "watch" sign as if bringing a class to attention. Once or twice before, he'd tried to brush it off and received short shrift, so now he did as he was told. Deep inside, part of him got a kick out of being bossed around by a pretty lady—it wasn't so different from marriage.

She loosely rubbed her hands together as if skating the palms off each other. He repeated it.

"'Picnic",' she said.

'Like a man and boy'll ever be riding out like this,' he chuckled.

'Boy? Young man, at least. Or "Bill".'

He reflected. 'I guess "son" I should know.'

'Yes,' she agreed firmly. 'And use it.'

'I promise. Teacher,' he added with a smirk.

'Good.' She held her left arm up, like cradling a baby, and brought her right hand down from her forehead to join it in cradling—something like a falling salute. '"Son".'

He copied.

'You're a quick study.' She did another, similar, but with the hand coming down from lips instead of forehead.

He copied.

'"Daughter",' she said.

He let his arms fall away, and his demeanour dipped.

'What?' she asked.

'We was hoping for a daughter to follow on.'

She took his hand. 'And we hoped for a son to follow on. That's all gone now, so don't spoil the day. It's too pretty up here for grey clouds from you.'

'It sure is.' He didn't know why that directness appeared—and gave an embarrassed smile.

'Coffee?' If she'd caught his compliment, it didn't show.

'That'd be kind.'

They clunked their mugs. He watched her drink and took in the view. The silence was idyllic yet clanging. Her gaze flickered towards him. His nerves jangled.

'I wanted to ask 'bout another sign.'

She smiled. 'You can always do that.'

He met her gaze, nervous, and looked down at the rug, then out across the vista. 'I wanna be… I need to be…. That is, I guess I'll need to be saying, "I love you"—down the road, sometime.'

'To Bill?'

He looked at her, then away. 'I guess. If a feller were standing up to be a real father. One who appreciated what he had.'

'Well, this works for anybody.' She raised her right hand, extended her thumb, first and little fingers and folded down the other two. 'It's as easy as this.'

He raised his hand, struggling to bend his second and third digits. She laid three fingers onto them and gently pressed down. Their eyes locked. She traced his little finger, then forefinger and thumb, then little finger and thumb. Her touch was tender, less purposeful than at school, and his skin tingled.

'"I. L. Y." I say it to Sarah most every day.'

A fizzing tickled his heart. 'Can't say it's something I'm rushin' to do. Ain't… manly.'

'Don't begrudge Bill that. Everybody needs somebody in their life—to wrap them up and love on equal terms. Take them for who they are—faults and gifts. Ride together on life's stallion—walk or canter.'

He smiled. 'Guessing that makes you some poet too.'

'Words are just words. Deeds make lives.'

'Like picking up a kid or riding to your house.'

'Or learning to sign.' She eyed him straight, moistening her lips. 'Or saying yes to lunch with a widow who should know better than come to remote places with grumpy old souls.

Grumpy old souls who had no reason to be so. Not anymore.'

He held her gaze until embarrassment welled up, so he looked away. The breeze tinkered with the leaves above.

She coughed. 'Lunch?'

He nodded. All he could hear was his heartbeat.

She served the assorted delicacies onto two tin plates.

'Laura?' She stopped. 'I got another question. Kinda… not 'bout Bill. Regarding… picnics and such.'

'Of course, you can ask me.'

'Why did you invite me here?'

Her brows tweaked. 'Apart from giving you a break from your labours, I've become quite happy with your company.'

'That's kind.' He fidgeted with his fork.

'And why did you accept the invitation?'

'I… that is… a woman's company is real pleasant, what with everything.' Why was his mouth so dry?

'Pleasant is the least I try to be.'

'And you are, Laura. Real easy on the eye too. The kinda woman that….' He failed at the last and nervously stroked his stubble.

'Yes?' She searched his face.

'That is….' He straightened his back and prayed for strength. 'Who would I be needing to ask if I wanted to come courting on you?'

Her face coloured as if lit from within; the burning coals of her soul turned over to rekindle their heat. There was also a nervousness—nothing like his unfamiliar disquiet—but it warmed him too.

'There's only Sarah besides me. Has been for so long. So if you wanted to ask her—not that I'm saying you need to—I think she'd be touched.'

'Could you learn me that?'

She guided him through the gestures. 'It's all coming pretty easy to you now.'

'Guessing one thing the Lord gave me was hands to do his work.' He smile awkwardly.

'That's true.' There was a pause that lasted half the afternoon. 'If that day came, what would be your intentions towards me?'

He thought. 'To become the kinda man what deserves you.'

'Aren't you already?'

'I ain't sure. 'Sides, I gotta get past Dennis Hayes first.'

'And you will. But if you're fixed on wishing yourself into a grave when the stagecoach arrives tomorrow, then perhaps it was a waste of time teaching you.' She shrugged and looked deliberately away.

He wiped his mouth with a napkin and touched her shoulder. 'I don't reckon it were.'

That's good to hear. Some men would be brazen enough to ask anyhow, knowing the courting was doomed, just to get a kiss with their last meal.' She smoothed the rug. 'Or picnic.'

Spooked, he eased back. His heart clattered. 'I don't…. That is….' He clenched a fist. 'Shoot.'

She toyed with a broken yellow blade of grass. 'I figure it like this. It might help you decide if you ever wanted to ask Sarah that question. We're not getting younger, so if you realised I wasn't the type for that question, or perhaps that… other sign,' she laid a hand into her lap and loosely figured "ILY", 'We'd know where we stood.'

He swallowed. 'Sure. Right enough.'

He reached for the canteen. She plucked it from the rug and handed it across. Their fingers brushed.

He drank. Their eyes met and held there.

'I don't mean to embarrass you.' She looked down, tucking hair behind her ear. 'I'm out of line. I'm sorry. I know it's been… difficult, but—'

'Yes,' he blurted, his heart forming the words rather than his mind. 'Condemned or not, I can't deny it's been on my mind.'

'I had a feeling.'

'Long time, truth be told.'

'Mmm-hmm.' Expectation pooled in her eyes.

Leaning in, he paused, waiting for a warning tug on his mental leash. It didn't come, so he gently kissed her on the lips. A drop of ambrosia from the Holy Grail.

Deep in the bowels of his essence, rusted-up gargantuan iron furnaces were lit by haggard old men roused from decades of slumber.

He pulled away, fearing an inferno of impropriety, sensing unwelcome aeons had passed with this touch, or Bill's aim had missed the snake, and he still lay feverish on the cold ground, merely dreaming of such un-met angels.

Her eyes searched his and sensed the struggle.

'Just say "No", Earl. It'll be easier on my heart and your gut. I've no desire to tear you up inside. I've been alone for many years. I get by. I need to be courted by a man who wants to, not one who thinks he has a duty toward me. Don't say "Yes" and break my heart later. It's not kind.'

He took her hand, feeling it as if for the first time.

'You see all this, what I try to hide, and still accept. Why?'

'Because I believe the Lord sent a sign. He brought you and Walter to find Bill. Then He delivered Bill to White Rock and Bill to you as a son—hard as you fought it. And He knows folks need caring and company in their lives, succour and support in dark times. He brought Bill to Sarah, and I think He brought you to me. He gives as well as takes, Earl.'

'Works in mysterious ways.'

She nodded. 'But nobody can make that decision for you—not Walter, me, not even the Lord. You can ask any of us, and we'll give you our mind, but we're not you.'

She laid splayed fingers over his heart. 'I made my peace. I know what Jim would want. And I know what I want.'

He contemplated the earth. 'I can't figure on ever being Jim to you.'

'Nor I, Mary.'

'Of all the folks who ever walked in town, this sorry fool is your choice?'

'I only ask to be treated properly, and I figure you'd do that. A man who'd be good for Sarah and me, who'd tread an honest path.' She smiled. 'Not so bad looking either. The only thing wrong is that a piece of your heart was taken away, and if it's mended, some love might grow there.'

He nodded slowly. 'I figure if anyone can fix me up, you're better'n most.'

'I'll take that as a compliment, if I may.' She winked.

'I ain't much good on compliments, neither.'

'Well, perhaps I'll try and fix that too.'

She touched his cheek, and he stroked her hair. Silent expectation bellowed in his ears. He licked the sheen of procrastination from his lips.

'Laura Mae, I'd be honoured to come courting on you.'

'Please do. And I hope Sarah sees likewise.'

'I'll try real hard to be that man. Do right by you. I ain't perfect.'

'Nor is anybody. But a good heart goes a long way.' She laid a pointed finger on his chest and traced the shape.

'That'd be something—having a heart good and forgiving as yours.'

'Perhaps my medicine is letting it be healed by love. By what I have, not what I've lost.' She met his eye. 'Or what I might have.'

Haggard old men opened the heavy furnace doors and piled on more wood.

He kissed her again.

Chapter 38

Earl's mind blazed throughout the ride back. The landscape was merely something that connected their origin and destination. The only sounds were eight hooves on dirt, competing poorly with the klaxons and whirrs inside his head.

As they rode, he replayed the scant seconds when he'd dared to hold her, the moments when their faces had been close or touching, the out-of-body recall of their idyllic position atop the hill—the lost pleasure of genuine company. Female company.

Once or twice his libido surfaced, asking his eyes to undress her of the skirt and blouse, which fluttered in the breeze as they cantered. Immediately he crushed the desire, jamming a gargantuan spanner into the rusted machinery that the haggard old men sought to oil and condition.

As the afternoon clouds covered the sun, he glanced heavenwards, waiting for the bolt that either God or Mary herself would hurl down to snuff out his tortured being.

Yet he reached White Rock unscathed, still bouncing between regret and curiosity.

Why not accept that it was real? He cared for Laura, found her increasingly irresistible, and enjoyed her company. His eyes couldn't keep off her, as if telling his mind that she could be—if she wasn't already—his new love.

They returned to decorous cordiality, went to the stables and stowed individual mounts in their places, coexisting like the friends who'd left a few hours earlier. Either she'd experienced second thoughts or sensed his disquiet and distance on the ride back. Hopefully, she was merely remaining socially aloof so as not to set tongues wagging.

They arrived at her house to find Bill and Sarah at the piano. They watched from the doorway, exchanging a knowing smile. He wanted to kiss her. Patience, he told himself. After many years of waiting, a few hours was a trifle.

The youngsters spotted them. The notes trundled to a halt and evaporated into the air. Sarah, then Bill, rose from the stool, and all four signed greetings.

'So, did you want to ask?' Laura said, low and without meeting Earl's eye.

'Yeah, I reckon I do. Can't say I recall the signs though, what with the distraction of… circumstance afore.'

She pondered. 'I have an idea. I'll guide you.'

She signed to Sarah and Bill, then cupped their shoulders, asking them to stay put. The youngsters exchanged an amused look.

Laura stood behind and between them, out of their sight but where Earl could see. Then she raised her hands in signing preparation, and he followed. A lump appeared in his throat, so he coughed it away.

Laura signed deliberately, and he copied. It was only a short stanza, but he could have been front of the stage at the Tucson Grand Theatre. His heart rattled along.

Bill and Sarah's faces lit, and they exchanged signs. Laura peered over, curious. The wait was interminable. Earl tapped his thigh. The clock ticked.

Daughter and son turned, raised fists in unison and bobbed them forwards.

Adrenaline coursed through Earl. Now, only his dumb reticence could prevent happiness.

Sarah hugged her mother. Bill gave her a loose buss, then shook Earl's hand. Sarah inspected his face with curiosity and signed.

Laura smiled. 'She says, "Please treat her right".'

'I aim to,' he replied.

Laura relayed that to Sarah, who signed to Earl, giving a cheeky wink. Laura smiled in disbelief.

'What gives?' he asked.

'She said you better had. Because remember—she can shoot now.'

Supper was like the calm after a storm.

At every opportunity, he drank in Laura's face and her bearing. The sweep of her hair, the curl of her ear canal, her brown eyes and the laughter lines bordering them.

For the first time, Bill and Sarah openly held hands. Perhaps the day's development had provided the courage to show their affection.

For Earl, it was too early to do similar: Laura might get used to it, and pretty soon, they'd be holding hands in town. That would beget judgement, trigger whispers, and become opinion and gossip. Things were already on a knife edge.

After supper, they all sat, talked, and read, and he was coaxed into rattling out a couple of tunes. Bill and Sarah stood with their hands pressed to the piano, absorbing the vibrations. Her face sat happily with recognition; his was a picture of concentration.

Earl imagined this must be what family life is like. He swiftly dismissed it. Once before, he'd experienced the warm emotional glow of home, and it turned into a suffusing inferno of loss. This was no time to idly dream or project a future. At most, it should be enjoyed for that moment.

So, he let the silent joy of the children subsume him and grew unashamed by Laura's closeness on the stool, her left hand popping a few complementary notes into the mix, sometimes holding the frame of the piano and allowing the tune to penetrate by more than ears.

Unnoticed, darkness fell. The longcase pendulum clock struck ten. Bill and Sarah noticed his glance at the timepiece, exchanged a sign, and offered them "Good night".

This was already in his lexicon, so he signed back, "Good night, son. Good night, Sarah."

When they'd left, the empty room pushed in on him.

Laura sighed contentedly. 'Thanks for a nice day.'

'Being with me's gotta be like planing down a hundred-year pine to figure a toothpick.'

'Nothing worth having is easy.'

'I figure you're right.'

She stood. 'Well, I'm turning in now.'

'Good food and a long ride'll take it from you.'

'And you have another day of carpentry ahead. Because I don't want to lose you now.'

'Nor I, you.'

She moved closer. 'Because it's official, you can kiss me goodnight. If you'd like.'

Foolishly, he glanced towards the room door in case someone was watching.

She smirked, as a teacher does when a student makes a misstep or fumbles their working. The hundred-year pine was still a telegraph pole at best.

She stroked his cheek. 'I know what's inside your head. You have to permit yourself this, ever since the moment you found Bill. You're asking yourself if it's right to do whatever's next. But the last thing you need is wondering whether you have anyone else's blessing.'

'I don't always… see so good.'

'Well, I hope you can see now.'

He nodded, drew her closer and kissed her.

Chapter 39

Earl woke refreshed in the Hotel and took a moment to reflect. Guilt and uncertainty weren't wholly banished, but they were diluted.

He dressed, took breakfast in the saloon, and then returned to the room to collect his bag.

The floor creaked behind him. His heart went off like a rocket. Was the stagecoach early?

He licked his lips, desperate for the tinge of Laura to nourish him at the end. He turned, good and slow, hands away from his waist.

Walter stood there. In his hand hung a brown bag.

'Missed you last night.'

Earl blew out a gale of relief. 'I made... other plans. You figuring to gimme a heart attack even afore the bullet comes?'

'Sorry, buddy. I was expecting we'd bend an elbow. Like we do?'

'Like I say, the day got away. I were out with Laura and then at her place late.'

Walter nodded slowly.

The air felt thin, like the world had taken an anticipatory inhalation and sucked the room of its oxygen.

'Look, Walt, say your piece—okay?'

'I got no piece to say. Except—happy birthday.'

Earl did a soft double-take and creased his brow in a rapid calculation. 'Shoot.'

'Yeah, so, maybe tonight you'll do me the pleasure of having that drink.'

'Shoot. Gotta be the first year we missed.'

'But on good reason, I guess.' A probing coated Walter's tone.

Best to come clean, Earl reckoned: the alternative was smart-ass jibes and looks for hours, maybe days.

'Laura and I are courting.'

Walter nodded as if it hadn't been a shock or surprise. He held out the bag. 'Then this goes double as congratulations too.'

'You make it sound like I won the rodeo.'

'The rodeo you're too old for—we both. Love, not so much. Now take the damn gift I brought you.'

Earl pulled open the bag and withdrew the familiar shape, considering an appropriate response. Refusing was out. Grudging acceptance was the only alternative.

'That's mighty generous.'

Walter tossed his hat on the bed. 'You hate it, and don't think for a second I don't know. Here's the news.' He gestured at Earl's already-full holster. 'That's about as much use as a paper horseshoe. For why? It's cursed. It's the memory of what you did and wished you hadn't. It's a millstone dragging you under. More likely to cost your hide than save it.'

'Guns are for weak men.'

Walter shook his head. 'Picking fights is for weak men. Protecting a man's self—and the folks he loves—isn't weak.'

Earl sighed, turning the new Colt over in his hand. 'I guess it's a real nice piece.'

'I'm asking you, as your friend, not to be a superstitious ass about this no more. Reckon you woke up pretty fresh today. Kinda like you don't hate being alive. Been a long time coming. So maybe I got a gift too—a piece of Earl Johnson back.'

He scanned the man's face, the greying temples—ageing he'd been partly responsible for. 'I hate you being right all the time.'

'You've got a woman now. I don't reckon I'll be right half as often as she will.' Walter winked.

'They can be, I guess.'

He unholstered his old gun, hefted it, tossed it on the bed and slid the new one into its place.

'Maybe you should find out for yourself? Seeing as how I broke my vow. Take your own advice, huh?'

'I'm fine.' Walter waved it away. 'I got... acquaintances anyhow.' He coughed. 'You know... uh... my old gun don't shoot straight in three years or more.'

'On account of you shooting with the wrong hand.'

'A left-handed gun isn't the cause. Old hands, maybe. So—are we good?'

Earl smirked. 'Gifting is doing well on you today, for a regular man without no birthday.'

Walter lifted the old gun. 'Not jinxed in my hand. Cleaned up a little. Check it over. Waste is a sin, and that ride you took cost more than we would ever have wanted. I'd sooner be ready for whatever comes next.'

'And me? Is this by way of trying to even the odds?'

Walter's face hardened. 'No. I didn't buy it so's you can put a bullet in Dennis's chest. You kill him, it won't bring back Bill's hearing, and I'd wager Laura won't look too kindly on it. You might even lose her. Worse, you kill Potter's cousin, Mayor'll likely kill you.'

The words thudded into Earl's chest. He sank to the bed, found a spot on his trousers and tried to wipe it off with his thumb. Everything new—this hard-won rebirth—could be snuffed out so easily.

'I weren't afraid to die afore. I am now.'

Walter sat beside him. 'You weren't afraid because you'd be with Mary. Now, you got something to lose. Two of.'

'If I wind up beside Mary, will she box my ears for taking up with Laura, even though we was barely two days together?'

'No. She'd be touched you thought enough of her memory to hold back for so long, not wanting to dishonour her. If you'd died that day—not her—and were looking down, would you want her to move on with her life, be happy?'

'Sure. Nobody deserved more on being happy than Mary. She were a light, a burning fire. I wouldn't want her to be dust and black ash, shut away and mourning.'

Walter patted Earl's leg. 'That's a fact. With a heart like she had, she'd hope the same for you. You mourned plenty. And now you're trying to do right by her boy.'

'Best as I can. Do me a favour?'

'Always.'

'Don't revenge me on Dennis. I fear Potter'd kill you as much as me.'

Walter tutted. 'Leave it alone, okay? Besides, he and Dennis aren't so close as they were.'

'Lyle were keen to see me in a box when he called by,' Earl recounted.

'What he wants is someone to do his work—like always. Dennis killed for him before and got no thanks. Potter could afford to fix up the man's porch, but did he?' Walter scoffed. 'Some loyalty, huh?'

'Maybe Potter's better the dead man than Dennis.'

Walter pushed himself to his feet. 'Enough talk about dead men. Not the stuff of birthdays. Nor even the day after.'

Earl heaved a sigh. 'I guess. Sorry for... running out on you. Clean forgot the day.'

'Not a problem. I reckon you had a fine time anyhow.'

'Give over. You was on my case for keeping my lone company these years, so don't you make insinuations 'bout my courting. If it sticks.'

'Ah—so you can be a grouch about even this.'

'Maybe I'm not good enough for her, Walt. I let Mary down, sure I can do it again.'

Walter gently but purposefully took a handful of Earl's shirt. 'Quit on that. Laura puts up with your baloney a damn sight better than I, so that makes her a keeper. Got that?'

'Guess it's true I gotta lot to be happy for—her heart, and beauty, and all.' A smile appeared.

There was warmth on his friend's face. 'Just don't get too damn happy yourself, or you'll be more insufferable than you've been these years.'

Earl winked and gave Walter a heavy slap on the back.

'Constant as the northern star, friend.'

Earl went to complete the renovations. Main Street buzzed with the morning to-and-fro. He identified the foreign sense in his bones—contentment. If Walter approved of his courting, it had to be the right decision.

He saw a familiar figure walking up and paused at the junction with Mountain Avenue.

'Morning.' There was a softness to her demeanour that surpassed anything he'd noticed before. Perhaps it was a little love leaking out?

'Morning, Laura.'

'Shall I bring some lunch over to the Hayes house after school?'

'That'd be mighty kind. Reckon I'll be finished up 'bout then.'

She looked up the street. 'The stage is due later.'

He swallowed. 'So I hope it's been a smooth ride to put the man in good humour.'

'Me too.'

The world fell silent to his ears—a deafening, portentous quiet. He wanted to kiss her but couldn't, not in full view of the town. Instead, he put his fists together, thumbs out, and circled them.

She smiled at his "together" gesture. 'I'll see you later.'

He knew she was trying to wash away his concern by imbuing the day with a sense of normality.

He touched the brim of his hat. 'Don't be bragging on the fine man you caught, you hear?'

She winked. 'Don't put a nail through those fine hands of yours.' She picked up her skirt and breezed away.

He continued his walk, ever more determined to live.

He set to work on the final boards of the porch, taking care of his gaps and levels. During breaks, when he took water, he checked the street for visitors—friendly or unfriendly. Done, he leant on the side of the house and, away from prying eyes, inspected the new pistol.

Should he load it? Would it be a sensible half-measure to aim for the man's gun arm or knee if matters came to it? Was it all moot? He dared not think how slow on the draw he'd be. Dennis Hayes was a good five years older, but the man had surely enjoyed more practice over the intervening years.

He imagined possible scenarios for the confrontation, and then came to a decision. He took another drink, hung the canteen on the porch rail, and then set about trimming the final board. He worked diligently, on haunches at the porch edge, knees in the russet dirt, fine saw burring away.

He leant back and ran a hand over the equal edges.

A pistol cocked.

Chapter 40

Earl's heart galloped.

As he waited for the bullet to hit, he pictured Bill, wanting that to be his last thought. Smart and shaved at Laura's table that day. Running with the newly-fixed wagon. Bearing joyful eyes at the approval of his new courtship.

Earl's mind cycled through hope, then fear. No regret, not now. That wasn't the way to go. Happiness was better. That's how he'd be leaving the world—with love, not guilt, in his heart.

When the pistol hadn't boomed, after five seconds which lasted five years, it was clear that Dennis—if it was him—wasn't cowardly enough to shoot a man whose back was turned.

He carefully set down the saw, rose equally slowly, and faced his nemesis.

Time had lined Dennis Hayes' face more than expected. Perhaps it was the burden of losing the eye. His black hair was grey at the temples, and either drink or home comfort had put pounds on him. Close by, Elizabeth's round face remained inherently kindly, but tension was writ on it now, as her husband stood with his pistol aimed at Earl's chest.

Earl was a right-handed gun, so he kept that hand aloft as he used his left hand to unbuckle and drop his gun belt. Walter had said the new weapon wasn't meant for Dennis, and Earl had gambled further—that an unarmed man was likelier to walk away from this.

Dennis watched the manoeuvre like a buzzard, finger tightly on the trigger.

Earl glanced up and down the street. No friends, no foes, just daily life. Whether or not he'd genuinely been serious about fighting his own battle, that was how it would pass.

'All these years, you staying away made me think you heard me that day,' Dennis said.

'I heard good.'

'So if you're not deaf, that would make you dumb?'

Earl winced—at the first insult, not the second. 'I know what you said, Hayes.'

'I said stay outta town. Now you do worse—you stand on my property.'

'Dennis—look.' Elizabeth pointed at the newly-laid porch floor.

The man only took his eyes off Earl for a second to appease his wife's interjection. Curiosity replaced the annoyance on his face. The gun wavered, and then Dennis regained his composure and levelled it again.

'I take it back. It's madness, not stupidity.'

Earl looked at the woman. 'It'll be safe for you now, Mrs Hayes. Not a rotten board left.'

'Why, Mr Johnson—'

Dennis' left hand snapped up, cutting off his wife's misplaced gratitude. 'Get in the house, Beth.'

A shiver ran down Earl's back. Yet it was hotter than hell inside his shirt.

Her face creased in contentment, big cheeks squashing her eyes. Still, her hand quivered. 'It's a really nice—'

'We've talking to do. Go inside.'

She shook her head. 'Don't be a fool, Den.'

'Only one fool here.' Dennis glared at Earl. 'Go in, Beth. I'll bring the valise presently.'

Elizabeth conceded, trod carefully up the steps, admired the porch as she passed through, and went inside. The door clanged shut as if locking Earl in prison.

Dennis cocked his head. 'Sneaky bastard, aren't you?'

'I lost a good woman, and I reckon a man needs a good woman, especially a man who's hurting.'

Dennis jabbed the gun forward. 'A man blinded—by you. And you've been a walking dead man every day since.'

'You can't know how much it felt like it.'

'Oh, I know enough about being less of a man.'

Earl's arms were tiring already. Sawing and planing were fine, but hands aloft were not in his muscles' lexicon.

'You got a nice place here, Hayes, and nobody deserves injury from a rotten board, least of all a good woman who's stood by a man for a whole lotta years. A good man.'

Dennis snorted. 'Hollow. It's all hollow. Like fixing to get the favour of still breathing by doing a man's chores.'

Earl sighed. 'I reckoned it were worth a try, is all.'

'Why? Why now? Thought I'd have forgotten?'

'Not a piece of it. I did it for my boy.'

Dennis frowned. 'Your dead boy?'

'He ain't dead, Hayes. He's found.'

'Is that so?'

'It is. And it's him I'm here for.'

'How do you figure?'

Earl let his arms fall, but Dennis flicked the gun's unblinking eye, so Earl raised them.

'You got a daughter, and you'd do anything for her, ain't that right? You been upcountry, building a house for her.'

'What of it?'

'So I got a son I thought were dead. And he's deaf, and I brought him here for getting help from Laura Mae. Because an afflicted man needs help—ain't that so?'

'Afflicted by you,' Dennis sniped.

They were still ten feet apart, and Earl had had his fill of spectacle, so he moved closer, as a bullet would reach him at any distance. He'd prepared a few words while working on the porch, based heavily on a narrative Laura had suggested. It was time to throw those last dice.

Dennis gripped the pistol tighter, and his gaze became warier.

Earl kept his tone measured and matter-of-fact. 'I were drunk that night. Weak and hurting. The punch were dumb and wrong, but the table were an *accident*.'

'You think that matters? Result is the same.'

'I do, Hayes. If you shoot me now, it's deliberate and cold, and I reckon cowardly—like whatever I said to you back then. I stayed in town a day and night, and you coulda had your shot, but you didn't. If you wanna revenge on any man for what went on, it should be on Lyle, on account of he put you in that posse and got you all cut up for his own ends. If that hadn't come to pass, there woulda been only one cut-up man in the saloon that night—me, in here.' Earl tapped his chest.

'It still went down.'

'And I had something go down. I lost a boy and a good woman to Mojave. I raised not a finger to revenge on them. Laura neither. Posse took her Jim, and she's walked tall with it. We're both hurting inside. Can't bring back Jim, can't bring back Mary.' He shrugged. 'Can't get back your eye.'

'Maybe I don't want to cork it up inside like you. Maybe I want to let the pain out—by killing you. Like I promised.'

Earl swallowed, puffed out his chest almost defiantly, and thought of Laura. 'So—shoot away. Some folks, I guess, do keep a grudge in their heart. I hope your good lady forgives you what you do.'

'That won't be your concern.' Dennis eyed the house.

'No. I got only one.' His throat was dry now. He loosened his collar.

Dennis angled his head. 'What might that be?'

'Take a minute—after—to talk to my good friend Walt. Only we got some questions.'

'About what?'

'That posse raid.'

'Why would I rake over that old shitshow?' Dennis asked.

'To do right by another man whose senses got took—be it accident or purpose.'

'Your boy?'

'That's so. I wouldn't cross you for anything, Hayes, and I sure as hell wouldn't shoot you in defence of what I done, but I'm here for my boy and the truth of his past. Dumb, you might call it, to risk a bullet for kin, but you risked plenty for that cousin of yours, and what I do it for is a damn sight more upstanding than killing Indians and stealing gold. Hell, if my boy's courting with Sarah Anderson comes to marriage, maybe I'm doing this so's I can build the kid a house, like what you did for that wedded girl of yours.'

He tossed his hands in supplication and resignation, then looked up the street to check for witnesses. Out of Dennis' eye-line, an angel stood rooted to the spot, a lunch basket in one arm, another hand to her mouth. Closer and across the street, another familiar figure covered his gun.

Earl didn't know whether to feel better or worse, more nervous or more empowered. Certainly, he ached for Laura. Her arms, her lips. Hours, days, months and years to be with her.

'Cousin Lyle told me not to spare my bullets this day,' Dennis murmured.

'He would. Me bringing a deaf boy here—one what's saved the Bank, got a fair job and done right by a sweet girl— that's too much for the man. Some folks gotta hate. So, you'd be doing him a favour, I guess. Whatever comes of it for you—losing friends or such like—Lyle won't care.'

Dennis inspected Earl's face and glanced towards the front window where Elizabeth gazed out, then his posture softened, and the gun dipped.

'It could be the case I've had my fill of doing Lyle's bidding. Getting hurt for it and receiving no more cut of gold than any of the dead men. He gave barely fifty dollars towards that house by way of a gift to my girl.'

'That don't surprise one mite.'

Dennis snorted, reflecting. He ignored a couple of neighbours across the way who'd stopped their chores to watch with intent, and instead focused on the man further away.

'I see your friend Walter Doonan there. I'd be right in thinking he has a bullet for me if I kill you straight?'

Earl's organs churned. If he said yes, it would sway Dennis and likely save his life. Still, honesty was best. 'No. He's sworn to talk to you, like I say.'

'So, it's important?'

'I stand here with your gun to my chest. I reckon you can figure it.'

Dennis stroked his beard. 'Hell, I only crossed the states and set axe on a few trees for my daughter. You're figuring to die for your boy.'

Earl hadn't thought of it like that. Anyway, it was too late now.

'That I am, Hayes. So what's your word?' He tensed his stomach—redundant as the gesture would be.

The deathly black eye continued to watch. A tiny muscle spasm in Dennis' hand—deliberate or involuntary—stood between Earl and the hereafter. Such slim margins man had created between life and death. A few grams of metal to summarily dismiss any argument.

He hoped nothing startled Dennis. He swallowed hard and wished it wouldn't be taken as weakness.

Dennis gestured over his shoulder. 'Laura Mae bringing coffee to the working man, is that right?'

'On account of me finishing up here and… her being a good woman I got the honour to court on.'

Dennis' eyebrow lifted. 'So you moved past Mary?'

'Took long enough. Some things gotta rest, though.' He shrugged. 'Can't fix the past. Only make a future.'

Dennis flexed the thumb on his gun hand.

Earl froze. Only his eyeballs moved, noting where Laura remained statuesque.

Dennis released the hammer. The gun lowered.

Earl watched it all the way and willed it to stay down. His muscles locked while the Colt moved to the holster and slid inside. He exhaled hard.

Dennis focussed on Earl's face. 'I can't let you walk away. Folk watching would think me a coward.'

'I deserve what's coming to me.'

'That's right.' Dennis lunged forwards and rammed his fist into Earl's solar plexus. For an older man, he hit hard, and Earl crumpled to the ground. His gut screamed in agony.

Dennis bent down. He spoke low and slow. 'Forgiving ain't forgetting—know that.'

He grabbed Earl's shirt and hauled him up. 'I gotta get the valise in for Beth, get some chow and rest after that ride. My mind ain't fixed to talk to you now. Someday, though.'

Earl coughed. 'Sure,' he wheezed.

'I'd sooner have my eye than a new porch.'

'Goes double here.'

'All the same, man's gotta take his licks.' He drew back his arm and crashed a fist into Earl's face.

Earl clattered into the building's siding, head blazing in pain, and collapsed to the dirt.

Dennis tugged his waistcoat taught, span, yanked up his travel case, mounted the steps and went inside the house.

Chapter 41

Laura had been further away than Walter but reached Earl first. Her skirt flailed, and the basket caroused as she ran. Walter was more measured in his arrival.

Earl's head swam. He swore it was worse than Dennis' punch years before—due to the dulling of his previous inebriation and the increased fragility of his fifth decade.

Laura was talking. All he gleaned was the sentiment. The words were unimportant—she'd be mollifying, concerned and reassuring.

Earl was helped to his feet. He touched his forehead. There was blood. Walter clutched firmly, supporting under one arm. In a discombobulated fit of embarrassment, he shrugged it off and did his best to stand straight. Walter huffed, then mentioned taking care of Earl's tools and gun.

The trio laboured up Mountain Avenue, back down Main Street, and by the time they fetched up at Laura's picket fence, Earl had stopped seeing double, but his head felt like it had been in a vice.

He'd doubtless attracted looks as they made their way, but didn't care. Looks didn't hurt, unlike bullets or fists.

Bill and Sarah weren't inside, and Earl didn't ask about them—it was mercy not to have an audience for his nursing.

Laura eased him into a chair in the living room. He didn't fight it or grouch. Being stubborn now was a dumb man's game, and he'd been keen to tell Dennis that nothing about this endeavour was dumb.

Coffee and a cold compress were brought. While Laura sat close, tending to his wound, Walter disappeared and returned a few minutes later with laudanum.

Earl said nothing, managing only gestures in reply to her gentle enquiries and soothing words. More than once—when Walter was absent—her lips brushed his. That alone made being alive a handsome reward for the altercation with Dennis.

Soon after, an unfamiliar desire to sleep overtook him, and he acceded to it.

The smell of dinner woke him. His bones were stiff, though his fuzzy head only grumbled. He touched his cheek—it was tender and cut.

Bill appeared in his field of view. "Pa?"

He dredged up a response on his fingers. "Son. I am fine. Are you?"

Bill frowned. "Yes, of course." He put a hand on his father's shoulder.

"Good." Earl sat up straight.

Sarah, across the room, stopped sewing. "Ma said you were hit."

"That's true."

"Why?"

How to answer this? "Later," he signed, waving in dismissal.

He gingerly stood. When he was still upright after a few seconds, he took that as his body's approval to go to the kitchen.

Laura stepped from the stove, softly touched his uninjured cheek and fixed caring eyes on him.

'What did you tell the youngs?' he asked.

'That you got into a fight. A quick one which wasn't your fault.'

'That's half fair.'

She caressed his hand. 'I won't need to lay flowers for you, Earl. The cut will heal a lot faster than my heart would have.'

'Building the porch were your idea. You did this. Saved me.' Gratitude and desire welled up.

'Yes. But the words were yours, and whatever they were, they prevented a bullet.'

'The man is just smart enough, is all. And you and Walt being on the street, I reckon that didn't hurt neither. Maybe you being a friend to Elizabeth stopped the man doing wrong by you.'

'He knew we were courting?'

'I'll tell any man what'll ask and any that don't. When a woman saves a man's tempers, then heart, then life, he'd be a stone fool not to be proud as punch to brag on it.'

She kissed his cut cheek. 'That's sweet. Now, I assume you'll stay for dinner?'

'I'm not minded to go to the saloon. Potter'll be spitting blood that I ain't a customer for the undertaker and his boy Tom what works there.'

'You need to rest. Did you make arrangements to speak to Dennis? Assuming he didn't give you the chapter while he had a gun at your chest?'

'I'll see him soon as he's minded. I'll tell Bill not to look the wrong way at Dennis for hitting me. I got what were coming, and it's to be left alone.'

'One night in the cell, and you've put your soul on trial for years. For what? Something lesser men do every week—those not knocked six ways from Sunday because they've lost a wife and child. One night of weakness doesn't make you a weak man, Earl. It only makes you human.'

'All the same, I'd sooner it hadn't gone along.'

'So do I, but then we might never have met.' She smiled.

He mulled that. 'I guess. I guess a man's deeds make him and where his life goes.'

'It's brought you here. Only you can judge whether that's a good or bad thing.'

'Here—is a good thing. All that afore, not so much.'

'I agree.'

A moment's silence fell.

'Walt was done watching me decorate that chair, I guess.'

'He thought you better off in the hands of a lady.'

Earl embraced her waist. 'Even better off in the arms.'

Chapter 42

Earl slept until late at the Hotel and arrived at Laura's around ten o'clock the following day. The place was empty; she at school, the youngsters up at the stables, or perhaps Sarah out on howdies with customers.

The burden lifted from Earl was significant, but there were still many matters to figure out. How would he balance spending time at home, at his trade, and seeing enough of his belle? He had to work to be able to provide for her and earn her courting. He also had to learn how to pass the time in White Rock while staying out of trouble. Making peace with Dennis meant only fewer potential aggressors towards him and Bill.

He brewed coffee, checked the gun drawer out of curiosity—the weapon lay there—and chewed through a couple of biscuits. Still, despite the absence of concern, it was odd to be alone in a house that wasn't his own.

There was a rap on the door.

In the hours and days that followed, he wished he'd had the sense of mind to stand still and let the visitor move on. After all, he couldn't be the person the caller sought.

On the porch, the leftmost face was Walter's. The next was Sheriff Bowman. The other three he didn't recognise from a hole in the ground: they were all younger than he, bristled but not bearded, and deadly serious.

His hand came to his waist, but he'd hung up the belt in the hallway.

Walter held out a cautioning hand, more against temper than bullets. His face was unusually direct.

'Earl.' Bowman had hands on hips, his belly straining at the belt.

'Sam.'

He didn't like it: this wasn't a belated birthday drinking invitation from well-meaning strangers, nor a welcoming committee.

Walter, ever the peacemaker, spoke up. 'Buddy, these are three deputised men from Clark County. They're looking for a young man with crimes to his name.'

Earl went rigid—everything except his heart and mind, which competed for the honours of fastest runaway.

'What of it?' he managed tersely, throat dry.

'Show him, gentlemen,' Bowman said.

The man in the middle of the three, the tallest and with a scar on his cheek between nose and mouth, held out a piece of off-white paper.

The legend read, "WANTED. For Rape, Murder and Property Violation. REWARD $1000." In the centre was a picture.

Earl tried to deny it with every fibre of his being, but it unquestionably bore a fair resemblance to Bill.

He clutched the door, steadying himself. 'That ain't my boy,' he said through gritted teeth.

'These men say the suspect is a deaf kid,' Bowman replied.

'Suddenly, there's only one in the whole state?'

'You have to admit the likeness.'

Earl shook his head. 'I ain't admitting nothing, and it ain't my place to.'

'Where is he?' the tall man asked.

'I got no clue. Who're you to ask anyhow?'

Bowman edged forwards. 'Wade Baskin, Gabe Evans, Corey Harman. I checked with Sheriff Everett at Four Pines. It's all legit.'

Earl eyed them suspiciously, then snatched the paper from the man's grasp. 'Gimme look at that.'

'I wouldn't fight this,' Walter cautioned.

'There's only a fight if there's cause to. There ain't. My boy did none of this.'

'It was two years ago.'

'Two years?' Earl looked at the three alleged deputies. 'Don't say much for your finding of men, do it?'

Inside, a tussle raged between the part of him which didn't believe a word of it and the part which sought a solution.

The right-hand man—Corey Harman—lunged forward, but the centre man tugged him back. 'We only been on the trail six weeks. But we got a tip there's a deaf boy in town.'

Earl glanced at Walter. 'No guesses who from,' he sneered.

Bowman spoke up. 'This is no lynch mob. The kid will get a fair hearing from me.' He lowered his voice. 'But it doesn't look good.'

'What says a deaf man done these things? Bill looks no worse than you or I or these fellers to pass on the street.' He slapped the paper. 'And Bill's nose ain't like that.' It was like Mary's—distinctive but just right.

'Listen, there's a girl in the whorehouse at Four Pines who says Bill was there. A man too vouches—he didn't speak up before due to not wanting to… admit he was on the property.'

'It was a whore got killed,' the tall man, Gabe Evans, added.

Earl's heart pounded. The details were irrelevant—a man, woman, lawman, jeweller, senator, vagrant or whore—murder was still murder. Unless it was self-defence. Bill had endured more than his fair share of insults—White Rock alone proved that.

Would the boy have gone that far without his Mojave upbringing? Earl wished he'd been there to raise Bill. Even more now, he despised the impact of his absence and actions.

'And this property issue?'

'A gate got opened up on a ranch north of the town. Horse got taken. A hundred head of cattle escaped. They were rustled before the owner got to round them.' Bowman looked at Earl directly. 'And, no, the owner didn't leave the gate open. No man with livelihood in stock would, isn't that so, Walter?'

'I guess it is.'

'Real grateful for your support,' Earl snipped.

Bowman put hands on hips. 'So, as it stands, you harbouring him would make you accessory. Where is he?'

'Sam, on my heart, I dunno. Guess the stables or maybe out riding.'

'Well, you know the score. He's to report—'

'Sheriff,' Walter cut in, indicating away to the street.

Bill was walking up. Earl's spirits fell, ready for a knife to the heart, the unpicking of everything he'd done.

Bill's face filled with curiosity as he opened the gate and came up the front walk. The quartet of lawmen parted like the Red Sea, watching the boy with suspicion.

"What's up?" he signed.

"Men to see you," Earl fumbled. His signing remained patchy, and he kept words to a minimum.

'No funny business,' Bowman cautioned.

Earl looked daggers. 'It's all I can do to have civil conversation with my boy. Funny business ain't reached Laura's lessons yet.' He faced Bill. "They say you are Wanted." He gestured tersely for the paper and held it out for Bill to see.

Bill looked at the flyer, the men, then at Earl. Fear blossomed on his face.

Earl laid a comforting hand on the boy's shoulder, dearly wishing someone would lay their hand on his—because he was fraying at the edges, rankled and despairing. He prayed that Bill's reaction was worry about a false accusation, not guilt.

He didn't want to sign the following phrase but had no choice. "Did you do these things?"

Bill's fingers quivered. "Some."

'Lord in heaven.' Earl's heart turned to stone.

'He admits it?' Bowman asked.

'He says "some".'

'So say you,' Evans sniped. He addressed the Sheriff. 'Earl can make the boy say whatever he wants. All this heathen hand talk is a smokescreen, or they can make it that way.'

'Then why did the boy—or Earl—not turn it down flat?' Bowman asked.

Earl saw an inkling that Sam wasn't immovable in his attitude. There was a glimmer of hope that Lyle's sidekick could be swayed by reason and decent morals.

Evans opened and closed his mouth; his objection was shot down.

'Some?' Bowman asked Earl.

"Explain," he signed to Bill.

After a hesitation, the agitated boy's hands set off at an incredible pace, and within moments Earl lost touch. Bill could have been describing his first horse or recounting his ambush: Earl simply wasn't equipped to translate, let alone follow. Even when he gestured for Bill to stop, he had to take the boy's hands and physically calm them.

However torn up inside Earl was, Bill was suffering more.

'Sam,' Earl said, forcing a calm tone. 'My signing ain't so good. We need a straight story. I ain't shirking that. We gotta hang fire until Laura's back. She can talk to the boy.'

'Sheriff, this isn't right,' Evans said.

Bowman mollified him. 'It's been two years. Nobody here's evading the law. I want justice as much as you. Hell, I don't want a criminal in our town, deaf or not. But we need the full story, not a patchwork blanket from Earl.' He tugged out a pocket watch. 'Laura finishes at the schoolhouse in two hours.' He looked at Earl. 'We'll come back.'

'Sheriff—' the last man began.

'Wade, quiet yourself. We'll get the boy, sure on that. He'll confess his deeds. There's guilt on him as large as a bull. Come for a drink. Then we'll head back and get words, not hands.'

Earl wanted to lay Bowman out for his tone but had another battle to fight.

'Don't go anywhere.' The Sheriff looked sternly at Bill, then led the men away.

"What's happening?" Bill asked.

"They come back later. You tell Laura."

Bill's face fell. He made a fist and circled it on his chest.

Earl remained immune to it. Apologies were no good. He needed a miracle, and soon—before he detonated with rage.

The kid's past had destroyed their future.

Chapter 43

Every minute while they waited for Laura to arrive, Earl churned with worry and disappointment, mainly at Bill but also at himself and Walter.

As a distraction, he tinkled on the piano. Bill paced and bit his nails. Walter made coffee.

They'd played Good Samaritan but seemingly given succour to a bad seed. He strained at the leash to give Walter a piece of his mind—a vast chunk of it—but had to hold fire until the whole story was out: Bowman could have fabricated the entire affair, likely on Potter's say. Sam wasn't a bad guy, but he kept poor company.

Walter came to the piano, mercifully about another matter. 'Your head okay?'

'It'll heal. I said I didn't need you to back me up against Dennis.'

'Sure, but I reckoned what if I don't back you up, and something happens. If I'm not there when I should, I'll wind up like you've been—and I didn't want that.'

Earl reflected. 'I guess I wouldn't wish that on nobody.'

The front door thunked, and Laura and Sarah entered.

'Hey.' She pulled off her cape, came over and offered a kiss.

Embarrassed in front of Walter, Earl let her lips slide onto his cheek.

She looked at the three men, her face serious. 'What's the matter?'

'Deputies in town. They reckon Bill here is… accused of crimes.'

She flinched, and peered at Bill with suspicion and curiosity. 'Tell me more.'

'That's the problem,' Walter interjected. 'We can't get Bill's story without you. He tried to explain, but good as your teaching is, your beau's no expert.' He sighed. 'And you know Sam, he'll call foul anyway, given a chance, on evading the law by false translation.'

'What did Bill do?' she murmured.

'Theft, rape… murder. So says Sam.' Earl swallowed hard, hating the sensation of those words leaving his mouth. For the first time in so long, he craved a drink and to hell with the consequences.

Her eyes widened. 'Lord in heaven.'

'I beg you ask. He denies some, is all I know. Sooner the story, sooner the fix.'

Sarah signed to her mother, who responded. Sarah's hand came to her mouth, and she stepped away from Bill. He reached out as if begging for forgiveness. She sank into a chair and clutched herself.

Laura interrupted the exchange, faced Bill and began the interrogation.

Bill's hands moved faster, more staccato, as the pressure of his defence took its toll. Equally, Laura's cool evaporated, her expression intensifying. Without warning, Bill flung down his hands and barged out of the room.

Earl made to follow—more angry than concerned—but Walter tugged his shirt and held him back.

'Get your hands off me.'

'Leave the boy alone,' Walter cautioned.

The front door slammed. Laura jolted.

'On account of you know a hell of a lot 'bout parenting?' Earl sniped.

'Walter, Earl! There's a young woman in the room. I'll have no brawling in my house.' Laura shot Earl a warning glance.

He puffed a heavy breath. 'What gives?'

She patted her hair, calming herself. 'He says he's not responsible for the murder. He was in Four Pines at the time, two years ago.' She sank into a chair. 'He admits visiting a whore, but denies relations.' She blushed faintly.

'Dirty—' Earl bottled his ire but made a fist.

'The gate? The horse?' Walter asked.

She nodded. 'He got picked on, taunted. He knew the man and wanted revenge. He'd had his horse taken. So he went to the ranch during the night and let the steers out.'

Earl pounded that fist into his palm. 'I knew he were a bad kid, Walt. I warned you!'

'Let's calm down now,' Laura said.

'Good for you to say. Yours ain't the kid riding around the state a wanted man.'

She recoiled. 'You act like you believe Sam Bowman!'

'I dunno what to believe, but I gotta take accusations serious, not knowing the boy and how he carried on these years. The kid stole—said it hisself, hid it from us. What else has he got?'

'This is your son!'

'Son or no, I don't defend murderers and thieves.'

On her feet in a flash, Laura jammed her hands on her hips. 'Earl Johnson, I don't know you right now.'

He banged the piano lid.

Sarah jumped, fear in her eyes, able to sense the confrontation in the room. She glanced at them all, picked up her skirt and darted out.

'Now look what you've done!' Laura snapped.

'I did nothing except pick up a lying thief of a boy, and he's lucky he ran out afore I wrung his damn neck.'

'Watch your tone, Earl,' Walter cautioned.

'Take a hike. You ain't helping none.'

The front door slammed. Laura dashed out of the room.

'You stupid ass,' Walter grumbled.

'I don't need your self-righteousness.' Earl caught his breath, paced, and tried to slow his racing heart.

Laura's voice carried from the hallway. 'Lord in heaven!'

Earl bundled past Walter to investigate.

She shook the biscuit barrel. 'Now look! My daughter's run out with a gun in her hand!'

'We was only doing the best for the kid,' Earl protested. 'Fetching him to someone who understood him.'

'And how's that worked out?' she demanded. 'Showed an innocent girl how to shoot a gun, and now what? Last time it was only a pail on Tom Potter's head. If she comes up against trouble—against a hearing person who can't sign, can't explain—someone who's a threat, what then?'

Earl jabbed a finger. 'I warned you, Walt, didn't I warn you? I told you cripples was bad. Always are.'

Laura went off like a firework. 'What?!'

Earl's stomach imploded, recognising the inference. 'I weren't meaning—'

'That's not what I heard. Bill and Sarah are the same. The same! And now they've run off.' She locked a stare on him. 'Which in my book makes him your son because running off is what you do very well.'

He didn't know whether to destroy the piano, bawl to the heavens, or sock her in the mouth. He chose an easier target. 'This is on you, Walt. This is your doing.'

'I'm not his father. None of us is guardians of his past.'

'And we wouldn't be neither. All the crimes would be out there,' he pointed, 'With him on the dirt. Why'd you have to pick him up?'

Walter faced him, nostrils flaring. 'Because I looked after another no-good kid once, to try and make him right. Give him a chance, a future. And he used to be my friend.'

He spun, strode out, and the front door clattered.

Earl leant heavily on the piano—a shell of a man with a shattered heart which unaccountably still rattled in his crushed ribcage.

Laura stood her ground. Her chest heaved. Their eyes locked. Love was temporarily absent from hers.

She set her tone firm, the teacher issuing an explicit instruction—unemotional and uncompromising.

'I'll make this easy. Get out. Get out and don't come back without my daughter.'

Chapter 44

He left Laura's house in a daze. He stood at the gate, leaning on the post for support as if weak from blood loss—his heart pierced and leaking into the dirt. He gazed across the buildings, trying to spot Sarah and Bill, standing large as life and making the quest laughably easy. Yet he wasn't seeing, only looking, as if in a trance. He had no idea where to start and hesitated to do so in case his search was in vain.

Nobody had died, Earl set as his mantra as he marched up Main Street. Nobody had died—not like before when his world had collapsed, and life felt a pointless endeavour.

The possibility of losing a son for the second time and causing the loss of an innocent girl—shattering apart two families—struck him rigid.

The sledgehammer gut-punch took him back…

He crested the rise a mile from the old house. A wisp of smoke rose—black, not homely. Instantly his throat tightened. He spurred the horse on, bile churning in his gut as he prayed it was only a bush fire, but as he grew nearer, the hope vanished.

The roof timbers were aflame.

He dismounted in motion, stumbling under legs weakened by distress. He yelled as he ran, calling out Mary's name in despair, hoping she'd managed to hide before the raiders got close. He strained his ears above the fire's crackle, desperate for baby Alden's howl.

Then he was in the house. In subsequent years, he didn't recall what pushed him to such danger, how his life was so expendable in the pursuit of those he loved. Smoke from the thatched roof and burning furniture suffocated his lungs and strangled his desperate cries. He fought through the small property, retreating only when an ember caught his sleeve and threatened to torch him. He burst into the clear air, tore off his shirt, hacked up smoky breath and wiped his streaming tear ducts.

Only when he'd collapsed to the dirt, coughing and retching, hopelessness pumping tears from his eyes, did he regain some semblance of voice and used it again to call for his family…

He shook away the daydream.

There was equally little point calling out now.

This time, he had a choice. He had an opportunity to rescue the situation, minimise damage and stop a tragedy. He could do what he hadn't—couldn't have—done before.

He could search.

The prairie was no smaller now, only much less dangerous. The marauding Mojave were gone. He had no enemies to encounter in search of his boy. There would be no peace to broker, no bargain necessary. All he needed was a strong will and a clear mind.

He needed to channel love. Love and determination that the embers of accusation should not catch alight and burn down an emotional household. And, if he didn't find the youngsters, he'd again wish to be dead. Dead, having avoided death and embraced new life.

There was no sign of them in town—as he'd fully expected—so he pelted, breathless, to the stables, the first sensible calling point.

Bill wanted a sanctuary. A safe place to examine, wallow, and rail—assuming the kid worked the same way Earl did. Whilst they were blood, Bill had no point of reference. A biological parent, but not a father. Earl half-hoped the kid was nothing like him: Bill behaved much better in many ways. Yet the echoes said it wasn't the case.

He didn't call out when he reached the stables, as that would be weak, desperate, and betray his fragility.

Abe was there, inexplicably saddling Jack.

Was Earl in so much of a daze—the lack of air to his brain from all the panic and running?

'What gives?'

Abe tightened the girth. 'I figured you'd need your horse.'

The penny clanged down like a church bell on Christmas. 'Abe, you're some piece of work.'

'I like the kid, Earl. Doesn't mean he's perfect.'

'He come here? Where'd he go?'

'I didn't see him, but Tanner is gone. Then Sarah came. Then Walter.'

'You ask Sarah? Was she crying?'

'No, but pretty cut up. She wanted my advice. She expected him to be here—like you, I guess—up in the loft, hiding from whatever. The law, she said.'

Earl nodded. 'Yeah. Bill's in for it, some ways. Deputies reckon he done crimes.'

'And did he?'

'Search me. Either he's run scared from a leathering from me or for bad deeds. Both ways, Sarah running too is a real fix.'

'She sure wanted to go find him. I said, "you don't have to love him enough to be his wife, only enough to care about saving his life". She thought some. Maybe she had an idea.'

'But didn't say?'

Abe shook his head sadly. 'No, but she cut off like bricks. So all this is what I told Walter.'

'He took off too?'

'Only back to town. If the kids weren't here, I guess Laura needs comfort. I'd go, but Walter said thank you, no. Said I'm best here in case they come back.'

'Or stall those three deputies if they look to ride out.' Earl stepped closer, conspiratorial. 'Maybe lose some tack, argue on monies and such.'

'I can't stand against the law.'

'It's lies—or some is.' He scratched his head. 'Or I gotta tell myself such.'

'A boy's gotta learn from his mistakes, be he still a boy or a man. Own up to truths, stand up to lies.'

Earl nodded. 'And he will, on my soul. Less he's gone.'

'So don't waste a minute.' Abe eyed the leaden sky. 'Rain by dusk, mark my words.'

Earl put a boot in the stirrup. Water sloshed in the canteen as his knee knocked it.

'You packing me up as well?'

'On Sarah's account, not yours. She's no water nor bedroll. Either she finds Bill, or you find her, or it'll be a hard night for a young woman.'

Earl's heart fell further. He didn't even want to mention the gun, which put the youngsters at greater risk.

'So, no more minutes on lecturing, all due respect. I'll take prayers and luck.' He eased into the saddle.

'Then take them.' Abe patted Jack's haunches.

Earl nudged the horse into a walk, feeling twice his weight but knowing the horse couldn't sense the insubstantiality of obligation.

Quickly he passed the town boundary, cantering undirected. He sought a destination, anything better than aimless wandering, relying on hope and luck over planning.

He went first to the hillside where he and Laura had picnicked. It was a lame guess but one of the few landmarks that might be familiar to Bill. Sarah knew the place, and maybe the two of them had spoken about it or even visited.

As he approached, he scanned the area for roped horses but found none. Similarly, the hilltop was empty. Only the wind whistled, strong from the west, where the nascent storm was blowing in. A thick cloud was drenching a rocky outcrop a few miles away.

For a few seconds, he remembered Laura's kiss, and it flooded his insides like the finest whiskey, spurring him. He tugged Jack around and set off towards the copse at Andrews Creek, where they'd stayed that first night.

The charred remnants of their camp were his only find.

He let Jack drink from the creek and took water and biscuits himself, trying to fuel his brain for inspiration.

If only he'd spent more time with Bill and Sarah. Learned to sign earlier or faster. Asked more questions. Cared. Except these were just the tip of the "if onlys".

Past is past, and future is future—that's what Laura had said.

He mounted swiftly and set off for his last, desperate option.

Chapter 45

Laura cried.

She could have fought it but didn't. She allowed herself to be weak—not because nobody was there to witness her perennial strength evaporate, not that she could selfishly get away with the crime of being vulnerable, but because it was the right thing to do.

The easy option would be to gird herself—as she'd done against prejudice, misunderstanding and ostracism—and keep everything inside, festering like a boil. Her daughter and friends might assume she'd got over the whole episode— when it ended—and have a fulsome heart, free of nagging resentment.

She needed to let despair out so it didn't explode later, disproportionately, and destroy one or more relationships.

She sat in her favourite chair and let the tears flow. It wasn't for what was lost—she hadn't given up—but for what she might lose, even if Sarah and Bill returned. A crack had opened up in the crust of her world, and she feared something insubstantial would fall in. Tendrils of disharmony, distrust and recrimination reached up from the void and sought to pull her, or those she cared about, into a one-way trip beyond redemption.

In truth, that shock had spoken many of the words which issued from all their mouths in the last hour.

Children have tempers and run away, even when children are no longer young.

The taking of the gun spooked her the most. Other than that, it might have been sweet—Sarah running off to check her beau was safe. But, undeniably, he'd put the gun in her hand, and Earl had put the boy in her house. It was cause and effect.

She pulled a handkerchief from her cuff. Sarah's yellow stitching was tiny and perfect. She dried her eyes until the material took no more moisture. It was essential to find perspective. Cause and effect were unending and unprovable. The men had brought Bill here because Sarah was deaf, and Laura signed. Perhaps her deafness was the cause. Or her birth. Or even Laura's marriage.

The root cause was undefinable and couldn't be changed—so it merited little thought. She'd been judgemental. Earl had acted similarly, and she'd told him to get over it. He'd been mourning a son who was still alive. She must not think the worst.

The tears stopped.

She went to the bedroom and checked her face in the mirror. She dabbed makeup to cover the redness around her eyes.

It was silly to be sad. She had a man who loved her and a boy who loved her daughter. So much was good about this whole situation: today's events were merely a bump in the road. All lives and relationships had them.

She clenched a fist, forcing this truth to swamp her.

She smoothed the bed blanket and wished for company and support. She visualised the town sprawl and its position in the landscape. She tried to picture Sarah, aiming—laughably—to connect with her on some level, to visualise where she might be.

But she came up empty, so she knelt, put elbows on the edge of the bed, palms together, and prayed.

There came a knock at the front door. She hastily ended her supplication, rechecked herself in the mirror, and went to face the inquisition.

Mercifully, there was none. Only Walter, hat held deferentially across his belly, neutral expression on his careworn face.

Behind him, the sky churned, stormy and portentous.

'Laura Mae.'

She cocked her head. 'Are we at loggerheads?'

'I caught a lotta bad words before—said a few too. Though, I don't know what good apologising does. It doesn't bring young people home.'

'That's true. So… was this for an apology anyway? I won't refuse one, but I won't ask for one. Nobody made deliberate hurt on anyone else.'

'Reckon so. I wanted to call back to say I checked all over town and spoke to Abe and….' He lowered his head and sighed. 'Bill done rode off. Sarah too. Place not to be known.'

She closed her eyes, forcing down the hurt. When she opened them, Walter's face was brimmed with concern and empathy.

'Would you… would you come in?' she said.

'I figured we weren't welcome no more, after bringing an outlaw to cut up your home.'

'If you or Earl missed the boy's true character, I'm in no position to hold a grudge against you because I'm as guilty. You didn't cause this. You did a good deed—so I should. Come in. The answer to this isn't throwing away our friendship. It's using it for the good of the situation.'

He nodded. 'If Sarah has half your wisdom and heart, we'll have a good situation by day's end.'

They stood in the kitchen, watching the coffee pot. Numbness lifted from her, yet the house felt disproportionally empty, as if walked by two ghosts.

'I don't mean for telling you how to live your life, Laura, but I'd gladly give up our years if you'd forgive Earl. The man's a lot more to lose with you than I do.'

'That's very sweet.' She filled the cups.

'He musta done something right to turn your head after all these years.'

'It's not for pity, Walter. I won't court or marry for the sake of not being alone, but if I wanted not to be alone, it would be with Earl. None of us is perfect.' She sighed. 'He has a cloud across his heart—that much is clear.'

'No. A thunderstorm. But you're the sun.'

That brightened her. 'The world is full of light. Only people, luckily few, are dark.'

He stroked the worktop. 'I guess it's not easy when it's your pa.'

She let the mug rest on the table. It was spotlessly clean, where she'd been earnestly doing chores to take her mind off the problem.

'Earl's father?'

He nodded. 'Long time ago. Name of Charlie. He was a carpenter, like Earl. For some crazy reason, he got a fight picked in a bar. Over nothing—looking a moment too long at a woman, Earl reckons. He was good with his hands but a slow draw, so his hand got shot up pretty bad. By luck, the other feller didn't shoot for killing, only warning. But Charlie couldn't work now, not doing what he wanted, and that tore him up. Real bad. He took to drinking. Got called a cripple.'

Walter shook his head. 'He wasn't a father no more, nor a husband. He hit her—Ma Johnson. She'd done nothing, but he'd gone all to pieces. Objected to having to provide for a boy, not being able to.' He drained the mug. 'So Earl saw. He was a kid. They see everything. And he was done with it, so he ran.'

'My God,' she breathed. Wisps of cloud passed across her heart. 'Ran where?'

'One morning, I found him in my barn. I only had a few years on him, but I'd been a working man since fourteen. Grows you up.'

'And you took Earl in?'

'Bed and board. Real grum he was. Got him working. Made a man of him, best I could. Wouldn't carry a gun, though, because guns make damaged men, and damaged men are no good.'

'Like Bill,' she murmured.

He shook his head. 'Bill's not the same. He's nobody to rail against for how he is. Only those who can't see inside a person. See beyond what a person can't do, to what they can.'

'You can't let go, can you? Of Earl?'

'Maybe without a kid of my own, I gotta look after someone, and Lord knows there's been days he needed a friend.' He smiled weakly. 'Weeks. Years.'

'You mended him twice. At the start. Then after Mary....' She hung her head, forlorn for the man she cared deeply about.

'Guess I did. Much as you took him still not fixed.'

'You think I can fix him all the way?' She poured more coffee.

'I reckon he wants you to, 'stead of me. I did my best these years, but your goodness has broken him like a steer. Maybe this time, he's no space in his heart for guilt. Reckon you've gotten inside and pushed it to overflow and fill with something better.' He toyed with the mug. 'Love can come again, most times.'

She heard introspection in his tone. 'Most?'

He sipped, searching her face as if for a signal to proceed.

'I was sixteen with Lily. Then seventeen. That's all it took, and we were to jump the broom. I can't think two people ever more put on this earth to be together.'

His face aged five years in moments, bearing the weight of history. 'She got sick and died.'

He puffed a heavy breath. 'So that was the end. There'd be nobody else. No way there could be. I'd be doing wrong by another woman every day, knowing she wasn't Lily. But that's me, what I choose to do. Earl doesn't know, and I won't ever tell because I never wanted him to believe Mary was meant the same way for him, not when they were together, not when she was gone.'

Her eyes creased in sadness. 'My word is my bond.'

'Call me crazy for closing up my heart and telling him to open his, for all the good it did the stubborn fool.' He gave a maudlin chuckle.

'But he has, and to the person whose door you came to on an errand of mercy.' She picked at a fingernail. 'You regret closing your heart? Perhaps you should take your own advice. Earl's proven that there are second chances.'

'I guess. But the Lord doesn't make circumstance easy.'

'I think the Lord decided long ago that neither Earl's nor my circumstance should ever be easy.'

'Let's hope this isn't a test to match what's gone before—for either of you.'

She laid a hand on his arm. 'The difference is that we fought those battles alone. This time we can do it together.'

Chapter 46

Earl wanted to build a fire, but it wasn't an intense enough distraction or release. The ride had caused too much delay anyhow, with pressure in his skull building like a steam boiler. As he had charged to the destination, he knew there would be release, whether through success or failure.

As he approached his house, its environs bereft of life, he momentarily considered it a blessing—for Bill. He would have irrevocably damaged their relationship by lashing out angrily at the boy. Maybe not a straight-out punch, but certainly a detonation disproportionate to circumstance.

Still, the boiler *would* blow.

He dismounted and went straight to the workshop. He heaved all the uncut wood from the shelves and thundered it to the floor. It bounced and nipped at his ankles, laying bruises.

He took the basket of small offcuts, darted out and threw the ensemble at the outside wall. The cacophony rattled like gunfire. He picked up the nearest shrapnel and bowled it back against the wall, then again with another, and again, over and over until it made no difference to his mood.

So he went back into the workshop and saw the defunct angel cross he'd rescued from Bill's grave. He snatched it up, dashed out and lobbed it at the wall. With a crack, the tapering leg splintered away, missing him by inches. He cursed, picked up the remainder and hurled it again with greater force.

When it didn't break, he grabbed a hand axe and scooped the offending article from the ground. He took it to a chopping log and set about it with gusto, his teeth clenched as he tried to shatter his handiwork into molecules.

Movement flashed in his peripheral vision. He left the axe aloft, mid-strike. Perspiration tickled his upper lip. His chest heaved.

A rider was silhouetted against the sky, approaching at a trot.

Earl let the axe fall, shifted it to his left hand, and covered the butt of his pistol. Soon, his hand relaxed, but his mood didn't quiet.

'I weren't running, Walt,' he rapped. 'I reckoned he might be here.'

'Whatever you gotta tell yourself.'

'A kid like that is no son to me. I got no defence to the actions of a boy I don't know. Thieving and murdering, then running off all yellow. I seen an afflicted man think he's above the law. I seen that already.'

Earl's eyes begged Walter to see through his lens of experience.

Walter threw his arms up. 'So that's it? You give up on Bill? How about I'd seen you in the barn that day and reckoned, "Nah, the kid'll probably work out fine without my help". How about that, huh?'

His voice was louder now. 'How do you think I'd feel, going on with my life?' He disdainfully looked Earl up and down. 'And for all I tried, what did I get? One ungrateful, mistrustful asshole. Should have saved myself the years. I wish I'd let you drink or fight yourself to death.'

Earl held the axe out straight. 'You shut your hole. I'm done with your preaching and your knowing-better words from a man who never had a kid, let alone one such as Bill.'

Walter scanned the shards of immaculately carved wood.

'The damn stupidity. You—a boy who ran because he couldn't be cared for. And I find you here—cowering again from facing up to situations. You keep running, Earl, one day you'll run off a cliff.'

Earl stepped in, heart racing, skin prickling. 'You shut your damn hole. I ain't no kid.'

'No. That kid of yours has more balls than you'll ever have.' Walter turned away.

Earl dropped the axe, grabbed the man's shoulder, yanked him around and laid in with his fist.

Walter dodged just in time. The blow missed him by inches, and he brought his fist hard into Earl's belly.

The shock and pain radiated through Earl like lightning, costing what felt like hours before he lashed out again, altering his aim at the last moment to catch Walter's jaw. Agony seared through his knuckles. He held in a howl.

Walter reeled, feinted with his left and crashed his hand across the side of Earl's temple. Dennis' cut reopened.

Earl stumbled and went down. His ass smacked hard into the earth, and he jammed out both hands to stop himself from going out flat. A few feet away lay the axe. He roll-scrambled to it, snatched it up, found his target and prepared to throw.

Walter's gun was out of its holster before Earl's arm was fully back. He cocked the trigger.

Earl stared down the unblinking eye. Pain crackled in his hand, fighting the grip on the axe. His body quivered, self-hate coursing through every fibre.

'Do it, Walt. Do it now. Leave me for dead. I got nothing.'

The man moved closer, gun unwavering and arrowed at his friend's head. He knelt at Earl's side and brought the barrel within a foot of his face.

'Your eyes look open, but they're closed. You see like a blind man. Or hear like a deaf boy—one or other.'

'I see good.' He held his voice steady despite his innards convulsing.

Walter shook his head. 'Your eyes lie. It's not a want for death in there. It's fear because you got things to lose now. You say you want to die, huh? It would have only hurt me before. Think who it hurts now, you selfish ass.' He spat on the ground.

Earl's gaze flitted between the gun barrel and Walter's hard-set face. The hammer remained cocked. What a way to go: a bad twitch of the finger again, but not from an enemy. What a waste that would be.

'You ain't shootin', are you?' His voice squeezed through a constricted throat.

Walter clicked the hammer back to rest. Earl's bowels exhaled.

Walter holstered the gun, rubbed his jaw and winced.

'I could never do it. Not only now, when you got the love of two new people. Any day, because a man needs a friend. So you can stay here, lose your boy and your courting girl, and waste all what we worked for. You want to break all that like you broke these things?' Walter tossed a hand at the splintered wood, then jabbed a finger at his friend. 'Or you want to be smart?'

The keening breeze flicked up dust around Earl's prone body. He let the axe fall mercifully from his grasp.

Walter offered his hand.

Earl took it, and they stood. He touched his forehead and found blood. It hurt like the dickens. It wasn't the first injury he'd taken in past days—and both had the same cause: love, weakness and self-hate.

He scanned the mess of wooden shrapnel and picked up a slice of planed face which read "ARLE". He fingered the name.

'I near took a bullet for my boy. I got hit for penance. I made peace. And Bill? The boy lived without a place afore, and a girl by his side and the law on his tail is reason enough to leave behind this sorry asshole. They're gone, Walt. Eloped, I reckon. Don't you see?' He tossed the wood aside. 'He ran 'cos he don't want me.'

'Maybe he was ashamed of letting you down. Show you forgive him. Now, when he needs you most. You risked death to help him—like you said. What's a little rain now?'

Earl sank to the smoothly-worn log. 'I'm the one what did the letting down. Being away that day made him the kid he is.'

Walter sat on their friendship seat. 'This isn't about the past. It's about now. You listened to me for thirty years. You stayed by my side 'cos you needed to lean. If you want out of this, it's now or never—or those years mean nothing.'

He clasped Earl's arm, and his gaze pierced his friend's soul. 'We gotta try.'

'How?'

'Back to White Rock. Get some ideas. Maybe say a prayer. If Bill isn't fixed on staying running, there's a chance. I don't have the strength I had to save you again. My days of carrying you are done. You've two folks to give and get love from. It's your choice: them or nobody.'

Earl shook his head. 'I reckon I lost Laura, though.'

'Her door's not closed.'

He scrutinised his friend's demeanour for bluster or bluff. 'I dunno, Walt.'

Walter stood and surveyed the landscape. 'World's turning. Storm's coming. Time's pressing. I'm cutting a path.' He fixed on Earl's face, then, when no response came, he headed for his horse.

Earl's last breath of resistance left him. 'You don't gotta save me. I'll come. You done enough. I'll leave you in peace now. If I got my girl back and all.'

'I guess some days you can be smart.'

Earl dusted himself down. ''Bout damn time, huh?'

'Yeah.' A silence fell. 'Dumb question, but you got whiskey here?'

'I ain't letting you ride drunk after my boy.'

'No.' Walter rubbed his jaw again. 'For healing. Not sure I had the strength for saving you this time neither.'

Earl flexed his aching hand. 'What you got in that jaw anyhow? Rock?'

Walter tapped Earl's forehead. 'Better than right inside, that's for sure.'

Chapter 47

The cave appeared darker and colder than before, but that was the spectre of being alone. Bill shivered. The sudden shower in the last few miles had drenched him, yet worse was to come.

Mrs Walker had described thunder by having Bill rest his hands on the small dining table and hammering it, quickly but with a crescendo, with her ageing fists. His arms quivered; he watched her eyes widen in calamity, accentuating the impression of the sound.

The storm would bring thunder, lightning, and very tangible rain. Those were fine—they couldn't hurt him, not like bullets from the guns of judgemental, unfeeling deputies.

Running had been the wrong decision, but it was for the greater good. He was a man, not a kid, and he'd pursued his path for long enough. Made mistakes. Nobody else should suffer for that, especially not the people he loved.

Loved. It was true. Though, much as he cared, he couldn't tie Sarah up in this.

He scoured the dark landscape. The clouds boiled, though the wind was only moderate. Nearby, Tanner huddled closer to the rocks.

Bill retreated inside the cave and stripped off his sodden shirt and pants. He gathered wood from Sarah's store at the rear of the cave, dug the flint and tinder from his hastily-assembled war bag, and set a small fire burning in the recess near the cave mouth.

There was a small risk that a passer-by might spy the glow, but he needed warmth. Besides, only a fool would ride out in weather like this. Another fool, he mused.

He jammed his wet clothes into a crack in the wall, so they hung by the fire. He vigorously rubbed his long johns to get heat into his bones and warmed his hands over the low flames.

He scanned the cragged roof and imagined running his fingers over the sharp creases. He wouldn't mind cutting himself—he deserved punishment. He imbibed the smell—a dry, dusty, mineral odour, deeper than the simple scent of a flower. Being inside something whose essence enveloped you, seeping through the skin and nostrils, was an unusual experience. It didn't waft; it subsumed. Not a loving embrace, more a sanctuary.

He couldn't understand how Sarah fixed her melancholy when she came here. It wasn't life-affirming—there was no joy. If he felt sad—as now—he'd want happiness from something less stark. A rainbow, perhaps. A warm swim, a daring ride, or a trusted friend to absorb all the negative energy and offer hope and encouragement.

This loneliness seemed greater than during the past decade because now he'd experienced an alternative. He had more to lose. Despair and sadness leached in with the cold.

Light moved at the cave mouth. He looked around in alarm, moved deeper into the gloom, found a rock and took it, ready to throw. He flattened against the wall, though it provided no defence against a determined invader. His heart was surely beating so loud it would alert the intruder. He should have hitched Tanner further away—the horse was a tell-tale giveaway.

He wished he had a gun or even that he'd trodden the straight and narrow in the past. He felt terrible for thinking ill of Earl—he'd welcome him now with open arms.

The single weak shadow on the floor grew, and it hardened as the fire gave it definition. It wore no hat nor had an outstretched hand that might bear a gun. Below the waist was a block of darkness, not two limbs.

If he could hear, he'd listen for voices—the deeper ones of men, perhaps the click of a pistol hammer. Mrs Walker had said it sounded like the tap of a knife on a metal plate or the snap of a twig. He'd gone into her garden and cracked some dry twigs, trying to sense the noise.

His breath still held—for the good it would do if danger were near—but it exploded from his lungs like a .303 when he saw who was there. Still, he didn't move, in case the visit wasn't one of friendship. He peered beyond her for other shapes, but none appeared.

The rock fell from his grasp.

Her expression was of relief, not admonishment.

"How did you know?" he signed, quivering with aftershocks of worry and anticipation.

"It's where I would come."

"Who else come?"

Sarah shook her head. "Just me."

"You should go. You'll be in trouble."

She stepped out of the backlight. Her clothes were limp and matted by the rain. "I don't want to leave you."

"But I did wrong. I let those animals out. I told lies to you."

"Did you... be with that woman? Did you hurt someone?"

He shook his head, took a finger from his lips and patted the open hand against his left fist. "I promise."

She cocked her head, exploring his eyes. In the awful delay of her indecision, he became acutely aware of his undress. He clapped both hands over his groin, then nodded towards the fire, explaining his actions.

Her face creased into mollification. "It's okay. You shouldn't catch a cold."

"You should be warm too."

She moved close to the fire. "Why did you run?"

"To save you, and Pa, and Laura."

"But we are here to help." Her face beseeched him.

"I should have left with Tanner when I got him."

"Why? To be alone?"

"I always been alone. Even in the camp. Even with Mrs Walker. They were in the same place as me but still apart."

"But you're not apart from me, or Ma. Or even Earl. He loves you, though he finds it hard to show." She clasped his hand with cold and fragile fingers. "You came here to protect me and Ma. You fought Tom to save me. You ran into the Bank. You want me to be safe."

"But you came here. You should have stayed."

"I want you to be safe. I want to be with you. We are courting—remember?"

He stroked her cool, damp cheek.

"Yes." He bit his lip. "Will they come?"

"They don't know about this place."

"So we are safe. Good. Did you bring water?"

She shook her head. "Did you?"

"Some."

"Food?"

"Biscuits."

"I see." Her face fell. "I brought the gun. Perhaps we'll see something to shoot and eat."

His eyes flared. "You brought the gun? Ma will be mad."

She looked at the ground. "Yes."

"This is why you should have stayed. Ma—Laura—will be mad at me too."

"Do you want me to go?"

In a flash, a war raged and ended in his head. "No."

She held his hands. "I'll stay."

His heart swelled. "Thank you."

She responded with a smile that spoke volumes. He curled his fingers into a sign he'd never made before.

It opened a ream of appendices in her smile. "I love you too," she replied.

A fork of lightning lit up the cave. She jumped and clutched him.

He felt the damp blouse that clung to her. "You will catch a cold."

"I have no choice."

"I won't tell."

She bit her lip, looked at the fire, and then at him in his underclothes. She had begun to shiver. The air wasn't cold, but the rain had been.

He pointed. "You left a blanket. With the wood. And I have one in my bag."

She nodded, though her brow remained knit. He scooted to the rear of the cave and grabbed more wood and the blanket. He set out the blankets, stoked the fire, and then rubbed her hands. A smile broke on her lips.

He removed the belt which gathered her dress, then found himself unfastening the dozen or so tiny buttons at the front. His fingers shook with nerves, not cold.

She pulled off her wet blouse, then, with her eyes, permitted him to slip down her dress.

He worked mechanically, not wantonly, then folded the clothes tightly, went to the cave mouth and wrung them out. Warm rain pattered onto his ankles.

He shook the clothes straight, found cracks high in the wall, and jammed in a corner of each garment, so they hung beside his shirt. All wafted in the hot air rising from the fire.

She shuddered, so he took her in an embrace, rubbing her back to generate warmth. He jolted back into the reality of the situation. His heart hammered in his chest.

She looked concerned. "It's okay."

Then she cupped his cheek, and he pressed in and kissed her without restraint. Overbearing sorrow for his previous actions mingled with a need for hope and comfort in a dark moment. She tasted like salvation, and it was as if the lightning outside swept through his every nerve.

With a gentle tug of her hand, he encouraged her to sit on the blanket. He folded the other blanket across their legs. The fire crackled. Two shadows danced on the walls.

Amusement sparked on her face. Her finger gingerly moved to the hole in his long johns, exposing a glimpse of inner thigh. He inhaled sharply as she touched the margin of material and flesh.

She snatched back her hand. "I'm sorry."

"I reckoned to buy a new one this week."

"I could stitch it. Then you'd save a dollar." She winked. "And buy me a present instead."

He pressed his breastbone, willing his heart to quit its alarm. He felt a fool, yet with just cause.

"Your heart is beating fast," she signed.

She touched his chest. She cocked an ear as if listening, minutely adjusting her hand's pressure and position, then closed her eyes to sense his rhythm.

He noted the curve of her cheekbone, the slender neck leading to her bare upper chest.

Her eyes flicked open. "My heart is beating fast too."

"Good." He was lost for what else to sign.

She took his hand and laid it over her heart.

He stroked the gentle frill of the cotton, pressed harder to sense the transmission of her heartbeat, and closed his eyes— to draw focus away from the sight, to channel all sensation to touch alone.

Indeed, her rhythm was pacy, which he hoped was as much from nerves—rather than excitement—as his was.

He opened his eyes and removed his hand.

She shuffled closer. "See? This is our journey. Together."

He looked away.

"What is it?" she asked.

"You are too good. Why do you be with a bad man?"

"You are not bad."

"I opened that gate, and I…." He bowed his head. "I did go to that woman." He sprang up and darted to the rear of the cave, abandoning warmth and care he didn't deserve.

In a moment, she was beside him. "Don't run. Not from me. Or the truth." She took his hand and led him back. They sat.

"You said you were never with a woman. Is that a lie?"

"No. But…." He lost faith.

She lifted his chin. "What is it, Bill?"

"I'm ashamed of what happened."

His frame quivered now—the prospect of losing her, the deceit, the remembrance of past embarrassment, the nerves about what might happen, what Earl and Laura might think. He was a fool. A weak, undeserving fool. A boy, not a man.

In just one of those rattling heartbeats, he could have leapt up and ridden away at full pelt. She was an angel, and devils didn't deserve angels.

She grabbed one of his tremulous hands and squeezed.

"Tell me. I won't be cross. If you care, tell me."

He searched her face for anger and criticism but found only concern and warmth. "I never been with a woman, so I wanted not to be joked at no more. To be a man. So I saved my dollars, and I went to see a lady." He took a deep breath. "But I didn't…. That is…." He clenched his fists and screwed his face against the awfulness of it.

Again, she cupped his cheek, bringing him back to her.

He swallowed. "We took off clothes, 'cos I wanted to do it, truly. And we was on the bed. And I saw her… lady parts. And I was," he swallowed more nerves and looked at his waist, "Ready."

"I see."

"And we didn't kiss or nothing. But she… touched me, my leg." He fingered the torn long johns, then tapped nearer his groin. "And. And I…."

He snapped his head to the side to avoid seeing her judge his shame. When a few seconds had passed without signs or action, he looked back.

She gently kissed him. "You were… too quick on the draw."

He pursed his lips and barely nodded.

"Thank you for telling the truth," she signed. "I am not a child, Bill. I know boys want girls in that way. Like Tom did in the stables."

"I would not have done it if I knew I would meet you. I went because I thought nobody would love a deaf boy raised by Mojave."

"I love you. Nobody is perfect. Not me."

He pushed damp hair from her forehead. "You are."

She shook her head. "At school, I hurt a girl who teased me. I pulled her hair something awful. Ma was cross. And I took the gun—remember? I hit Tom with that pail. He could have been hurt bad. And…." She bit her lip.

"What?" He stroked her cheek.

"Tom and I kissed. And… we came here. And he touched me," she tapped her chest.

He grimaced. "But you didn't…?"

Her eyes flared. "No. I wouldn't. I couldn't. Tom doesn't care. Not like you. He wants the bragging. He's rough."

"And he's a hearing person. He doesn't understand."

She nodded. "No."

"Like the… lady. She didn't understand. I couldn't sign with her. She laughed. Because I was a cripple in my shorts, like in my ears."

Compassionate, she held him.

His blood still raced, but no longer through nerves of what he needed to say. The tidal wave of relief mixed with the fizz of tender togetherness—something not present in that three-storey building in Four Pines on his eighteenth birthday.

Her hand laid on his thigh, then he touched hers. When they parted lips, she unbuttoned his long johns to the belly button—calmly and deliberately.

She slid her hand inside, over his chest, and laid it there, ostensibly imbibing his heartbeat. Her hand was warm, and the touch heady.

Naturally, his heart pulsed hastier now.

She removed her hand and offered a querying look. He reached out but snatched back, swamped by fear.

Loving concern washed over her face. "I won't mind. Whatever happens."

"Even if—?"

"Yes. Because it means you think I'm pretty. I'm nervous too. For a girl, it… hurts the first time. Or Ma says."

He arced back. "I don't want to hurt you."

"It doesn't matter. I want to be with you, Bill." She smiled and stroked his head.

He kissed her. She caressed his chest, then held his head beside hers, ear to ear, merely comforting him. He let his hands fall on the outside of her thighs.

"Don't worry," she reiterated.

He touched a finger to the skin of her breastbone and felt the soft warmth of her in that tiny contact. A second finger touched, and a third.

His hand eased flat, then across, over the curve of her. He closed his eyes and drowned in the surge of endorphins. His lips felt hers touch, first gently and soon more keenly.

The fire crackled. One shadow danced on the walls.

They began the journey.

Chapter 48

Warning raindrops spotted on Earl's hat as they neared town. Sundown was distant, but nightfall seemed upon them. They'd burned an extra hour's ride swinging past a couple of spots which Walter suggested, but the result of the search was as predictable as he'd left unsaid.

Two acceptable outcomes remained: Bill and Sarah were either back at Laura's or somewhere sheltered. Rain wouldn't kill a man—or his courting girl—but lightning could, and fast-riding horses might slide on mud and bring injuries to themselves or their riders. If Bill had been a fool to run, Earl hoped the years of plains riding had imbued a sense of when to find a good spot and wait out the storm.

Distant thunder cracked as they walked from the stables to Laura's. He gazed skywards, hoping the main cloudburst would pass by and not turn the place into brownish mud. Nonetheless, women quickened their pace, and shutters were being closed up.

'I'm right grateful you sold Sam Bowman half a lie,' Earl said.

'Result's the same—Bill's gotta face charges and make the deputies see the truth, or he'll be ever hunted.'

As they approached the house, a lump formed in Earl's throat. Time for another apology on this spot—the hardest yet.

He removed his hat. Steady rain pattered his head and slid down his cheek, dipping inside the collar of his moleskin coat.

Laura opened the door gingerly—perhaps expecting the deputies' return—then flung it wider when she saw them.

'Well, don't bring in more water than you have to.' She beckoned them inside.

He went to put his Western on the peg, then held back.

She rolled her eyes. 'Hang your darn hat up, Earl Johnson. You're no more stranger than you were this morning.'

So he did as bade, and they went through to the living room. Droplets plopped dark spots onto the rug. The fire was warm and comforting.

'I'm real sorry.' He wanted to get his apology in first. 'I didn't bring Sarah, and you said—'

'I say a lot of things.' She studied his face. 'Have you—did you have an accident?' She touched his forehead, and he winced.

'I guess I... took a knock somewhere.' He casually eased a hand behind his back. He'd ridden one-handed to give the swelling a chance to subside, but it was still colouring purple.

She glanced at Walter, who responded with uncharacteristic sheepishness, and narrowed her eyes. 'Have you boys been fighting?'

'No, ma'am,' Earl blurted.

She reached around, took his hand and held it up for inspection. Then she studied Walter's jawline. 'Pardon me?'

'That is, yes, ma'am,' Earl admitted.

'Did you run it in the river to reduce the swelling?'

'No, ma'am.'

She looked at them with disdain. 'I oughta knock your heads together.'

'I reckon we done enough of that.' Earl fingered his aching temple.

She exhaled with deliberate disappointment. 'Walter, sit yourself down. You, mister—help me with the coffee pot.'

The friends exchanged the look of scolded children, and then Earl followed her into the kitchen.

She spoke quietly. 'What are you trying to prove? Did you not get your fair share from Dennis Hayes already?'

'I'm sorry, and I'll try better. I were at the end of my tether and all, right scared for my boy and your girl.' He shook his head. 'And I'm cut up over what happened, and we'll find the boy, and Sarah, and if no damage is done, and there's forgiveness in your heart, I'd like to keep on courting. If you'd have me.' He inspected his feet.

She lifted his chin. 'We were never *not* courting. I know you'd ride to the end of the earth for those two and to make amends to me. You have a better heart than you believe, and that's what Walter was trying to prove to you—but not the way I would.' She pushed up on tiptoe and kissed his bruised skin.

Relief and endorphins cascaded through him. He held her waist and kissed her lips. 'End of the earth is nothing. I'd go to the moon and the stars.'

'Just don't stand on your friend to get there.'

'Yes, ma'am,' he replied cheekily.

The intervals between the thunderclaps steadily grew shorter, and the windows rattled with rain. The three sat in pensive silence.

There came a noise unlike thunder—a heavy rap on the door.

She sprang up.

'They'd be fools to come hunting now,' Walter said.

Earl followed her to the door, ready to offer support. For a second, his heart bounded on the chance that it might be Bill, Sarah, or both.

Abe stood on the doorstep, sodden by the rain which hissed on the ground and battered the flowers into submission.

'Golly, Abe, don't stand there.' She urged him inside.

He shook water from his coat and hat, then plunged gratefully into the house. His short, tightly curled hair was dry as a bone, but his grey stubble was dotted with spray.

'Coffee?' Earl offered.

'That'd be good.'

Earl brought the pot through. Abe gratefully took the mug and nodded thanks.

'It's either big good news or big bad for a man to come out in this weather,' she suggested.

'I'm hoping good.' Abe drank. 'It's rainin' to beat the Dutch.'

'Well, don't keep us itching,' Earl said.

'We should reckon some of that Want poster is a fabrication.'

'A mistake, perhaps,' Laura said.

Abe shook his head. 'I heard some things, and I don't think the mistake has come lightly.'

Earl clenched a fist. 'I figured something weren't right.'

'I was taking a drink for calming my worries about not stopping your two riding out. Three fellers took to sit at the next table, so I kept quiet and low. Except something knocked at my brain like I knew a face.'

'Is that so?'

'Well, they got to talking, and I heard about a deaf boy, and I drank real slow. And it comes to this—the one says we'll get the kid back for ratting on your brother and taking away his gains. And I saw it—the red hair of that no-good man who tried to turn over the Bank.'

'That so?' Walter replied. 'Harper, was it?'

Abe clicked tired old fingers. 'Harman.'

'They're fitting up Bill because he stopped that robbery.' Walter rubbed his cheek as he considered things.

Abe nodded. 'And this Harman—what got clean away— must'a went crazy over the unlawful money he didn't get.

And he railed on it to this feller, his brother, and by choice or accident, he's gone out to even the score.'

Laura rapped the arm of the chair. 'No-goods beget no-goods.'

'So it's all bluster and fixing revenge,' Earl said.

'Hold your horse,' Abe said. 'The one guy, he'd seen Bill around in Four Pines and knew some folks ragged on the boy. The… woman… what got killed, she told tales on Bill and how they'd been together, making the boy a laughing stock. So the guy figures—sure, kid could wanna kill her. But they got no proof. They only got that Bill was in town.'

'But looking to make a case all the same,' Walter said.

'Ah, but the steers is different. That come later, and Bill cut town after. Maybe he crossed paths with that rancher and did a boy's prank. Rancher put out the reward, but breaking a gate? That's not rape-murder. That's what they want Bill for. And get this—' Abe jabbed a finger. 'They sold Potter and Sam on it too. State put up a reward for the killer, and Potter added more if they could pin it on Bill.'

Earl leapt from his seat in a heartbeat.

'Sit down,' Walter snapped.

'You heard, Walt!'

'Words of strangers—words they'd swallow if you said a thing to Potter. Because they'd know who to say "Yes sir" and "No sir" to—and it's not you.'

'Sit down,' Laura echoed. 'We're fighting Bill's battle, not yours.'

Seething, Earl sat.

'Listen,' Abe continued, 'I called by Sam Bowman after that. He's got Want posters in there, always does. There's one on the wall for a rape-murder in Four Pines—except the same face with a handlebar. Older feller too, but not unlike Bill besides.'

Earl slammed his fist on the chair and yapped in pain—his punching hand already bruised from smacking his friend's cheekbone.

'So this is *good*,' she said firmly to quell his rising discontent. 'Bill told the truth. Look at the good side, for Lord's sake.'

'I guess,' he said through clenched teeth.

Walter stood. 'All we have now is to get one of them to admit the ruse and find the youngs before the law does.' He peered through the window into the half-dark, where the rain lashed and town lights burned. 'Good news being no sane man would ride out in this hell, less his life depended on it.'

'Well, I reckon Bill's does,' Earl replied. 'He won't understand what they say, and he might get riled and raise a fist.'

'Or a gun, if Sarah's found him,' Walter added.

Laura winced at this.

Earl went and put an arm around her. 'Don't worry, sweet. She'll have took cover. She's smart and tough, like her ma. She won't know where Bill is, and the deputies won't know where either one is.'

Laura frowned. 'Then why would she ride out after him if she had no clue?'

'How in hell do I know?'

'I wasn't asking you. I was asking the world, I suppose.' She shook her head. 'I'm too worried, that's all.'

She stood and fussed around, tidying where no tidying was needed.

'She'd have come back if she could.' Walter shrugged. 'So maybe they do have a secret place. Everyone has someplace they go to when the world's too much.'

Earl ignored Walter's gaze. He paced. 'Excepting this is their home, and Bill don't got none besides the forge anyhow.'

'Neither does Sarah. She'd go to her room or....'
Realisation dawned on Laura's face. 'There is a place,' she
said—softly, as if convincing herself. 'Perhaps?'

Earl crouched in front of her. 'Where?'

'There's a cave, about a half-hour ride from here. I went
once. Actually, one more time, when Sarah was laughed at in
the schoolhouse. She ran away—well, not properly away. She
wanted to be alone. To cry, I suppose.' She sighed. 'Perhaps
they went there.'

He stood. 'Then we ride out.'

'Don't be a fool,' Walter snapped. 'It's not a night for man
nor beast. The deputies won't ride—they're filling bellies and
livers. If Bill's there, he's safe—from folk and the storm.'

'Is that so?' Earl asked Laura.

She nodded. 'I can't think anyone knows of it but us—
certainly as a hidey hole for Sarah.'

Abe rose. 'Tomorrow morning, we'll ride out.'

'Not you, Abe,' she said. 'Stay in town, or it might look
suspicious. You have Lyle Potter's ear, and we might need
that afterwards. Don't annoy the man.'

Abe reluctantly agreed.

Walter peered out the window. 'Come night, there's no
moon ever gonna break those fat clouds, and unless a man
knows where to look, the youngs are good and safe.'

Earl sat on the chair arm and stroked Laura's hair. 'Maybe
it was a good sense for Bill to go after all. He bought time for
us to figure things, and having Sarah gave him a place to go.'

'The friends' retreat,' she mused. She sat bolt upright.
Distress rang in her face. 'Tom Potter.'

'What of him?'

'He and Sarah—they could have been there. When he was
making to court her. She could have shown him, for a ride
out of town, for being sweet.'

'Dang.'

Walter ruffled his hair. 'Only if he and Lyle talk and they grow brains and do some figuring... but I guess it could be.'

'First light it is,' Abe announced. 'You get some rest. I'll bring the horses over before the sun, quiet as you like.'

'That's very good of you,' she said.

'You forget, I'm short one stablehand and one favourite little lady.' Abe winked. 'Figure I'll step out for a free bath now.'

Walter followed Abe to the door. 'That's for sure. Before Main Street's a river for swimming, I'll go to the forge and take Bill's bed in case he returns quietly to his own spot. But Laura, if the kids come back, you'll be sure and send Earl to holler?'

She nodded.

Walter flashed her a smile and lowered his voice to Earl. 'I'll leave you to... make up properly.'

Earl smiled. 'Keep your head low out there.' He nodded uptown. 'We ain't out of this yet, and Lord knows we still gotta figure how to winkle out those deputies' lies.'

The room lit violently, and thunder shook every wall.

Walter shrugged. 'Well, I reckon we've all got a night awake to work on it anyhow.'

Chapter 49

Earl dimmed the light in Sarah's room and prepared the covers. Being in the house, ready to support Laura, was the best thing to do. Still, the girl's absence only crystallised their worries about the situation.

He sat on the bed, ankle-deep in regret and disappointment. Then he examined the facts, and it allowed him to wade back to emotional dry land.

A faint sniffle broke the silence, so he padded across the hall and peered around Laura's door. She was more than ankle-deep, and her tears only added to the tide.

Gentlemanly reserve ran through him at the sight of her underclothes, but she'd seen him, and her face spoke more of "come" than "go", so he sat on the bed and brushed saltwater from her face.

'What if they don't come back?' she murmured.

'What if they do?'

His uncharacteristic positivity put a query on her face. She tugged a handkerchief from her sleeve and dried her eyes. 'Do you think?'

'You said 'bout the cave, and that's what I figure. If it were only Bill gone, I'd be getting words from you that the Lord already took once from me, and he ain't that cruel to do it twice.'

'Not for me either, I would hope.' She took his hand and entwined their fingers.

He looked around, seeing the room for the first time. Rain lashed the window, enough to extinguish a wildfire.

He sighed. 'I didn't have nobody when they was taken.'

'At least I had Sarah, that day Jim didn't come home. I shouldn't cry now.'

'Yeah. You should. I did. Not afraid to say as much.'

'No crying tonight?' she asked.

'No. They're fine. Last time I told myself they was gone and dead, and I were wrong, so it'd be dumb to think the same now. We just gotta wait.'

'And I have you here. You are a blessing in my life at any time, but especially now.'

'Still can't figure what you're doing with a feller like me. You're too good.'

She patted his chest. 'Perhaps it rubs off on another person. And burdens are better shared.'

An echo came to him. He gazed into a spot in space and haltingly dredged up the recall.

"When a trouble nears and presses
She would rout it with caresses;
Hide my face in sunlit tresses;
And her laugh is softer, crisper,
Than a bird's song or a whisper."

Earl shrugged and picked at his nails.

Her mouth hung ajar in wonder. 'And then you surprise me again.'

'From the old country. Brother to my father. He wrote some. He didn't come across the water. Said we had no grass here to speak of.'

'It's lovely.'

'Used to be for Mary. I had a bad day—it'd all go away when she were beside me.'

She stroked his hand. 'I'm honoured in comparison.'

'I won't do it no more.'

'You be who you are. I hold no jealousy.'

He nodded. 'Nor ill-will neither. I'm a lucky man.'

'I need to rest now. We start early.'

He pointed out the door. 'You want me, you holler.'

She bit her lip. 'Hold me a while?'

'Sure. If it'd help.'

She moved around the bed, pulled back the covers and slid in. He turned the light down low, but flashes of lighting leaked through the curtain gaps.

He lay on the covers, she turned her back, and he laid a hand on her shoulder.

For a couple of minutes, the only sound was a few sniffles mixing with the patter of water on glass.

'Are you comfortable?'

'I guess,' he replied.

'Get under the covers if you'd like.'

He debated, then acquiesced, stroking her sleeve. She pulled his hand across into a loose embrace.

'You can hold me, lovely man, but this isn't an invitation.'

'I'd be a heel to take advantage.'

She gently squeezed his hand. 'I know, to my very soul.'

He held her tight, and she him, clinging onto each other like life rafts amidst the emotional deluge which sought to match heaven's cascade.

His mind circled: without Bill, he wouldn't have met her; without Bill, he wouldn't have this hoo-hah, and they wouldn't need each other's support. So he bathed in her scent, listened to her soft breathing as she slipped into sleep, and knew he owed Bill as much as he could give.

Bill and Sarah held hands at the cave mouth, their other palms pressed to the wall.

The rain came down in sheets, and the tiniest fraction drummed on the neck of the canteen, which he'd jammed, open and upright, between two stones just outside. They might go hungry but not thirsty.

Even as the lightning persisted, every bolt made them jump as it lit up the landscape, silhouetting saguaros and highlighting the impromptu streams forming on the soggy prairie floor below.

He released her hand. "Tribe said storms mean God is unhappy."

"God is unhappy that men spread lies. He is not unhappy with you."

"How do you know?"

"There was no storm after the Bank robbery or after Tom tried to hurt me. Those are worse things than breaking a gate."

He remained unconvinced. "I don't want to go to jail. And I don't have money to pay back the rancher."

She touched his cheek. "There's another way. There must be."

"What should we do?"

"I don't know. If you run away from me, my heart might break."

He smiled awkwardly, riddled with guilt and indecision. "Love is bad if it makes hearts break."

"Will your heart break?"

"I don't want to find out. Shall we go away? Together?"

She frowned. "I didn't mean that."

"I can't go home. Earl will leather me, even if the law finds the truth."

"You must take your punishment."

He squeezed her hand as if pushing acquiescence in through her skin. "I'll get a good job and buy a piano and look after you good."

"I can't leave Ma."

"She has Earl now," he protested. "She won't be alone."

"I know a girl leaves her ma some time. But not to run from the law."

"Even for a boy she loves?"

She smiled—but awkwardly, and turned away.

His spirits sank. He didn't care if God was unhappy. He knew love and companionship now, and that's all he wanted.

In the morning, he'd ask her again. He'd hold her close that night and convince her she needed him, and he'd ask her again, and then they'd run away.

He was now a man, and she a woman. They were masters of their destiny.

Chapter 50

In the morning, the going was hard. Earl hadn't seen the like in five years. It was as mentally tiring for him and Walter as it was physically for Jack and Dusty. The air was dry, but the light stygian. Walter rode ahead, scanning the undulating landscape, weaving between patches of thick mud, new streams and prairie obstacles.

Earl kept clear yards behind and to the side, avoiding the clods of ochre gloop Dusty kicked up. He thanked his stars for taking Laura, her arms tight around him, rather than letting her ride alone—especially on an unfamiliar horse, as Sarah had taken Hester. Still, Jack bore a heavy load under horrible conditions.

Laura steered Walter occasionally, cupping her mouth to call ahead, and they heeled over in unison.

Soon, Earl picked out the rocky range she'd described, dull and unimpressive in the milky early sun, and he eased Jack on faster, leaving Walter to trail.

As they drew near, his pulse accelerated to the pace of the hooves.

They hadn't arrived first. A cluster of horses on the craggy hillside marked the location.

'Dammit to hell.'

He temporarily had no care for any discomfort the words caused her—this was a dispute between men, and she'd better expect more cussing. As long as guns stayed in holsters, blue language would be a dream outcome.

The last yards were interminable as Jack picked his way between slippery half-buried boulders, every plant of the hoof making a tiny slither in the muddy scrub grass. The two riders rocked like a stagecoach with a busted spring, and Laura clenched tighter to Earl. They looked up the rise to where their arrival became a sport for the spectators.

Mercifully, the five men—three deputies, Sam Bowman and tell-tale Tom Potter—had their guns still holstered. Bill and Sarah stood by, hands clasped together between ramrod-straight arms which told of nerves and defiance.

Yet, seeing their numbers now equal, big Gabe Evans touched the butt of his gun as the threesome came to a halt ten yards away.

'Easy and slow,' Walter said from the corner of his mouth. He dismounted, boots slapping the moist earth, and held out a hand for Laura. She slid down, found her balance, and hurried towards Sarah.

Earl quickly hit the ground, patted Jack, and followed.

'We'll overlook any further charges, Earl—for running and such—if you can square this,' Bowman said.

'Reason we brought Laura Mae.' Earl looked daggers at Evans. 'So any man what touches his gun in the presence of these ladies will be sucking up stormwater.'

Some of this was bravado, some was through love for Laura, and some was a need to save Bill.

Laura and Sarah were now in a loose embrace, with Bill beside them. Sarah's gun was jammed into his waistband.

"Put the gun on the ground," Earl signed.

"Pa?"

He repeated the phrase, mustering a face of what parental insistence might look like.

'No secret signs!' Sheriff Bowman barked.

'Jesus Christ, Sam! Whole reason we come here is to talk like you folks can understand. Ain't no secrets. Just telling my boy to lay down his gun. He's no killer any more'n I am.'

Bill, with commendable caution and transparency, did as he was bid.

Only Tom Potter's hand grazed his holster. Earl considered the young man as dangerous as any of his companions: Tom's disregard for Bill and Sarah had shown before. No doubt, he swam in self-congratulation from masterminding this attempted capture. The Mayor would be so proud of his boy.

Earl wanted to wring Tom Potter's neck.

Instead, he went to Bowman. 'We talked to Bill. He admits letting loose them steers.'

Evans smirked at his colleagues. 'What'd I tell you, boys?'

Earl grizzled at him. 'Bill's problem ain't only his own for what he done. It's on sons of bitches who'd rag on him being deaf, and take advantage. It's on men who'd deny him fair work and take his horse.'

'But thieving isn't the answer,' Bowman insisted.

'And I don't agree with it,' Earl said. 'But a man's gotta live, and get by, and not be cut down by hate.'

'And that rancher has to live, and make his way, and not be thieved on.'

'All the same, you know how a man of our acquaint got stolen from and stole back. A man in your town what holds hisself above the law and rails against this kid, and what's he got? Raising a posse of men, most now in the ground, for thieving back gold.' Earl wrinkled his nose.

'You want to watch your mouth.'

'Double from me,' Tom Potter called.

Earl didn't even dignify that with a glance. 'So call off your dogs, Sam.'

'That still doesn't answer to the rape-murder.'

Earl turned to the deputies. 'Any of you men recognise Bill as the man what done this? Any of you in the whorehouse that day? That maybe you don't wanna talk 'bout? Or is this all hearsay and baloney?'

'We've got a clear description of the person who was there that night,' Evans replied.

'Says who?'

'Another whore, a friend to the dead girl.'

'And she give the date, the time? She see clear in dark corridors? Huh?' Earl demanded.

'She saw good enough,' Cory Harman piped up.

'Why, you acquainted with her? You take to visiting? Maybe go back this past week? Pay a few dollars extra for a good story?'

Harman looked at the ground. Something behind his expression indicated that if one of the three were to crack, it might be him.

'That'll do,' Evans cautioned.

The petrichor drifted over them, even as the sun leached warmth into the early morning. Tiny pools in the dips of boulders glimmered with the weak light.

'What date? You gotta know that, right?' Earl insisted. 'Date she got killed?'

'July twenty-seventh,' Sam replied.

Earl beckoned Bill over. Sarah let him go, then took her mother's hand.

"What day did you see the whore in Four Pines?" Earl signed.

Bill was unsure, embarrassed. Earl nodded for him to continue.

"July twenty-fifth. My birthday." Bill looked at the ground.

'July twenty-fifth, gentlemen. That's the day Bill was there.'

'You expect us to believe that?' Harman scoffed.

Earl smiled inside—the red-haired man grew riled because his story was showing holes, and he wouldn't be able to revenge his bank-robbing sonofabitch brother.

'Reckon I do, on account of it's the boy's birthday. Every man knows his birthday.'

'He could be lying. We hear he's a half-breed Indian raised by thieves.'

Earl moved within a foot of Harman. 'My boy was born on July twenty-fifth, and raised by folk what had their land took from under them. All the same, they learned him this way of talking for his betterment.'

He lowered his voice. 'Now, we got word the man you chase has a moustache and maybe five years on Bill here. What d'you say to that?'

Harman swallowed. 'Any man can visit the barber to escape justice.'

'Why, you show that paper of yours to the barbering man for witness and proof?'

'Now, Earl—' Bowman interjected.

'We saw it happen,' Wade Baskin blurted.

'Is that so?' Earl asked.

'Yeah. And you can't prove I didn't.'

'Well, ain't that convenient?'

'It... is for us,' Evans said.

Earl eyed them all. 'So you seen Bill here getting his face shaved and did what? Nothing? You see a Wanted man, ripe for taking, and you got on with your lives?'

'We was... we wasn't deputies then,' Wade stammered.

'All the same, you recognised the man and had no call to do your civic duty? To walk over to your Sheriff... Everett and raise the alarm that a murderer was sat in the barbershop, clear as day?'

'He hadn't been identified then,' Evans announced smugly.

'Ain't that convenient again? This was next day after the killing you seen this feller? July twenty-eighth it'd be?' Earl stood in front of Wade Baskin. The man was shorter than he, weaselly, with sallow skin.

'Yeah, I reckon so,' Baskin replied with clearly forced gumption.

'And near on two years later, you recall as crystal the man you seen that day? You spend plenty of hours watching other men get their barbering? Gazing at 'em?'

'You son of a—'

Wade lunged, but Earl stood aside, and the man stumbled forwards, catching himself before he spreadeagled on the dank ground.

'You horse's ass, Wade!' Evans rapped.

'This is baloney, Sam,' Earl said. 'This ain't nothing but trying to take money from you and the State for false arrest. And being gutless yellow scum for hating a deaf boy who done nothing but fight back against men like these.'

'He's guilty,' Tom called.

'You shut your hole, kid, or I'll clean your plow. You ain't even been to that town, much less have the guts to go to a whore who'd laugh at you for what you carry.'

Tom rushed forward, but Walter grabbed his shirt, and Tom stopped as if he'd hit a wall.

Earl ignored the look of disgust and went to Gabe Evans.

'Jig is up, and you know it. Either you bring a wagon of witnesses what say my boy done this, or you saddle up and find the real coward varmint—afore he breaks another poor woman's neck.'

'What about our reward?' Harman chipped. 'I ain't takin' the little end of the horn!'

Evans jabbed him in the ribs.

'It isn't over, Earl.' But Sam Bowman's shoulders had slumped. 'The boy admitted to crimes. State demands five hundred dollars for restitution, and a month in the cell.'

'For breaking a gate and taking a mare?'

'The law's the law,' Evans interjected. Earl looked with disdain at the man's lopsided badge.

'You and Bill are treading a fine line, Earl,' Bowman cautioned. 'Remember, the boy tried to escape justice.'

'False justice, I reckon. I thought better of you than defending men like these. Give a man a tin star and sight of dollars, and he'll sell any poor kid down the river.'

Bowman held up a warning finger. 'Again on that line. Be grateful we're holding off those other charges. A young man—or any—isn't beyond learning he's got to pay for mistakes.'

'I learned plenty myself these weeks.'

Bowman nodded. 'So, what's it to be?'

'The kid don't got five hundred dollars. Neither do I.'

'Then he'll stay in the pokey at night and work it off in the day. Six months should do it.'

Earl clenched a fist in supplication. 'Dammit, Sam, have a heart.'

'I got a badge, and that's what matters. Fact is, these men found a thief, and the victim's got to have recompense.'

Lost for words, Earl scanned the faces of his compatriots. Walter stood alone, resting against the cave mouth. His hand casually but deliberately hovered by his holster. Earl wanted to ask advice but had come this far under his own steam, and Laura's ultimatum rang in his ears.

He was tantalisingly close to victory. He'd grown the balls; now he just needed to find the money.

He took off his hat and massaged his hair as he ambled over to her. 'No doubt about it, we're in a spot.'

She squeezed his arm. 'I explained to Bill. He'll do it.'

'I don't want him to do it.' His care and love for Bill hit a new high.

'It doesn't look like there's a choice. I have a hundred dollars saved, but I don't suppose you'd take it.'

'I couldn't. You done more'n enough for the boy anyhow. It ain't your place.'

'Then I don't see a solution.'

'It's a hard row to hoe, no mistake.'

He rapped his hat back and forth on his thigh as if trying to knock an answer from it, like a magician's rabbit. The boy had suffered enough, both for what he'd done and for what the world had done to him. Yet, justice had to be served. Earl couldn't fail now, after everything he'd been through.

He saw the cave properly for the first time, overlooking a world waking from Noah's deluge—an ark in which two kindred creatures had sheltered. He contemplated the landscape. Out there stood an old, dead home Bill had never known, and another he'd likely never need.

An idea came to him.

Chapter 51

Earl replaced his hat. 'Don't recount this to Bill,' he told Laura as he passed.

He gathered himself in front of the Sheriff. 'I figure my place is worth five hundred or more, with the acres.'

Bowman's brow furrowed. 'You're handing over your property?'

'Proceeds to pay Bill's debts, and he'll be bound over not to leave the county.' He heaved a breath. 'That's my say-so. How do you figure as fair shake?'

Bowman looked at Evans, who acceded with a disconsolate nod.

Earl saw the pain in Laura's face, but she conceded and pulled Bill to her.

'I'll give you one week.' Bowman lowered his voice. 'A single bad step or word, it's the jail cell for Bill. And I hope to hell the Mayor sees it the same. I doubt it, though. Man's a... law unto himself sometimes.'

'No argument on that.'

'It's a crock of shit,' Tom snapped.

Earl ignored it. 'I'm grateful, Sam. I paid hard for my misdoings, and Bill's account gotta be settled likewise. So, let's make that an end to the matter. These ladies don't need to be out on a cold morning no more.'

Bowman nodded tersely. 'Come on, gentlemen.'

The four walked to their horses, hitched to a saguaro fifty yards away.

As Bowman mounted up, voices were raised between the three. Baskin and Harman shoved each other. Evans urged calm, but voices went up another notch. Both men drew their guns.

Earl tensed. Laura clutched Sarah, and they faced away. Walter moved to a better position, ready to cover the ladies.

Tom Potter, isolated nearby, twitched his gun hand.

Gabe Evans barked again. Bowman, atop his mount nearby, waved a calming hand. Baskin and Harman's demeanour loosened.

Earl breathed.

Faint words drifted across from Baskin's mouth. Harman drew at a snap and fired. The gunshot rapped Earl's ears, smacked onto the stone outcrop, and ricocheted across the landscape. A bird squawked away from its nearby perch.

Baskin crumpled to the sodden dirt.

Earl covered his gun. Flinching, Laura steered the youngsters closer to the cave where Walter stood, hand on holster.

Evans grabbed Harman's shirt and imparted something blunt. The smaller man recoiled, holstering his gun. Bowman merely shook his head and barked an instruction. Evans and Harman picked up Baskin's lifeless form, took it to a horse and awkwardly laded the body across the saddle. Then they mounted their steeds, Evans pointed Harman to take Baskin's reins, and they turned towards White Rock and ambled away.

Earl breathed again, more deeply. Just deserts for deceitful scum.

'See what you did?' Tom called.

Earl ignored him and squelched up the slight incline to the waiting trio. He took Laura in an embrace, and Bill held Sarah likewise.

Hooves tapped on the subsurface rock.

'See what you did?' Tom said softly, eyes narrowed at Bill.

'Get outta here,' Earl replied.

'No good, thieving cripple,' Tom mumbled.

Earl clenched a fist.

'Raise a whole damn litter of 'em, see what I care,' Tom added.

Then, as Tom turned to lead his horse away, leaving those words in the air, gutlessly cast in front of those who couldn't hear, Sarah made a quick sign. Earl didn't recognise it.

Tom did because he dropped the reins and surged forwards. Earl caught him. Tom tried to swing a fist in Bill's direction, but his movement was restricted, so he writhed. Earl gripped harder.

'Lemme at him, old man.'

'No fear.'

'I guess not. The kid wouldn't fight anyhow. He's a runner.'

'That so?' Earl beckoned with his head for Bill to come forwards. Bill queried, but Earl nodded permission.

'Turn your back, Laura,' Earl said firmly. She didn't argue.

When the women looked away, Bill made a fist.

Earl nodded again.

'You cripple coward,' Tom spat.

Bill laid a single hammer blow into Tom's solar plexus. Earl let the boy collapse to the mud, coughing and clutching his midriff.

He crouched at the boy's side and lowered his voice.

'You or your pa touch me, my family, or these ladies, I'll kill you all.' He picked up the reins of Tom's horse and threw them onto the boy. 'Get up and go home.'

He didn't watch the reprobate leave, though he listened to ensure the sound grew fainter. He clasped Bill, then helped the young lovers gather their belongings and walk along the rock line.

Walter had unhitched their mounts and was tendering a canteen. Sarah took it, drank, and passed it to Bill.

'I don't know what to say,' Laura ventured.

'I ain't sure either.' Earl wiped a fleck of mud from her forehead.

'He has to know he's relieved of the burden.'

'Not sure I got enough signs for telling.'

She rested a hand on his shoulder. 'So, I'll do it. All the same, you're without a home.'

'Better me than Bill. I got a few dollars for rooms.' He glanced at Walter. 'Or maybe there's a free floor someplace.'

Walter nodded.

She shook her head. 'I won't hear it. You'll move into the house.'

He eased back. 'I don't reckon—'

'You're a stubborn soul, so I won't argue with you. I'll only ask my courting gentleman nicely.' She pressed her lips to his cheek. 'There's a space for you, and I'd like you there until we find another way.'

He looked at Walter, who'd purposely turned to admire the landscape. Bill and Sarah munched gratefully on biscuits, and he wondered about their thoughts.

However, he was a grown man and could make his own damn decisions. 'That'd be… real nice.'

'Good. So, let's go home.'

He assessed the horses, the conditions underfoot, and the brightening day. 'I figure I'll stop by my place. Check for storm damage and such. See if it's still five hundred dollars' worth. Sure hope so.'

She nodded. 'That's an idea.'

'And take Bill.'

'That's a better idea.'

'Walt,' he called. 'You see these good women back to town.'

Walter doffed his hat. 'My pleasure.'

Bill was intrigued, still undoubtedly unaware of what had transpired and what was due.

'Laura, would you tell Bill what went on?' Earl asked.

'My pleasure too.'

He retrieved Jack and Dusty, and walked to where Walter held Tanner and Hester.

Bill's eyes searched Earl's—his head now full of the how and why—and he was a coiled spring. Earl expected a battle of wills, a request to backtrack on his gesture, or possibly a bear hug.

Instead, Bill simply signed, "Thank you, Pa."

"No problem. Son."

Walter guided Laura and Sarah together onto Hester, then mounted Dusty.

'I want Walt in the house 'til we're back,' Earl instructed.

'And coffee on the stove.' Laura blew a kiss.

The trio turned and cautiously picked their way down the treacherous slope towards the prairie floor a hundred feet below.

"Let's go," he signed to Bill. "I got things to show you."

Chapter 52

They only rode for a half-hour before stopping to let the horses drink from a swollen stream. Tanner hadn't eaten in maybe eighteen hours, and Earl didn't want to push too hard—there was a long day ahead.

By mid-morning, the sun burned warm, and the ground they traversed had been less drenched by the storm. They upped the pace, and the imaginary scent of the stove coffee pot tickled his nostrils.

Meantime, he bathed in having this time with Bill. His frame seemed taller. The air felt cleaner. Unarguably, life had fewer troubles.

The creek which bordered the house ran strong, strewn with twigs and leaves, so he took care over the crossing point upstream of the property. Caked mud washed from the horses' legs, and welcome spray kicked up into the men's faces.

He led Bill to the small corral, and they heaved one of winter's last hay bales from the feed store behind the house and took it to the animals. The trough had brimmed overnight, and quickly the horses nourished themselves.

Earl patted Tanner. "He's a fine horse."

"I have a real thief to thank for that," Bill replied with a smile.

Earl recalled the hundred-dollar reward. "The Sheriff should count your good d-e-e-d-s more than your bad."

Bill was patient while Earl finger-spelled—even using it himself when Earl hadn't followed.

As they wandered to the house, Bill spied the outdoor fire pit and signed "wood".

Earl nodded. Any way of getting coffee and beans hot was good enough. His stomach growled. Bill looked worn out and pale, having only been nourished by a girl's company. Earl thought of Laura and couldn't wait to be in her arms again.

Bill peered into the workshop. Earl took him inside and showed him the prepared wood, tools, and works-in-progress.

Bill picked up a carved walking cane. "You are good."

"I make my way."

"Why would you sell this all for me?"

"A house can be r-e-p-l-a-c-e-d. A son can not."

Bill nodded humbly. "Thank you. I am sorry I ran."

Earl clasped the boy's shoulder. "I ran too, afore. When I had nobody."

"Now we do."

He saw Mary's eyes in the boy. "I was mad at you. I am not sorry for that. Don't run, Bill. Always face up to what you done."

Bill's face creased. "I will."

Back outside, they collected the detritus from Earl's earlier rage. Bill paused, inspecting a rudely butchered piece of carving. He held it up, and his finger traced the grooves in the mesquite: "ALDE".

Earl puffed out a breath, searching for the right words and how to express them with his hands. "This was your cross. Until you lived again."

"A-l-d-e?"

"That was your birth name. A-l-d-e-n."

Bill waggled the wood. "At the old house?" Earl nodded. "Why broken?"

"Because… because I can be a weak man."

Bill canted his head, introspective, then brightened. "Strong too. For me."

"I guess."

"Where should I put it?"

There was no remaking the cross—Earl had no desire and no need. He wanted to carry the shards—or maybe just that piece—in his saddlebag for all days as a reminder of his weakness. Yet, it would also bring an echo of what he'd long thought lost but had now regained.

It was a relic of a past life. One he needed to let go.

"Put it on the fire," he signed.

Bill queried, so Earl reaffirmed with a nod.

They gathered the pieces of the cross, plus the hand axe with which he'd threatened the life of his dearest friend, and tossed them on the smoky fire.

They sat and ate and drank, and he imbibed the silence of the homestead. The whisper of the wind, the chatter of the creek and the crackle of the wet wood.

After an hour, they shut up the house, kicked wet earth across the small fire's ashes and took to the saddle.

They rode for three hours across the drying scrub. Birds wheeled, seeking treasures uncovered by the rains.

He'd told Bill their destination—no point in making it a surprise.

As they neared the old house, he worked harder to suppress negativity. When they arrived, he said and signed nothing but let Bill dismount and tentatively approach the ruined walls.

The rusted trough had filled with water, so he led the horses over to drink.

He watched his boy pick through the wreckage, pausing to examine the blackened and slimy stone as if trying to sense history by touch alone.

Involuntarily, Earl wandered to Mary's grave. Beside it stood the unmarked rectangle of stones which had longtime represented Bill—no, Alden. Seeing his son here, large as life, reawakened something crammed deep down inside—that these were only ever memorials, tributes in loco of actual forms beneath the ground.

On a good day, he counted his stars that he'd not returned to two bodies—shot, scalped, or burned—but merely the absence of his family. Despite the crushing, all-consuming grief and regret, a minuscule flame had remained alight in case he was one day, inexplicably, reunited with them. Over the years, however, that flame had died—or he extinguished it. Living with the possibility of redemption was even more challenging than dealing with the finality of loss—and he'd done poorly on that too.

He'd disappeared into a daydream, and Bill was at his side.

"This makes me sad," Bill signed.

"Sad is right. But she's in a good place now." He glanced upwards and stroked one of the stones.

Bill knelt and caressed the carved legend on the remaining angel cross. "You made this, like for me."

Earl nodded his fist.

Bill gently fingered the petals of the recently planted stems. "These was Ma's [—] flowers?"

Earl flashed a query—a word had slipped him by.

"F-a-v-o-r-i-t-e," Bill spelt.

"Yes."

Bill let that sink in. "Laura likes these."

"That's true."

"What was she like? Ma?"

Earl girded himself. "Good. Pretty. Brave to marry me. An angel."

"Tribe said she gave herself for me."

He had to look away and breathe hard. "That was Mary."

"You made a nice spot for her."

"It was just a spot. She ain't here." His legs ached from crouching, so he stood and looked over the vista, trying to take it for what it was, not what past it held.

Bill caught his eye. "I think I know where."

The sun fell from zenith, blasting in their faces as they headed west. Earl pulled the brim down low while still able to follow Tanner's tracks.

After two hours—breaking for biscuits, water, and jerky—Bill halted atop a low rise.

In the valley below, two small rivers merged in a crooked V, sandwiching a fertile plain maybe a mile across. Sunlight glinted off the rippling water.

Earl scanned the horizon. All was clear. He pulled off his hat and wiped sweat on his sleeve.

Bill pointed. "The old camp."

Yet there was only a place in Bill's young memory.

Earl imagined scattered tepees, horses corralled up, food animals penned, and smoke rising from fires dotted through the village. Dark faces, dark hair, foreign tongues. Fear and revenge, hatred and misunderstanding. A small corner where a white boy could be accepted, grow, and be taught to sign, ride, care, and a million other things.

He nodded a reply and replaced his hat.

Bill tapped Tanner's flank and led them down the slope.

As they got closer, Earl didn't fear Mojave, their ghosts, or an ambush. He only feared failure because now he knew Mary had a resting place, he couldn't think to live without at least seeing it once.

The land levelled, and Bill weaved his path, searching for an exactness within his general recollect.

Five years had passed since the Mojave were taken to their new Reservation, and nature had reclaimed the once-cleared spots of ground, filling in the holes from driven stakes and poles. Yet if Earl looked closely, there were scraps of evidence, though they weren't his actual quarry.

The wind susurrated through the longer plumes of grass, and the rivers burbled in stereo.

Bill nudged Tanner into a faster trot, so Earl spurred Jack. A hundred yards on, Bill saw the spot and slurred to a stand. They dismounted and left the horses ground-hitched, allowing them to munch gratefully on the lush greenery.

Bill was impassive in his approach; Earl tentative. The reality screamed in his ears and burned his retina.

It was indeed here—a simple unmarked cairn of stones.

They stood a respectful six feet away. Earl removed his hat, and Bill followed suit, checking his father's face as if learning how to grieve.

Earl's heart yawed—one moment leaden, the next moment floating.

"Mother," Bill signed.

Earl forced away the lump in his throat. He pulled Bill close and breathed deeply and evenly of the cool air.

There was a sign he'd asked Laura about, never knowing when he'd use it. He took back his hand, as both were needed.

"Wife."

He fought tears, and then didn't. Bill now understood how to grieve, and did.

After a couple of minutes, with salty residue drying on his face, Earl went to Jack and unhitched the wooden angel. Bill walked down to the river's edge.

They met at the cairn. While Bill held the cruciform steady, Earl used a wet stone to drive it into the ground. It slid easily into the fertile earth, and they checked it was straight and firm. He laid the stone on top of the cairn, clasped his hands together and closed his eyes for a minute. He was pretty sure Bill did the same.

There was nothing more to do.

He studied the surroundings and committed them to memory. This unfamiliar land was the home of a longtime scourge race that he should hate but didn't. The land of his son's unseen upbringing.

He looked at the cairn again and steeled his nerves. His signing was poor, but he did his best as he spoke.

'I'm saying goodbye now, Mary, but I have our boy, and another angel to guide me.'

Bill signed, "Goodbye, Ma."

Quickly, before more tears came, he took Bill's arm and walked back to the horses.

Each took to the saddle, turned for the rise and set off.

Neither looked back.

Chapter 53

The route back was unfamiliar—retracing their steps wasn't the direct way to White Rock.

Earl took the lead and struck out southeast, and when they reached the first high ground, he scanned the undulating horizon, used the sun as a compass, and picked out a route. He reckoned he could see ten miles and aimed for another high ridge. From there, he expected to find a landmark—maybe Tipping Rock.

"Are we lost?" Bill signed.

"Do you know this land?"

Bill shook his head.

Four Pines lay way off east—though Earl had never visited. "We're good. Home by sundown."

He jabbed Jack's flank, and they set off.

The going passed flat and easy, and they reached the ridge in good time. At its foot ran an arrow-straight stream that had cut down through a vein of soft rock. A pair of Palo Verde provided shade, so the men dismounted and let the horses eat and drink.

They stripped a few dead branches from the trees, Earl dug out his flint and tinder, and they worked up a fire for coffee. Bill refilled their canteens in the brook and dug dried fruit and biscuits from his war bag.

As they sat there, Earl listened to the water tinkle and the leaves murmur.

He felt sad that Bill would never experience these small beauties of nature. Equally, the boy didn't want pity or special treatment.

How would he have reacted if Bill had trodden precisely the same path—endured the same scrape, needed the support and bailout—but been a hearing person? It opened forks of past happenstance, idle wondering and then, quickly, introspection, so he shut it down and concentrated on the moment and building the future.

Bill dug into his tan waistcoat pocket and unfolded the crumpled news cutting presented weeks before at another campfire. He set it under his boot. "I'm not Bill no more."

"Your name is who you want, son."

"It never was."

"What did… they… call you afore?"

"C-o-w-e-s-s-e-s-s. It meant 'little child'."

"Mary could have told them your name."

"She did. When she was gone, they wanted an Indian name."

Earl nodded. "I guess."

"I didn't mean to be like Wild Bill."

"Not wild. Just Bill."

"Yeah."

"Well, that's fine on my account."

Bill shook his head. "That's past now."

"Whatever you want, son."

"Alden. I'm Alden Johnson." He finger-spelt it.

Earl swallowed raw emotion. "Sure. That'd be… real good."

Bill tugged the paper from under his sole and placed it on the fire. They watched it catch and burn quickly to ash.

The sun glowed hot orange, a few handspans from the horizon, as they slowed to a trot at the town limits.

Earl was struck by the enormity of the decision to give up his home, and the resulting burden on them to make a future in White Rock. There was no sensible alternative and equally little way to turn all hearts and minds in their favour. Perhaps he'd sunk their only lifeboat.

They stabled the horses and went to Abe's hut to advise of their return. In the ten-foot square wooden shack, with a dark patch on the floor where the storm had breached the old roof, Abe was in an old chair, hand to his forehead.

He rose as if startled.

Earl sensed something amiss. He glanced around in case of marauders or ne'er-do-wells, but all was calm.

'Earl, Bill,' Abe said, signing a greeting.

'What gives?'

'Gives?'

Earl saw the bluff because he'd noted the cut and nascent swelling above the man's left eye. Reflexively, he touched his own jaw. 'What happened?'

'I fell. Tripped on a damn rope.' But his face betrayed him.

'Never figured you a liar, Abe.'

The man shuffled on his feet.

Earl clasped the man's arm. 'You helped my boy. You gave us the words of them deputies, and it fixed the mess. You're a stand-up guy, and we're real grateful. So, I'll ask again—who did this?'

Abe's dark eyes scanned his visitors. 'Potter came calling.'

'I coulda figured.' Earl ground his teeth.

'Look, I guess the deputies caught sight of me last night. I'll live—it's fine.'

'Nothing fine 'bout it. It's low down to beat on a man what's only looking to get the truth.' Earl spat. 'But the truth don't matter to Lyle Potter where the boy's concerned.'

'Walter told me what happened out there. I'm real glad.'

'Men already got shot and killed for lies and greed. You're lucky not to take more'n a fist.'

Abe gave a faint shrug. 'Mayor and I have an understanding.'

'From past deeds?'

'Deeds and… debts.'

'Well, ours is debt too. So come to the house, and Laura'll fix you up.'

'I'm good.'

'That ain't an invitation. 'Sides, I reckon there'll be a spread laid out for having like a prodigal son come home.'

There was a spread, but it lay untouched on the table for a long while. Laura attended to Abe's wound.

'I never figured Lyle had the balls to lay his fist on another man,' Walter said.

'Gun butt.' Abe winced under the smart of the iodine.

'I thought you were impervious,' Laura said.

'You can test a loyalty too far.'

Earl sneaked a crispy strip of bacon from the table, wolfed it down, and brought a finger to his lips when Sarah gave him a motherly shake of the head. She and Alden were jammed into a chair that had been brought from the living room. They looked sorely tired. His head rested on her shoulder.

'What's he gotta be owing you for?' Walter asked Abe.

'His life, and maybe silence.'

'What the hell d'you go and save his life for?' Earl scoffed.

Laura gave him a warning eye. 'Mind yourself. Most folks in town haven't got grudges against the man.'

'You're among friends, Abe,' Walter said, encouraging him.

'I'm sworn secret.'

'Are you sworn secret 'bout this cowardly assault?' Earl asked. 'If no, I'll make it my business to tell whoever asks.'

'Please, Earl, no. I don't need to give the man any other cause.'

'Then how come a good man like you is beholding to a guttersnipe like Lyle Potter? On account of he runs this town and pays your wage?'

Abe sighed and eased Laura's hand away from his head.

He nodded thanks and took the coffee she offered. 'The raiding posse—with good Jim—that's when it happened.'

'No shame in saving a man's life—whatever man,' Walter suggested.

Abe took a long draw from his mug. 'So, we rode out to get Potter's gold. We surprised them. All the same, Mojave made it a real fight. Jim and Potter and me high-tailed out when we got the gold. Some men fell. Sam Bowman's brother too. Dennis was last out.'

Earl clicked his fingers. 'Damn. I still gotta talk to him.'

The man nodded slowly, distant. 'Yeah.' A sigh. 'We holed up that evening, straight after, to lick our wounds. And for Potter to check his loot. Dennis, me and Jim—all that got away with our wits and limbs. My and Potter's horses took rounds and were hurting.'

Earl went to Laura and held her hand. He didn't know how much of this was old ground to her, but sometimes the rawness of recollection can take a person unawares and kick them in the gut.

Abe continued. 'We made up a fire and filled our bellies. Jim took first watch. I was off taking a piss. Three of 'em came. One got to Jim before I got my shot off.' He pulled an apologetic, supportive expression. 'Dennis killed the second. The other feller had Potter by the throat, ready for scalping. I didn't have a clean shot. They fought. That's how he got hurt—cut a tendon in his thigh. I had to pull the raider away. Managed to duck his swing and get two good shots.'

He bent forwards, fiddling his hands together. 'So, Lyle owes me. And Sam never really forgave him, though he follows Lyle around like a puppy. And Lord knows what I'd do if it was the same camp and we brought deafness to your boy. I thought enough suffering went on anyhow.'

Earl drew Laura closer. She was signing to Alden and Sarah, recounting the tale as the youngsters held hands.

Walter looked at the two pairs of sweethearts. 'Call me an old soak, but more than gold came out of that day. I could break that man's bones as much as anyone, but let's eat, give thanks for what we got and not stir up any more hornet's nests.'

Earl nodded sombrely. 'All well and good, but you ain't the one got stung.'

They filled their bellies, and then Abe made his excuses and left.

Laura played copycat phrases on the piano with Sarah to raise spirits, but Earl remained subdued.

'We never took that birthday drink,' Walter murmured. 'I reckon you could use it tonight.'

That was accurate. 'I guess now's the day I gotta ask permission.'

'Don't think I won't chaperone you.'

'One day, you won't be needing to.'

'That'd be a good day,' Walter said with a smile. 'So, will we raise a glass to a better year than many?'

'I guess so.' Earl stood. 'Laura? Walt and I are heading to the saloon. We got kind of a tradition for taking a drink around my birthday, and I don't wanna let the man down.'

Her face lit. 'Birthday, is it?'

'A few days back.'

He hadn't bothered to mention it, not expecting a gift so early in their relationship and certainly not wanting to make her guilty for missing something she couldn't know about. He had to find out her special day so as not to feel an ass when the time came. Walter's was November twenty-fifth. Aside from Mary and Alden's, this was the only other date he ever cared for.

'Why didn't you say?' She rose from the stool and squeezed his hand.

'Only person ever minded these past years was Walt, so I never had a reason to give it much thinking.'

'Well, I hope the supper made up for me not knowing.'

'Having you and Alden in my world is better'n any gift.'

She smiled, then fell sterner. 'The saloon? Tonight, of all nights?'

Walter held Earl's shoulder. 'There'll be no trouble.'

'No,' she said firmly. 'Not unless you want to sleep in the stables.'

Earl raised his hand in affirmation. 'I'll lay a finger on no man.'

'Nor bullet, nor bottle,' she added.

He pecked her cheek. 'Guess I got a lotta earning trust to do.'

'Perhaps a little. Now go with your friend. And if you want a bed, come home sober too.' She winked.

'This is why I never got married,' Walter murmured.

'I heard that, Walter Doonan,' she said.

Earl nodded farewells to Sarah and Alden, then paused. Something tugged at his insides.

Chapter 54

The moon sat low and full in the sky as the three walked up Main Street. Many hours had packed into that day, and weariness crept in. Earl would have passed on Walter's offer, but the man had to get back to his life. This burst of intense proximity in their friendship was ending. Everyday life was resuming, although, for Earl, it would be nothing like the old normal. It would be immeasurably better.

This would be a "see you around" drink.

'Now I feel like a third wheel.'

He looked at Walt. 'How d'you figure? I got more to talk 'bout with you than my boy—and easier ways of doing it.'

'You should take him with you to clear out your old place. Maybe he'll help with your signing.'

He chuckled. 'I never felt so old.'

'Funny. I never seen you so young.'

The music drifting down the street grew louder. The surface was choppy underfoot, where the mud created by the storm had dried unevenly and not yet become powdered and flattened by boots, hooves and wheels.

The saloon buzzed—he reckoned many folks had held over yesterday's drink, not wanting to get drenched on the journey. With Walter at the rear, Earl led Alden in and spied an empty corner table. Alden gazed around, oblivious to the piano's rag overlaying the clamour of chatter and rap of glass on wood. Smoke coiled above many of the tables.

They went to the long bar, its surface decked with a sheen of spilt beer. Walter was quick to get money ready. Earl turned to Alden and signed, his right hand a palm, drawing it, index finger touching, down his cheek.

Alden nodded.

'Beer for the boy,' Earl said.

'You—ginger ale?' Walter asked.

'Whiskey,' he replied. 'And cut out that look. Things change.'

'Well now, I guess they do.'

Walter caught the barkeep's attention and ordered. Each collected their drinks. Alden nodded his thanks, and Walter headed away.

By luck, their table lay on the opposite side of the room to where Bowman and Potter sat. All the same, Earl had no illusions that their sojourn would pass unnoticed.

He laid some coins on the top and looked the barkeep straight. 'That's for damages.'

'What damages?'

He merely turned and went to join the others.

The first sip of whiskey smarted through unfamiliarity, then Walter offered his glass and they all toasted.

Alden signed "Happy", which Earl recognised, then touched his index finger chin to chest, and Earl had a pretty good idea what that word was.

"Thank you. Son."

He watched the boy and drank pensively. 'So, I guess I'll take Alden to my place like you said. Gonna miss it, I reckon.'

'If you've spare time—what with your boy, good lady, learning signs, and your woodworking—to take to maudlin over a pile of logs that housed a worse man—a man you oughta forget, maybe my lecturing days aren't fully over.' Walter smiled to show he was only half-serious.

Then the smile faded.

Earl looked up—there were two visitors at their table.

'Evening, Sam, Lyle,' Walter said flatly.

Earl's hackles rose, but he kept them in check. 'What can I do for ya?' he asked with forced politeness.

'Nothing at all.' Potter eyed Alden with undisguised distaste. 'Just checking on this... happy gathering.'

'Civil drink is all, wetting throats at the end of a helluva day.'

Potter nodded. 'Sam told me.'

'Well, good. Then you know all debts been paid.'

'Debts? Maybe. All the same, it doesn't erase what happened.'

Earl rose carefully. 'What's on your mind, mister Mayor?'

'I'll recall giving you and the cripple boy an ultimatum. Any trouble with the law, and he leaves town.'

Earl sneered. 'You take that word back.'

'Man's got a place to say what he wants. Especially in his own town.'

'And a man's got a right to defend his boy. And another man's daughter if he must.'

Potter leaned in. 'Why, Laura's bed getting sympathy from one she knows?'

Earl narrowed his eyes. 'Time used to be a man in your position would defend the town from ignorant accusing un-gentlemanly folk, not be one.'

Potter's hand came to his gun. 'You want to watch your words, not even being a citizen. And the deaf boy—did he ask to come here? Did he ask to stay? Did he speak it? Mojave are thieving rats. How's it feel to have your boy raised by them?'

Earl covered his shiny new weapon.

Potter sneered. 'Gun again, is it? You see, Sam? That's a real bluff!'

Earl's belly churned, yet Walter's stare was a tight rein, and the thought of Laura was an angel on his shoulder.

'Only difference between you and my boy is you'd hear the bullet coming.'

Potter's eyes widened, his fat cheeks reddened, and he glanced around. 'There's a lot of witnesses in here to threats like that.'

'And a lot to slurs on good character.'

'Why? Which of you and that there,' he glared at Alden, 'Is good?'

Earl looked at Potter's right hip. 'And which of you is the cripple?'

'What did you say?'

'Blight by innocence is no crime, but cripple by guilt and greed is an affront to the Lord. We ain't leaving town, and that's an end to it.'

Potter's brow creased. 'Is that so?'

'Only one man here has blood on his hands. Alden put the good of your damn Bank afore hisself, and the truth of his past above the lies of those deputies.'

'And he laid hands on my boy.'

'Everybody gets what's coming.'

'Pardon me?' Potter brought his whiskey breath closer.

'We're going on with our lives now, Mayor. You have a good evening.' Earl sat, heart pounding.

'I don't like your tone.'

He stood again. 'I don't like your words. And I don't like what happened to my boy.'

'What's your meaning in that?'

'We all got burdens. And times we need a drink to ease them. So, we'll sit.'

'Sit and make the hands of the red man, language of heathens.'

Earl smiled conspiratorially. 'Yeah. And say what we wanna 'bout you and this town, which you'd never know, nor get proof on.' He signed "Asshole" to Alden, who let a smile loose and looked away.

'I won't have that in here,' Potter reaffirmed loudly.

'You can't outlaw a man moving his hands. Ain't that so, Sam?'

Bowman looked sheepish. 'I guess, maybe.'

'Back me up, Sam,' Potter demanded.

'Been enough false talking of the law today,' Earl said.

The Mayor's nose moved close to touching distance. 'You better know your place.'

'I sure do. Here, with my boy and my good friend Walter. Trying to take a drink and not be ragged on by cheats and bad-mouthing sons of bitches.'

Potter snarled, then cocked his nose towards Alden. He stepped back. 'You're not worth it.' He turned.

'My thinking too.'

Potter rounded, nostrils flaring, and his fist lashed out.

Earl dodged left.

Potter's arm missed by a clear margin, powered forwards and dragged its rotund owner into overbalance. His left arm flailed, pawing at the table. Alden leapt back, grabbing both glasses.

Potter caught the edge of the table, toppling it away, and crashed to a heap on the ground. He rolled onto his back, eyes ablaze, face red.

Earl held up his palms. 'Not a finger on the man, Walt. You too, Sam. Swing and a miss.' At the nearby tables, chatter had evaporated, and movement had slowed. The piano fell silent.

Bowman extended a helping hand, but Potter flapped it away and pushed himself to a stand.

Walter covered his gun. Earl left his alone. But Potter merely turned brusquely and weaved away through the tables. Smatters of laughter followed in his wake.

Alden sat down and nervously fingered his glass.

Earl set the table upright and eased into his chair.

He insisted they stay and have a second drink, not wanting to be rushed away or walk out as if a job was done. They'd have to be honest with Laura, but his conscience was clear.

The piano struck up. Hubbub returned to normal. One of the neighbours even nodded in approval. Earl bobbed a curt appreciation but didn't want to get into dialogue—he'd no desire to be dividing up sides in town. Every man had enemies and friends, and he was no different. Perhaps worse, as the head of the town wouldn't be shy in preaching the evils of the Mojave, alleged half-caste boys, and the scourge of the deaf and their heathen ways.

"Will he ever stop?" Alden asked.

"Someday," Earl replied, not knowing when, how, or why. Everything dies, he reminded himself. Even hate.

Walter returned with the second drinks, and on his heels was Dennis Hayes.

Dennis nodded. 'Earl.'

'Hey.'

'I saw what went on.'

Earl worried that Dennis might see the altercation as an echo of his accident, and it could give credence to the notion that Earl was no good. But this time was different for many reasons.

'What of it?' he asked.

'Gravity's no friend to a man of Lyle's… deportment.'

Earl managed a faint smile. 'That's so. We still got a beef?'

'No. You wanted to talk. This your boy?'

'I got that pleasure.'

Dennis touched the brim of his hat. 'Good to know you.'

Alden tapped his forehead and nodded.

'Will you take a drink?' Earl asked.

'Thank you, no. That would be consorting with the enemy a mite much for Lyle's demeanour.'

'I get that.'

Dennis tugged over a spare chair. 'What do you want to know?' He stroked his whiskers.

'That raid. Was it on a river fork?'

'Yeah. One way in and out. Smart people. Not so smart to cross the Mayor, though.'

'Abe says you was last out, and there was dynamiting.'

Dennis bowed his head and puffed. 'That's true. Lyle's direction. "Leave the red sons of bitches a message".'

Walter's brow knit. 'What message?'

'I dropped a pound of dynamite in the cooking pot outside the Chief's tent. Damn near took my ears off at many yards.'

Earl stood like he'd been stung on the ass. 'What'd you say?'

'A parting shot. A warning not to cross Lyle again.'

Earl fizzed like a bad keg. 'Alden done told us some of how he comes to be deaf, and stone me if we didn't get the devil's side.'

Walter gestured firmly, and Earl sat.

'He was there?' Dennis asked.

Earl nodded, his teeth clenched. 'Kidnapped as a baby. Revenge or a surrogate kid. I got no care 'bout reasons. Fact is, explosion took his ears, killed his ma—my Mary.'

Dennis closed his eyes. 'Shoot.'

'Can you be certain it was you?' Walter asked.

'Look, I didn't mean for—'

'We already called even, you and me,' Earl said. 'I just gotta know.'

Dennis wrung his old hands. The lines on his face deepened.

'I rode away, and I guess I saw a woman with a youngster making to run.' He covered his eyes. 'I thought them Mojave, but....' He bowed his head.

Earl steeled his frame, seeing himself in the person before him, as a younger man with the world crushing down. A man who'd needed a friend and confidant, someone to shake him and show the error of his self-recrimination.

'Hayes, I hold no grudge against you. Get this straight—it ain't your doing.'

'To kill that poor woman—your wife, Earl—and take this young man's hearing?' Dennis' head shook as if casting away demons. 'I can't bear look at either of you.'

'A man don't gotta forgive hisself for what weren't his fault. I learned that some. I wish it weren't so, but our deeds is meant with good reason, and we can't be riled up for circumstance we had no knowing of. That posse raid, that explosion—that's on the head of another man. A lot worse man than you. A greedy, gutless coward. So, like I say, we'll go on with our lives.'

Dennis gripped Earl's arm. 'I'll carry it with me, as I will everything that day and the next, and if I had my time again, I'd turn Lyle down flat.'

Earl removed the man's hand. 'I carry what I did to you. So, there'll be no hitting here.'

'You're a good man.'

'Well, that's as maybe.'

Alden tapped Earl's arm. Earl scanned the boy's face. What to say? He tried his best, in a few simple sentences—the facts, with no side. Alden absorbed it all and grew sullen. The other three men exchanged glances. Earl sipped his drink.

Alden put his shoulders back and signed.

Earl breathed a sigh of relief and turned to Dennis. 'He forgives you.'

'Convey my apologies.'

'I already did.'

'Do it again. Please.'

Earl did. Alden nodded to Dennis and forced a thin smile, which was returned. Dennis stood.

Walter deliberately cleared his throat. Earl recognised that kind of nagging and identified the reason why.

He stood. 'I forgive you, Hayes.'

Dennis rubbed a fingertip over his missing eye. 'Likewise.'

'If it's all the same, keep it from Lyle,' Earl asked.

'I intend to. I couldn't bear to see him happy. Frankly, it's all I can do to keep civil with the man.'

'You and me both.'

Chapter 55

They parted with Walter at the adjacent Hotel, and Alden returned to the forge after giving his father a grateful hug. Earl walked the last few hundred yards, serenaded by cicadas, muted voices and distant music.

Sarah had turned in, but Laura was up.

He decided it was best to be upfront about events. 'You oughta know, Potter tried to make me draw tonight.'

She took his hands. 'And?'

'He can rail on me all he likes. That's a man's grudge. But on Alden, or you, or Sarah? I only got so much steel in me. But I didn't lay a finger. Walt saw—he'll say.'

'That's wise. Lyle's a fast draw for a big man.'

'Well, if it's the Lord's wish, maybe one day soon a faster gun'll come to town.'

She touched his cheek. 'That man's name is used too much in this house.'

'For certain now. Dennis talked.'

'Oh. So?'

His head fell. 'It was the posse what done that to the boy.'

She closed her eyes. 'Oh, Lord.'

She led him to the sofa, where he explained all. Silence fell. The clock ticked. They let the revelation permeate.

'Dennis is a beat man for what he done.'

She nodded. 'I'm not surprised. But it wasn't his idea.'

'No. And if they wasn't close afore, I don't see him and Lyle breaking bread no more.'

'Sarah won't like it. Perhaps it's good that she and Alden share something, even if it's loathing for the same man.' She stood and adjusted some ornaments.

He followed, concerned the news might rile her. 'I don't reckon Alden's the loathing type. But maybe he took enough hate in his life, and it washes off easier than Sarah.' He held her waist. 'She's had you to keep her from the shadows of the world.'

'I do what I can.'

'We gotta look forward—you're always telling me so. Talking to Dennis were the thing, and it's done. He can't go back, no more'n you or I. 'Sides, I sign pretty good now, huh?'

She smiled. 'You learned a few tricks, old dog.'

A thought occurred to him. 'Walt was saying you all have a Fourth'a July dance and such? We should make it a… kinda family affair. New frocks and all. Put our happy faces on.'

'Is that an invitation, Earl Johnson?' Her eyes twinkled.

He took a mock bow.

'I'd be real proud if you'd accompany me to the dance, Laura, ma'am.' He pulled her close. 'It'd be a single honour.'

She did a so-so of her head. 'I'll sleep on it.'

He patted her backside. 'Sleep—that'd be an idea. The day's been a week or more.'

'Will you walk up to the Hotel? Or would you not make it that far—seeing how tired you are?'

He took this on board. The haggard old men looked up from their stools and pulled cigarettes from their lips, ready to grind them out with boot soles.

'I guess… I guess that'd be another way.'

He sat on the edge of the bed, pensive. A night here was no longer a treat or a luxury, but a necessity, unless he wanted to spring for a hotel room or take to his blanket for an uncomfortable sojourn under God's ceiling.

'Regretting your decision today?' she asked.

'Ain't nothing to regret. Parents gotta make sacrifices for their kids.'

'You and Walter worked hard building that house.'

'Yeah. But it were just a house. Not a home. Not like this.'

'Believe me—there were many days it felt cold and empty. Much nicer with you here.'

She dimmed the lamp, and the flickering light threw their shadows on the wall—standing shadows which embraced, pressed close and merged.

They paused, and he helped her turn down the bed.

'There's still time to get your hat,' she said softly.

'I figure putting on more clothes is the exact opposite of how it goes.'

'I don't enter into this any more lightly than you.'

'I'm glad on that.'

'We both had our courting years and hoped never to see them again.' Her fingers moved over his shirt.

'But we neither of us forgot.'

'No.'

They kissed, and then he stood calmly as she unbuttoned his shirt, and he hers. She managed her skirt, and he removed his pants. The shadows merged again, the cotton of her undergarments soft to his touch.

What broke the spell was a sense memory, a good one that triggered reticence, caution and an echo of guilt. As often, she noticed it and let him break their embrace. A querulous expression flitted on her face.

He forced a smile. 'You'll be getting the idea this ain't easy—and that's right. But don't take that it's not nice.'

She stroked his hair. 'I know.' She gently bit her lip. 'Listen, it's a warm night, so I'm undressing and getting under the covers. Rest is fine, and talk is fine.'

'Those is fine, for now.'

She moved to the far side of the bed and unbuttoned her camisole, so he turned his back, went to the near side of the bed, sheepishly pulled off his long johns and choreographed himself unseen under the covers. It was like thirty years had never happened. He was like a young buck again, fizzing with desire.

He relaxed onto the pillow. The sheets were cool and less starchy than at the Hotel. She lay beside him, covers loosely pulled up around her neck, her face glowing in the light from his side cabinet lamp.

Distantly came the clatter of hooves on dirt and the rush of wheels. Then quiet, and the reality of the situation.

'You're awful pretty and forgiving of a man's ways.'

'You can call me pretty any day you like.' Her hand rested on his chest, and her knee brushed his thigh. The covers slid off her shoulders.

'Whole world looks prettier today, having our children back and all.'

'I suppose even an old woman in the altogether could look pretty on a night like this.'

His gaze moved from her impish eyes to her upper chest.

'I reckon that, altogether, the altogether is fine any day.'

'Is that so? Well, the truth is, even on a warm evening, I do sleep in nightwear.'

'Meaning?'

'That's it. I'm not undressed because it's warm. I'm undressed because you're here.'

'Ah. Yeah.'

She clasped his upper hip, exerting gentle inward pressure. He kissed her lightly at first, then with less restraint. His hand lay on her waist, then moved to the warmth of her back, and he pulled her close.

Haggard old men stamped out their smokes, rolled up their sleeves, and set to long-forgotten tasks.

Chapter 56

The following morning, as the conscious world subsumed the subconscious, Earl's first sensation was of someone in the bed beside him. Quickly, he placed that as logical and pleasant. Secondly, he didn't recall any night terrors or crushing self-doubt preventing him from falling asleep.

Frankly, it all felt pretty damn fine.

He lolled his head over. She was looking at him, not in adoration—more in apprehension.

'What? I snore?'

She smiled. 'No. How are you feeling?'

'Fine, I guess.'

'So, what do you want to do first—fix up a bath so you can wash off the sin, or hurry up to the church and pray for forgiveness?'

But he spied the twinkle in her eye. 'You gotta spoil a perfectly good night, huh?'

'Silly me—assuming you enjoyed anything on this earth without chewing yourself up for a time.'

He pulled her close. 'That ain't fair. I enjoyed your cooking and your teaching, and I guess inside, I enjoy your ribbing too, 'cos it means you care.'

'Anything else?'

'You fishing, Laura Mae Anderson?'

'Perhaps.'

'I enjoyed your... company.' He ran a hand over her backside. 'Your company was... real nice.'

'So was yours. I think I can put up with you a while longer.'

'I figure putting up is a good place to start.' He kissed her.

Earl met Alden at the stables. They hitched Jack up to the old wagon, Alden mounted Tanner, and they set off for Earl's house. They didn't stop on the way but made up coffee and bites for mid-morning fuel when they arrived, then set about fitting some of his few possessions onto the wagon.

All the while, he remained workmanlike, and Alden's company kept any sense of fond parting at bay. There should be no reluctance to leave behind this empty chapter of his life.

When the horses had taken their fill, he set Jack to the wagon, tested all the fastenings, crossed himself that the ensemble would hold together, and they retraced their steps to White Rock. That passed without incident, so the following day they repeated the endeavour. Anything from the house that Laura had a better example of was left behind or consigned to the handsome fire they used to cook lunch and burn rubbish.

As he munched on the bacon and beans, cross-legged opposite his boy, the smoke of memories curled up to heaven. Nothing much had survived from the old, ruined house, so no decades-old fondness went up in ashes.

Bellies full, they damped down the fire, brimmed canteens from the river, saddled the horses, and, neither looking back, left for the last time.

Laura's place was well furnished, so there was no way they'd fit everything in—especially his tools. He needed a separate workshop again, but that would have to wait. A few things were dotted around the house, some went to the forge, and the remainder were put under a tarpaulin in a spare corner of the stables. Abe took a couple of dollars for the trouble and agreed not to breathe a word to the cantankerous owner.

They returned home to find Laura and Sarah comparing new dresses for the dance. Each did a twirl for their respective beau. Alden signed something to Sarah, which Laura translated, so Earl used it for his perspective on Laura's attire. "Beautiful."

She took his hand and shimmied, leading him to whatever tune played in her head. He tried to follow her, but his hips and rhythm were as underused as his gunplay.

She stopped. 'Now Earl,' she said, motherly, 'I'll be right that your invitation to the party this weekend means you can actually… dance?'

'It's been more'n twenty years. Reckon you can tell.'

'You're a real fixer-upper, you know?' She gave a familiar smile.

'I don't need telling. Only fixin'.'

'Then we'd better practice, hadn't we? I'm sure Alden's not one for twirling the ladies, either. If he wants to keep his girl, he should learn. And that might go for you too.'

He cupped her cheek. 'Letting me go would be as good as stone-cold murder. My heart'd break so fast.'

'That's very sweet. So, stow that hat, and let's get to it.'

They cleared a space in the living room, and Sarah took a first turn at the piano. Alden stood by, absorbing the rhythm, as Laura, with much laughter and a few trips, coaxed life into Earl's two left feet. The part he enjoyed most was finishing with a theatrical flourish, dipping her back and landing a fine kiss on her lips.

To follow, Laura took to the piano, and signed the rhythm and tune to Sarah.

He watched as, more methodically and with greater aplomb, Sarah showed Alden some steps. Whether it was their youth, the finesse of her guiding hand, a better sense of rhythm, or a tighter physical bond, there was no competition for which pair would win the house rosette on Saturday night.

A voice inside Earl suggested ears were perhaps an unnecessary luxury in the pursuit of life, love and happiness.

On Saturday afternoon, Laura announced they'd all take baths to be gleaming examples of upstanding White Rock citizens. She offered Earl first dip in the water, but he chivalrously passed over the honour and used the time to wander up to Drake's for a shave and haircut.

He took Alden, and they waited a good hour in line—with half the town having the same idea—but it was worth it.

"Sarah said there are fireworks tonight," Alden signed.

"Yeah. You ever seen them?" Earl replied.

"One time, at Four Pines. They are loud, folks say." The boy's face betrayed sadness at missing out on this part of the experience.

"Beauty is in looks, not sounds. Sarah proves that."

Alden nodded firmly. "I'm a lucky man."

"We both are."

In the bedroom, Laura was dressing after her bath, and he took no shame in admiring her as she checked his clean-shaven cheekbones and shorter locks.

'I got out quick because I knew you'd be a devil and try to climb in with me.'

He cupped her waist. 'You looking to fix that hankering part of me?'

'No. Only I want to stop you sloshing water over the floor in pursuit of… affections.'

'Then I'll be pursuing 'em later, after dancing.'

'If you have any life left in those old bones.'

He pulled her closer. 'Oh, don't you worry 'bout that.'

'Now run along, mister.'

In the bathroom, he checked his lined and sun-drenched face in the octagonal mirror, pulled off the odorous underwear and slipped gratefully into the warm water. He tilted his head back and submerged, so his ears were underwater, then washed water over his head. He lay there, warm as in a womb, eyes closed, and willed the water to absorb his scant worries.

The light level changed, and he sensed movement on the floorboards, transmitted through the bathtub and into his hands which rested on its inner surface.

He was initially concerned that Sarah or Alden had walked in, and redness of embarrassment wanted to leach from every pore. Yet the visitor hadn't darted out in a panic, so he calmly opened his damp eyes. Laura sat on the stool at the foot of the tub, watching his face.

He lifted his hands from the water. "What?" he signed.

She held up a soap bar and tossed it over.

He caught it and took it under the water. "Thanks."

"You're welcome."

"Is this a show now? Old man in the tub?"

She smiled. "No. Do you want me to go?"

"No."

The warmth wasn't merely in the water now but in his soul. He moved his hand under the surface, created the sign, and held it up. He was confident in it now: it spoke of what he'd known for days but had held back from admitting.

Her face broke into joy.

She picked up the stool and sat beside him. "ILY too."

He reached out, took her dry hand, and stroked her fingers. Her mouth moved, but he heard only a dull murmur. He pushed his ears above the surface and wiped the water away.

'There's something, ain't there?'

She smirked. 'Does your father know about Alden? He got told whys and wherefores last time?'

He knew "last time" meant she didn't want to unnecessarily bring up Mary's name. It wouldn't matter— there could be no offence. Still, he'd long ago filtered out the spots of nagging and 'fixing' which had doubtlessly gone on for those precious five years, leaving only angelic memories. Mary made him a better man, and that was worth it all.

'She insisted I wrote him when the boy were born. Ma had gone by then. Had enough of his doings.'

'And you wrote when Alden… when they….' She faltered.

'Walt insisted I say they was taken.'

'So, Charlie should hear that you have Alden back again.'

'Old fool never wrote. Can't think he cares. Didn't make to find me when I ran.'

'Perhaps your running disappointed him too much.'

He looked away. 'His riling and beating disappointed me a heap more,' he mumbled.

'Nobody's perfect. Not even you, Earl Johnson.'

'Some run, some fight. You know what man you picked here.'

She kissed his forehead. 'I know you'd fight our corner for your son and us two. You already proved that.'

'Well, I shoot 'bout as good as I dance, so let's hope no more quarrels come a-knocking.'

Chapter 57

For a joyous occasion, Earl felt too reflective, which disappointed him.

Only he could spoil the Fourth of July. Only he could taint the joy of two new relationships with the buzz of selfish musings on what might have been. The old grouch still held on by his fingertips.

He stood, leaning against a pillar in the dancehall, while music sprang, and bodies stomped and twirled. If his brain had to be distracted from the here and now, it should be fondly recalling another dancehall in another town in another decade, bathing in those moments where he fought to hold his attention on the pretty girl on the far side of the room, the one Walter said he should meet.

Now, he watched a courting couple as they blended seamlessly with the townsfolk, interconnected invisibly and silently, marking out the steps and the time, smiling and clapping. Alden looked like a dashing man, sporting a new shirt. They'd even let him wear a holster belt and Laura's gun—so he fit in with the menfolk—and he'd polished the buckle up good. Earl's chest swelled with fatherly pride.

'Okay, what's eating you tonight?'

He felt her tell-tale touch, sighed at his negative introspection, and held her waist. Honesty, as ever with Laura, was the best policy.

'You reckon they'll get wed?'

She followed his eye-line to Alden and Sarah. 'I think there's a chance. You look like that'd be the end of the world.'

'I'd be an old fool for thinking bad on others' happiness.'

'Yes, you would. Now—why?'

He'd been rumbled again. 'I barely got to know the boy, and soon he'll be leaving.'

Her face betrayed disbelieving amusement. 'Well, if you aren't the king and champion of seeing bad in every little thing.' She leaned closer to avoid a raised voice over the harmony of piano, fiddle and accordion. 'You're as good as wishing they'd break up otherwise.'

He hung his head. 'It's only wanting back them years we never got.'

'People don't stop growing, learning, and changing when they're young, like our two. Every day's an adventure. You're six feet of wonderful example about how new people and things can come to us.' She signed, "Understand?"

He bobbed his fist, pecked her cheek, and returned to gazing around.

On the periphery, Walter was in conversation with a familiar face.

'I seen Walt with that woman afore.'

'Mrs Fletcher. Yes, I've noticed them talk.'

'You figure…?'

'I don't know. She's a widow, that's true. But Walter… he said his courting days were past.'

'Fools say that sometimes, huh?'

She smiled. 'Perhaps this old dog has taught that one a new trick?'

The music ended with a flourish. Applause, whoops, and hollers barrelled through the cavernous hall.

Alden and Sarah held hands and skipped through the crowd towards the door.

Earl watched other folks watch them go, alert for signs of disquiet. Mostly, they were treated like any two people. To attract no attention was sometimes the best result because worse was possible.

In the far corner, Potter offered a flicker of worse and resumed his conversation.

Walter approached, doffing his hat theatrically. 'May I have this dance?'

Laura curtsied. It was a warm evening, and her dress was light in fabric, deeply pleated on the skirt, and a striking blue which marked a significant change from the autumnal hues she usually wore. She appeared younger, fresher—the belle of the ball—but her happiness undoubtedly contributed to the glow she radiated.

Earl wasn't too dumb to know he'd been partly responsible for that. He was the luckiest man alive.

'I didn't know you danced, Walter.'

'Well, I'll let you be the judge.'

She took Walter's arm, flashed Earl a wink, and was escorted into the centre of the room as the tune struck up.

His friend had been sandbagging and moved with rare aplomb. How the heck had Earl missed this aspect of Walter's character? For a single man without mention of courting in his life, he stepped and twirled like the best of the townsfolk.

Nearby, Mrs Fletcher watched attentively. There was something in this, he mused.

Below the pitch of the instruments came a distant thud, then another. Earl stepped to the window. Two fireworks lit up the sky in red and blue. Youths, he mused, keen for their own display before the main event took place later, out back of the dancehall.

He returned to worrying how his faltering footsteps would compare with Walter's masterclass.

Still, Laura wouldn't mind—it was merely another in her list of things to 'fix'. He watched her swirl and sway, laugh and bob, and didn't care that he wasn't perfect because she was still his gal.

When the tune finished, they walked back over, and Alden and Sarah had re-entered the room and caught the tail end of the dance.

Sarah signed to Laura, who looked at Walter and replied.

'Yes, you're a dark horse, aren't you, Walter Doonan? Really cutting a swell tonight.'

'My ma was always a dancer, and even if a boy hasn't got a girl, he's got a ma who'll nag on him to get one and teach him the steps for when he does.'

'Then I think Sarah will take a dance too.'

He tipped his hat. 'After some air, it'd be a pleasure.'

The music began again, and Walter took his leave.

Earl clasped Laura's hand, Alden took Sarah's, and they joined the throng on the busy boards of the hall.

He would have danced better—or more in tune with Laura—if he'd let less attention wander to how the youngsters performed, wondering at their understanding of the ebb and flow of the tune.

His attention flitted between them, the flow of other bodies, and Laura's twinkling brown eyes, and he felt grateful for what he had—which was much.

As they span towards the street end of the hall, the main doors burst open, with Walter in a full head of steam. He barrelled in, unconcerned by how many carousers he shoved aside.

'Laura,' he bawled. 'The house is afire.'

Chapter 58

Earl ran.

He sensed Walter at his back as he burst out from the hot, noisy atmosphere and willed his legs into more speed through the warm evening bathing Main Street. He barely registered the twilight sky as a palette of dark blues, and the fading symphony of happy celebration.

The flickering orange glow at the far end of the street was unmistakable.

A younger, fitter man passed him at a canter, a bucket of water sloshing in his hand.

'I hollered for the bowser,' Walter shouted from behind.

Earl didn't look back—he only cared that strong company was there, and the alarm had been raised. Laura was an irrelevance—he didn't want her or Sarah anywhere nearby, despite it being their home.

The distance was interminable, Main Street as long as the whole of Arizona, and with every wasted second, the futility of his upcoming task increased. Yet he pushed on, lungs bursting, gun thwacking against his thigh. The tinge of smoke in his nostrils grew with each stride.

The left side of the house was alight. Flames licked up from the dining room window towards the main bedroom.

He threw open the gate, almost tearing it from its hinges.

Walter called his name, but it was no barrier. Earl charged through the open front door, ignored the wisps of smoke which coiled in the still air, turned left, grabbed an armchair and clattered it back through the lounge door and outside.

'Don't be a fool,' Walter urged.

Earl dumped the chair on the road twenty yards from the house. 'Find water or be a help, not an ass,' he snapped.

Walter jammed his hat on a fencepost, darted up the path and inside the burning building. To their left, two people tossed meagre buckets of water on the flames. The crackling siding hissed and smoked.

'Real grateful,' Earl yelled, then hung his hat likewise and ran inside.

Smoke was seeping into all the rooms. He tugged his neckerchief over his nose and mouth like a bandit, yanked two tapestries from the wall and dashed back into the clean air.

Alden stood at the gate, breathing heavily from the jog down. Behind him, Laura and Sarah, skirts gathered up in their hands, trotted closer. Their faces were torn with despair.

He dropped the tapestries on the armchair.

"Stay here," he signed.

But Alden lobbed his hat aside, pushed past and jogged to the house.

'Damn kid,' Earl cursed, setting off in pursuit.

'Earl!'

He ignored Laura's voice, tugged off his jacket and lobbed it across the fence, where it caught awkwardly. He didn't care—jackets were cheap but houses weren't.

Walter and Alden were in the living room, so he took the stairs two at a time, plunging into the denser smoke which rose and wafted through the upper floor.

He coughed hard and kicked open the bedroom door. Heat slapped into him.

The far wall was aflame, but water spattered on the windowpane as a good-natured citizen directed the hose.

He went to the dresser, yanked out a drawer and swept everything from the surface into it—jewellery and keepsakes, including the carved brooch he'd brought for her those weeks ago.

In the corner of the room, flame licked through joints in the boards.

He dropped the drawer on the bed, threw open the wardrobe, grabbed as many clothes as possible, tossed them on top of the brimmed drawer, scooped the ensemble up and fought back through the door space.

His elbows painfully rapped the jambs as he passed. His chest hurt, and his eyes smarted.

He rattled down the stairs, burst outside, blew hateful smog from his lungs, dumped the drawer on top of the growing pile in the roadway, and turned back to the house.

A hand caught his arm. He spun.

'Let it go!' Laura's face pleaded.

'It's our home!'

'I can't live in a saved home with a dead man.'

He mashed his lips to hers. 'I ain't dying.'

Two men shouted as they grappled with the hose and bowser, its output starting weakly to combat the developing inferno. Further round, Abe directed a chain of the volunteer bucket brigade to lob their water over the side of the house. Amongst them was Dennis Hayes. Elizabeth waved.

Potter and Bowman stood at a safe distance, hands on hips, offering neither support nor harm.

Laura clutched Sarah and winced as the bedroom window exploded and spat shattered glass onto the garden.

Walter and Alden bundled more belongings out. They'd trawled upstairs, rescued some of Sarah's things, and their faces were grey with ash. The porch was tinged with flames. Soon, only a fool would go back in. They couldn't save anywhere near as much as Earl wanted.

'Last time,' he shouted over the fire's crackle.

Heat scalded his face as the threesome fought through the front door. Unspent water spattered down from above and beside. The dining room door stood ajar, and only orange was visible through the gap. He tugged the door tightly closed, vainly trying to stop it from encroaching on the hallway.

The last piece of furniture was the piano, which Alden was pulling from the wall. Earl shook his head vehemently, pointed at the piano stool, and barked at Walter to grab the other end instead.

Alden flashed an expression of insult but gathered up the stool and disappeared into the smoke billowing through the door.

They manhandled the instrument, hacking with coughs, towards the front door. It teetered under their weakened efforts, and Earl dropped it on his foot, cussing unapologetically. Sweat poured from his brow. Walter's eyes were red and streaming.

Earl heaved up his end of the piano. Walter did likewise. It yawed and smacked hard against the frame of the door. Walter yelped and pulled his hand back, then shook it, his face creased in pain. He steeled himself against the injury, and they dug deep into their last reserves to lug the bulky mass to the front door.

Earl took a deep breath, turned his face from the flames that reached for them, and pushed his leg muscles harder. They staggered out onto the path and dumped the piano down hard.

Alden arrived and took hold with gusto. Earl fed off that willpower, hefted the load, and quickly the three of them were clear of the gate and set the instrument on the dusty roadway.

As soon as the weight was off, Earl bent at the waist, drunk deep of the fresh air, and coughed out smoke.

Walter rudely grabbed Alden's jacket as the boy sought to return to the house.

'Stay here,' the man rapped.

Alden went to Sarah and held her hands. As her dress could be laundered, she pulled him close and buried her head in his neck. She sobbed.

Walter clutched his injured left hand.

'Sorry, Walt,' Earl said.

Walter shook his head to say it didn't matter, tugged off his neckerchief and wrapped it around his hand, wincing.

Laura came to Earl's side, her face red with tears and anguish, and crushed him to her. 'Oh Lord, Earl.'

He held her steady. 'Nobody died, nobody died.'

She pushed away and tried to smear the dusting of dirt and ash from his cheek.

A report of shattering glass rang out.

'You stay here,' he instructed, then jogged away to relieve the man on the hose.

The front doorway was alight now, but the fire on the side of the house had subsided under the steady stream of water.

He glanced around—maybe thirty people were marshalling themselves to collect buckets from all-comers. Abe stood in the garden, perilously close to the flames, urging commands, his face lit orange. Spilt water made slop of the roughened flower beds, and Laura's gaillardias were trampled flat.

There was no time to be maudlin. Walter stood at the bowser, pointing to where Earl should direct the reedy jet of water.

The seconds crawled past as he willed the herculean effort to overcome nature's destructive force.

Slowly, the flames receded, leaving blackened timber and jagged holes. He peered through the gaps at the loss and heartache.

'Don't get much luck with fires, do you, Earl?'

Acid rose in his throat. He thrust the hose at Walter and turned to Potter. 'Grab a bucket, Lyle, or shift your fat ass.'

Potter eyed the scene. 'Maybe this is the Lord's way of saying that time's right to be making your way.'

'You sonofabitch.'

'That's no language in front of ladies. Good thing not all of us hear it.'

Earl darted forwards, but Walter yanked hard on his sleeve. Earl rudely shook away his friend's warning.

'Lord's way nothing,' he rapped at Potter. 'This fire is your doing.'

'Is that so? Word is a firework caught the roof.' An all-too-familiar smirk played on the Mayor's lips.

'Like hell.'

Potter stepped closer. 'Prove otherwise. Fire is God and the World's nature, a sign to renew. I think you'd do well to move on.' Hot orange flecks reflected in the man's cold, dark eyes.

'I said, you lay anything on my family, you answer to me.' Earl fingered his gun butt.

Potter did likewise.

'Earl,' Walter cautioned, struggling with the hose. He beckoned a man and passed the duty on.

'You should be looking to save what you have, not lose it. Again.'

Earl's nose wrinkled. 'This is you what done this.'

'I've been inside the hall this whole time. Isn't that so, Sam?'

The Sheriff nodded.

Earl shot burning daggers at Potter.

'I saw a man running,' Walter interjected. 'When I come down first, before I raised the alarm. Young man, maybe.'

'Young man, what set the fire?' Earl asked.

'I don't know, okay? Most folks are at the dance. I reckon the Powell kids set a couple of fireworks way off yonder. But the feller was that way.' Walter pointed to the far side of the street, towards the dancehall.

Behind the houses, the white moon rose into the deep blue. On their windows, licks of orange shimmied, reflected from the dying conflagration.

Earl scanned the scattered few dozen people. A safe distance away stood Tom Potter.

He jabbed a finger at the Mayor. 'Your boy. Your boy done this, you cowardly bastard.'

'I'd say he was dancing, wouldn't you, Sam?'

'Could be so,' Bowman replied. But he couldn't look Earl straight.

'You can't burn a man out of town,' Earl said through gritted teeth.

Potter shrugged. 'It's not your house. Not your decision.'

Earl's hand twitched. Laura and Sarah were a few yards away, their fingers entwined. Beyond them, Alden's frame was tense, his hand ready. Earl wanted to call out and tell the boy not to do anything dumb, but it would be unheard and worthless.

'Go stand with the ladies, Walt.'

'Earl—'

'Go stand,' he snapped.

Walter walked behind him and stood beside Sarah, his makeshift bandaged hand across his chest.

Earl faced Potter. 'We ain't leaving on your say so.'

'I gave the cripple boy thirty days, less he made trouble. He made trouble, clear as day.'

'You shut your hole 'bout my boy. He's a good kid.'

'You don't know the first thing about him. You didn't even try to save him that day.'

Earl's blood boiled. 'Saving were suicide. Only a fool man goes up against raiders.'

'One man did—and rescued what he lost. Which of us is the coward now?'

'You ain't even have the balls to set this fire yourself. Used your boy, who's as much an evil sonofabitch as you.'

Potter's hand snapped to his gun but paused on the butt. Earl twitched but didn't draw. Tom had moved closer.

Potter smiled and let his arm fall loose. 'Least I got a boy who can hear and talk.'

The camel's back snapped clean in two.

Earl snatched at his gun and slid his finger into the trigger guard. The manoeuvre came slow, but it was all there, a dormant sense memory created three decades ago.

Potter drew in a heartbeat, found aim and fired.

The gun was torn from Earl's grip with the crack of a bullet on metal. It thumped to the dirt four feet away.

A woman shrieked—he expected it was Laura.

He stood rock still, beaten, and not enough of a fool to go for his downed weapon.

Walter's hands flew up defensively: another man who was no fool—he might best Potter on a good day but now could barely hold a gun, let alone draw it with a bandaged hand.

But beyond them, Alden tugged out his borrowed gun.

In that split second, Earl wondered whether a shouted warning would be of any use—if the boy would sense or even stop on command. Signing was too slow. At worse, it might distract Potter and draw his fire. Yes, Earl might take a bullet, but he'd prefer that than his son get hit.

Potter didn't need more than a split second. He shifted aim and fired.

Laura's scream came so hard on the heels of the shot that they could both have come from the barrel of the same gun.

Again, Potter's aim was true—mercifully. Alden recoiled as the gun was blown from his hand, and then he went down hard as the ricochet took the bullet past his thigh.

Earl's body screamed at him to bolt over to the boy, but self-preservation won. He was rooted to the spot, nerves fizzing.

Laura was aghast, her dress quivering.

Alden reached for the gun which lay beside him.

'No!' Earl yelled.

Potter raised his gun again.

Six feet from Earl, Sarah's right hand lunged for Walter's holstered gun, tugged it from his left side and jammed it out front, bringing her second hand to support the weight. It was far from steady, but the aim was clear.

Potter saw her move, and his arm swung.

She fired.

Chapter 59

Potter thudded to the dirt.

Sarah dropped the gun like it was hot.

Walter stepped in front of her, drawing the aim of whatever lowdown scum might challenge a young woman.

Twenty yards away, Tom Potter gripped his gun.

'Hand down!' Abe calmly drew his weapon, stepped forward and jammed the barrel into Tom's side. The boy looked daggers but put his arms half up.

Earl quickly scanned the crowd. Many had backed away or taken cover. The hose hissed uselessly on the ground. The fire remnants crackled. Sam Bowman covered his holster, watching for the next sudden move.

Potter lay like a beached whale, gun clamped uselessly in his hand.

Alden rolled on his side, holding his upper leg, his face etched with pain.

'Gonna help my boy, Sam,' Earl called, loud enough for all to hear. 'Self-defence, Sam— I want it written.'

He passed behind Walter and the ladies as Laura picked up the discarded gun. She clasped Sarah's hand in support.

'Aye from me,' Walter added. He called out towards the bowser. 'Get on that hose, Marty!'

'We all got witnesses,' Sam replied noncommittally.

'I want his boy in custody on suspicion,' Earl demanded. He reached Alden. "You hit?"

"Don't know."

He threaded arms under the boy's shoulder and helped him up. Alden shakily stood on his own, face wretched, blood leaking into his trousers. Earl scooped up the gun.

The sky boomed.

He jolted, shocked.

Canopies of colour erupted above and away, cracked and thumped, then fizzled into sparks that winked out against the deep blue. All eyes turned heavenwards in alarm, then in wonder.

Earl ignored it and encouraged Alden to lean on him. The boy swayed. Earl holstered the gun and clutched hold with both hands.

The sky detonated again. Reds, blues and whites bloomed in his high peripheral vision. On the ground, a shape stirred—something which shouldn't be moving.

Potter grunted, lifted a shaky arm and brought it to bear.

Earl grappled with Alden, frantically trying to free his gun hand as the distant barrel found its mark on them.

The air cracked but without colour.

Potter jerked and fell back.

Another gunshot ripped the air, and a second bullet found its home in the man's chest.

Earl looked urgently for the source.

Laura's shaking arm lowered the gun. She swayed. Walter lunged in and clutched her. Sarah buried her head in her mother's back.

The bowser hose hissed.

Distant music rippled unseen through the still air.

More fireworks detonated in loud rainbows of ironic joy.

Licked by waning flames, the charred timbers of the house spat and groaned.

Mayor Potter lay still and silent.

Chapter 60

Earl let Alden down to the ground.

Sarah broke away from Laura and came to keep the boy company. She pulled a handkerchief from her pocket and pressed it to the leg wound. Then she put her lips to his, boldly declaring her love to the whole town.

Earl took Laura in an embrace, watching as the last of the bucket brigade tossed their water on the ebbing flames.

She held out the gun like a dead rat. 'Get it out of my sight.'

He took it, and she buried her head in his chest. He passed it across to Walter.

Walter turned it over in his hands. 'Guess your old gun weren't so useless after all.' He holstered it gently. 'Good enough to deter those who'd put danger on your family.'

Earl nodded, sober, then indicated Alden. 'Go get the Doc, quick sharp.'

Walter set off at a trot.

Earl cupped Laura's tear-stained cheeks and kissed her softly and languidly. 'Nobody died, sweet. Least, nobody worth talking of.'

Her face creased into despair. 'Our home did.'

'That's a house—wood, nails and effects. Home is people and love, and we still got that. Don't we?'

She rubbed flecks of black ash from his face.

'Love always wins, Earl. That's how it works.'

Doc Cartwright came. They helped Alden to the neighbour's porch, and Laura held a lamp while the boy was checked over. The bullet had sliced his clothes on its way into the dirt and gouged a deep six-inch cut in his thigh.

The undertaker, Jeb Malone, had been fetched from the dance and prepared to take Potter's body away. The man moved steadily but the worse for drink.

Earl left them to their work and went to clear the air with Sam Bowman.

'He'd a shot me or the boy, or both.'

Bowman gestured for calm. 'It's a hell of a night.' He nodded at the smouldering house. 'You got other concerns.'

'I weren't drawing to shoot—only by way of warning.'

'Take your family and get some rest. Town's supposed to be celebrating, not figuring how to put folk behind bars.'

'He killed Mary and deafened the boy,' Earl said firmly.

Bowman patted his shoulder. 'You got the future to worry about, not the past. Besides, I'm not in the habit of arresting women and girls for self-defence. They need succour, not chains.'

Earl inspected the man's face for double meanings and hidden agendas but found none. Then Bowman walked away.

Abe approached, marching Tom Potter at gunpoint.

'What do you want doing with him?'

Earl shrugged. 'I ain't the Sheriff. Let him go.'

'You trust him?' Abe asked in surprise.

'The boy works for Jeb—that so?'

'Sure.'

'Then let him help bury his pa, who lies there on account of making cowardly quarrels with good ladies who never done him a speck of harm.'

He eyed Tom, good and strong. 'So, unless he wants to be picking out his own damn coffin, he'll go on with his life, especially being a rich man now, from his father's... doings.'

Abe gave Tom Potter a good shove. The boy slunk away.

'I'm real sorry, Earl.'

They looked at the half-gutted property. 'We paid in ash, not blood, and that's a blessing.'

'If you need a place—'

'You're a good man, Abe. The women need beds, not straw, nor more kindness from this town. We'll take rooms yonder and find the world tomorrow.'

'I'll fetch Jack and the wagon.' Abe noted the rising moon. 'We got light enough to take those things to the barn. Check the house too for anything able to be made good.'

Earl reached into his pocket, pulled out all the dollars, and pressed them into the man's hand.

'You don't got spares for giving me,' Abe protested.

'My place sold yesterday. I cleared my debt to Sam and the county. Had a few coins over. That's enough on it.'

Abe nodded in resignation. 'I'll get the wagon.'

Earl pulled Laura tightly to him under the covers. He smelled appallingly of smoke, and his hand burned sore from the whiplash of Potter's bullet.

Down the corridor, he was sure Alden was similarly comforting Sarah.

'Sun'll come up in the morning,' Earl murmured.

'Jim bought insurance,' she replied into his chest. 'He was organised like that.'

'The boy's skin'll heal up.'

'We never finished our dance.'

He inhaled her scent. 'Next year.'

She pressed even closer. 'Stay with me,' she whispered.

The quiet of the Hotel room was tinged only by distant footsteps and the ticking of the clock, which showed long past midnight.

'That'd be marriage,' he ventured.

'Yes. Yes, it would be.'

Walter was already at the house in the morning. Sarah and Alden remained in their room while she re-dressed his wound.

Laura and Earl toured the sad, blackened timbers strewn with detritus of half-burned bedclothes, broken crockery and splintered glass.

'I'm no steeplejack,' Walter said, 'But sense says tear down and start over. Watered wood rots like a man's bad deeds kept covered.'

Laura turned to Earl. 'In hindsight, I should have sold up and bought your place. Then debts would be paid, and we'd have been out of the way of all this.'

'But this is your town,' he protested. ''Sides, my place'd be tight for two, let alone four. And anyhow, who was it said the past is gone, and we only got the present?'

She smiled but sadly. 'The present is fine. It's the future which needs work.'

'So, we better figure on making it.'

'You'll need a workshop,' she suggested.

'And space for the young folks. For now, anyhow. And to keep the horses close, save on stabling.'

'Not on this town lot,' Walter said.

'That's what I figured,' he replied.

The following day, Walter met them again outside the charred house.

Earl pulled something from his jacket pocket.

'See this makes the mail coach.'

Walter looked at the envelope. 'Sure. You give the new address?'

'Yeah.'

'Good.'

Expectation hung in the air. The three horses whinnied, getting reacquainted.

'You come by, Walt. Any day, door's open. I'll take it real personal if you don't.'

'Or I'll see you in town.'

Earl nodded. 'Ladies gotta make their trades. Me and Alden too.'

'If you need another hand on the saw—'

'Like I said—coffee pot's always on.'

Laura called down from her saddle. 'It'll be winter before we're even there if you don't quit yapping.'

Walter lowered his voice. 'At least Mary couldn't shoot.'

Two hours later, the three horses and two wagons crested the rise overlooking a familiar area of the prairie. Sunlight glinted off the narrow brook, which meandered past the ruined stone house.

'Are you sure?' she asked.

'Only memories I care for are ones we're gonna make.'

Epilogue

By September, the main house became the product of many days hard labour. Earl and Alden cut the wood—the boy was starting to show real carpentry skills. Laura and Sarah took turns keeping them fuelled while the other was in town, at the schoolhouse, or running errands. Laura had rescued a few gaillardia stems from her old house and created the beginnings of a new garden.

Walter occasionally stopped by with endeavour and company.

When they all had a roof, work began on Alden and Sarah's house, sited a few hundred yards distant—close enough for company but far enough for independence.

It was finished in late November, before the worst of the winter arrived, but Alden wouldn't move in until certain matters were attended to. So, one day, Earl sent Walter into Ridgeway, and he returned with the Pastor.

When the ceremony was done, Earl saw a look in Laura's eye and asked the man to go ahead one more time.

Later the following year, Sarah was delivered of twins, Mary Laura and James Walter.

Their hearing may or may not have been good. It doesn't really matter.

Acknowledgements

For editorial assistance:

Maddy Glenn at SWS
Jess Lawrence
Beth Miller
Heather Fitt

Advance readers:

Deborah Klée
Laury Silvers
Ingrid Weel
Roy Towndrow
Stuart Moore

Cover design:

Carl Thompson

Chris Towndrow has been a writer since 1991. He began writing science fiction, inspired by Isaac Asimov, Iain M Banks, and numerous film and TV canons. After a few years spent creating screenplays, in 2004 he moved into playwriting and has had several productions professionally performed.

His first published novel was 2012's space opera "Sacred Ground". He then focussed on "hard" sci-fi, and the Enna Dacourt pentalogy was completed in 2023.

He has always drawn inspiration from the big screen, and 2019's quirky romantic comedy "Tow Away Zone" owes much to the Coen Brothers' work. This book spawned two sequels in what became the "Sunrise trilogy".

His first historical fiction novel, "Signs Of Life", was published by Valericain Press in 2023.

Chris now returns to his passion for writing accessible humour and will largely focus on romantic comedy novels. There are three of these in development.

Chris lives on the outskirts of London with his family and works as a video editor and producer. He is a member of the UK Society of Authors.

Visit his website at: christowndrow.co.uk

X: twitter.com/TowndrowBooks

Instagram: instagram.com/towndrowbooks

If you have enjoyed this book, please do leave an online review. An indie author's ability to generate valuable sales is enhanced by the reviews of kind readers.

Also by the author:

An original romantic black comedy with a dash of the unexplained.

When a travelling salesman with monochromacy finds a town that doesn't exist, he must choose between love and a long-held promise of untold riches.

"A gripping yarn - quirky characters, a pacy plot and a setting like you've never read before. A fun ol' read."
- *Paul Kerensa, Comedian & British Comedy Award-winning TV writer*

Printed in Great Britain
by Amazon

32800030R00229